DATE DUE

SEP 2 3 1998	JAN 2 0 2000	
OCT 06 1998		
OCT 23 1998		
FEB 05 1999		
AUG 2 5 1999		
MAR 1 8 2000		
JAN 24 2001		
NOV 1 8 2003		
FEB 1 8 2006		
APR 1 9 2007		
DEC 1 7 2008		

THIEF OF DREAMS

Mary Balogh

JOVE BOOKS, NEW YORK

THIEF OF DREAMS

A Jove Book / published by arrangement with
the author

PRINTING HISTORY
Jove edition / May 1998

All rights reserved.
Copyright © 1998 by Mary Balogh.
Cover photo by Wendi Schneider.
Cover art fan courtesy of A Ladies Gallery, Longmont, Colorado.
This book may not be reproduced in whole
or in part, by mimeograph or any other means,
without permission. For information address:
The Berkley Publishing Group, a member of Penguin Putnam Inc.,
200 Madison Avenue, New York, New York 10016.

The Penguin Putnam Inc. World Wide Web site address is
http://www.penguinputnam.com

ISBN: 0-515-12274-2

A JOVE BOOK®
Jove Books are published by The Berkley Publishing Group,
a member of Penguin Putnam Inc.,
200 Madison Avenue, New York, New York 10016.
Jove and the "J" design are trademarks belonging to
Jove Publications, Inc.

PRINTED IN THE UNITED STATES OF AMERICA

10 9 8 7 6 5 4 3 2 1

ONE

THE DAY WAS GOING TO BE an extraordinarily busy one. A birthday was to be celebrated—the one and twentieth of Lady Cassandra Havelock, Countess of Worthing.

Normally such a birthday would have been of no great significance to a lady. But this was an exception. The late Earl of Worthing had died a year ago to the day, leaving behind him an only daughter and one of those rare earldoms that devolved upon the female line in the absence of a male, the idea being that the new countess would hold the title in trust for her own son. The late earl's brother had been appointed her ladyship's guardian during her minority. She was not married and it was impossible for her guardian to arrange a marriage for her during the year of her mourning.

The birthday that was to be celebrated, then, was an enormously significant occasion. The Countess of Worthing—a mere *woman*—was to achieve her majority and her independence. There was no one in her life—no *man*—with the power to order that life for her. Yet it was an indisputable fact that no woman could live her life independent of a man's superior wisdom and guidance, especially when that woman was titled and wealthy and the owner of a large estate in Somersetshire.

The fact that she was also beautiful, lively, and charming merely compounded the problem.

They were all agreed upon that—her uncle and former guardian, her aunts, and the one male cousin who was old enough to be allowed an opinion of his own.

There was the evening's ball for which to prepare—it was to be the grandest ball within the collective memory of the neighborhood and its environs for miles around. There was to be a full orchestra, and so many guests had been invited—and had accepted their invitations—that the event was expected to rival even some of the more modest squeezes of the London Season.

In addition to the preparations for the ball—and none of the countess' relatives was willing to admit that the brunt of *that* task would fall squarely upon the servants' shoulders—there was to be the whole business of greeting and entertaining the houseguests during the afternoon, and then there were those who were coming from too far away to be expected to return home in their carriages after the ball was over. Almost all of the spare bedchambers were to be occupied.

Once the afternoon came, the day would be carried along on its own hectic momentum. They all realized that. But the morning was relatively free. And a family conference was imperative. One was called in the morning room. There was the whole question—the whole *problem*—of Cassandra to be discussed.

Conveniently, Cassandra herself was away from home during the morning. She had walked over to the dower house to call upon her cousin and friend, the Honorable Miss Patience Gibbons. More to the point, she had gone there for a final fitting for the gown she was to wear to the ball. The mantua maker and her two assistants, who had been brought down from London in order to create ball gowns for all the ladies, had been lodged at the dower house rather than at the house itself.

Cassandra did not know of the family conference that was held in her absence—and in her interests.

The Honorable Mr. Cyrus Havelock presided from a

standing position before the empty fireplace. No one disputed his leadership since he was the only brother of the late earl and indeed had missed the title himself by a mere half hour, having been born the younger twin by that exact margin of time. Not that Mr. Havelock was in any way embittered by his subordinate position, as he was frequently at pains to assure his family. He had been dealt with generously on the death of his mother, when the neighboring estate and manor of Willow Hall had been made his. And he was fond of Cassandra.

The other members of the family in attendance were Mrs. Althea Havelock, Lady Beatrice Havelock, unmarried sister of the late earl, Lady Matilda Gibbons, widow of Baron Gibbons and also a sister of the late earl, and Mr. Robin Barr-Hampton, the son of Mrs. Havelock by her first marriage. Robin could not be called a member of the family in the strict sense of the term, but he was four-and-twenty years old, he was a respectably prosperous landowner in his own right, albeit on a somewhat smaller scale than either his stepfather or his stepcousin, and he was a sensible and amiable young man.

"The question is," Mr. Havelock began after calling the meeting to order by clearing his throat with a low rumbling sound and lifting onto the balls of his feet before settling back on his heels again, "what are we to do about Cassandra?" He slid one hand inside the button opening of his long blue silk waistcoat and looked about him. It was perhaps fortunate for him that according to fashion, his skirted coat with its full side pleats and wide cuffs curved away at the front edges and was not even expected to button across his broad chest.

"I shall remain here with her for as long as she needs me, brother," Lady Beatrice said in the strident tones that characterized her. "I no longer consider myself her chaperon but her companion and friend and guide. I shall remain all three for many years to come if the good Lord is willing. I am not in my dotage yet."

"Zounds, Bea," her brother said, "no one is suggesting

any such thing. But what we are to *do* about her is the question."

"Worthing should have taken her to London years ago," Lady Matilda said. "Beatrice could have gone to chaperon her. *I* would have gone and taken my dear Patience with me. I spoke to him about it on the rare occasion when he came home, but he always said Cassandra was too young for such frivolity and she was better off in the country. Who was I to argue with him? But I do think *you* might have had a word with him, Cyrus."

"Frivolity!" Mr. Havelock shook his head in exasperated disbelief. "What can be more serious business than finding a husband for one's daughter? He did not wish to be bothered with the gel, that was what it was. She should have been married off years ago."

"I suggested as much to him the very last time he was at home, if you will recall, my love," Mrs. Havelock said. "London was the place to find a suitable husband for dear Cassandra, I told him, especially under the circumstances of the inheritance. 'Tis still difficult to believe, I do declare, that she is now a countess in her own right and that Kedleston Park is all hers. Poor dear Cassandra—all alone."

"I have done my duty by her as her guardian during the past year," Mr. Havelock said, lifting onto his toes again before rocking back to a more stable position. "But my hands have been tied. We have all been in mourning for Worthing until this day. How could I choose her a husband at such a time?"

"You could not, brother," Lady Beatrice said. "You have nothing whatsoever for which to blame yourself. None of us do. Your guardianship is at an end, but you are still her uncle and we are still her aunts. We have a grave responsibility to her."

"Which brings us back to the point," Mr. Havelock said. "What are we to do about Cassandra? She is no longer a minor, she has the title, she is owner of all this"—he swept one arm about in a wide arc—"and she will be prey to every fortune hunter in the country. Mark my words. There are already a dozen young men just within this county who have been waiting for this day with bated breath."

"Cassandra is a sensible girl," Lady Beatrice said.

"You were quite right to use that word. Cassandra is a *girl*, Beatrice," Mrs. Havelock said. "She is lovely and sweet and trusting and really very—young. She will need a great deal of guidance in fending off fortune hunters and choosing a sensible and steady young man who will be a good steward of the property for their son."

" 'Tis the end of May and too late for her to be taken to London for the Season this year," Mr. Havelock said with a sigh of frustration. "Perhaps we should plan it for next year. Present her with gentlemen of her own rank; men with fortunes of their own. Let them take a look at her. Do the whole thing up properly as it should have been done three years or more ago."

"And I will take Patience," Lady Matilda said. "She will be nineteen by then. 'Tis only right that the daughter of a baron and granddaughter of an earl be introduced to society and presented at court. And she has grown very pretty, though not as lovely as Cassandra, I will admit. 'Tis settled then, Cyrus?"

"I will go, too," Lady Beatrice said. "Your time will be taken up with Patience, sister. I will see to Cassandra's interests. I have no doubt that she will make a very splendid match indeed."

"Perhaps we could go as well," Mrs. Havelock said. "Shall we, Cyrus? We will be closer to dear Rupert at school, and Amy and Hannah will enjoy seeing the sights. Besides, 'twill help if Cassandra has an uncle in place of her father to pick out suitable young men for her and to discuss a marriage settlement on her behalf. We have not been to London in a long age, I do declare."

" 'Twould seem to be the best plan," Mr. Havelock said after pushing out his lips and lapsing into silent thought for several moments. "Though she will be well into her two-and-twentieth year by then. 'Tis an advanced age for an unmarried lady."

"Pshaw!" Lady Beatrice said impatiently. "She is a very infant, brother. 'Twill merely be thought that she and her family are discriminating. Cassandra has beauty and position and wealth enough that there has been no necessity to snaffle up the first half-presentable young man to stammer out an offer. She will seem the more desirable for her caution. Why, *I* received more offers after the age of two-and-twenty than I ever received when I was considered of more marriageable age.''

"We certainly do not want Cassandra to be quite as cautious as you were, though, Beatrice," Mrs. Havelock said with a titter. "You were free to do as you wished with your life. Cassandra has the duty of bearing a son to whom to pass the title. Or a daughter at the very least."

" 'Tis settled, then," Mr. Havelock said, lifting onto the balls of his feet once more before resuming the more solid stance. " 'Tis a relief, I must confess. I shall speak with the gel tomorrow after all this excitement of a birthday is over."

"Egad, but you have forgotten something, sir," Robin Barr-Hampton said from the window, where he had taken up his stand at the beginning of the meeting. "You have all forgotten something."

They turned to look at him with raised eyebrows.

"Cass may not wish to be borne off to London," Robin said. "She may flatly refuse to go. And as of today, she has every right to do so. She cannot be forced."

"But we are making plans for her own good, dear," his mother said.

"She might resent the fact that others are planning for her," Robin said. "She might very well resent the fact that this meeting is being held at all—in her own home and in her absence."

"We are her family, Robin," Lady Beatrice reminded him. "We love her. We have every right to be concerned about her future happiness."

"Zounds," Mr. Havelock said, raising one hand to scratch at his unpowdered bob wig, " 'tis not as if we are trying to marry her off to a wicked old curmudgeon who will dissipate her fortune and beat her daily, Robin. Quite the contrary. She may choose whom she wishes, provided

I approve—provided *we* approve. We have older and wiser heads than my niece.''

"But she may not ask for your approval," Robin said. "She is under no compulsion to do so, sir, if you will forgive me for saying so. Might I be permitted to suggest an alternative plan?"

His stepfather pursed his lips and all attention turned Robin's way again.

"Cass has never been to London and has never expressed a wish to go there," Robin said. "She is happy here. Cass is always happy. I would think it desirable to arrange matters so that she can remain happy. That can be accomplished best by helping her keep her life very much as it is and always has been—or such is my opinion."

"But she cannot be happy if she remains unwed, Robin," Lady Matilda said, and then bit her lip. "I do beg your pardon, Beatrice."

"But I agree with Robin," Lady Beatrice said. "The single state is well enough for a woman of strong character, but Cassandra would not be happy remaining in the single state. That girl needs a husband and children."

"I would humbly offer my services on both counts," Robin said. "Cass has always been fond of me and I of her. Other people might accuse me of fortune hunting since my own property and fortune are meager in comparison with hers. But *you* would all know that 'twere not true. I would keep Cass happy, and I would provide the male protection she needs. I would be a careful steward of the property both for her sake and for that of our son. I would allow her to be—well, to be Cass. I would like to offer her my hand tonight, before she can be confused by fortune hunters—and they will very soon be on her doorstep. But I would not do it without your approval, sir, or yours, Mama, or yours, Aunt Matilda and Aunt Bea."

He had brought silence to the room. Everyone simply stared at him.

"That is a splendid offer, dear," his mother said at last. "I know you mean it just as you have expressed it. And 'tis true that you and Cassandra have always been fond of each other.''

"It might indeed be the best plan of all," Lady Matilda said. " 'Tis true that Cassandra loves Kedleston and might not like to be taken away from it by a man of property from another part of the country. And we know you to be an honorable man, Robin. I daresay 'twould be a love match.''

"The marriage could take place this summer," Lady Beatrice said, "and we would not have to go to all the trouble of traipsing off to London next spring. I never did like London—nasty, smelly place, full of beggars and vermin. And I would not have to grow accustomed to the presence of a stranger in the house after Cassandra married. I approve of the idea. What do you say, brother?''

Mr. Havelock looked at his stepson with pouted lips and a thoughtful frown. He rocked to the balls of his feet. "Zounds, but it might work," he said. "You have proved a capable manager with your own property, Robin. Yes indeed, it might well be the best solution of all. Tonight, you say? I could make the announcement at supper. Or from the orchestra platform before the end of the ball. We can talk over the marriage contract tomorrow, my lad. There is too much else happening today. Your own property can be willed to your second son. Yes, by Jove, I like it. I was uneasy about having to wait almost a whole extra year, I must confess. We can have the first banns called on Sunday.''

"You forget one thing, sir," Robin said, smiling.

All eyes turned his way again.

"Cass may say no," he said. "She has every right to say no.''

"But there is no reason in the world why she should, dear," his mother assured him.

The meeting ended satisfactorily. Cassandra's family, those who loved her and wished for her happiness and future security, had arranged for both. None of them, with the exception of Robin himself, was troubled by doubts about their niece's finding the plan quite as satisfactory as it was to them.

Cassandra, Lady Worthing, lifted her face to the sun and drew in a deep breath of the warm fresh air.

"Mm," she said, and she stopped in the middle of the grassy avenue, held her arms out to the sides, and twirled all about, laughing. "Is this not the most beautiful day there has ever been, Patience?"

Her cousin stopped and watched her. "Well, it *is* a lovely day, Cass," she said, "even though it rained this morning. But of course to you it looks lovelier than it does to anyone else. Today is your birthday."

"And I am *free*," Cassandra said, twirling once more. Her petticoat and the skirt of her muslin open gown billowed out around her before settling back on the small walking hoops she wore beneath them. She set her head back to rights, and the brim of her wide straw hat, tilted forward on her head over her round-eared lace cap, shaded her face from the sun again.

"La," Patience said, laughing, "were you in captivity before then, Cass?"

"I was," Cassandra replied. "I was in mourning. Is it not wonderful beyond belief to look down at oneself and not see unrelieved *black*? But of course, you did not wear mourning as long as I. He was not your papa. And today I am of age, Patience. No more guardians. No more men ruling my life. I am the most fortunate of mortals. How many other women can say on their twenty-first birthdays that they are free and mean it?"

Cassandra had lingered at the dower house long after the fitting for her gown was completed. She had lingered just *because* she had been eager to return. But no houseguests could be expected until the middle of the afternoon at the earliest, and there was nothing to do in the ballroom except get under the feet of the servants, who were far more competent than she and to whom she had given perfectly detailed and lucid instructions. As soon as she returned to the house, she knew, she would be like a caged bear. Although this was the happiest day of her life, she was well aware that the happiest part of it would come this evening with the ball. She could hardly wait. And now she was on her way back to the house, walking up over the hill from the dower house and along the lime grove until the tiered flower garden at the side of the house and the house itself came into view in the distance.

"Uncle Cyrus has not played the tyrant with you," Patience said. " 'Twould be as well, Cass, not to express the cause of your exuberance in his hearing."

"Oh la, no." Cassandra looked conscience stricken. "He has been the most indulgent of guardians. I would not have his feelings hurt for worlds. But he does treat me as if I am a child, you know, Patience. As if I were a peagoose. It does not help that I am so despicably *small* and look years younger than my age. Perhaps I would be taken more seriously if I were six feet tall." She laughed merrily and her cousin joined her.

"But 'tis the nature of men to treat women so," Patience said, "and the nature of women to be so treated. I do not know what I would do without Uncle Cyrus to watch after me. Mama is not the most practical of persons, though 'tis disloyal of me to say so out loud. Besides, Cass, soon enough you will have another man to watch over you who will be more to your taste than Uncle, I daresay."

Cassandra frowned. "Why are we such good friends?" she asked, but she did not wait for an answer. "We are so very *different*, Patience. You are speaking of a husband, are you not? Everyone believes that I will now choose someone in great haste because I *have no choice*. I could not possibly manage without a man. I would crumble. Kedleston would crumble."

"La, Cass," her cousin said, "and neither could you manage."

"Phooey!" Cassandra exclaimed inelegantly. "This all belongs to me, Patience." She waved her arm to indicate the lime grove and to suggest a far larger area of land beyond it. "And today I have the freedom to enjoy what is mine in my own way. Why should I give it up to a man who would assume that I am a mere frail woman in need of his superior guidance? Why *should* I?''

''But you have to marry someone, Cass,'' Patience said with great good sense.

''Why?'' Cassandra asked. ''Aunt Bea has never married and she seems perfectly happy with the single state. Yet Aunt Bea is unfortunate enough to be dependent upon her relatives for a home. I do not have even that impediment to perfect happiness. I am a wealthy woman and I own my home. I have no intention of marrying. Ever. Well, perhaps I do not mean I will *never* marry. But only if someone very special were to come along. I do not expect him. I will never marry merely because I ought.''

''But, Cass—'' Patience looked at her aghast. ''You are going to need—I mean—do you not *like* men?''

Cassandra laughed. ''Of course I do, silly goose,'' she said. ''I enjoy the company of gentlemen—they are often far more amusing than ladies. I enjoy dancing with gentlemen. I even enjoy flirting with them. But I would not enjoy being owned by one of them.''

''One does not think of ownership when one marries for *love*,'' Patience said.

''Oh pooh!'' Cassandra lifted her face again as they left the lime grove behind and there was nothing above their heads but blue sky and sunshine. She sighed with contentment. ''How many people do you know who have married for love, Patience? Most ladies *say* they are in love when they marry, of course, and some of the gentlemen, too, I suppose. But soon enough the marriage settles into a very ordinary dullness. Sometimes the partners can barely tolerate each other before the first year is out.''

''That is unfair,'' her cousin said. ''Uncle Cyrus and Aunt Althea are fond of each other.''

''Fond!'' Cassandra said scornfully. ''There is no spark in the word. But it describes their feelings for each other to perfection. I do not even believe there is such a thing as romantic love. 'Tis wishful thinking on the part of those who wish to or who must marry.''

''You are wrong, Cass,'' Patience said.

"I suppose you know from personal experience," Cassandra said. And then she looked at her cousin, arrested by the thought. "Have you been in love, Patience? *Are* you in love?"

"La," Patience said, blushing, "what a question to ask, Cass."

"You *are*," Cassandra said, crowing with laughter. "Oh, this is famous. Who is he?"

But Patience had become very prim. "You are mistaken," she said.

"No, I am not." Cassandra's eyes were dancing. And it was not difficult to guess who Patience's secret beau was. It was blind of her not to have noticed. They had been friends for so many years, the three of them, that it had not occurred to her to think of romance in terms of the other two. " 'Tis Rob. Oh, wonderful. He is quite handsome and amiable, I grant you, Patience, though perhaps a little too solid a citizen to be described as dashing. But nonetheless, oh yes indeed, he is perfect for you. I approve. I give you my blessing." She chuckled with merriment. "And does he love you, too? Does he languish for you? Does he suffer sleepless nights, tossing on his fevered bed, unable to stop thinking about you and longing for you?"

But Patience was not enjoying the joke. Her flush had deepened and she looked acutely embarrassed. Cassandra sobered instantly when she saw the effects of her teasing. This was all very serious to her cousin.

"Forgive me," she said. "But 'tis Robin, Patience? You love him?"

"And he does not know I exist except as a very much younger cousin to be indulged," Patience said. "You are not to say any more about it, Cass. And you are not to breathe a *word* to him. I should *die* of mortification."

"But 'twould be a perfect match," Cassandra said. Why had she not thought of it before? Why had she not noticed? She and Patience were very close friends. But she had been wrapped up in the circumstances of her own life during the past year, ever since the death of her father on her twentieth birthday. How selfish and self-centered she had become.

" 'Twill never be," Patience said, sounding almost cross. "Robin likes *you*, Cass."

"*Me?*" Cassandra stopped to look in amazement at her cousin. "Of course he likes me. We have been friends and playmates forever. But you do not mean that, do you? You mean he *likes* me. That is absurd, Patience. We are like brother and sister."

"Nevertheless," Patience said, and allowed the one word to speak for itself. "But I daresay he will never say anything to you, Cass. You are too far above him. You are a countess. And you own Kedleston."

Cassandra was too amazed to speak for a few moments. "Famous!" she said at last. "So you sigh over Rob and Rob sighs over me and I—am quite fancy-free. I am to dance the opening set at the ball this evening with Robin. I shall confront him. Oh no, I suppose I shall not. Bother! Now I shall become self-conscious with him—with *Rob*. Is he to dance with you?"

"The second set," Patience said.

"Well there!" Cassandra said triumphantly. "He has asked us both. Me out of duty—I daresay Uncle Cyrus suggested it—and you out of inclination."

"The other way around," Patience said. "I was there when he asked you, remember? How could he not ask me, too?"

"Well bother!" Cassandra said again. But the front of the house had come into view and she brightened and quickened her pace. "Look, a carriage. I cannot see whose it is, can you? 'Tis too far away. Though I daresay I would not know it anyway. The houseguests have begun to arrive and I am not there to greet them. What a way to begin my adult life—in absentia. But Dexter will have everyone shown to the right room and everyone will gather later for tea in the drawing room. Patience, if I were any more excited, I would burst at the seams, I swear. How does one act the demure, mature lady when one feels like an exuberant child—and looks like one, too. Well, tomorrow I shall be transformed." She laughed gaily.

"We will be there in five minutes," Patience said.

"Whoever it is has arrived rather early. I do not believe you should blame yourself, Cass. I wonder who it is. 'Tis just one person, not a whole family."

They hurried up the sloping lawn toward the terraced flower garden, but turned before they reached it so that they might enter the house through the front doors.

Her happiest day was about to begin in earnest, Cassandra thought.

TWO

BRIGHT SHAFTS OF SUN-
light slanted through the branches and leafy canopy of the
old forest and alternated with moving bars of shade on the
face of the traveler, turned toward the window as it was.
From the winding, sloping driveway up which his carriage
traveled he could see that the trees extended to either side
as far as the eye could see.

"Gawd!" his companion said from the other seat.
"Nothing but bloody trees forever and ever, amen. Like
you imagined it, is it, then, Nige?"

"Mm," Nigel Wetherby, Viscount Wroxley, replied,
only half hearing what had been said. "No, different somehow, Will. But then I have spent all my life imagining this
place without ever seeing it until now. One can never quite
picture something as it really is."

It was vaster, more impressive. In imagination one saw
only the visual and in only one condition of light. Now he
could smell the foliage and the earth, on which this morning's rain had fallen. He breathed in deeply and held the
breath. And though the sound of his horses' hooves and his
carriage wheels drowned out most other sounds, he was
aware of birdsong in a higher register than the prevailing
noise.

"'Tis vaster than I expected," he said.

"Gawd!" his companion said again, throwing a world of disgust into the one word and crossing his massive arms over his massive chest.

Everything was massive about William Stubbs, from his huge, almost hairless head—he steadfastly refused to wear a wig, calling them fleas' nests that should be worn anywhere but on a man's head—to his sturdy legs, which rivaled the tree trunks beyond the windows in girth. He was also almost incredibly ugly, with a nose that had been broken an indeterminate number of times and never set properly, great yellow teeth, one cauliflower ear, and one eye still in its socket but glazed and quite sightless. He was, as his present companion and employer was fond of telling him, not the sort of character one would care to encounter in a dark alley at night—or in broad daylight, for that matter.

Nigel, Viscount Wroxley, could scarcely have offered a greater contrast. Tall, graceful, handsome, he was also the epitome of elegance and refinement, dressed as he was in the height of London fashion, his clothes made by the most skilled and the most expensive tailor in town. Anyone who did not look closely enough to detect the breadth of shoulders and chest beneath the elegant coat and embroidered waistcoat and the keen, worldly-wise intelligence in the heavy-lidded blue eyes might have set him down as an indolent town fop.

"I'faith, Will," he said, "I suspect God did have something to do with the scenery. You must accustom your mind to the idea of kicking your heels in the country for a while—for a long while unless you decide to leave me. But I should hate that."

"And I, too, Nige," the unlikely valet said. "Gawd, you'd go and get yourself killed for sure if I turned my back on you."

Nigel raised his eyebrows and regarded his man with cool hauteur, but he did not answer him. He was in no mood for prolonged conversation. There was too much curiosity to be satisfied in the scene beyond the window. He was, in fact, close to the fulfillment of a life's dream, which had become more obsession than just dream during the past nine years. He had reached the culmination of a whole long year of planning and self-imposed waiting—unnecessary waiting if Will was to be believed. But it had been his plan and he had never been one to listen to advice when it ran counter to his own inclinations.

He wondered if even now he was being overeager. Perhaps he should have stopped for the night at the village inn and waited until tomorrow to make his call. He had shaved and dressed with care that morning, but it was afternoon already. He always liked to look his best when going into company. He had become almost fanatical about it—since he had had a choice in the matter, that is. His lips compressed for a moment and his eyelids drooped farther over his eyes. But he had not alighted at the inn. He had merely sent his footman inside to reserve a room for him.

He had done the right thing to proceed, he thought. After all, it *was* but afternoon, and he had lived a long time for just this moment. He would perhaps have realized that he was nervous if he had been accustomed to thinking of his own feelings in such terms.

He drummed his long, well-manicured fingers on the window ledge and breathed in deeply of the rich scents of foliage and soil, keeping the window down. A small herd of deer was grazing among the trees to his left. He noticed that they did not take fright at the sound of his carriage. They must be quite tame. And then he was aware of the stronger fragrance of rhododendrons, and sight followed smell. The carriage moved beyond the forest into a more cultivated, though almost as shady, stretch of the park.

Soon now, he guessed, he would see the house itself. The driveway had been gradually climbing out of the valley in which the village was situated, and sure enough, the rhododendron bushes and other cultivated shrubs soon fell away behind them and only a broad expanse of green lawn was left to border the road. In the distance, higher again, the ancient forest resumed.

But between the end of the lawn and the trees was a building. Kedleston itself, huge and magnificent—though he had expected a mansion, of course, and had even been able to picture what it must look like. Except that again the reality surpassed the dream. It was a Jacobean house, built of mellow red brick with white stone window dressings. Its tall windows reflected the light of the sun. Its profile ran quite counter to the classical symmetry of more modern buildings. It was pinnacled and gabled. Nigel's eyes roamed over it. Ah yes, he thought with quiet satisfaction, he was not at all disappointed.

"Gawd! Cor blimey!" William Stubbs had twisted about in his seat to gaze behind him through the window. "Is this *it*, Nige? 'Tis like a fairy palace, like in them stories they tells little nippers."

"But 'tis real, Will." Nigel's voice was languid, but his eyes were keen enough beneath the lazy lids. Yes, it was very real indeed. At last. At long last.

Would she be at home? he wondered. He had not sent any warning of his coming. Deliberately so. He had not wanted her warned. Her absence, of course, would play havoc with his plans, but he did not believe she would be absent—not for any length of time, at least. She never left Kedleston. She had never even been to London. And a month ago she had been here, as she had been three months ago and six months ago. He had sent to find out. Of course she would be here now.

He wondered if he would find her as lovely as he had heard she was. She was said to be a beauty, though no one had ever described her to him and he had never asked. He had never seen a portrait of her. He wondered what manner of woman she was. Gentle and shy? That was how he had always imagined her, basing his assumption on the fact that she had never left her home, that she had lived her life in the countryside. But she might as easily be a shrew, for all he knew, or a loudly assertive country woman who loved nothing better than riding to hounds.

He really did not care what she looked like or what manner of woman she was. His plan had been made and he was not likely to deviate from it now merely because of her appearance or demeanor.

"And you 'ave waited an 'ole year for this," William said, shaking his head, "wen you could 'ave come immediate like I said you should. You got to be dicked in the nob, Nige. And all because of a country filly wot's prob'ly cross-eyed and pocked."

"And innocent," Nigel added with a sigh.

"You're cracked, Nige," his valet said with marvelous disrespect. "Queer in the attic."

"All of which compliments you have paid me many times before, egad," Nigel said. "But 'twere best not to pay them in the hearing of Kedleston's inhabitants, Will. Or to address me by quite so familiar a name. 'Tis not done in polite society, as I have been at pains to explain since you insisted on taking service with me. They might suggest that I string you up from the nearest tree—and there are plenty of them—for insubordination."

"No one 'as yet succeeded in knotting a rope about old Stubbs's neck, m'lord," his valet said, without looking in any way quelled by the setdown. He often referred to himself by the aged adjective, though in fact he was only three years older than his employer—thirty-two to Nigel's twenty-nine. "But you do know as you are doing this all wrong, I s'ppose. I does more than s'ppose. I knows. I been telling you for long enough, Gawd knows. We never did toughen you up proper, lad." He crossed his arms again and gazed with a fearsome fondness at his elegant, haughty employer. "Do it your way, then. But when this piece o' petticoat ties you in knots, don't come to old Stubbs to untie you. That's all I got to say."

"For which mercy may the Lord be praised," Nigel said dryly. "Not that I believe you for a single moment. By my life, Will, I do not know why I tolerate your insolence." He looked coolly at the ugly giant on the opposite seat while fingering the handle of his quizzing glass. He did not raise it to his eye—perhaps because William Stubbs looked fearsome enough without being magnified.

The carriage swung about the final curve and drew to a halt before the front doors of Kedleston. A groom approached with purposeful strides from what must be the stable block, which they had passed on their approach to the house, and the doors opened even before Nigel's coachman could descend in order to rap on them. A footman ran down the steps and prepared to open the carriage door for him to alight. Another servant, the butler at a guess, stood on the top step, looking keenly but respectfully at the carriage. He would learn nothing from its appearance. It was recently purchased and plainly painted without any identifying crest.

"Gawd a-lordy," William muttered. "We been an' gawn and died, Nige, an' come to 'eaven. I always 'xpected to go to the other place."

"Good day to you, sir," the butler said, bowing with stiff formality from the waist as Nigel got down from his carriage and looked about him with indolent curiosity—it really was enough to make one feel significantly dwarfed. "I have the pleasure of greeting . . . ?" He paused politely.

"Wroxley," Nigel said, without withdrawing his eyes from his surroundings. "Viscount Wroxley to see the Countess of Worthing."

The butler frowned in thought. "M'lord," he said, half bowing again. "I do not believe I have your name . . ."

Nigel looked at the man unhurriedly, raised his eyebrows, and waited.

". . . on the list of expected guests, m'lord," the butler said, completing his sentence belatedly. "Doubtless an oversight. If you would step inside, m'lord, I am sure we can—"

"I am not expected," the viscount said. "I wish to speak with her ladyship. Kindly tell her so."

"She is—" The butler was definitely frowning now. "I am not sure her ladyship is at home, m'lord. I will have to inquire." But he looked over the visitor's shoulder to note the superior quality of the carriage, plain though it was, and of the horses, and he looked at the viscount himself to note his fashionable and expertly tailored coat and waistcoat and breeches, his immaculately styled and powdered hair, his three-cornered hat held correctly beneath one arm, his silver-headed cane held carelessly in one gloved hand—and his air of haughty good breeding. And then William Stubbs stepped out of the carriage and stood before its door, feet apart, arms crossed over his chest. "I believe she *may* be at home, m'lord. Would you be so good as to step into the crimson salon?"

"I would indeed," Nigel said faintly.

The crimson salon lived up to its description, though the color of the furniture and draperies had mellowed with age. It was a room that suggested past opulence and present less prosperous times. It was very slightly shabby, though less so than Nigel had suspected might be the case. The shabbiness had been less apparent in the hall with its old-fashioned oak paneling and high plaster ceiling.

He crossed the room to the long window and looked out through one of the square panes. He was looking back the way he had come with the carriage just a few minutes before—across the wide and sloping lawn to the shrubs below it and the trees below them. And to the valley and the rolling hills beyond. The village, he noted, was hidden from sight by the trees. It took no effort of mind to understand why the house had been built on this particular spot. The view was magnificent. It was paradise on earth—Will had been half-right. It was England.

He felt the old familiar pain clutch at his heart. England! The thought of it at one time had been both his despair and his one sustaining hope. England *was* paradise—or so it had appeared to him then—and as seemingly unattainable in this life as the heavenly paradise that was said to lie beyond death.

Of late he had not been given to such flights of fancy. But yes, he would allow himself a moment of enthusiasm. He had earned it.

It was a long wait—all of ten minutes. He was beginning to think that she really was from home or that she refused to see him—a somewhat amusing possibility. It seemed that she was expecting other visitors today. Perhaps she believed she had no time for him. Would he insist? Or would he be content to wait until tomorrow? He wished to avoid any unpleasantness if he possibly could—that had been the whole point of the long wait and the careful plan.

He could, of course, even now throw the whole plan to the winds. Will Stubbs, his friend and his confidant and only incidentally his valet, had always thought it a foolish plan. Nigel Wetherby, Viscount Wroxley, should go to Kedleston and assert himself as he had every right to do, Will had always insisted. It never made good sense to tiptoe gently about a woman's feelings, especially when that woman was a stranger and probably squinty-eyed and knife-tongued into the bargain. Nigel should disregard the woman, Will had always said. She was nothing to him and he owed her nothing.

Perhaps even now he should do things Will's way instead of his own. Or perhaps he should at least retreat to the inn to think things over one more time.

But it was too late. The door opened behind him and he turned slowly, wondering who had been sent to deal with the inconvenience of his call. But it was not the butler standing there or any other servant either. She was clearly a lady—a young lady. The lady of the house, if he was not mistaken.

Mr. and Mrs. Havelock were in the hall speaking with the butler when Cassandra entered the house with Patience, breathless and apologetic.

"You were here to greet the first guest?" Cassandra asked, reaching up with both hands to untie the ribbon bow at the nape of her neck that had kept her hat in place. "How dreadful of me to have missed him." She had a nasty thought suddenly and grimaced. "I do hope he *was* the first?"

"Dexter came for us, Cassandra," her uncle said. "The caller is not one of your invited guests."

Cassandra grimaced again. "Oh la," she said. "Whom did I forget?"

"No one, dear," her aunt assured her. "He gave his name as Viscount Wroxley. We have never heard of him. He is certainly not from anywhere close to here. Cyrus will see him and discover his business."

"You need not worry your pretty head," Mr. Havelock said, with the sort of hearty joviality with which he had treated his nieces since they were infants. "Run along with Althea and Patience, m'dear."

Viscount Wroxley? Cassandra had never heard of him either. "Did he ask for me specifically, Dexter?" she asked the butler.

"Yes, my lady," Dexter said with a bow. "I showed him into the crimson salon, my lady. But Mr. Havelock—"

Dexter, too, treated her like a child. All the servants did. Not that they were ever disrespectful—far from it. But there was something in their manner, something gentle and indulgent, as if they would tell her, if they dared, that she need not worry about a thing. *They* would see that the household ran smoothly, and *they* would see to it that she was pampered and protected for the rest of her life—or until she had a husband to do the pampering and protecting in their place.

Yesterday, she thought, she might well have given her uncle one of her sunniest smiles and run along with Patience. But there was all the difference in the world between yesterday and today. Today she was an adult. Today she was free.

"I shall see him, then," she said, favoring everyone with her most dazzling smile. She turned to stride off in the direction of the crimson salon. Her aunt and uncle, she realized before she reached the room, were coming along behind her. A footman, doubtless signaled by Dexter, scurried ahead of them to open the doors.

Who on earth was Viscount Wroxley? And what was his business with her? It was an intriguing mystery to greet her on her birthday. So rarely in the heart of Somersetshire did one meet strangers. Life was very secure and very pleasant here—and frequently quite dull.

Cassandra paused in the doorway of the crimson salon before moving inside so that her aunt and uncle could approach, too, and be effective chaperons. Her visitor, Viscount Wroxley, was standing by the window, looking out, though he turned at the sound of the door opening. He was indeed a stranger to her. She had never seen him before, of that she was certain. She would not have forgotten him if she had.

He was a young man, certainly not older than thirty years of age. He was somewhat above the average in height, and slender, not thin—certainly not thin. He was handsome, too, in a rather thin-faced, prominent-nosed way. But what struck her most in the few seconds that passed before anything was said was his immaculate, understated elegance. She knew immediately that he must have come from London, or at the very least from one of the fashionable urban centers.

Everything about him suggested wealth and taste and elegance. His dark blue frock coat was curved outward at the front to reveal a long silk waistcoat of a lighter shade. His coat was cut along slimmer lines than was the older fashion favored by her uncle and most men of her acquaintance, with fewer side pleats. It emphasized his graceful form and his height. His light gray knee breeches buckled neatly over his white stockings—her uncle still rolled his stockings over the tops of his breeches. He had neatly powdered hair with side curls and the length hidden in a black silk bag behind and tied at the nape of his neck with a black bow. Yet even as she curtsied she was aware that Viscount Wroxley was not wearing a wig. It was his own hair. His three-cornered hat and a cane had been set down on a table close to where he stood.

This was an intriguing moment indeed.

He made her an elegant bow and she noticed with what natural grace he moved.

"The Countess of Worthing?" he asked. He had, she realized then, been examining her appearance during those few seconds as closely as she had been observing his. How unmannerly of them both! She smiled.

"Yes, my lord," she said, advancing a little farther into the room. "And my uncle and aunt, the Honorable Mr. and Mrs. Cyrus Havelock. May I ask to what I owe this honor?"

"I understand," he said, after bowing to her aunt and

uncle, "that today is your birthday, my lady. I know also that it is the sad anniversary of your father's passing one year ago. May I offer both my congratulations and my sympathy?"

"Thank you," she said, startled. "Did you know my father, my lord?"

"Yes, indeed, by my life," he said. "The Earl of Worthing was a friend of mine. A particularly close friend. I still mourn my loss—and yours, madam."

Cassandra smiled warmly. Her father had always spent several months of the year in London on business. During the last five years of his life, after her mother's death, his stays there had become longer and longer, so that by the end she had rarely seen him. She had felt that she scarcely knew him any longer. He had never invited her to join him, even during the months of the spring Season, when other young ladies of her rank were taken there to meet prospective husbands. She had never particularly wanted to go for *that* reason, but she would have liked to spend more time with her father. And she would have liked to see London.

"You were a dear friend of my father's?" she said. "How very pleased I am to make your acquaintance then, my lord. Have you come all the way from London just because today is my birthday and the first anniversary of Papa's passing?"

He inclined his head to her. "I could conceive of no better use to make of my time," he said. "I would not intrude upon you during your mourning, madam, for though dear to your father, I was a stranger to you. Today seemed the appropriate occasion on which to pay my respects. I hoped you would not be from home."

"Oh," she said with a somewhat breathless laugh, "I am never from home, my lord." She felt warmed through to the very heart. A man who did not even know her had come all the way from London to wish her well just because he had been Papa's friend. He had come such a distance not even knowing for sure that he would find her at Kedleston. He must have been an amazingly dear and loyal friend. She might have met him sooner if her father had invited her to London.

"I congratulate myself upon my good fortune, madam," he said.

And then she realized as she smiled at him in sheer delight that she was keeping him—and her aunt and uncle—standing. "Please will you be seated, my lord?" she said. "Shall we all be seated? I shall have a tea tray brought in and you must tell us all about your friendship with Papa. Everything there is to tell."

He had the most charming of smiles, she thought. He was the handsomest of gentlemen.

"While one feels the deepest reluctance to forgo such a courtesy," Mrs. Havelock said, " 'twould be well to remember, Cassandra, that there will be guests arriving all afternoon and that you should be free to greet them. Perhaps his lordship, if he is staying in the neighborhood, would care to return to take tea with us tomorrow?" She smiled graciously at Viscount Wroxley. " 'Tis my niece's birthday, my lord, as you are aware. She will be busy with the celebrations for the rest of the day."

Mr. Havelock cleared his throat with a low rumble. "We will be pleased to receive you for an hour tomorrow afternoon in the withdrawing room, m' lord," he said, "if you can spare the time to stay in the area and are not on your way elsewhere. May I recommend the village inn? I understand that the beds are tolerably clean, the food quite palatable, and the landlady respectable."

"I am intruding upon a busy and happy day, madam," Lord Wroxley said with a keen look at Cassandra from his rather heavy-lidded blue eyes that did curious things suddenly to her breathing. "I will be delighted to take tea with you and your family tomorrow afternoon. And I have already taken a room at the inn, sir."

But Cassandra had a sudden thought and clasped her hands to her bosom. "But you will not sit in the inn parlor all night being dull, my lord," she said, ignoring the sudden movement her uncle made with his hand, as if to stop her. "You will be a guest at my birthday ball here this evening.

You will be my special guest.'' Her aunt and uncle would not be allowed to expel him to the inn until tomorrow merely because Papa had never made them acquainted with his friend. She was Papa's daughter and mistress of Kedleston.

"Doubtless, Cassandra," her uncle said in his gentle avuncular voice, the one that said by its tone she was just a child and did not know what she was saying, "his lordship would be uncomfortable at a country entertainment at which he has no acquaintances."

"But he is acquainted with us," Cassandra said. She would not withdraw her invitation or discourage the viscount from accepting it. He had been Papa's friend and was therefore hers.

Viscount Wroxley had kept his eyes on her. " 'Twould be my pleasure to accept, madam," he said, speaking to her in a somewhat lowered tone, as if his words were for her alone even though her uncle and aunt could hear them clearly. "I can conceive of nothing I would rather do this evening than dance at your birthday ball. 'Tis to be hoped that your hand has not already been bespoken for every set?"

"Only for the first," she said, smiling at him and regretting that even that had been promised.

"Then I will make so bold as to request the honor of the second?" Lord Wroxley said with raised eyebrows.

"Thank you." She stood smiling at him, feeling very pleased with herself indeed. There would be a stranger at her ball, a handsome, wondrously elegant stranger to add novelty to the occasion. And she would dance the second set with him. What a very splendid day this was turning out to be.

Her uncle gave his rumble of a cough again. "You will excuse her ladyship now, m' lord," he said. "Your carriage is still at the door, I do believe."

"Indeed it is," the viscount said, taking up his hat and his cane from the table and setting the former beneath his right arm. "I will not keep you longer from your duties, madam."

But Cassandra had had another thought and she acted upon it without taking time for further consideration. "But you must not stay at the inn, my lord," she said. "I could not possibly allow a friend of Papa's to stay there. I do not doubt that the beds are horridly lumpy even if they are clean and that the food is dreadfully plain even if it is palatable. You shall stay here at Kedleston. There are rooms not yet taken. I shall have Dexter show you to one and send a groom to the inn to cancel your reservation."

"Cassandra—" her uncle began.

"Oh lud, my dear," her aunt said at the same moment.

But it was perfectly unexceptionable to ask Viscount Wroxley to stay. The house was to be full of guests, including her aunt and uncle. Besides, he had been her father's friend and had come a long way to pay her the courtesy of a visit.

"I must insist," she said. "I *do* insist. You will stay, my lord?" She wondered if he would notice the obvious disapproval of her uncle and aunt, though they said nothing, and refuse.

He raised one eyebrow and looked instantly haughty and quite unmistakably aristocratic. "If *you* insist, my lady," he said, "I must, as a gentleman, capitulate."

"Oh, splendid!" Her hands were still clasped at her bosom, her straw hat suspended from them by the ribbons. She reached out one arm toward her new guest. "Come then, my lord, I shall take you to Dexter, and he shall see to your comfort."

She set her hand on his wide cuff when he had crossed the room to her, and preceded her ominously silent aunt and uncle from the room after smiling brightly at them. But she no longer had to fear the scold that she knew was imminent. She was mistress of Kedleston. She was free. She could invite whomever she chose to stay there. And so she did.

THREE

She was a beauty. She was small and well shaped and dainty, with dark unpowdered hair beneath her lace cap—somehow he had imagined her as a blond—with dark gray eyes, whose long lashes added both size and allure to them. She had lovely white, even teeth and a dimple in her right cheek when she smiled. She smiled often. She had been dressed charmingly for the country in a light muslin open gown with only small hoops. She had obviously just come in from the outdoors. She had held a wide-brimmed straw hat, and her cheeks had been glowing with healthy color.

She was more than a beauty. She was not the shy, timid, lusterless creature he had pictured in his imagination, but was warm and vivid and charming. He had been invited down to tea in the drawing room and had found it filled with other guests as well as her family members. He had certainly not been the only man unable to take his eyes off her. Indeed, she had been very much the center of everyone's attention, and he did not believe that it was just the occasion that had caused it. She must have any number of suitors—even more than he had expected her to have. It would be not only her rank and her wealth that would attract. Indeed it was amazing that she had not married before Worthing's death.

He had felt quite secure during the past year, of course. No suitor would have been encouraged or accepted during the year of her mourning. And so he had delayed his coming. But tonight she might well be besieged by attentions. And in the coming days and weeks she undoubtedly would be. She was one of the most eligible young ladies in the country.

Nigel stood in his shirtsleeves at the window of the bedchamber allotted him, looking out over a three-tiered flower garden that descended the slope to one side of the house. Beyond was a lawn and then the trees again, with a wide path curving with the slope to the right of them. *Paradise on earth.* Yes, indeed it was. Any person living here, owning all this, would never need to go away again. All the beauty, all the serenity, all the energy a man could ever need were here.

It was so much more than he had spent a lifetime imagining.

He could hear Will Stubbs busy in the small adjoining dressing room, unpacking and setting out his shaving gear and the evening clothes he would need for dinner and the ball. He smiled to himself. Will could not possibly be anyone's idea of a typical valet. But he would not be a hanger-on, he had declared quite emphatically two years before when they had been unexpectedly reluctant to part company. He must earn his keep. Nigel had not yet hired a valet; Will had declared his intention of filling the vacancy. They had been perhaps equally surprised—and equally amused—to discover that the new valet not only liked his job but also did superlatively well at it.

Nigel's thoughts returned to the Countess of Worthing. It pleased him that she was beautiful—and charming and vivacious. He looked forward to the evening, looked forward to dancing with her, conversing with her—she had played the perfect hostess at tea and had not conversed at any great length with any one guest to the exclusion of any others. She had exchanged only a few brief words with him.

How fortunate that he had arrived today instead of tomorrow. He had not expected to find it so easy to begin their acquaintance. He certainly had not expected to spend his very first night here in the house itself. At Kedleston.

She liked him, he thought. She had welcomed him and his story with warm, unsuspecting delight—unlike her uncle and aunt and the other two aunts he had met at tea, who had treated him with the proper courtesy and very obvious caution. But of course today she did not have to look to her relatives for guidance or advice. And today she was acting with remarkable lack of caution.

It was a good thing he meant her no harm. Quite the contrary, in fact.

He meant her only good. He meant to deal fairly and generously with her, when he was under no obligation to deal with her at all.

It was her problem if she behaved without caution.

"Hark ye, Nige," William Stubbs said, poking his head around the dressing-room door without first knocking, "if we 'as to get you all togged out to trip a reel or two, you'd better stop your woolgathering and fetch yourself in 'ere."

Will's superlative services did not include anything resembling the proper deference a valet was expected to show his master, Nigel reflected as he turned obediently from the window.

Lady Beatrice's private sitting room was the appointed gathering place. They were all dressed in evening finery, but it was not yet time to go down to the drawing room to mingle with the guests before dinner. They were all deliberately early.

"And what did *you* make of him, Bea?" Mr. Havelock asked. He looked disproportionately large standing before her dainty fireplace. His peacock-blue satin waistcoat added to the impression of vastness.

"He has distinguished manners, brother," she said. "He might even be described as charming, if a trifle—"

"Foppish?" Mr. Havelock suggested. "Hmmph! And you, Matty?"

"He certainly has the best of tailors," Lady Matilda said. "One can always tell. And he is an extraordinarily handsome young man. I cannot agree that he is a fop, Bea.''

"His carriage is new and extremely well appointed,''
Mrs. Havelock said. "I daresay he is a wealthy young man,
and of course he has the title, which must always impress.
But 'tis unfortunate that Cassandra spoke up without con-
sulting Cyrus first. Perhaps 'twas little more than a common
courtesy to invite him to the ball since he *is* a viscount, but
to invite him to stay at Kedleston! Lud, the child has no
idea how to go on. I was fit to swoon.''

"Zounds,'' Mr. Havelock said, "he may be distinguished and charming, Bea, and he may be elegant and
handsome, Matty, and he may have an elegantly appointed
carriage, Althea, but what has been proved? Who the devil
is he? Pardon me, but strong language seems called for.
Before I would have invited the young man to spend longer
than an hour in the drawing room tomorrow taking tea with
the whole family present, I would have demanded to know
who he is, who his father is, where his property is, what
his prospects are. Is he respectable? Charming he may be,
though I thought him arrogant to a fault, but is he someone
we ought to receive? We have done far more than receive
him, thanks to Cassandra's youthful impetuosity. I feared
just this sort of thing. Worthing should have married her
off years ago.''

"He is a titled gentleman, Cyrus, as Althea has pointed
out,'' Lady Matilda reminded him. "And he *was* Worthing's close friend.''

"Which is not necessarily much of a recommendation,
Matilda,'' Lady Beatrice said. "And we have only his word
for it.''

"You think he may be an impostor, Bea?'' Lady Matilda
asked, looking and sounding deeply shocked. "But why?
He has such a very handsome smile.''

"Why, Matty?'' her brother asked, clearly exasperated.
"Why? Because Kedleston is potentially one of the richest
properties in England and probably soon will be now that
it no longer has to support Worthing's expensive habits.
And Cassandra owns Kedleston. That is why. I do not say
Wroxley is an impostor, but I do say he is very probably

a damned fortune hunter—pardon me. He would have us believe that he has come all the way from London merely to wish the daughter of his late friend a happy birthday. Pox on it, does he think we are all green girls here? He came because he is in dun territory and he smelled the chance of a fortune. That is why he came, you may depend upon it.''

''Do not work yourself into an apoplexy, brother,'' Lady Beatrice said. ''It may well be that you speak truth. Cassandra did a very unwise thing, but 'tis of no very great consequence. The house is full of guests, many of them equally eager to get their hands on Kedleston. It will not happen. We have decided that. We have already settled Cassandra's future in her own very best interests. Once she is safely betrothed to Robin, the Lord Wroxleys of this world may stay in London where they belong and squabble over the heiresses there.''

''Bravo, Aunt Bea,'' Robin said, laughing. ''I cannot see that any great harm has been done, either. Cass has never been a giddy girl, despite her smiles and her youthful high spirits. She has always been sensible, if a little impulsive. She will not allow her head to be turned by handsome looks and practiced charms, you may be sure. She scarcely glanced at Wroxley during tea. She did not noticeably favor any of her possible suitors.''

''She is indeed a sensible girl, Robin,'' Lady Matilda agreed. ''And if she invited a young man to attend the ball and to stay at Kedleston, then we may be sure she did so because today is a very special day for her. And he was Worthing's friend. How could she have turned him away? We have nothing to fear. By tomorrow—la, even before tonight is over—she will be affianced to Robin and will live happily with him for the rest of her life.''

''I should not demand some answers from Wroxley to-night, then, you think?'' Mr. Havelock asked, looking from one to another of them, a frown on his face. ''About who exactly he is, I mean?''

''I think not, my love,'' his wife said. ''Tomorrow he will leave, especially after he understands that there is no point in remaining to pay court to Cassandra. We will never see him again and it will not matter who he is."

"He seems very young to have been a friend of Worthing's," Lady Beatrice said. "But I agree, brother. Apart from satisfying our curiosity, I can see no advantage to questioning the young man this evening. He is to dance the second set with Cassandra, you said, Althea? Well, there are enough young bucks who will be clamoring for her hand after that. And tomorrow he will be gone."

" 'Twould be demeaning to ask pointed questions, sir," Robin said to his stepfather. "He might conclude that you were treating him as a serious suitor."

"Zounds!" Mr. Havelock said. "You are right, m'lad. We will proceed as planned, then. By this time tomorrow all will be settled and the gel will be as happy as a lark. She will be pleased we have chosen you, Robin. The more I think about it, the more convinced I am of it."

"And why should she not?" Mrs. Havelock asked, smiling fondly at her son. "She has loved Robin all her life. Lud, it amazes me that we did not think of this obvious and happy solution sooner."

"We could have done nothing about it before today, Althea," Lady Beatrice said. "We were in mourning. No time has been lost. You may come and kiss your aunt on the cheek, Robin, and then offer your arm. It is time to go down to the drawing room. 'Tis to be hoped that Cassandra and Patience have finished dressing and will not be late. Girls can very easily be late when they have balls and beaux on their minds. I can remember well how it is."

She offered her cheek to a laughing Robin.

It had been the happiest day of her life. Cassandra felt no doubt of that fact even though she knew that perhaps she should feel guilty at such a conviction in light of the fact that her father had died exactly one year ago. But she had always dutifully loved him while he lived, and she had mourned him for a full year. She would always respect him in memory. Life must move onward. And she was happy.

This evening would be the perfect culmination of a perfect day. She stood up after her maid had finished pinning the frivolous lace cap to her carefully curled and powdered hair and arranging the long lappets down her back. She looked at herself in the full-length pier glass and was satisfied with her appearance.

Oh, she was more than satisfied. She felt wonderful, and though she would not say so aloud to another living soul, she thought she looked rather wonderful, too. Aunt Beatrice had been quite right about the colors. Cassandra had wanted to wear something vividly bright for the ball. She had not wanted to look like a very young lady about to make her come-out, and she had desperately wanted something that contrasted totally with the unrelieved black she had worn for so long. But Aunt Bea had insisted that delicacy was more in her style than vividness.

Her embroidered silk mantua was of pale gold. It was an open gown, the bodice opened to reveal a darker gold, and far more heavily embroidered stomacher, the full skirt, draped over wide hoops, opened to show the white silk-and-lace petticoat beneath. The robings or borders of the mantua were also embroidered more heavily than the rest of the garment. The three white lace frills of her shift flared beneath the elbow-length sleeves of the bodice. Her heeled slippers were of gold silk, her fan of patterned ivory.

She thought she looked rather beautiful, but very much too short of stature and too immature of feature for her age. It was her constant complaint. She looked like a delicate, helpless child, and everyone treated her as such. Oh, with affectionate indulgence, it was true. But with condescension nevertheless.

"Oh, you do look beautiful, Cass," Patience said with a sigh. There was a note of envy in her voice.

Cassandra had almost forgotten her cousin's presence. Patience and Aunt Matilda had been invited to dress at Kedleston so that they would not get windblown during the lengthy walk from the dower house—Aunt Matilda always declined the offer of a carriage.

"Do I?" Cassandra asked, tipping her head to one side and continuing to gaze at her image in the glass. "Then

that makes two of us.'' Patience was dressed in the palest
blue and looked extremely pretty, even though her coltish
figure had still not developed curves womanly enough to
satisfy her and perhaps never would. But at least, Cassandra
was in the habit of telling her with quite sincere envy, she
had some height. She was almost four inches taller than her
older cousin.

"Everyone is going to want to dance with you," Patience said. "There will not be enough sets to be granted
to all who will ask."

"That is because it is my birthday," Cassandra said,
"and everyone is duty bound to dance with me. But you
will have your fair share of partners, too. Of course you
will. Have you been imagining that you will be a wall-
flower? Phooey!" Patience was incurably modest about her
own charms. Yet even apart from her coltish beauty she
would have a sizable dowry from her father's estate when
she married.

"Viscount Wroxley will wish to dance with you," Patience said. "He is very handsome and very elegant, Cass.
Perhaps you will change your mind after dancing with him
and fall in love after all. 'Tis quite like a fairy tale, I do
declare. He has arrived out of nowhere in time for your
birthday ball. He was Uncle's friend. And he has deliberately sought you out, coming all the way from London."
She was half laughing, half-serious, Cassandra saw when
she turned to look at her.

She laughed herself. "But I have no glass slipper to wear
or to lose," she said. "Besides, Patience, I cannot run from
my own ball at midnight, can I? He is wonderfully handsome, I must confess, and he has already solicited my hand
for the second set. I shall enjoy dancing with him and that
will be that. Tomorrow he will be going back to London,
I do not doubt, though I hope to speak about Papa with
him before he leaves."

"And perhaps he will fall in love with you," Patience
continued, as if she had not heard a word of what her cousin
had just said. "Uncle probably told him how beautiful you
are and he has wanted to come all during the year of your

mourning. But I am glad he has waited. You look so much lovelier without your blacks. He will fall in love with you and marry you and carry you off to London, where you will be the belle of every ball.''

"Mercy on me," Cassandra said, laughing and twirling about before the pier glass again. "And they lived happily ever after. How horridly dull it sounds. We had better go down, Patience. 'Twould not do if I arrived last in the drawing room like a favored guest rather than the hostess, would it? I shudder at the thought. But I have forgotten something.''

She hurried to the dressing table and removed the lid from a small box that she drew from a top drawer. She rummaged inside it with one finger.

"You come and choose one, too," she said.

"Patches?" Patience said, leaning toward her. "You are going to wear a *patch,* Cass? But where are you going to place it?''

"Let me see," Cassandra said, withdrawing a small round black circle from the box. "Beside my eye? I think not. On my cheekbone? No, my dimple interferes with it there. Beside my mouth?'' She placed it there carefully and turned to face her cousin. "What do you think?''

"But you know what a patch next to the mouth is said to suggest," Patience said, giggling.

"The willingness to be kissed?" Cassandra said. " 'Tis also meant to *tease,* Patience. No one would dare try. Shall we go? Are you going to wear one?''

"You are going to *leave* it there?" Patience said, staring at the provocative patch her cousin wore. "We have only ever worn them in private before, Cass, since Uncle brought them home for you that time. I will not wear one in public. I should die of embarrassment.''

"But tonight I am a woman," Cassandra said. "And tonight I shall dare to be fashionable even here at Kedleston. Let us go before I lose my courage.''

But in reality she was not without courage at all, she thought as they left her dressing room and began the descent of the staircase to the drawing room. The happiest evening of her life was about to begin. And tonight all things seemed possible. Tonight she was no longer a girl. Somehow, mysteriously, since just yesterday she had been transformed from a girl into a woman. She had charge of her own life. It was a wonderfully exhilarating feeling.

She wondered suddenly if Viscount Wroxley would approve of her appearance tonight. She had been dressed quite plainly for the country outdoors this afternoon. Perhaps she had appeared quite rustic to him. She knew that tonight's gown was fashionable—the mantua maker had come from London and knew all the latest styles. And then she smiled to herself when she caught the direction of her thoughts. Her head *had* been turned a little by the arrival of a handsome stranger. But she did not care. Today was her day and tonight was her night and she had admitted to Patience this afternoon that her aversion to marriage had nothing to do with a dislike of gentlemen.

She hoped the viscount would think her fashionable and perhaps even a little beautiful. He had been Papa's friend. It was only natural that she should wish to impress him.

They were not the first to arrive in the drawing room, she saw as soon as she entered the room with Patience. Her uncle and her aunts and Robin were already there, as well as four of the houseguests. One of the latter was Viscount Wroxley.

He was dressed very magnificently indeed in a coat of emerald satin lavishly embroidered with silver thread to match his silver waistcoat. The linen and lace of his shirt and cuffs sparkled white. His gray silk knee breeches and white stockings hugged powerfully muscled legs. His shoes had high heels and buckles embedded with emeralds. His hair was freshly powdered and worn in two rolls at the sides with the length bagged in black silk and tied with black ribbon at the nape of his neck, as it had been earlier. The hilt of the dress sword he wore at his side glistened with emeralds. His appearance suggested wealth and elegance and taste. Cassandra caught and held her breath at the sight of him. *This* was how gentlemen dressed for a London ball?

He had, Cassandra realized as she opened her fan and

waved it slowly before her face so that her nervous hands would have something to do, been examining her appearance quite as thoroughly—and surely as appreciatively—as she had been observing his. Just as he had this afternoon. He raised one eyebrow and bowed to her.

Somewhere in the depths of her abdomen she felt a flutter of something that in all honesty she could only describe to herself as desire.

And somewhere else—in her heart, in her head—she felt the almost overwhelming exhilaration of knowing that now it had truly begun, this happiest evening of her life.

Nigel had deliberately come downstairs early. He had wanted to be at leisure to look about him. The house, or the little he had seen of it, really was quite magnificent, he found, and not nearly as shabby as he had expected or feared. He wondered if there was a portrait gallery somewhere. He longed to see it. But tonight would not be the time to ask. Perhaps tomorrow. Or the day after. He was in no great hurry. He had waited long enough. He would not rush now.

He was the first to arrive in the drawing room, but the family members came soon after him—Mr. and Mrs. Havelock, Lady Beatrice, Lady Matilda, and Mr. Robin Barr-Hampton, who, he gathered, was Mrs. Havelock's son by a previous marriage. He made his bows to them all and understood before many minutes had passed that none of them liked him. Not that any of them deviated by even one iota from perfect good breeding, but they talked pointedly about how eager he must be to return to town after a few days in the country, about how busy they were all to be in the coming days, especially their dear Cassandra, who was preparing for her—future. Lady Beatrice paused significantly before using that particular word and he understood that she intended him to believe she had meant to use the word *marriage*. But being too well bred to speak of such a thing before it was properly announced, she had used a vaguer word.

They meant him to understand that Lady Worthing was

to be married soon. Yet clearly there was no betrothal or they would have been only too delighted to be more specific.

They thought he had come to woo the countess. And they were strongly opposed to his suit. Nigel listened politely and made the appropriate responses, an enigmatic half smile on his lips.

He wondered who the intended bridegroom was. Barr-Hampton perhaps? He was young and he was part of the family. And certainly the stiff disapproval he succeeded in conveying to his supposed rival without saying more than a dozen words in all would suggest that he felt a certain proprietary interest in his stepfather's niece. But were the older people willing to countenance a nobody as a marriage partner for the countess? It was possible. They would still maintain some control over the affairs of Kedleston in the event of such a marriage, he supposed. And Lady Worthing herself was unlikely to fight them even if she felt no special fondness for her cousin. She was a sunny-natured girl. But there was the rub—she was a *girl* and doubtless biddable and easily influenced.

They saw him as a threat.

Three other guests arrived in the drawing room and were served with drinks. And then finally the doors opened again to admit the countess herself and her young cousin Miss Gibbons. Nigel did not even try to hide the fact that he watched only the countess herself as she hurried inside, came to a stop partway across the room, a look of eager anticipation on her face, acknowledged everyone's presence with that look, and finally rested her gaze upon him. Her expression told him clearly that she approved of what she saw. As he approved of what he saw, by Jove. Dressed all in white and pale gold, her hair powdered, she looked very fetching indeed. Like a teasing little temptress. The startlingly black patch beside her mouth offered a bold invitation that should have been matched with sultry eyes. But her eyes were wide with innocence.

Nigel held her eyes with his own—not with intensity, but with an amused sort of appreciation.

"An angel come down from heaven, i'faith, for the delight of mere mortals," he said, making her his deepest, most reverential bow. "Your father would be proud of you today, my lady."

The blush of color in her cheeks merely enhanced her beauty. Her eyes sparkled at him. "You flatter me, my lord," she said. "But I would have you tell me more of your friendship with my father. I saw little of him during the last few years of his life."

"'Twould be my pleasure, madam," he said. "But 'twere best done when you are more at leisure to devote an hour or so of your time exclusively to one guest. Tomorrow, perhaps?"

She smiled into his eyes, seemingly quite unalarmed at the prospect of spending an hour or more alone with him. "You do not have to hurry away to some other engagement tomorrow, then?" she asked him. "We will have time to talk? I am very glad, my lord. I shall look forward to it eagerly."

She was making it all very easy for him. Far easier than he had expected. So far he had not had to relate any of the stories he had prepared concerning his connection with Worthing. He had not been called upon to offer any proof of the friendship he claimed with the late earl. He owed his success purely to the innocence of a trusting nature, he knew. If she had not returned from her walk when she had this afternoon and he had met only her aunt and uncle in the crimson salon, he would now be kicking his heels at the village inn, preparing tomorrow's strategy.

"If I had another engagement, i'faith," he said, "I would surely break it, madam, in the knowledge that my doing so would make you *very glad*."

She laughed—a pretty, happy laugh. But she was clearly aware, too, that she was hostess of the dinner that would be served soon and of the ball that would follow it. She turned to greet the other guests in the room and the new ones who were arriving every minute. Robin Barr-Hampton, almost but not quite glowering, was soon at her elbow. She turned her head to favor him with a sunny smile, though it seemed to Nigel that there was nothing of any special fondness in it.

He rather hoped she was not in love with the fellow—or with anyone else. He had no wish to cause her any great unhappiness. It had been the whole point of his lengthy delay in coming to Kedleston.

FOUR

THE BALL OPENED WITH A minuet. Cassandra danced it with her cousin, reveling in the sights and sounds about her. The ballroom looked like an enchanted wonderland, decked as it was with flowers and filled as it was with their scents. The candles were lit in the chandeliers and their light was reflected in the newly polished mirrors and off the jewels worn by the guests. And those guests, both male and female, added the myriad colors of silks and satins and the mingled sounds of conversation and laughter. The orchestra, seated on the dais, was adding the harmony of music to the sounds of revelry.

It was all for her. It was her ball. It was the ball that celebrated her coming of age.

"Egad, cous," Robin said, "you look monstrous pretty tonight."

"You sound *surprised*, Rob," she said, smiling fondly at him. "But *monstrous* pretty sounds a fearsome thing to be."

He looked disconcerted for a moment and then threw back his head and laughed. "Dainty words do not come easily to my lips, Cass," he said. "But you do look pretty, for all that. Pretty enough to eat."

She was pleased. Robin did not usually compliment her

on her appearance. "You had better not do it," she said. "I might not enjoy it."

He chuckled.

"Would you believe that *six* gentlemen apart from you asked me for this first set?" she asked.

"I would believe it." He grinned. "And the poor devils have to wait for the next. Though only one of them can dance even that with you."

"Not even one," she said. "Viscount Wroxley has already spoken for it."

"I had forgot." His grin faded. "Is it wise, Cass?"

"Wise?" She raised her eyebrows. "To grant a set ahead of time? I did it for you, Rob."

"To so favor a perfect stranger," he said, "about whom we know nothing whatsoever. He might be a rogue, Cass, or an adventurer. He might not even be who he pretends to be."

She frowned. "He was Papa's friend."

"Did your father ever mention his name?" he asked.

"Of course not," she said. "I rarely saw Papa, Rob, or had a letter from him. You know that. And you are being very foolish. Why would he say he was Papa's friend if he was not? Why would he have come all the way from London just to wish me a happy birthday if he was not? 'Twould make no sense."

"Cass," he said with affectionate reproach.

The conversation had not progressed very quickly. They were frequently separated by the steps of the dance and could exchange words only when they were close. Trust Robin to think of impostors and rogues and adventurers, she thought. Robin had always peopled the woods about Kedleston with villains when they were children and obviously had not changed much.

"You are not to spoil my evening," she told him when next they were together, but she smiled to show that she was not overly cross with him. "You must confess, Rob, that he is exceedingly handsome and very splendidly dressed. I am determined that I shall be able to boast tomorrow and for weeks and months to come that I danced

with him. And tomorrow he is to tell me about his friendship with Papa. What have you to say to that, O Doubting
One?''

''Just that you are a very child, Cass,'' he said, shaking
his head, ''and need someone with an older and wiser head
to look after you.''

''Uncle Cyrus?'' she said. ''He ceased to be my guardian
yesterday, Rob, and I cannot say I am sorry. And if you
dare call me a child one more time, I shall stop dancing
and stamp my foot and toss my head and create A Scene.''
She laughed lightly.

But Robin, she could see, was out of sorts. He was
frowning.

''Oh Rob,'' she said the next time she was able. She had
been struck with a sudden thought. ''Did you mean yourself? Were you offering your own older and wiser head?
Were you offering to *look after me*? I will always be happy
to see you at Kedleston and to consult you with any problems I may have and to listen to your advice. You must
know that. I am not going to stop loving you, you know,
merely because I have come into my own at last.''

But he continued to frown as he stepped away from her.
Viscount Wroxley, Cassandra could see, was not dancing.
He was talking with the Reverend Hythe and elderly Mr.
Wintersmere—and he was watching her. She almost despised the way her breath quickened as she acknowledged
him with a smile. She noticed that he held a quizzing glass
in his hand. Had he been observing her through it?

''Pox on it,'' Robin was saying, '' 'tis impossible to converse while dancing. Talk with me later, Cass, when we
are at greater leisure. At suppertime. We can eat and then
leave the dining room early and find a quiet nook.''

''Why?'' she asked in some surprise.

''We need to talk,'' he said.

''Do we?'' She did hope he was not going to become
stuffy, imagining that now she was free of Uncle Cyrus's
guardianship she was going to need his guidance at every
turn. She loved Robin like a brother and she would never
be so hardheaded that she would not listen to advice, es-

pecially from a man who had successfully run his own estate for several years. But she really did not need him or
any man to *look after her*. How alike all men were! It was
probably a general assumption that she would choose a husband in some haste now that she had achieved her majority,
in the certain knowledge that she could not possibly cope
with life unless she had a man beside her to tell her when
to breathe.

"Meet me at suppertime," Robin said as he bowed to
her and she curtsied, the minuet at an end.

"Very well," she said, "if 'tis so important to you,
Rob."

"It is," he said.

And oh bother, she thought, Patience had not been right
about Robin, had she? She fervently hoped not.

"I am very glad, i'faith," Nigel said as they began to
dance a cotillion, "that I had the presence of mind—or
perhaps the audacity—to reserve this set with you this afternoon. I have seen that your admirers flock about you,
like bees about their queen."

Her smile brought out her dimple. He idly imagined
touching it with the tip of his tongue. The dimple was far
more alluring than the patch she wore daringly close to her
mouth.

"Or perhaps," he said, "they are more than admirers.
Perhaps they are suitors, each desirous of being the first to
petition for your hand now that 'tis yours alone to give."

"And perhaps," she said, laughing, "they are just gentlemen showing courtesy to their hostess, my lord, or desirous of dancing."

"By my life," he said, "'tis remarkably pleasurable to
show courtesy to such a hostess as you, madam."

She looked like a lovely child, sparkling over the treat
of a birthday party. Except that she was not a child. She
had a woman's allure, though all was unspoiled innocence.
She was not skilled at parrying gallantries with repartee or
with feigned indifference. She could only smile and show
both her awareness and her enjoyment of his flatteries.

She could be very easily shaped to a man's will.

"But I would wager a fortune," he said, "that all is not mere courtesy with a number of the gentlemen gathered here, madam. Who are your particular admirers and suitors? I wonder. Mr. Barr-Hampton most certainly. And he had the distinct advantage of being first to dance with you."

"Robin?" she said, startled. "He is my cousin, my lord, not my suitor. He is like a brother to me. We climbed trees together and fought thieves and robbers in the woods together and went riding together."

Perhaps he had misunderstood, though he did not believe so. Barr-Hampton had not yet declared himself, apparently, but he surely would. Her words reassured him, though. Fond she might be of her stepcousin, but she was not in love with him. He could not tell if Barr-Hampton loved her, but that was not his concern.

"Well, then," he said, "the young gentleman in blue velvet with enough lace to sink a smuggler's brig. *He* admires you, madam, and has hopes of doing more than admire unless I am much mistaken."

"Mr. Raftan?" she said, following the direction of his eyes. "He is exceedingly shy and has the unfortunate tendency to stammer when he is nervous—and he is frequently nervous. I take pains to converse with him at entertainments, my lord, as so many ladies avoid his company."

And so Raftan had conceived his hopes. But she did not love him—she pitied him.

"Ah," he said, "then by my life it must be the gentleman whose valet spent at least all afternoon curling his wig. The one dancing with the lady in pink."

"Sir Isaac Bingaman," she said. "He spent two months of last winter in London with cousins and wishes us all to know how *rustic* we are. He has become remarkably foolish."

"But not in his admiration for you, madam," he said. "And the only sense in which you might be called rustic, i'faith, is in the way you embody all the loveliness of the English countryside for which men yearn when they are on foreign shores."

"Oh." She forgot to smile for a moment, but her eyes grew larger and her flush deepened. "You do have a way with words, my lord. I do declare you must *practice*. Have you been on foreign shores? Have you ever been away from England for any length of time?"

Seven years. For a few moments he felt that he could scarcely breathe, even though all the French windows had been thrown back to admit the somewhat cooler air of the outdoors to the ballroom.

"As most gentlemen have," he said, inclining his head.

"Ah," she said, "the Grand Tour. How fortunate gentlemen are. How I should love to see other countries. Did you see all the most celebrated and picturesque places?"

He had seen hell on earth. "Nothing," he said, "to compare with—what were the words I used a moment ago?— the loveliness of the English countryside for which all men yearn." He looked deeply into her eyes as he spoke—with deliberate intensity this time—knowing she remembered that those words had been used to describe her.

She gazed back at him with parted lips, too innocent to conceal the pleasure she felt at his lavish compliment. But he never found it difficult to lure far more experienced women than she under his spell. Only a couple of weeks before one of his mistresses, a married woman of some sophistication, had told him almost crossly as she had bowed to his will that he could charm the birds out of the trees if he set his mind to it.

He was setting his mind to it now.

"I suppose, madam," he said, "that every set for the rest of the evening is spoken for and that there is at least one understudy for each ready to jump out from the wings should one of the favored few expire before his turn comes?"

She laughed gaily. "This is a country ball, my lord," she said. "We behave with far less formality than do people in London. Gentlemen rarely reserve sets ahead of time."

"Then country gentlemen are decidedly foolish, by my life," he said, "and deserve to lose the partners of their choice. I would dance the set after supper with you, madam, if you would be so good as to reserve it for me."

" 'Twill be remarked upon if I dance with the same gentleman twice at my own ball," she said, but she spoke lightly, almost teasingly. She wished to be persuaded.

He lifted his eyebrows. "Indeed?" he said. "Your *guardian* will demand to know my intentions?"

She laughed. "I have no guardian, my lord," she said. "I am my own mistress."

"Then, madam," he said, "you are free to allow the singular fact that you dance twice with the same gentleman to be remarked upon."

"And so I am," she said. "But I am also free to refuse to allow it to happen, my lord."

Ah. At last. She was flirting with him. She was enjoying herself. He fingered the handle of his quizzing glass with his free hand as he danced and half raised it to his eye.

"I must remind you then, madam," he said, "that I was your father's friend. Perhaps even his dearest friend. And that I have traveled a long distance to greet you on your birthday. And that I am a guest in your home. And that I am humbly begging you to dance again with me."

She was laughing with delight. "Then you leave me with no choice after all, my lord," she said. "The set after supper is yours."

And the set after supper, he decided, would not be wasted on the dance floor, where a conversation could be conducted only in fits and starts and could be overheard by anyone intent upon listening. There was a terrace beyond the French doors, and the tiered flower gardens he could see from his bedchamber were beyond that, and a lawn beneath the tiers. It was a warm night and one that was bathed in moonlight.

It was a perfect night for—a little romance. A very little. He would be patient.

Cassandra had no chance to sit with her supper partner. Everyone, it seemed, wanted to talk to her, to congratulate her on her birthday and on the success of the ball. And it *was* a success, she believed, not just for herself because she had decided it was to be the happiest evening of her life, but for everyone. All the young ladies had had partners for every set, including—of course—Patience, who had not had to sit out even one with Aunt Matilda and who looked endearingly surprised at her own success. And all the gentlemen had seemed less reluctant than usual to dance. Even Aunt Bea had danced one set with portly Mr. Latimer.

Cassandra was looking forward to the next set. She was also a little embarrassed about it. What would people think or say when she danced for a second time with Viscount Wroxley? But really, she decided, she did not care. She *wanted* to dance with him again. She would never have the chance again after tonight. People might say what they wished.

But first, of course, there was to be her private talk with Robin. He had not forgotten about it, she saw when he came striding toward her, took her by the elbow while Mrs. Timmings finished relating an anecdote about her son-in-law's brother-in-law, made their excuses for her, and steered her from the dining room into the empty ballroom.

" 'Tis a splendid ball, cous," he said. "You are enjoying it?"

"More than I ever dreamed possible," she said. "Is it not wonderful beyond belief to be one-and-twenty years old? Can you remember the feeling of being finally free, finally your own person?"

"But I am a man, Cass," he said. "There is a difference."

She could have argued the point. But had she done so she would have become heated with anger, and this was not a night for anger. She smiled instead. "What was so important that I had to be hauled away from my supper?" she asked.

"I think, Cass," he said, "you had better marry me." He grimaced while she stared at him in shocked incomprehension. Patience had been right. "Pox on it, but that was not well expressed. I am not good with words or I would have prettied it up. You know I am just a plain man and can say only what is in my mind. I think you had better marry me.''

"Rob?" she said, still staring. "*Marry* you? Marry *you*? But why?"

" 'Tis very peculiar, you must admit,'' he said, "for a woman to be able to inherit all this, Cass. Fortunately it has never happened in your family before, but now it has. Uncle should have foreseen it and made sure that you were well married long before this birthday. I suppose he did not expect his own early demise—most of us do not—but it was irresponsible under the circumstances not to prepare for the worst.''

"The worst," Cassandra said quietly, opening her fan and waving it absently before her face. "I am part of the worst, Rob?"

"Egad, Cass," he said, "you do put words into a fellow's mouth.''

"Let me hear your words then," she said, snapping the fan closed again. She was beginning to feel angry after all. Very angry. She had not expected this of Robin.

"I do not wish to insult Uncle," Robin said. "He was your papa. And what is done is done—or rather, what is *not* done. The fact is, Cass, that you have been left with all this and without a man to protect you.''

"And you think you should be that man," she said.

He looked at her, frowning. "You look cross," he said. "You ought not to be, Cass. It is what is best for you. We are all agreed on that. We—''

"All?" she asked, interrupting him. "We?"

"Stepfather," he said. "Mama, Aunt Bea, Aunt Matilda. We are all in perfect agreement, Cass. I know I do not have your rank and my property would fit into one corner of your estate. But you know me. You know that greed is not part of my nature. We are fond of each other. And I will—''

"Look after me," she said, finishing the sentence for him. "You will *all* look after me, but you most of all. You realize, I suppose, Rob, that the property would not become yours on our marriage?''

" 'Twill be held in trust for our son," he said, flushing.

She supposed she should feel grateful to him. Robin, she knew, would never be motivated by greed. But he did have a strong sense of responsibility and a fondness for her. Was Patience *really* right?

"Do you love me, Rob?" she asked. Poor Patience if his answer was yes.

"You know I am fond of you, Cass," he said. "I always have been."

" 'Twas not what I asked," she said. "I asked if you *love* me. Do you?"

"With all due respect, Cass," he said, "love is for women, you know."

"Thank you." She smiled at him, relieved, though there was still fury boiling deep inside her. "That answers my question. And *my* answer is no."

"No?"

"I will not marry you," she said.

He closed his eyes. She wondered if he was surprised. The family had decided that she was to marry him and it would have occurred to none of them that perhaps she would refuse to do so. Though it might have occurred to Robin himself. Robin knew that she had a mind of her own.

"But, Cass," he said, "whom will you marry?"

"No one," she said. "I will marry no one."

" 'Twas the way I asked," he said, lifting a hand to run through his hair, remembering that he was wearing a wig, and gesturing futilely with the hand instead. "I should have practiced a pretty speech."

"Phooey!" she said.

"But you have to marry someone," he said. "You can see what has happened today already, Cass, and it will continue to happen more and more frequently. Now that your mourning is over, now that you are of age, everyone has designs on you. Mine is not the only offer you will hear in the coming weeks. And you will invite fortune hunters, men who do not care a farthing about you, only about your wealth. Look at Wroxley, for example."

"You believe he is a fortune hunter?" she asked.

"Egad, cous," he said, sounding exasperated, "what do you think? That he came down here all the way from London because he was Uncle's friend? Because he wished to greet you on your birthday? The man is a conceited fop. He was *flirting* in the most outrageous manner with you before dinner. He was flirting with you when he danced with you. He will probably try to dance with you again tonight."

"I am to dance the next set with him," she said.

He made a sound of frustration. "Can you not *see*?" he asked her.

"Obviously not," she said. "But I can see the contempt in which I am viewed by my own family. I am without understanding, without *brains* because I am a woman."

"Not contempt, Cass," he said. "Egad, we *love* you! And you are not without either understanding or brains. 'Tis just that you are young and female and need the protection and guidance of a man. 'Tis the nature of men and women. There is no contempt in our desire to protect you. He is after your fortune, Cass. You may take my word on it. The next thing you know, he will be announcing his intention of staying another day."

"He is to spend an hour with me tomorrow, telling me about his friendship with Papa," she said.

He clucked his tongue. "Listen to older and wiser heads, Cass," he said illogically. "If not to mine, then to stepfather's and the aunts'. Stepfather expects to announce our betrothal before the night is out. Let him do it. You will be safe then. I promise you will be safe. I will never abuse your trust."

She felt almost blinded with fury. How *dared* they! But she was not really surprised. And perhaps it was unfair to be angry. They had not had a chance to see that she was capable of managing her life and her estate very well on her own. And undoubtedly they thought they had her best interests at heart.

"I know you would not, Rob," she forced herself to say as gently as possible. She could not raise her voice anyway. Most of the guests were back in the ballroom and the orchestra members were tuning their instruments. "But there will be no announcement tonight. Or tomorrow. Or ever concerning you and me. You must stop thinking of me as your responsibility. I am not. And I shall tell Uncle Cyrus the same thing."

"Cass, you are not—" he began. But he was interrupted before he could tell her what she was not. Viscount Wroxley was bowing to them.

"I cannot allow you the advantage of private conversation with the lady any longer, sir," he said to Robin. " 'Tis my turn, i'faith. Madam?" He extended his hand for Cassandra's.

He looked faintly amused, almost as if he knew that the conversation he had interrupted had not been entertainment. He was no impostor, Cassandra thought, setting her hand on his. He was all ease and grace and warm charm. He had a sense of humor. And he was clearly a wealthy man in need of no one's fortune. She would not think of Robin's strangely disturbing marriage proposal until later—or of his warnings either. She would not allow him to spoil what remained of this happiest night of her life.

" 'Tis my pleasure, my lord," she said, smiling at Viscount Wroxley and deliberately not turning her head to see the scowl she was sure must be on Robin's face.

No one was going to spoil this night. Or her life. Not without her express permission.

FIVE

VISCOUNT WROXLEY LED
Cassandra onto the dancing area where the sets were beginning to form—and across it toward the open doors of the French windows. She could feel a welcome coolness as they drew near. How lovely it would be to step out there. Before supper some of the guests had strolled out on the terrace, where lanterns had been lit for their pleasure and convenience, but she had not set foot outside herself. Mr. Snyder had invited her out there just before supper, but she had refused. Mr. Snyder, who often held her in conversation outside church on Sunday mornings and who often invited her to make up a table of cards with him at evening entertainments, was on the verge of offering her marriage, she had sensed. She had avoided the moment. The thing was that she *liked* him as she did most of the gentlemen who were rapidly turning from friends and neighbors to suitors. She did not want to hurt any of them and create an awkwardness that would make social intercourse difficult for some time to come.

She had not seen it coming with Robin, of course. She still could not quite believe what had just happened. She thought of Robin almost as a *brother*. She felt quite unprepared to enjoy the dance she had looked forward to for several hours. Her mind felt as if it had been caught up in some sort of whirlwind from which it could not pull free.

"I'faith, madam," Viscount Wroxley said, "your ballroom is like a tropical garden, filled with exotic blooms. 'Tis unfortunate perhaps that such gardens are by their very nature overwarm for comfort. Perhaps you would be willing to forgo the pleasure of dancing in order to step out into an English garden bathed in moonlight and cooled by an English breeze."

They were at the doors and had stepped through them before she could answer. The terrace was deserted so soon after supper. The air felt instantly cool and fresh. The sounds of conversation and the tuning of instruments from the ballroom seemed instantly muted. She breathed in deeply and closed her eyes. She felt her mind begin to stop whirling.

"It *is* lovely," she said wistfully.

"Yes, by my life," he said, so softly that she opened her eyes and found him gazing at her intently.

He was flirting with her again. She did not know much about the art of flirtation. It had never before been practiced on her. Though she had had suitors even before Papa's death, they had all been serious, even earnest in their attentions to her. She had never been particularly unhappy that Papa had never invited her to London to be presented at court and to participate in the social entertainments of the Season, though both Aunt Matilda and Aunt Althea had thought him neglectful of his duty as a father. But she would admit that sometimes—as now—she felt that something was lacking in her education. Though it was such a *relief* to be dealing with light flirtation after the disturbing seriousness of her talk with Robin.

"*Shall* we stroll?" the viscount asked her. She noticed that he had stopped just outside the French windows, that he was not trying to force her into doing anything against her will. "Shall we deprive your ballroom for half an hour of its most lovely and most exotic bloom?"

She laughed softly. "Do they teach you such gallantries at school?" she asked him. But she wanted to stroll outside with him. She wanted to be free of the crowds and the noise for a short while before returning and enjoying the rest of her special evening. She knew that she was perfectly safe with Viscount Wroxley. Despite Robin's foolish warning, she knew that he would not embarrass or distress her by suddenly blurting out an unwanted marriage offer. "Yes please, my lord. A stroll would be heavenly."

"Aye, heaven indeed," he said, leading her across the terrace rather than along it, and down the flight of shallow stone steps to the graveled path between the top and the middle tiers of flowers. "I knew, madam, as soon as my carriage began its ascent from the valley through the woods this afternoon, that I was approaching heaven. I knew that I had arrived there when I saw the house and when I gazed from the window of my room at this very scene. 'Tis paradise on earth. Anyone who belonged here would be foolish indeed to wish to leave again for any length of time."

They were words of lavish gallantry about her home, and yet they appeared to have been spoken with a certain conviction. She looked at him in some curiosity.

"Why *did* you come?" she asked him. " 'Tis a long distance from London and you had never met me. Did you truly come only to pay your respects to me, or is Kedleston on your route to somewhere else?"

"Why would anyone wish to go somewhere else when there is Kedleston?" he asked. "And the mistress of Kedleston. Your father spoke of you frequently, madam, and with deep affection. He spoke of his home with feeling."

"Did he?" she asked, and wished after the words had been spoken that she could take the sound of surprised wistfulness from her voice. Her father had been deeply affectionate toward her when she was a child, but he had changed in later years. It had not seemed important to him to spend more than a few weeks of the year with her. He had been content to live away from Kedleston for months at a time.

"The Earl of Worthing," he said, "was not an entirely happy man, I regret to say. I believe—pardon me, madam, for speaking frankly of something that is none of my concern except that he was my friend—I believe he cared deeply for your mother?''

Had he? Certainly he had stayed at Kedleston for far greater lengths of time while Mama was alive, and there had been a time when he had seemed a happy man. But had he loved Mama so deeply that being at home, where she had lived, had become painful to him after she was gone? It was difficult to know for sure. Cassandra had been only twelve years old when her mother died. Children just did not think of their parents in terms of close and intimate relationships. They were simply Mama and Papa.

''I felt that I almost knew you,'' Viscount Wroxley said. ''I would have come immediately on his passing, madam, but—pardon me again—cowardice kept me away. What can one say to comfort a grieving daughter? I waited to allow the worst of the grief to pass, and then I waited longer for no good reason at all. Finally I recalled that your father's passing had coincided with your birthday—your twentieth. What better occasion to come, then, than now, today? And so I came. And your father was perfectly right—about your home and about you.''

His voice had dropped. He was leading her down the steps at the other end of the terraces and turned to stroll with her along the path between the middle and lower tiers. The music from the ballroom was clearly audible, but it seemed strangely to be coming from very far away. From another world. The evening air was heavy with the perfumes of the flowers and soil. She could hear insects whirring and droning off in the darkness.

He spoke with sincerity. He had come because he felt an obligation. He was gallant and charming and even flirtatious, but he was no fortune hunter. He had no ulterior motive in calling upon her. Robin was wrong. Uncle Cyrus and the aunts were wrong. And finally she was able to think for herself and act on what *she* believed to be the truth.

''I am glad you came,'' she said. ''You have made an already wonderful day quite perfect.'' She wondered if it was wise to express her feelings so honestly, but she knew no other way than to say what she thought and what she felt.

"I'faith, madam," he said, "what more could I ask to make my own day perfect?" He had stopped walking and turned to face her. He had turned his hand beneath hers so that her fingers slid more deeply into his palm. "I, too, am glad I came." As she watched he raised her hand to his lips and held it there.

It was something that had happened to her dozens of times. Numerous gentlemen had kissed her hand, several of them this very evening as they had passed along the receiving line. But never before had it seemed like something intimate, something forbidden. Perhaps it was that they were in such a secluded place—she ought not to have allowed him to bring her down off the upper terrace. Or perhaps it was that his eyes held hers the whole time—except when for a moment he looked down at her patch and perhaps at her lips, too. Or perhaps it was that a wave of strange weakness fluttered through her heart and her stomach and her knees.

He lowered her hand and looked upward. " 'The moon shines bright,' " he said. " 'On such a night as this. . . .' " He looked down at her and smiled.

He really did have a way with words. But they sounded familiar. She frowned in thought. "Those words are from a poem," she said. "No, a play. By Mr. Shakespeare."

"Ah," he said, "an educated beauty. Sometimes the words of poets express our meaning far more eloquently than we can do ourselves."

She remembered then. *The Merchant of Venice.* They were words spoken by two lovers, each trying to outdo the other in describing events that had happened on such a beautiful moonlit night. They were lovers' words. Viscount Wroxley was flirting with her again—but with gentle humor. The tension had gone. She smiled at him.

"I have not found you lacking for eloquent words of your own, my lord," she said. "You have said some outrageously flattering things to me."

"Outrageous?" he said, raising his eyebrows. "Flattering? Zounds, madam, you have not looked in your glass lately if you truly believe that I have *flattered* you. Is the night beautiful? I believe it is. There is the freshness of the air, the scent of the flowers, the spill of blooms over the terraces, the smooth lawn, the trees beyond. There is the moonlight to lend the scene all the charm and mystery of a dim nocturnal light. But do I see all this beauty? Or does it all fade into insignificance beside the loveliness of the exotic flower I plucked from the ballroom?''

It was the most outrageous compliment of all. It had been spoken with a half smile and with his free arm gesturing elegantly and with deliberate theatricality. And with eyes very steady on her own. She laughed softly and at the same time felt all the force of the preposterously flattering words—even though she knew they *were* flattery and was amused by them. It was all very confusing.

"I see you will not answer my question," he said. "I will answer it for myself then. It all fades into insignificance, madam. By my life it does.''

She was startled. All the light humor, all the deliberate artificiality had gone from his manner. Only his eyes remained the same—but for so few moments that she was left feeling foolish at the intensity of her own reaction. Then he was smiling at her again, his eyelids half-lowered over his eyes.

"Perhaps after all," he said, "I can acquit myself well enough without the assistance of Shakespeare. I must return you to the ballroom, madam, or at least to the respectability of the upper terrace. I did not realize, i'faith, that I had brought you so far. 'Twould not do for your reputation to be compromised on such a happy occasion as this.''

"I am of age, my lord," she said as he led her toward one flight of steps. "And I am my own mistress. I do not feel the need to be flanked by chaperons at every turn.''

"For which fact I must be thankful this night," he said. "But you are a lady, madam, and have been gone from the company of your family and friends for long enough.''

For a moment she felt indignation at being treated as a child yet again—especially by a gentleman who was es-

sentially a stranger. But only for a moment. Then she felt
a rush of warm gratitude. He was not treating her as a child
but as a *lady*. Though he would flatter her and flirt with
her, he would do nothing to harm her reputation. If he were
a fortune hunter, he would. He would use everything to his
advantage.

She liked him very much indeed. And this half hour, to
which she had looked forward quite eagerly since he had
reserved it with her during the second set, had been very
much more wonderful than she had anticipated after all.
And this was not even the end of her acquaintance with
him. He planned to stay for at least a part of tomorrow.
Indeed, he had come down from London just to see her.
He was not on his way elsewhere. Perhaps she could persuade him to stay for a few days? And why not? Uncle
Cyrus and Robin were staying until the end of the week,
as well as Aunt Althea, of course. And Aunt Bea was a
permanent resident. It would be quite unexceptionable for
her to have another male guest, especially a friend of
Papa's.

It would be enjoyable to have a new acquaintance and
one who was so amiable and so amusing—and so something else, too. She could not quite put it into words. Attractive? Yes, he was very attractive. And why should she
not engage in a little flirtation, even perhaps a little romance? She would enjoy it thoroughly, but she would not
run the risk as she would with a neighbor of trapping herself into raising expectations she did not mean to satisfy.
Viscount Wroxley would return to his life in London very
soon—of course he would. In the meanwhile . . .

In the meanwhile the music had stopped and they were
climbing the last flight of steps to the lantern-lit terrace.

" 'Tis an enchanting ball, madam," Viscount Wroxley
said, leading her toward the French windows. "Forgive me,
then, for admitting that to me the best part of it has been
the half hour I spent away from it."

How could she admit that the same was true for her when
the ball was hers? "La, sir," she said, "do you feel no
shame?"

"None whatsoever, madam," he said, pausing to sketch her an elegant bow.

His answer gave her enormous pleasure.

Mrs. Althea Havelock was drying her eyes with a lace-edged handkerchief while Lady Matilda Gibbons patted her on the shoulder and Robin stood before her, frowning. Lady Beatrice watched her brother, whose frown was far more thunderous than his stepson's.

" 'Twas no personal insult to me, Mama," Robin said. "Indeed, I believe 'twas almost completely the opposite. She sees me as a real cousin and even as a kind of brother. She cannot yet see me as a prospective husband."

"Yet," Lady Beatrice said. "You say truly, nephew. Cassandra needs to be given time. The idea is new to her. But with our affectionate guidance she will come to see the sense of the match and even the desirability of it."

"Time?" Mr. Havelock roared, and then looked about him self-consciously to assure himself that no guest had wandered back into the dining room. But there was no one except a few servants to overhear the conversation. "She needs to be given *time*, Bea? The gel is one-and-twenty. She should have been married four years ago—five! And for what will she use this time? For what has she used it since Robin spoke with her?"

"I feel the insult, Robin, my love," Mrs. Havelock said, producing a few more tears to mop up. "Lud but I do. You are not good enough for your stepfather's own niece? Yet if Cyrus had been but thirty-five minutes older . . ."

"There, there, my dear Althea," Lady Matilda said soothingly.

"There was no insult intended, Mama," Robin assured her again. " 'Twas the wrong time to speak up. I should have waited until tomorrow, until all the excitement of the ball was over."

"I shall have a talk with her, nephew," Lady Beatrice said. "She is a sensible girl. And 'tis not as if there were someone else she would prefer. She has encouraged none of the gentlemen we know to be prospective suitors."

"But by thunder she has encouraged that—that popinjay," Mr. Havelock said, his voice approaching a roar again. "She has proved everything we most feared. Left to herself, she behaves as if she did not have a brain in her head. And neither does she. Cassandra needs guidance. She needs protection. Not only did she grant him another set when there are a dozen gentlemen clamoring for her hand. She also left the ballroom with him."

"They were not even on the terrace when I looked out there," Robin said. "They were down on the lowest path, and they were standing still, facing each other. For two pins I would slap a glove in this Wroxley's face. Poor Cass has no idea how to deal with practiced charmers and deceivers. And he has declared his intention of staying on for a while tomorrow in order to regale her with tales of his friendship with Uncle, if you please."

"I shall demand to know his intentions before they do speak," Mr. Havelock said. "I shall have a plain answer from that young man, mark my words. Zounds! That it should come to this merely because Worthing did not do his duty by that gel. And you have your talk with Cassandra, Bea. Robin will speak with her again later in the day. You may dry your eyes, Althea. She will have him once she has had time to think about it and listen to sensible advice. We are her family after all. She will do what we know to be best for her."

"But we have to remember, sir," Robin said, frowning, "that she is under no compulsion to do so. And I have the distinct feeling that Cass is going to be stubborn. Perhaps, as Aunt Bea suggests, we should give her a little time, let her try her wings for a while. We can watch over her and be ready to catch her when she falls."

"Provided," Mr. Havelock said ominously, "she has not been gobbled up by a bird of prey before then. Zounds! Why in thunder did that scoundrel have to come today of all days to turn the gel's head?"

"The answer should be obvious, brother," Lady Beatrice said. "Viscount Wroxley deliberately chose today of all days. 'Tis the day on which my niece's head was most likely to be turned.''

"Lud but I still feel the insult," Mrs. Havelock said. "Indeed I *do*, Matilda. You understand how I feel, do you not? You are a mother."

"There, there, my dear," Lady Matilda said.

Nigel was sitting on one of the steps leading from the lowest tier of the flower garden to the lawn below. The ball was long over. Everyone else, even the servants—even Will Stubbs, damn his eyes—had retired to bed. It was almost dawn. Indeed, there was a distinct lightness to the eastern sky beyond the trees ahead of him.

He was not wearing his ball clothes. He had retired to his room just like everyone else, but he had found himself quite unable to sleep. He was overtired, perhaps. Or overly aware that at last he was here, at Kedleston, that at last his carefully conceived plan was being put into action—and was succeeding admirably. She was an almost dangerous innocent.

Or perhaps his sleeplessness was Will Stubbs's fault. He had waited up—of course. All good valets waited up to undress their masters and brush the powder from their hair. All good valets did *not* also scold—or admit to eavesdropping.

" 'Ere, Nige,'' had been his opening gambit. ''Wot's this about the moon and the nocturnal wotever and the stink of blooms paling into insigrif—into nothing wotsoever important beside an exhotic flower grabbed from the ball-room?''

"Zounds," Nigel had said, raising his eyebrows, "you were all ears, Will. But there is some old adage about leopards changing their spots that would suit you admirably. It would have served you right, by my life, if you had leaned so far out of the window that you had fallen out. Not that you would have killed yourself. But with good fortune you might have dented that hard head and acquired a minor headache."

"It fair made me puke," his valet had said, talking not

about the headache but about the flowery speech of flattery he had overheard.

"But then you know nothing of courtship, Will," Nigel had said languidly, picking up his brush and tackling his hair powder himself, if only to annoy Will, who was taking his time about hanging up his coat. "Your idea of wooing a woman, I daresay, is to stuff a coin into her cleavage and stride off in the direction of the nearest haystack, trusting that she will follow to earn the coin."

"Oi, oi," William had said, "old Stubbs was never such a soft touch and don't you accuse 'im of no such thing. A wench 'oists 'er petticoats and gives good honest 'ard labor before she gets 'er coin. But this one is a silly little filly, Nige, with not a farthing's worth of sense in 'er 'ead. She's no match for you, lad."

"All the better," Nigel had said. "Wooing her is no hardship, Will. By my life, she is easy on the eyes."

"You tell 'er the truth," William had said, waving the brush, which was now in his hands, menacingly in the air. "Like you ought to 'ave told 'er an 'ole year ago. I tell you wot, Nige. You're an 'andsome devil and you 'as that tongue wot earned you nothin' but grief in a place we both knows about but wot works like a charm on little fillies wot don't know no better. She is going to fall 'ead over buttocks for you, mark my words, and then wen you does tell 'er the truth, you will never 'ear the end of it. Scold, snivel, snivel, scold—it won't matter which she does more of, Nige. There'll be no escaping it. You knows very well wot it feels like not to be able to get away from trouble. Women like 'er is trouble."

But Nigel had not been about to change his plans at this late date. "Some of us still have a conscience, you know, Will," he had said, his tone so bored that it had seemed to give the lie to his words. "There are tears aplenty ahead for that little bundle of sunshine and innocence. But at least my conscience will be clear." He had been out of humor and close to being out of temper, too. But from long habit he maintained the outer appearance of boredom. "Put the damned brush down. If you think to cow me by threatening me with it, you may think again. I do not bow to threats."

"Now, 'tis not right to provoke old Stubbs," William had said, glowering at his master from his one working eye. "You knows that from experience, Nige. I could put you to sleep in a moment, like I done once before, and you would wake so sore all over you would beg me to put you back to sleep with one more pop to the chin." But he had set the brush down and then grimaced. "Little bundle of sunshine. Gawd! Little bundle of—you didn't *mean* wot you was saying to the filly out there, did you, lad? Now I really could puke."

"Out!" Nigel had commanded. "Get out. You are dismissed. Your services are no longer required. Good night."

"That little filly is nothing but trouble," William had said again, insisting as he so often did on having the last word. "You take 'er on, Nige, and you will be sorry. Will Stubbs will 'ave no sympathy for you then. I might even give you a thrashing for being one obstinate son of an 'ore." He had not slammed the door as he left. Will never had need of resorting to empty gestures. When Will wished to make a gesture, he made the real thing. He had once pounded Nigel Wetherby, Viscount Wroxley, to within the proverbial inch of his life.

And so Nigel had found himself unable to sleep. He had dressed and come back outside, intending to take a brisk walk about the park, to explore, to discover all the parts of it he had not yet seen. He had come out through the ballroom and one of the French windows and run nimbly down the steps toward the lawn. But he had stopped before he reached it.

It would be unseemly to wander about the park, exploring unknown areas, before anyone had invited him to do so. He was merely a recently arrived and very temporary guest, after all. In point of fact, of course, he had every right to explore, but he had not come to assert his rights—not yet. He had arrived with a plan. He had waited a year because of the plan. He must have patience and carry it through piece by slow piece. It still seemed to him the best possible approach, despite Will's continued opposition. But then even Will did not know the full truth. No one did but him.

Being human, he had hoped to find her both beautiful and amiable, Nigel thought. Perhaps he had even hoped to find her desirable. She was all three.

She was also disturbingly innocent.

He had come to lure her with his wealth and elegance, with his wit and charm. He had come to beguile her with stories of his friendship with her father. He had come to make her fall in love with him.

It was all going to be very easy.

He could just wish, perhaps, that she did not seem so much like a wide-eyed trusting child—even while she looked like an enchanting, eminently beddable woman. He tried to concentrate on the latter image, but the other persisted.

She reminded him too strongly, perhaps, of another wide-eyed, trusting child, of another dangerous innocent—himself at the age of nineteen.

Fortunately she was not fated to fall as hard into reality as he had done. The very thought could turn him to ice inside.

Nigel glanced down suddenly at his right foot and realized what he was doing. He was flexing it and turning it counterclockwise in wide circles, his heel resting on a lower step. An old habit. There was no longer any pain in his ankle, though the marks would be there until his dying day, a constant reminder—*of hell.* He shuddered and stilled his foot.

And now he had arrived in heaven. It was a fair exchange. He had earned it. By God he had earned it. It was amazing he had come out of hell with any feelings of compassion left to him. It had not been easy to hold humanity together when all his efforts had been needed just to keep life intact. But he *had* held on.

It was mainly hatred that had kept him going, of course, and the necessity of exacting revenge. But he had always been aware of *her* caught in the middle, so to speak. She had become, perhaps, his one hold on humanity, the one being who had kept him from being consumed by hatred. The destruction of innocence was a dreadful thing, and he had decided not to destroy it. Or not entirely so, at least.

She would feel destroyed, of course, when the truth was finally revealed to her.

The birds, hidden in the trees below the lawn, were setting up a loud and joyful dawn chorus. It was going to be a lovely day. Yesterday morning's rain appeared to have settled the weather. He had paved the way to spend an hour or more alone with the countess this morning. He would have the chance to use all his stories. He would be able to manipulate that innocence and naïveté. He would be able to lure her a little deeper into love with him.

In the meanwhile he must try to get at least a few hours of sleep. He got to his feet and began the climb back up to the terrace and the ballroom door he had left slightly ajar. It was only when he was halfway across the ballroom that he realized he was limping. He stopped, shut his eyes very tightly for a few moments, and then deliberately corrected his gait.

SIX

THE DAY LACKED ONLY TWO hours of noon, Cassandra saw in some alarm when her eyes came open and she looked at the clock. She *never* slept beyond eight at the latest. For one moment she thought that the clock must be broken, but its steady ticking was irrefutable evidence to the contrary. Besides, there was a distinctly late-morning look to the way the sunlight was streaming through the window. And when she turned her head to glance at the small table beside the bed, she wrinkled her nose at the disgusting sight of the cup of chocolate standing there, a gray, greasy-looking film across its surface. It must have been there for *hours*.

It was only then that she fully remembered and forgave herself—though she had certainly intended to rise early. There had been her birthday and the incredibly busy, almost unbearably exciting day. And the ball that had lasted not quite until dawn, though it had come close. It was the most wonderful ball she had ever attended. She was partial, of course, but numerous guests had told her the same thing as they made their departure or climbed the stairs to their beds.

It had been a day and a night she would always remember. She stretched luxuriously and then sat up and threw the bedclothes aside. It had been the first day of her adulthood. A frivolous day, it was true, but a fitting celebration

of her new status. Today—what was left of it, she thought
ruefully—was intended for far more serious business. There
were guests to see on their way, of course. But today she
was going to summon Kedleston's steward and she was
going to start learning all there was to learn about estate
business. He would look at her with amused condescension,
she did not doubt, and Uncle Cyrus when he got wind of
it would assure her that she did not have to worry her pretty
little head about such matters—with the emphasis on the
little, she suspected. But she would stand her ground.

Today she was going to begin her adult life in all earnest.

She was halfway to her dressing room before she remembered more. She winced. Poor Robin. He had been
talked into offering for her, and he had agreed to do it
because it was just like him to sacrifice his own happiness
in a family cause, although he was not, strictly speaking, a
member of the family. And she had bitten his head off in
return. But really she had been very cross with them all—
not with *him*. They could not possibly conceive of the
idea—not even Aunt Bea—that her life was now her own
and that she was perfectly well able to live it for herself.

She would see Robin as soon as possible, she decided.
She would apologize for being cross with him. She would
make a joke of the whole thing and they would have a good
laugh over it. It would be too bad if an awkwardness should
develop between them and spoil a friendship she had always valued very much indeed. She wondered how Patience had enjoyed her dance with Robin. Certainly
Patience must not be allowed to discover what had happened last evening. It was all so *foolish*! And she did not
for a moment believe that Robin really did have tender
feelings for her.

And then, just as she reached her dressing-room door,
she *remembered*. Papa's friend. Viscount Wroxley. She felt
a little flutter in her stomach and bit her lip, smiling at
herself. She believed—yes, she really believed she was a
little in love with him. How splendid! She had never been
in love. She had always thought it was a foolish and self-
induced emotion—and perhaps it was. She had not thought

that it might also be very pleasant, that it might make the day seem brighter and make one want to hurry through one's toilette so that one might rush downstairs and see him again.

How very silly.

And how very delightful. She was going to enjoy the few days of his stay—she was quite determined that it would be a few days and not just today. She would charm him into staying longer. She was going to flirt with him as he flirted with her. She was going to enjoy this foolish feeling of being in love.

And she would see her steward, too—and pit her will against Uncle Cyrus's. Oh, *how* she was going to enjoy this new life of hers. How wonderful freedom was. She was indeed one of the privileged few women to experience it. This was how all men felt all the time. Free. In command of their own lives. Able to plan their own futures. Able to enjoy the more frivolous pleasures, like falling in love, without being seriously diverted from the more important business of life.

How fortunate she was. She pulled on the bell rope in her dressing room to summon her maid.

Nigel was late down to breakfast. But then so were most of last night's guests, it seemed. The breakfast parlor was full, though the Countess of Worthing was not herself of their number. The talk was mostly of the ball, of the lateness of the hour—no one was willing to admit to being generally a late riser—and of the necessity of being on the way home as soon as might be.

Lady Beatrice Havelock asked him if his carriage had been ordered brought around—he would doubtless wish to make as early a start as possible since he was returning all the way to London.

Nigel inclined his head to the lady and informed her that he had no plans for an early start.

Mrs. Havelock informed him that he must be dreadfully dull in the country, accustomed as he was to town life and town amusements. He must be simply *longing* to be back in London.

Country air and country scenes were a pleasant diversion from the stuffiness and sense of confinement one felt in the city, he told her with another inclination of the head.

They all had an impossibly busy day planned now that his cousin's birthday was over, Robin Barr-Hampton said to a soon-to-be-departing guest, though he raised his voice so that it might be heard farther afield. He rather believed that Lady Worthing had arranged to spend the day with her aunt at the dower house—something to do with the mantua maker who was there to sew a whole new wardrobe of clothes now that her ladyship was out of mourning. She would really have no time for anything else today.

Nigel smiled to himself. The family of the Countess of Worthing was letting him know, without the slightest breach of good manners, that he was unwelcome at Kedleston. Fortunately, perhaps, the countess's family had no power at Kedleston—not any longer. Influence they might have, but they must themselves be uncertain as to the full power of its scope if they felt it necessary to hint and nudge him on his way. Were they afraid that the lady would invite him to stay longer?

The lady *would* invite him to stay longer. And he would grant her wish.

She had come downstairs by the time he left the breakfast parlor, but she was busy seeing departing guests on their way. She was going to be busy for some time. He caught her eye, raised his eyebrows, and sketched her a bow, but he did not try to engage her in conversation or to lead her aside. She had her duties to perform and was conscientiously doing them. He could wait. She smiled back at him, her cheeks rosy with awareness, he was interested to see. She was looking remarkably pretty in a light-colored sack dress, fitted close to her neat little figure at front, flowing loose at the back. Her hair beneath a frivolous cap was unpowdered.

But his attention was called away from her even before he could move away of his own volition.

"I understand you are not leaving this morning with everyone else," Mr. Cyrus Havelock said to him, the words quite deliberately chill and accusing. " 'Tis wise of you to wait awhile, my lord. One hates to have one's carriage caught in a slow-moving line."

"I avoid it at all costs," Nigel agreed.

"Perhaps you would care to step into the library with me until the house has grown quieter," Mr. Havelock said, indicating the way with one arm and half bowing for the guest to precede him.

They must be very unsure of their influence over the countess, Nigel thought. They were all doing their part this morning to protect her from the threat they sensed in his person.

The library was surprisingly well supplied with books. At least one previous earl must have been a collector and perhaps even a reader. There were also numerous paintings of horses and various sporting gentlemen on the walls. It was a masculine domain, a cozy room despite the faint air of shabbiness from which several others he had seen in the house so far also suffered. But shabbiness was not unbecoming a room such as this. It made it look lived in.

"Who are you?" Mr. Havelock asked, closing the door behind him. Obviously he had decided to get straight to the point without any more pretense of courtesy and social niceties.

"I beg your pardon?" Nigel raised his eyebrows and fingered the handle of his quizzing glass.

"Your family? Your property? Your connections?" The older man looked squarely at Nigel and slid his hand inside the button opening of his waistcoat. He had not sat down or invited the guest to do so.

"I do beg your pardon, sir," Nigel said. "Have I overlooked some fact that would explain your interest in such matters?" He raised his glass briefly to his eye and surveyed Mr. Havelock through it.

"What was your connection with my brother?" Mr. Havelock asked. "Were you drinking partners? Did you even know him?"

"Am I to understand," Nigel asked, lowering his glass and speaking slowly and quietly, "that you believe me to be a liar, sir?"

"Zounds!" the older man said, losing his temper. "My niece is a green girl, sir, and I believe you know the fact very well and have played upon it from the start. We have only your word for it that you are who you say you are. And even if you are—who the devil is Viscount Wroxley? We have only your word for it that you were Worthing's friend. And if you were—what sort of recommendation is that? My niece has been seduced by distinguished looks and charming manners. *I* have not, sir."

"As the devil is my witness," Nigel said, lifting one eyebrow, "I should certainly hope not."

Mr. Havelock flushed a dull red. "I demand to know your intentions," he said. "Your intentions toward my niece, Wroxley."

Nigel raised his quizzing glass again and took his time about replying. "You speak as her ladyship's guardian?" he asked.

"I do," Mr. Havelock said firmly, lifting onto the balls of his feet and then settling back on his heels again. "Someone has to look to her interests. I am her uncle, her father's brother, sir, and I speak for her aunts as well as myself."

"But the lady, I do believe," Nigel said, "is of age, sir, and has come into full possession of her fortune and property. Do you speak for the *lady*, sir? Has she asked you to demand of me my intentions? If so, I would prefer to explain them directly to her, by my life. If not, I decline the honor of answering at all."

"Egad, 'tis as we thought," Mr. Havelock said in a voice that probably carried beyond the confines of the room. "You do not need to tell me who you are, my lord. I *know who you are*. You are a villain and a rogue. And you do not need to tell me your intentions. I *know what they are*. They are to gain possession of my niece and of her property and fortune."

"Ah," Nigel said softly, "then you did not need to ask

the questions, sir. But do you not find that social conversation is ever thus? We ask questions to which we already know the answers—or to which we *believe* we know the answers—merely as a courtesy, to keep the conversation going, to avoid the discomfort of silence." He smiled arctically.

"You will not succeed," Mr. Havelock said. He had regained control over himself, though he was breathing heavily. "Lady Worthing is a sensible gel. She listens to her elders. We are a close family. She will not be allowed to fall prey to your schemes."

"Well then." Nigel smiled again. "You have nothing to fear, sir, do you? You will advise her ladyship on her choice of a husband and she will make the wise choice. Who *is* your choice, if I may make so bold as to ask?"

"My stepson, Robin Barr-Hampton," Mr. Havelock said. " 'Tis all settled. All that remains to do is for the announcement to be made and the banns read."

"Ah yes," Nigel said pleasantly, "and the bride to give her consent, I suppose. A trifling matter in such a close family. Such a cozy arrangement will doubtless work to the advantage of all concerned. Such marriages usually do, even if they also tend to be a trifle—dull, shall we say?"

Mr. Havelock's nostrils flared. "As you can now see," he said, " 'twould be as well to have your valet pack your bags and to have your carriage brought around, *my lord*. Perhaps in London you will be able to find an heiress with a less vigilant and less loving family."

Nigel released his hold on his quizzing glass and strolled toward the door of the library. "But you forget, sir," he said. "Her ladyship has her heart set upon hearing about my friendship with her father. 'Twould not be gentlemanly of me to depart before I have obliged her."

He left the room and shut the door behind him and stood for a few moments before proceeding on his way. One never grew accustomed to hearing contempt and loathing in men's voices, he mused, or to listening to unveiled insults. One convinced oneself sometimes—when one's very sanity was at stake—that one had so hardened oneself that nothing and no one could ever hurt again. But one always found oneself feeling new wounds when they were created.

All of yesterday's guests had left—all except one. An appointment had been made with the steward for later in the afternoon—and yes, she had explained, it was indeed Lady Worthing herself, and not Mr. Havelock, who wished to speak with him. The awkwardness with Robin had been dealt with.

"Rob," she had said, going directly to him on the terrace as soon as the last carriage had driven away and linking her arm through his, "I do beg your pardon if I dealt harshly with you last night. I am more grateful than I can say for what you were prepared to do, but we must both admit in the cold light of day that 'twas nonsense. We must agree to forget about it or even better to laugh about it, for we are friends and I would hate more than anything to lose your friendship." She had smiled her most beguiling smile at him.

"Cous—" he had begun. But he had been looking altogether too serious and he had had the beginnings of a frown on his brow. She had set two fingers firmly against his lips and laughed.

"Tell me we are still friends," she said.

"Egad, Cass," he said, exasperated, pushing away her hand, "of course we are still friends."

"And that we will forget last night's nonsense," she said.

He had sighed. "If you say so," he said. "I rushed you. We all rushed you. We are concerned about you, Cass, a woman on your own."

"The world will continue to turn," she told him.

"Just promise me that *you* will not rush, cous," Robin said, "or allow yourself to be rushed by someone who has your interests less at heart than we do."

"I promise to live my life with all the wisdom of my years and experience, Rob," she said, laughing. "I have to go. There is something I really wish to have time for before I keep my appointment with Mr. Coburg."

"Coburg?" he said. "Kedleston's *steward*, Cass? *You?* But stepfather—"

"But Uncle Cyrus does not own Kedleston, Rob," she said firmly. "I do."

He would understand in time, she thought. They all would. But she would not argue the point with any of them. She would never convince them through arguments. They would learn through her actions that woman though she was, she was perfectly capable of being the Countess of Worthing. She would do better than her father had done. Papa had neglected the estate. He had lived away from it in his later years and drawn large sums of money from it without putting anything back into it. She would see that that situation was reversed, that Kedleston prospered under her ownership, the house and the estate and everyone who lived upon it.

But for a few hours, before it was time to see Mr. Coburg and begin an education no one had thought it necessary for her to acquire, she would devote herself to something far more frivolous and far more pleasant.

Viscount Wroxley was looking very handsome this morning and quite as elegantly and richly dressed as he had been yesterday. His hair had been freshly powdered and rolled at the sides. She had caught only a glimpse of him while she was busy with the departing guests, but his eyes had looked appreciatively at her and she had felt a rush of physical awareness, a feeling quite new to her. A deliciously wicked feeling.

He was in the hall when she went inside, examining the intricately carved designs on the oak paneling, quizzing glass in hand.

" 'Tis all original," she said, crossing the hall to his side. " 'Twas carved when the house was built."

"Exquisite, by my life, madam," he said, but he looked so intently at her that she knew he was flirting again.

"Papa used to talk of remodeling the hall," she said, "and replacing the wood with marble to give the house a more classical look and a modern air. But I am glad he never did it."

"You do not believe that what is fashionable must therefore be superior, then?" he said. "I applaud your taste and your good sense, madam."

"In his last few years," she said, "Papa was not here to make the changes—improvements he called them—he used to speak of. 'Twas as if he lost interest. You knew him during those years, my lord. Tell me about him."

" 'Twould be my great pleasure. But not here," he said, taking her hand in his and setting it on the wide cuff of his sleeve. "Exquisite the hall may be, madam, but the day outside is lovelier and I must discover how well you rival it."

She was still wearing the straw hat she had donned in order to step outside to see her guests on their way. It was a brightly sunny midday and seemed even sunnier for the fact that she was on the arm of a handsome man with whom she was a little in love. Just this time yesterday, she thought, she had not even known of his existence. Yet even then she had thought it the happiest day of her life.

"I wish you to see the park, my lord," she said when they were on the terrace, "but there is so much to see. Far too much to be shown in a single day, alas."

"Beauty is to be beheld slowly and savored," he said, bending his head to look steadily into her face in a manner that was becoming familiar to her. He was an expert, she thought, in saying one thing and implying another, in seeming to admire the beauty around him and yet suggesting that he saw only hers. And yet a smile seemed always to lurk far back in his eyes as if to assure her that his gallantries were not intended to deceive her, but only to delight her. " 'Twere best to spread the enjoyment of many delights over more than one day."

Was he saying what she thought he was saying? Was he willing to stay longer than just today? Would he stay for a few days? She had hoped so. Now it seemed altogether possible.

"Today I will show you the rose garden, then, my lord," she said.

"For today, madam," he said, " 'twere sufficient. There is no flower lovelier than the rose."

They were agreed, then, it seemed. He would be staying for longer than just today. There was no rush for anything. She could take her time enjoying his company. She led him toward the west side of the house and the high clipped hedges with the trellised arch that led through to the rose garden.

It was always a surprise to visitors. The lawns, the hedge, the trees higher on the hill behind the house—all were varying shades of green. Yet once through the arch, one stepped into a different world, into a riot of color and a perfection of form. Even the air was different, fragrant with the heady perfume of thousands of roses.

"This," she said, looking up into his face, "is my second favorite place in the whole park. One cannot come here out of spirits and leave again without feeling restored."

"Perfection, i'faith," he said, bending and cupping a half-opened deep pink bloom in his palms. "There is no flower lovelier than the rose, and there is no rose lovelier than this particular one."

She smiled and noticed how his hands, long-fingered, elegantly manicured, held the bloom in a delicate touch that would not crush it. And she noticed the marks of calluses on his palms, incongruous with the rest of his appearance, but giving his hands an undeniable masculinity. But then he was not an effete-looking gentleman for all his fashionable elegance. His broad shoulders suggested the existence of powerful muscles. His knee breeches and stockings encased legs that needed nothing added by way of padding.

She blushed when she caught the direction of her thoughts and realized how improperly her eyes had been roving.

He was plucking the rose, careful not to damage it. He was going to present it to her, she thought. But he had broken off the stem close to the bloom and when he turned to her he did not do as she had expected. He looked at the front of her gown, seemed to consider for a moment, and then lifted the rose to slide the short stem down inside the front of her bodice, into her décolletage. His fingers did not once brush against her bare flesh. He looked up into her eyes.

"There is no *flower* lovelier than the rose," he said. "But by my life even this most perfect of perfect blooms is not as lovely as its wearer."

It was such a lavish and such a ridiculous compliment— though no less pleasing because of that—that she first smiled and then laughed outright.

"And 'tis certainly not as perfect as you are with words, my lord," she said. "Tell me, do London ladies *believe* such flatteries?"

"London ladies are less modest than their country-bred sisters," he said. "Perhaps 'tis that they see less of natural beauty and feel themselves unrivaled except by one another. Ladies who have spent their lives in the country are surrounded by the loveliness of nature and do not know that they are a part of that loveliness and indeed sometimes surpass it. At least, madam, that appears to be the case with a certain young lady of my acquaintance who at this moment surpasses in loveliness the rose she wears in her bosom."

She bent her head to look down at the rose. It was pleasant to be flattered, she thought, when the flattery was light-hearted and without any motive other than to give delight.

"But you wish to hear of your father, madam," he said, offering her his arm again. "I see a rustic seat beneath the willow tree yonder. Shall we sit there in the shade while I speak?"

He was also an expert at knowing when flirtation had gone far enough. There was kindness in his eyes now and gentleness in his manner. They would sit and talk and perhaps he would become her friend, too, as he had been Papa's. Perhaps these few days would not end their acquaintance. Perhaps she would be able to write to him occasionally and he to her. It would not be improper. She was an adult, after all, and no longer a girl to be confined by all the rules with which female reputations were protected.

She hoped they would become friends. She hoped they

would remain acquainted even if only by infrequent letters. She did not like the thought of bidding him farewell in a few days' time and never seeing or hearing from him again.

Which seemed a remarkably foolish way of thinking, she admitted, when this time yesterday she had not even met him.

SEVEN

THEY SAT BENEATH THE willow tree for almost an hour, surrounded by the sights and perfumes of roses, while he entertained her with stories about her father. Some of them were true. Some were the truth only very slightly bent to show the late Earl of Worthing in a favorable light. Some were pure fabrication. Much of the time she watched him from beneath the forward-tilting brim of her straw hat, her face showing her reactions to his tales—amusement, interest, suspense, surprise. There was a total lack of artful subterfuge in her nature, he thought. He could almost pity her.

"I am so glad there were friends and laughter in his life during those last years," she said. "I always wondered. And you yourself said just yesterday, my lord, that he was an unhappy man."

"His friends helped him forget the death of your mother," he said. "Or if not exactly to forget, at least to find relief from his suffering."

"*You* helped him," she said. "I am so happy that he knew you. I was young and did not understand a great deal, but I can see now that Grandpapa's passing and then Mama's fewer than eighteen months later must have been too much for him. And a daughter of twelve years must have seemed poor consolation to him."

He took one of her hands in both his own. "No, i'faith," he said, "you will not burden yourself with the belief that your love was not enough for your father, madam." She had loved Worthing, that blackhearted scoundrel, he thought. " 'Twas too much for him. He spoke of your happy nature and your warm heart, madam, and of his reluctance to bring his own low spirits home to you—or to bring you to London, where you would be oppressed by them. He demonstrated his deep love for you by staying away from you."

Her eyes were swimming in tears when she raised them from looking at his hands holding hers. "Oh Papa!" she said. "How foolish of him. And now 'tis too late for me to bring him comfort."

He raised her hand to his lips. "I ask pardon, my lady," he said. "I should have said nothing. Your tears are like a knife to my heart."

"No!" She leaned toward him so that for one startled moment he thought she was going to kiss his cheek. She did not do so. She smiled instead through her tears. "You have been wonderfully kind. And now I know that Papa had friends to the end and that there were good times for him and even laughter. And I know why he rarely came home and why he never invited me to come to town. I have not admitted even to myself until this moment that I was hurt by what seemed to be his neglect. Now I can admit it and know that I have no reason to feel hurt. He loved me as much as I loved him."

He gazed at her from beneath lazy lids. Had he ever been this innocent? he wondered. But he knew he had.

"Thank you," she said.

He might have capitalized on her gratitude. He might have closed the few inches between their mouths. He might have turned her gratitude into something else and hastened along the moment for which he had come. But he was still remembering an innocent nineteen year old.

"Your uncle, Mr. Cyrus Havelock, looks much like your father," he said to change the subject somewhat. "The resemblance is quite remarkable, in fact."

"They were twins, you know," she said. "Papa was half an hour older than Uncle Cyrus. Twins run in our family. Grandmama once told me that they are always male and they always seem to be the eldest children."

"With the result that the younger twin misses the heirdom to the title and property by half an hour or thereabouts," he said with a smile. "I'faith, madam, it sounds painful."

"To his credit, Uncle Cyrus has never seemed resentful," she said. "He has been very kind to me, though I have sometimes seemed ungrateful, perhaps. One chafes at the necessity of obeying a guardian when one is twenty years old. But I have always tried to keep my annoyance to myself. He has spent almost as much time here during the past year as he has at his own home. And all the time he must think about how very nearly this was all his."

"And it has happened before?" he asked her.

"Not for several generations," she said. "I remember Mama telling me once how relieved she was when I was born and she knew that I was not twins." She laughed. "There are portraits. There are paintings of every family member for centuries back, but the ones I always like looking at are the portraits that show the twins. It has happened five times in all."

"And the portraits are here?" he asked. "At Kedleston? There is a gallery?"

"Yes," she said. "But I will not bore you with it, my lord. I know how tedious 'tis to be dragged about the portrait gallery of a family in which one has no interest whatsoever."

"Madam," he said, holding her eyes with his own, "my late and dear friend was a member of this family. And *you* are a member of this family. You wound me when you assume that a visit to the portrait gallery would bore me."

She blushed and then got to her feet. "Perhaps you are being gallant again," she said. "But if you are, then you must suffer the consequences. I shall take you there now. There is time."

They met Robin Barr-Hampton on the terrace close to

the front doors. Nigel had the distinct impression that the man had been looking for them—perhaps to play chaperon? He looked quite openly annoyed. But if she noticed, the Countess of Worthing chose not to comment upon the fact.

"Is it not a wonderful day, Rob?" she said with her usual sunny smile. "His lordship and I have been sitting in the rose garden talking about Papa, and now I am taking him up to the gallery to show him some of the portraits. I shall see you at tea after I have spent an hour or so with Mr. Coburg?"

She had made it perfectly clear that they did not want his company on their visit to the gallery. Who was Coburg? Nigel wondered. Barr-Hampton stayed on the terrace when they went inside.

She took him first to look at the large canvas that displayed the Earl of Worthing, her grandfather, with the countess and their four children. The little boys, the late earl and Cyrus Havelock, were identical in looks in the portrait.

"But 'tis easy to tell who is who," the countess explained. "Papa stands proudly at Grandpapa's shoulder, you see, while Uncle Cyrus stands beside Grandmama in a subordinate position. I always thought it rather sad that there had to be such a distinction between two sons who must have been far closer than brothers usually are. But such is the nature of life."

Nigel gazed at them with interest—at the late Worthing, at the younger brother.

"There is a portrait of Papa after he grew up," his companion said. "With Mama—and me."

"Then I must see it," he said, looking down at her with a smile.

The late earl was a young, good-looking man in the portrait to which she led him. His wife was a young beauty. It was easy to see from whom the present countess had inherited her dark coloring. She was a very young child in the painting, with curly hair and rosy cheeks and dimpled arms. She was smiling sunnily at the portrait painter, her elbow on her mother's knee, her chin in her hand.

"By my life," he said, "you were adorable."

"Past tense?" she said. "My lord, I do declare you have forgotten your gallantry."

"By my life," he said, "you *are* adorable."

They both laughed. But what had really struck him about the portrait was that Worthing had changed beyond recognition before he had known the man. Not physically, perhaps. The man in the painting was quite recognizably Worthing. But the man in the painting was also an eager, happy young man who looked upon the world with open, unclouded countenance. By God he had changed—unless the painter had erased the dark, brooding passions from the face of his sitter.

"He changed so very much," the quiet voice of the countess said from beside him, echoing his own thoughts. "I have only to look at this portrait to know that 'twas so. He used to laugh and joke all the time. He used to play with me and read to me and tease me and . . . Well, it does not matter. Perhaps it was Grandpapa's passing and the new responsibilities of the earldom followed so closely by Mama's death. Perhaps it was that they had not had a son. Who knows? But he did change."

"Perhaps," he said, offering her his arm, "we should look at some of the other family twins, madam."

The set before her father and Havelock were her great-grandfather and his brother. It was a portrait much like the other, except that fashions were very different and these two boys were older—about fourteen. They were quite identical. Which was which? he wondered. The elder brother, the viscount, was at his father's shoulder, of course. But really, which was which?

"The likeness is fascinating, is it not?" she said. "I used to come up here alone when I was a child and weave stories about all the twins. Did they ever take each other's place? When there was some tedious state occasion for the elder, did the younger sometimes impersonate him so that the elder could go carousing somewhere else?"

"Indeed," he said, " 'tis enough to make one feel aggrieved *not* to have been born a twin."

"There are none in your family?" she asked him.

"Not to my knowledge, madam," he said, leaning closer to the portrait. "Egad, but they are alike. What happened to the younger?"

"I do not know," she said. "There was a quarrel, some dreadful unpleasantness, but no one would ever give me the details. Grandpapa looked quite thunderous when I asked him about it once, but then Grandpapa often looked thunderous. And Papa did not know. 'Tis rather sad that one completely loses touch with relatives within a very few generations."

"If one did not, madam," he said, "one would have so many relatives to invite to such celebrations as weddings that one would have to hire the largest cathedral in England and then proceed to have extra wings built."

She laughed. "I suppose you are right," she said. "Do you wish to look at the twins before these two?"

He saw them all before she suddenly exclaimed in dismay.

"How long have we been here?" she asked him. "Oh la, I will be late for Mr. Coburg and give just the opposite impression from the one I am determined to give."

"Less than an hour, I do believe, madam," he said. "May I escort you to Mr. Coburg and explain that if you are tardy 'tis because you were showing an extraordinary courtesy to a guest? And if he will not accept that explanation, then he is a knave and a scoundrel and does not deserve your concern."

But she was breathing a sigh of relief. "If 'tis less than an hour," she said, "I am not late. Mr. Coburg is my steward and I would be willing to wager my fortune on the certainty that he intends to run this estate entirely alone— or under the directorship of my uncle. I will wager, too, that it has not occurred to either of them even in his most bizarre dream that I might decide to take a hand in the running of my own estate."

"And you have so decided, madam?" Nigel raised his eyebrows.

"I am a woman, my lord," she said with an impish smile

that brought her dimple into full evidence. "I am also a person. I even entertain the conviction that there is a brain hidden somewhere inside my head. But what is more to the point, I am a woman *with power*. Could you imagine anything more alarming? I am the Countess of Worthing, and Kedleston belongs to me. 'Tis mine for the rest of my life. And I am of age. I intend that my steward will be answerable to me. I intend to learn everything that he knows and perhaps even more than that. I intend to look after Kedleston as well as every earl who has preceded me and better than some." Her cheeks were flushed and her eyes were shining by the time she had finished speaking.

Nigel pursed his lips and thought about his crash from innocence. Had there been a definite moment when he had finally understood? Or had it crept up on him more gradually? He could dash this woman's innocence with one sentence if he so chose.

Her smile had gone. "You do not think I can do it either," she said. "Men never do. But I will show you all."

"On the contrary, madam," he said, making her a bow before offering his arm. "You must allow me to escort you to your meeting with your steward so that you will not be late. He will never expect a *mere woman* to be punctual. I would like nothing better, by my life, than to be a blot on the desk blotter during this meeting. 'Tis my conviction that you will assert yourself quite manfully—pardon me, quite womanfully—and gain the ascendancy over a *mere man*."

She smiled brightly and set her hand on his cuff. "I have looked forward with great eagerness all year to reaching my majority," she said. " 'Tis going to be such *fun*, my lord, to learn to be my own *woman*."

Just as other women might think it fun to be free to attend as many parties and balls and routs as they wished, he thought. He began to see—with some surprise—that the Countess of Worthing, in addition to beauty and a sunny nature and innocence, had some character.

It would undoubtedly have been better for her if she had not.

• • •

The hour Cassandra spent with her steward was not an easy one. For one thing she found herself confronting two men, not one. Her uncle was in the study, too, looking grave and fondly condescending. Mr. Coburg had a very similar expression on his face. But it was Mr. Havelock who explained to her that she must not worry her pretty little head about what would happen to her estates now that he was no longer officially her guardian. She could relax in the knowledge that Mr. Coburg was one of the most competent stewards in England and that of course he himself would be on hand to deal with any matter on which Mr. Coburg might need to consult him. Willow Hall was no more than ten miles away, after all.

With which words Mr. Havelock thought to terminate the meeting. His look and his smile were definitely dismissive.

But Cassandra smiled warmly at both gentlemen, walked about the large oak desk to seat herself in the great leather chair behind it, and asked to see the books.

The books might have been upside down and written in Arabic for all the sense they made to her at first. And even at the end of the hour she had learned enough only to realize that the books were not upside down or written in a foreign alphabet. She asked questions that must have seemed incredibly naïve, and even downright stupid, to the two men, and she asked to have certain explanations repeated in more intelligible English. She asked about subjects that made more sense to her than rows of figures that apparently all added up to indicate something extremely important—subjects like repairs to laborers' cottages and schools for the children of the workers—only to find that there were more figures relating to those matters and that everything added up to something called financial feasibility. In other words, she understood—was there enough money for such things, and if so, could the money more profitably be spent on something more important?

She had some of the books carried up to her rooms at the end of the hour, much to the consternation of both gentlemen. She intended to pore over them until they began to make sense to her. And she intended to continue to ask questions even if at first they would merely demonstrate her appalling ignorance.

"Egad," Uncle Cyrus said with hearty good humor as the two of them approached the drawing room for tea, "but you are a plucky little thing, Cassandra. You will learn that 'tis best to leave everything to Coburg, of course, but 'tis as well to make him remember that you *are* the Countess of Worthing. Even when you have a husband to oversee everything for you, you will still take precedence over him, after all—unless you marry a man of equal or superior rank."

Cassandra did not waste breath in putting right any of his misconceptions. She merely smiled at him and at the footman who opened the drawing room doors for them.

Mrs. Havelock, Lady Beatrice, Patience, and Robin were gathered in the drawing room for tea. Viscount Wroxley was not there, Cassandra saw at a glance. Apparently Lady Matilda had walked over from the dower house with Patience, and the viscount had gone strolling in the park with the former.

"I suppose, Cassandra dear," Mrs. Havelock said, " 'tis too late for his lordship to leave here today. Doubtless he will have his carriage brought around early in the morning. Mornings are always the best time for travel."

"He will be staying tomorrow, Aunt Althea," Cassandra said, crossing the room to the tea tray and accepting a cup of tea from Lady Beatrice's hand. "And perhaps for a day or so longer."

The storm broke, as she had expected it would. She could not really understand their objection to Viscount Wroxley. He was young, personable, titled, obviously wealthy. He had been her father's friend. He had come all the way from London to pay his respects to her. They were all very eager that she marry soon and marry well. From their point of view she would have thought that the viscount would be seen as something of a catch. None of her other prospective suitors came close to him in eligibility—not even Robin.

"A true gentleman does not arrive unannounced, invite

himself to your birthday ball, and outstay his welcome, Cassandra,'' Mrs. Havelock said. ''Especially when he is a total stranger to all of us.''

''When I took him aside this morning,'' Mr. Havelock said, his cup and saucer dwarfed in one large hand, the other hand pushed into the button opening of his waistcoat, ''he evaded my questions about his family and connections and he refused point-blank to state his intentions toward you, Cassandra.''

''He must certainly be made to answer all of Cyrus's concerns, niece,'' Lady Beatrice said, ''before you can even consider him as a suitor. He must be made to tell us exactly who he is and what his prospects are. We must discover if he is a steady young man, if he is worthy of the great honor you would do him by accepting him as your husband.''

Cassandra laughed at them all, not with derision, but with genuine amusement. ''My husband?'' she said. ''My suitor? I met his lordship but yesterday. I like him. He has been kind to me and has enabled me to see Papa as he was for the last years of his life. In a few days' time he will be returning to London and leaving me with pleasant memories. That is all. He is *not* my suitor and never will be. And it must be remembered that *I* invited him to my ball, and *I* invited him to stay here last night and for a few days. *We* need discover nothing about him that he is unprepared to tell us. *I* know all I need to know about him.''

''He was very charming to Mama and to me when we arrived earlier,'' Patience said timidly.

''Viscount Wroxley is very good at being charming, dear,'' Mrs. Havelock said. ''That is part of our concern. Girls like you and Cassandra are easily deceived by charm. If you were older, you would understand that steadier virtues are more desirable qualities to look for in a husband. Robin now—''

''We will leave my name out of this, Mama,'' Robin said. ''You will only succeed in making Cass even more stubborn. You should tell her the other plan. She may find it more appealing.''

They were still planning her life for her, then. It would

take a while for them to understand. Cassandra looked about the group of her relatives, eyebrows raised. "Plan?" she said.

"There will have to be an unfortunate delay, of course," Mr. Havelock said. " 'Tis unfortunate because you are already one-and-twenty, Cassandra. But your position and your fortune will make your advanced age of little account, I daresay."

"Granted the fact that I am almost an elderly lady," Cassandra said, laughing, "what is the plan?"

"We are going to take you to London next spring for a Season," Mrs. Havelock said, "and for presentation at court, of course. 'Tis almost criminal that that has not already been done. We will find you a husband worthy of your rank, Cassandra, dear, but one who will not take you away from Kedleston, 'tis to be hoped."

"I shall come with you, too, niece," Lady Beatrice said. "And Matilda will bring Patience. 'Tis time she made her come-out before she is too old. And she has a competent dowry from her father. Althea will be busy visiting the boy at school, and Matilda will be busy with Patience. I shall be there for you."

"And you, Rob?" Cassandra's eyes laughed at him. "Are you a part of this plan, too? Will you go to London to find yourself a bride? Perhaps she will even be me—or Patience."

"Oh la, Cass." Patience's hands flew to her cheeks, her eyes wide with dismay.

"I shall doubtless stay on my own land, Cass," Robin said with quiet dignity. "This is another plan, you know, not the old one in a different dress."

She had hurt his feelings, Cassandra thought. And she had deeply embarrassed Patience. She was instantly contrite. But she felt besieged from all sides and the temptation to spread out the pain a little more thinly had been too great.

"I am obliged to you all," she said, looking at them each in turn and realizing both that they loved her and that she loved them. "We shall see. Although I am greatly en-

joying being at Kedleston this summer, by next spring perhaps the prospect of a Season in London will be appealing.
But you must all understand that if I go, 'twill not be in
search of a husband. I do not intend to marry, you see. Not
for a long time, anyway.''

Perhaps eventually, she thought, after a few years, she
would feel confident enough in her control over her property to give herself in marriage to a man of her choice. But
not yet. If she married now, she would give up this precious
gift of freedom that so few women ever knew.

They were satisfied. They did not believe her, of course.
They were quite convinced that once they had her in London, they would have her married off in no time at all. And
there was nothing callous in their wish to do so. They truly
believed that without a husband to take command of her
life for her, she would not be able to live it for herself.
Even Aunt Bea thought it. Aunt Bea thought of herself as
a strong, masculine type of woman, and in many ways she
was right. But she saw her niece as softly feminine, as
being very much in need of a man.

The door opened at that moment to admit Lady Matilda
and Lord Wroxley. Someone spoke of the weather and the
topic was discussed to the point of exhaustion and beyond.
Robin pointedly reminded Cassandra that she would have
to spend all of the next day at the dower house since Patience had informed him that the mantua maker needed
more measurements and consultations with her before she
could continue with her work. Viscount Wroxley said that
he would be delighted to see the dower house since Lady
Matilda had made it sound so very charming, and that he
would be honored to escort Lady Worthing there tomorrow
morning.

Cassandra looked at Robin and smiled when she met his
eyes. He scowled back. *That* little ruse had turned out in
quite contrary fashion to what he had intended.

''Thank you, my lord,'' she said. ''How kind of you.
That would be very pleasant.''

EIGHT

NIGEL SPENT A VERY
agreeable few hours at the dower house the next day even
though he saw little of Cassandra, who was abovestairs with
the mantua maker. Lady Matilda Gibbons showed him
about the neat Palladian house at his request and Miss Patience Gibbons showed him the small park, which was really a part of the larger park of Kedleston, of course. It did
not look its best, she explained to him, since the sun was
not shining today and the wind was blustery and indeed it
looked likely to rain at any moment. He assured her that
both the house and the park were quite idyllically pretty.

Both ladies were easy to charm, and he unashamedly
charmed them. In time he would doubtless need all the
allies he could find.

He would allow himself today and tomorrow, he had
decided last night before sleeping. The almost open hostility of the rest of her family might make it difficult to stay
longer under present circumstances. Today, of course, there
was the frustration of having little time to spend alone with
her, but he would make the most of what he had. They had
walked the almost two miles from Kedleston to the dower
house through pretty wooded parkland despite the fact that
Havelock had predicted rain and the aunts had urged their
niece to take the carriage. The carriage would be sent, Barr-

Hampton had added after she had refused, if rain settled in before her return. Nigel eyed the lowering clouds all day, willing them to hold their waters for at least a few hours longer.

A carriage ride, though it held promise, would be all too short.

She came to her aunt's sitting room while the three of them were taking an early tea. She brought fresh air and sunshine with her, it seemed. She was laughing.

"I do declare, Aunt Matilda," she said, "I am going to take to wearing sacks. Not sack dresses, you will understand, but real *sacks*. I have done nothing all day but choose fabrics and patterns and then dither and choose other fabrics and patterns, only to start the process all over again. And I have stood on pedestals, my arms aloft, being prodded and poked and pricked and measured until I thought I would never be done. Oh la, are those the currant cakes your cook makes *so* well? Yes, do put a couple on a plate for me, Patience. I am starved."

"I'faith, madam," Nigel said, having got to his feet at her entrance, "you might wear a sack to the grandest ball and still outshine the queen herself."

They all laughed.

"Lud, my lord," Lady Matilda said in a mock scold, " 'tis treason you speak."

"On the contrary, madam," he said, " 'tis the truth."

" 'Tis gross flattery," the countess said, wagging one finger in his direction. "*And* 'tis treason."

"Is the queen beautiful?" Patience asked, and they all laughed again.

It was a merry little gathering. But Nigel got to his feet again when he saw a spattering of raindrops on the window.

" 'Tis time I escorted you home, my lady," he said, "before the heavens open."

"Oh lud," Lady Matilda said, looking toward the window, " 'tis raining. You should have come in the carriage, Cassandra, for even this morning the sky was threatening. Perhaps you should wait awhile. You will be soaked if you walk home in this. Perhaps the rain will stop."

"I think not, Aunt Matilda," Cassandra said. " 'Tis more likely to get heavier. We will leave immediately. I have no fear of getting my feet a little wet."

"Perhaps Uncle Cyrus will think to send the carriage," Patience said.

Nigel looked at Cassandra, but he was interested to note that she made no mention of her cousin's promise to do just that.

"Perhaps, madam," he said, turning to Lady Matilda, "you have an umbrella we could borrow."

"There is the big black one that was my husband's," she said. "I shall have it fetched, my lord." She looked anxiously toward the window again. "Oh lud, 'tis not easing, is it?"

"I have a small one you could borrow, Cass," Patience said.

"I'faith," Nigel said, "two umbrellas can be worse than none. They forever clash and force their carriers off the path into longer, wetter grass. The one umbrella will suffice, Miss Gibbons."

Cassandra, he noticed, did not contradict him. She was, he realized, as intent as he on not being deprived of the walk home, wet though it might be. Yes, he thought, today and tomorrow would be time enough. He need delay no longer than that.

The rain was just heavy enough when they left to necessitate using the umbrella. He held it over both their heads with his right hand. He offered her his left arm. At first she rested her hand correctly on his cuff, but that set too great a distance between them for the umbrella to be fully effective.

"Slip your arm through mine," he suggested, looking down into her face beneath the brim of her hat. "We will remain drier if you do."

All day he had feared that the rain would spoil his plans. It did not take him long to realize that quite the reverse was true. When she set her arm through his, he drew it against his side and in the process drew *her* against his side. The small walking hoops of her skirt were scarcely an impediment at all. The umbrella over their heads seemed to shut them into a closer privacy than even that offered by the deserted pathway they followed through the park of the dower house and up the hill to the trees. And the sound of the rain drumming on the surface of the umbrella closed them even more into a world of their own.

He deliberately did not make conversation. Neither did she, though whether it was deliberate or not he could not tell. Certainly she must feel the tension that grew between them—the tension he had deliberately created. The fact that she did not try to break it by prattling told him something. Something he wanted to know.

He turned to look back down the hill as they reached the trees.

"Ah," he said.

She looked back and then looked at him and half smiled. A carriage had drawn up outside the doors of the dower house and someone—Robin Barr-Hampton, he would wager—jumped out and hurried into the house.

Nigel felt quite confident in asking the question—else he would not have asked it. "You wish to return?" he asked her.

"No." She shook her head—and allowed him to hold her eyes with his own.

She had slid her arm from his when she had turned. But she had turned in toward him, as he had turned toward her. He made no move to offer his arm again so that they could walk on. She made no move to take it. He looked deeply into her eyes, allowed his own to roam over her face, focusing on her mouth for a few moments, and then looked back. He did not smile or move.

He was playing her like a puppet on a string, he thought as her hands crept up—as he had known they would—to rest lightly against his chest. And yet all was not coldness on his part. Her beauty and her warm charm had not left him completely unmoved. She was easy on the eyes, he had told Will Stubbs. Doubtless she would be easy on the lips, too—and on other parts of his body.

He moved his head closer to hers, lowering his eyes to

her mouth again, waiting for her eyelids to flutter and then close before parting his lips slightly and touching them to hers. Not dispassionately closed lips, he had decided, and not a passionately opened mouth. Not a deep kiss. Not a long kiss. A warm, tender, yearning, forbidden moment. He raised his head and looked at her through half-closed lids.

She opened her eyes and looked directly back into his again. Her lips had been softly pouted, he thought. They had pushed back tentatively against his own. It had very clearly been her first kiss.

"I should have stopped you," she whispered to him.

"Should you?" He allowed himself the merest hint of a smile at last.

"But I am glad I did not," she said. "I have wondered."

He felt almost jolted by the honesty of her words. No maidenly blushes and confusion for the Countess of Worthing. No blaming him for taking advantage of having her alone without a chaperon. No pretense of experience or ennui. Just—*I have wondered*. Wondered what? What it felt like to be kissed? What it felt like to be kissed by *him*?

"And I am glad you did not," he said. "I have wanted to do that since I first set eyes on you two days ago. No, by my life, before that. When your father used to talk about you. I knew I must see you for myself. I knew I must kiss you."

She smiled. "Silly," she said. "That is silly. Let us continue on our way."

Yes, it was enough—for today. It had prepared the way for tomorrow. But the rain was falling more heavily, and though they were among the trees and were in one sense more sheltered, there was also more chance of brushing against wet greenery or dislodging a whole stream of water from a low branch. He did not offer his arm. Instead he wrapped it about her waist and drew her close to his side. She made no protest.

And so they walked in silence about the side of the hill and along the avenue of the lime grove he had admired during the morning walk in the opposite direction and on toward the lawn at the ballroom side of the house. Her inside arm, he noticed after a while, had come about his waist.

"Yesterday," he said to her when they came to the lawn, breaking a lengthy silence, "you described the rose garden as your *second* favorite part of the park. What is the first?"

"The pool," she said. "Behind the house there is a steep descent and at the bottom of it a pool fed by a long waterfall from the next hill. There are ferns and wildflowers and trees and—oh, and utter seclusion. 'Tis not only the loveliest spot in the park. 'Tis the loveliest spot in the whole world, I declare."

"Tomorrow," he said, "I would have you take me there if you will, madam."

"Yes." She turned her head to smile up at him. "And I would have you see it, my lord, before you depart."

"And tomorrow," he said, holding her gaze, "at the pool I will kiss you again."

They had stopped walking once more. She moved her lips as if to speak but said nothing. She drew breath but said nothing. She bit her lip.

"What can you not say?" he asked her, moving his head a little closer, tilting the umbrella so that they would not be observed by anyone who happened to be looking from one of the east windows.

"I cannot say that you ought not," she said. "I cannot say that you must not. I should say both but cannot because I would be speaking untruths and that would be unfair to you. I will not be coy."

He had never met anyone like her. She wanted to be kissed tomorrow but she would not say today—as ninety-nine women out of every hundred would say under similar circumstances—that she did not. She would not place the blame for the kiss on his shoulders. It was something she wanted and she would not deny it. She was indeed a woman of some character.

"Madam," he said, "I honor your trust."

"Do you?" She half frowned. "I will take you to the pool tomorrow, my lord. 'Tis lovely there even when it rains. And I will kiss you there as you will kiss me. But I will trust you to remember that 'tis but a kiss as today's was—between f-friends.'' She hesitated on the final word, but there was no other she could use. They were not friends but they were not lovers either. They were neither—yet.

"I will never do anything to you, madam," he said, "that is against your will." He had planned it so—that all would be done with her consent.

Except that consent, he thought, could sometimes be deceptive. There was informed consent and uninformed consent. He had once consented with alacrity to an evening of cards and had hurried along to it with joyful, youthful eagerness. He had had no idea—not the slightest premonition—of what exactly he had consented to.

Just as the Countess of Worthing did not. She thought she was consenting to a kiss, a little romance.

There was really very little similarity at all, of course. His motives were not malevolent—though there would come a time when she would undoubtedly think they were.

The sun was shining from a cloudless sky again the next morning, just as if there had not been the day of gloom and rain in between two such summery days. Patience arrived at Kedleston in the middle of the morning. She came in the carriage Robin had sent for her.

Robin had had a talk with her and her mother the afternoon before, when he had gone to the dower house with the carriage to fetch Cassandra home—he had been determined, he had said, that she would not be alone inside it with that scoundrel Wroxley. He had been extremely annoyed to find that the two of them had already set out on foot for Kedleston, rain notwithstanding.

"I do believe our suspicions about his lordship have been unfounded, Robin, dear," Lady Matilda had told him. "He is a very charming gentleman, and it appears to me that he is genuinely fond of Cassandra."

But Robin had only scowled. And Patience had discovered during the course of the conversation that had followed that all her worst fears were well founded. Robin had *of-*

fered for Cassandra on the night of the ball, though she had rejected him.

But while she had been nursing her broken heart, Robin had turned to her and informed her that she must help him—and Cassandra, of course. Viscount Wroxley was going to stay for another day or two at least and of course he would do all in his power to go off alone with Cassandra—and Cass was so innocent and so gullible, Robin had added, that of course she would go off with him without a thought to his intentions or her reputation. Patience must come early to Kedleston on the morrow, and he and she would trot along in the wake of the other two wherever they decided to go.

She and Robin were to play chaperon, Patience had understood. It was not a role she relished, especially when she knew that Robin was merely trying to protect his own interests. Patience herself liked Viscount Wroxley and thought that he and Cassandra made a gloriously handsome and romantic couple. But she had been unable to say no to Robin. Besides, she had been unable to resist the chance of spending a part—perhaps a large part—of the following day with him.

And so she came to Kedleston by the middle of the morning only to find that Cassandra was still at breakfast. Not that she had risen late—Cass had always been an early riser. But she had spent a couple of hours with Mr. Coburg, Kedleston's steward, riding over to the home farm in order to learn something about its operation. Robin and Viscount Wroxley were in the breakfast parlor with Cassandra when Patience arrived, though neither was eating.

"Ah, good morning, Patience," Robin said, getting to his feet when she entered the room—the viscount did likewise and also bowed. "I am delighted you could come."

"Patience?" Cassandra looked surprised to see her. "How lovely to see you. Did you walk over?"

"Cassandra and Viscount Wroxley are going to take a walk down to the falls," Robin said. " 'Tis a long and arduous walk but a lovely day for it. I do believe you and I should invite ourselves to join them, Patience." He looked inquiringly at Cassandra. "That is, if you have no objection, cous?"

Patience knew her cousin well enough to realize that she had every objection in the world. Despite what Cassandra had said on her birthday, Patience was convinced that love had found her after all and that she had planned a few hours alone with the viscount. And what more romantic setting was there for a private tryst than the pool at the foot of the waterfall?

Cassandra smiled brightly. "That would be delightful," she said.

Before Patience could seat herself or feel the full awkwardness of knowing herself to be an intruder, Viscount Wroxley smiled his charming smile at her and spoke to her.

"Miss Gibbons," he said, "while Mr. Barr-Hampton keeps her ladyship company, perhaps you would care for a stroll outside with me. The sunshine is too lovely to be wasted, by my life."

"Thank you, my lord," she said. Patience liked him because, surprisingly, he appeared to like *her*. He was an extremely elegant gentleman and she had been quite awed by him at first. But he really was charming. She found that she could relax in his company and simply be herself.

"Miss Gibbons," he said when they were strolling slowly over the lawn before the house, "I can conceive of no greater pleasure than to have your company and that of Mr. Barr-Hampton while her ladyship shows me her favorite spot in the park. No, zounds, I lie and you know I lie."

He looked into her face with such lazily smiling eyes and such a conspiratorial wink that she could not possibly take offense at his words. Besides, she had already known the truth. Mama was right. The viscount really was fond of Cass. Indeed, Patience would not be at all surprised if he actually loved her. She found herself smiling back at him.

"But Robin feels the need to chaperon Cassandra, my lord," she said. "What am I to do to dissuade him? He will be cross if I simply say no."

"I'faith," he said, "I would not have him cross with

you. We need a little scheme, and one moreover that would throw you for a short while at least alone into the gentleman's company."

His eyes were now looking quite intently into her own. Patience felt herself blush. He *knew*.

"I understand," he said, "that the descent to the bottom of the hill and the pool is quite steep. There is a path?"

" 'Tis quite treacherous in parts, my lord," she said. " 'Tis strewn with rocks. One has to watch one's step. But Cassandra and I both know it well. 'Tis quite safe for us to use it."

"But 'twould be quite understandable if a lady were to— perhaps turn her ankle and be unable to go on?" he said. It was a statement rather than a question despite the inflection at the end of the sentence.

"Oh la." Patience had never been a good actress. But she knew exactly what was being asked of her. She was being asked to deceive Robin—Robin of all people! She was being asked to give Cass and the viscount time alone at the pool.

"One would not, of course, wish harm to any lady," Viscount Wroxley said. His eyes were now smiling kindly at her. "It would be as well, perhaps, to exercise great caution on such a potentially dangerous path."

He was not going to urge her further, then. And he would understand if she failed to do as he had suggested. He would leave the decision to her.

He was so right for Cassandra, she thought—so handsome, so charming, so warm, so *masculine*. If he married Cass, then Robin would not be able to do so. Robin would never do for Cass. There was dreadful pain in the very thought of the two of them marrying, but even apart from her personal bias, it would not be a good match. It was not that Robin was not masculine—that was *very* far from the truth. It was just that Robin was—well, he would allow himself to be dominated by Cassandra merely because he would feel the enormous responsibility of protecting her and Kedleston from those who would take advantage of a mere woman. He would *think* he was in charge, but he

would not really be. Such an arrangement would never satisfy either Robin or Cassandra.

Patience could not somehow imagine Viscount Wroxley
allowing himself to be dominated in any way at all.

And so it was that one hour later an accident happened.
They had strolled, the four of them, diagonally through the
rose garden and down the long sloping lawn beyond it until
they came to the trees and the steep slope down the back
of the hill behind the house. The path was indeed steep and
rocky, though the rocks were a help more than a hindrance.
They stopped one from hurtling down the slope and finding
oneself unable to stop. Viscount Wroxley assisted Cassandra on the descent, though she laughingly protested that she
was quite as surefooted as a goat. Robin offered Patience
his hand and gripped hers strongly, reassuringly. He even
smiled at her.

"Thank you for coming, Patience," he said quietly. "I
will not forget that I owe you a favor."

The words, smiting her conscience as they did, might
have caused her to change her decision if they had not come
just one moment too late. She stepped on the edge of one
rock—too close to the edge of it—and slipped heavily and
awkwardly down one side of it, losing her balance and
gasping as she did so. Robin's firm support prevented her
from toppling quite over, but he could not save her from a
severely painful ankle.

She really was no actress, Patience thought, gasping
again and sitting sharply down on the rock so that she could
grasp her ankle with her free hand. And she had been
served well for the deceit she had perpetrated against
Robin. She really had turned her ankle. She blinked away
the tears that sprang to her eyes and bit down hard on her
upper lip. She would not cry. She would not! The pain was
dreadful.

And then Robin was down on one knee in front of her
and was lifting her foot onto his thigh and examining her
ankle with gentle hands and looking up into her face, concern and contrition in his own.

"Oh, my dear," he said, "I am so sorry. Is it dreadfully painful?"

Two tears spilled over, but she swallowed determinedly. " 'Twas all my fault," she said.

Cassandra and the viscount were hovering over her, too, and exclaiming with sympathy and concern.

"We must go back," Cassandra said. "We must get you onto a bed, Patience. We must summon the physician. Is it broken, Rob?"

"Merely sprained," he said, "I hope."

Viscount Wroxley had the most expressive eyes she had ever seen, Patience thought, looking into them briefly before wincing as Robin touched the most painful spot on her ankle. She could tell that his lordship understood she was not playacting.

"I shall carry you back to the house, Miss Gibbons," he said quietly. "I am sorry about this. By my life I am."

But Robin visibly bristled. "That task will be mine," he said. "Egad, I blame myself for this. I suggested that we come. And I was the one assisting Patience to ensure that she came to no harm. Zounds!"

Never again, Patience decided, *never again* would she do anything to deceive another. Least of all Robin.

" 'Twas my fault," she said. "I was careless. I was looking about me instead of at where I was stepping. But you must not all come back with me. I would feel dreadful. This was *your* day, Cass. You wished to show his lordship the loveliest part of the park and you must do so. Please. Oh, please!"

They both protested—quite sincerely, she was sure. To his credit—and to her everlasting shame—Robin did not. He seemed far more concerned about her than with playing chaperon.

"I can walk," she said when it was finally clear to everyone that she would suffer severe distress if they all returned to the house with her. "You do not have to carry me, Robin. I am too heavy."

But when she tried to walk she stumbled on the very first step and would have fallen if Robin had not had an arm firmly about her waist. She hid her face against his shoulder and really did weep for a few weak moments. Not just at the pain—she *deserved* that—but at what she had done. The plan had worked beautifully. Cassandra and Viscount Wroxley had continued on their way down the hill. Robin had no idea she had wrenched her ankle deliberately.

He must be the strongest man in the whole world, she thought a few moments later as he swung her up into his arms and strode up the hill just as if he were carrying a mere feather. She set her arms about his neck and rested her forehead on one of them. And he was very masculine indeed. She might have thrilled to the excitement—and the embarrassment—of being so close to him if only she had not been feeling so very dreadful. And if her ankle had not been throbbing so painfully that it threatened to drown out all thought.

"My poor Patience," Robin said against her ear. "My poor Patience."

" 'Twas all my fault," she whispered. "Robin, I am too *heavy* for you."

"Sh," he said, such tenderness in the sound that she could have howled out her misery. "Sh."

NINE

THEY SHOULD HAVE IN-
sisted on going back to the house with Patience, Cassandra
thought as she and Viscount Wroxley continued on their
way down the hill. But it would have distressed Patience
if they had done so. She would have been convinced that
she had ruined the day for all of them. Besides, there was
nothing the three of them could have done. Robin was quite
capable of taking Patience back on his own and summoning
the physician to look at her ankle. And once they were at
the house, there would be Aunt Althea and Aunt Beatrice
to fuss over her and send for Aunt Matilda.

She was rationalizing, Cassandra thought. She really had
not *wanted* to miss the outing. And before the accident had
happened—though she had *not* willed anything like it to
occur—she had wished there were some way to lose Robin
and Patience. Now she felt guilty, almost as if she had
caused the accident. Poor Patience!

"I have a confession to make." It was as if Viscount
Wroxley had read her thoughts and spoken them out loud.
But it *was* he who spoke the words, not she. He had come
to a stop on the steep path, her hand clasped in his, and he
was looking into her face, slightly above the level of his
own. "I am afraid I was the cause of your cousin's accident."

"No." She smiled at him. "You were not even close to her, my lord." He, too, then, must have wanted Robin and Patience to go away.

"When I strolled outside with Miss Gibbons," he explained, "while you were breakfasting, madam, I suggested that she might pretend to have an accident." His eyes were very intent on hers.

Her own eyes widened. "It was *pretense*?" she said. "She was pretending? She did not hurt her ankle at all?"

"Alas, madam," he said, " 'twas no pretense. In pretending to stumble, it appears that she actually did. I am at fault, you see, for suggesting that she engage in such deceit for my sake. I meant her no harm, by my life, but harm came to her nonetheless."

They were deep in the wooded hillside, the tree branches and leaves like a shady roof over their heads, ferns growing profusely on either side of the path. There were the smells of earth and greenery, the sounds of birds—and the faint rushing sound of the waterfall. There was the feeling of total seclusion.

"And so you feel guilty," she said. "And I feel guilty because I wished it, too, my lord. Not the accident, of course. But—this." She hunched her shoulders but did not explain what she meant. She did not need to do so.

She was in deep waters, she realized. She had realized it yesterday after that walk home from the dower house, and last night when she had tried to sleep. She had realized it this morning when she remembered that they were to come here alone together and that he was to kiss her again. She was playing with fire. In deep waters and playing with fire. She half smiled at the mixture of images.

"Should we go back?" he asked her.

They should. For very safety's sake. And because they were both guilty and ought to punish themselves by turning back from the pleasant outing they had planned and anticipated with pleasure.

She shook her head.

Something had changed, she thought as they continued their descent. The lightness, the teasing, flirtatious quality had gone from their relationship at least temporarily. For the first time, perhaps, she realized how unwise it was to be so far from the house and from other people, alone with one gentleman.

But before she had time to wallow in more such troublesome thoughts, they reached the bottom and turned through the trees and out of them into a world of such enchantment that it always took her breath away even though she had seen it a thousand times.

There was the pool, tear-shaped and deep and always a rich dark green in color from the reflections of the trees on the hills and the ferns that grew thickly about its edges and overhung its depths. The waterfall cascaded over the steep rocky cliff on the far side of the pool. The rocks on either side of the water were mossy. Ferns and even a few small trees grew out of the crevices.

When one stood at the pool, the rest of the world always seemed universes away.

"I'faith," Viscount Wroxley said, " 'tis the Garden of Eden." There was only a slight touch of humor in his tone.

"But there are no fruit trees," she said.

He held her hand and laced his fingers with hers. It somehow seemed more intimate a touch than his arm about her waist the day before. But he was not flirting with her. He was looking about him with deep appreciation, almost with awe.

"Yes," he said at last, looking down into her uptilted face, "I can see why 'tis your favorite part of the park. I doubt such beauty could be improved upon anywhere in England."

"Or anywhere else in the world?" She smiled at him.

His lips tightened and something almost bleak flickered behind his eyes. But it was a fleeting look, soon succeeded by a smile to match her own. "Certainly not anywhere else in the world, madam," he said. "There is nowhere to compare in beauty to England."

"I came here often when I was a girl," she said. "Sometimes when I was sad, sometimes when I was happy. It did not matter. 'Tis a place to soothe sadness and a place to elevate happiness.''

"Your cousins came with you?" he asked.

"Sometimes." She smiled. "We climbed the cliff and swam in the pool, though the water is deep and 'tis dangerous for a child to swim there alone. Usually I came alone. 'Tis a place for solitude."

"And yet," he said, "you chose to bring me here, madam?"

"You are a guest in my home," she said. "I wanted to show off the best the park has to offer, my lord."

"Did you, by my life?" he said. "Do you bring all your guests here, then?"

She had never brought any stranger here—until today.

"No," she said.

"Just some?"

"None," she whispered. "Only you."

"Why?" His voice was low.

How could she answer him? Did she even know why herself? So that he would kiss her again? He had kissed her on the hill above the dower house. She had not needed to bring him here for that. And if that was her motive, it was a dangerous one. So that she would have some time alone with him in an enchanted world, then? So that she would have the memory of him here to look back upon? So that she could come back here next week or next year or ten years from now and remember just this—this moment?

"I do not know," she said quite truthfully in answer to his question. "Because you asked, perhaps?"

But she knew suddenly with almost frightening clarity. She wanted to draw him into the deepest, most intimate, most precious level of her life. She wanted . . . Something had happened in the three days since her birthday, something she had wanted never to happen, something she did not want to happen even now—not, at least, with this intensity. Something that had happened so quickly that she felt bewildered and breathless—excited and frightened. She gazed into the pool, trying to gather her thoughts.

"Yesterday," he said, "I told you that I would kiss you again when we were here."

That kiss had shaken her world—a very theatrical and silly thought. But she was unable to think of another way of describing to herself how it had made her feel. She drew her gaze from the pool and turned her head to look into his eyes.

"I would not take advantage of you when you are far from home and without a chaperon," he said, his eyes roaming all over her face, so that she already felt physically caressed. "I will kiss you only with your consent, madam. May I?" His eyes locked with hers again as he asked the question.

She was suddenly aware of her own shocking ignorance. Was he the gallant, honorable gentleman his words suggested? Or was he a skilled seducer? Was there any chance at all that her uncle and aunts were right about him? But she did not want to feel the doubts. She was in no danger. She *knew* he would not harm her in any way. And she wanted more than anything else to be kissed again—here beside the pool and the waterfall. By him.

She nodded.

He kissed her as he had kissed her the day before—lightly, warmly, lingeringly, his hands on either side of her waist holding her a little away from him. Today the touch of his lips against her own was less of a raw shock. Today she could even think sufficiently to realize that he kissed with his lips slightly apart. It was the reason for the shock and the sensation of intimacy, though it was only their lips that touched. She could taste him. And she could hear the rushing of the water and smell the ferns. Her hands, she realized, had moved up from his chest to rest on his shoulders. Broad, well-muscled shoulders.

It was wrong, she thought when he lifted his head and looked into her face again—his blue eyes looked dreamy and heavy-lidded and beautiful—to allow a man to kiss her when they were not even affianced and never would be. But it did not feel wrong. No harm would come of it. Except that she could not bear to think of his leaving tomorrow or the next day.

His hands, she realized suddenly, had been drawing loose the silk bow at the nape of her neck. He lifted one hand, took off her straw hat, and let it fall to the ground.

" 'Twas an impediment," he said, smiling.

And then thought and the ability to analyze fled as he slid one arm behind her waist and the other about her shoulders and her body swayed against hard-muscled masculinity. She could feel him from her shoulders to her knees—she had not worn hoops at all today. But even as she opened her mouth to gasp in air, his own was upon it, also open.

And this, she realized rather fuzzily, was what he had meant by kissing her at the pool.

She clung to him, one arm about his waist, one hand up behind his head, knowing with an understanding beyond thought that something irreversible was happening to her. She was discovering aspects of her femininity of which she had been unaware. Now that she *was* aware of them she would never be able to forget. Her whole body responded to the embrace. She ached and throbbed in places that were far removed from the kiss itself. And yet the kiss absorbed her. He touched her with his tongue, first lightly, circling her lips, then brushing up behind them, and finally pushing slowly and deeply right into her mouth.

She heard a moan and was not sure if it had come from her or from him. But perhaps it had been her. He withdrew gradually from the kiss and loosened his hold on her. She gazed at him, dazed and disoriented.

"By my life," he said, "you make me forget myself."

As she had forgotten herself. She looked about until she saw what she was looking for—the old log, half-overgrown with ferns, which had served her many times as a seat. She left him and walked to it on legs that felt only just steady enough and sat down on it. She looked across the pool to the bottom of the waterfall and up the cascading water until she could see the blue sky. She drew in a deep breath, held it, and released it slowly. She drew in another.

He stayed where he was for a long time and said nothing. She was thankful for the time he gave her in which to collect herself. How very naive she was. She had expected no more than a repetition of yesterday's kiss—and that had seemed shocking enough to her.

He came over to the log at last and set one foot on it. He rested his forearm across his knee. She did not look away from the waterfall.

"I have offended you?" he asked quietly.

She shook her head. "No," she said.

He touched the knuckles of his free hand very lightly to her cheek before removing his hand. "I meant no disrespect," he said. "My intentions were honorable, madam."

What did those words mean? She turned her head to look at him.

"I would not have kissed you so," he said, "if I had not for a few minutes allowed my passions to rule me. For that I beg your pardon. But I would not have kissed you at all, madam, if I had not been prepared to offer you my hand and my heart afterward. Will you do me the great honor of marrying me?"

She stared at him speechless. Her mind would not function.

"You must have known," he said quietly when she said nothing, "what my feelings have been for you since the moment I set eyes upon you. Since before that, though it sounds fanciful perhaps to say that I felt drawn to you even before I met you. You must have known that I would not bring you here to kiss you unless I meant to offer for you."

No, she had not known. Any of it. He had been Papa's friend. He had come out of kindness. He had engaged her in light flirtation. He was a sophisticated man of the city, of society. He was a viscount, a wealthy man. *And she was a countess, a wealthy woman.*

"No." She shook her head.

"You did not understand?" He took one of her hands in his, but she withdrew it firmly and set it with the other in her lap.

"No," she said. "I will not marry you. I do not wish to

marry anyone." She was having trouble breathing, just as if all the air had been sucked out of the valley into the blue sky far above.

"I have caused you distress, by my life," he said quietly. "Is my regard so abhorrent to you then, madam?"

She looked up very directly into his eyes then. She had to know. "Is it my fortune?" she asked. "My property? Were they right about you? Are you a mere fortune hunter?"

He did not answer for a long time. But he did not move away or look away from her. "By my understanding, madam," he said at last, "your fortune and your property will remain yours your whole life. They will not become your husband's. And by my observation, madam, the property has not prospered as it ought of late, or if it has, money has not been spent where 'tis needed. There are signs of shabbiness at Kedleston. I have a fortune of my own and as your husband I would gladly use it to make of your home the magnificent house it was intended to be."

She could not tell if he was angry or not. Certainly he was very serious. There was no humor in his eyes or in his voice. She had made a fool of herself. But no—she had had a right to ask. She was of age. She had no one to ask the questions for her—not unless she accorded that right to Uncle Cyrus. But she did not need her uncle to organize her life. She was quite capable of doing that for herself.

He wanted to marry her, then, purely because—because he felt a regard for her. He had fallen in love with her as she had fallen in love with him. And she *was* in love with him. Suddenly the thought of spending the rest of her life with him, of becoming his friend, his—his lover, was almost overwhelmingly appealing.

But only a few days ago she had been ecstatic at the knowledge that she was free. Even if her husband was given no ownership of her property, he would still own her in the eyes of both the church and the state. She would owe him obedience. And just a few days ago she had scoffed at the idea of romantic love. Was she to throw everything away that she had believed and dreamed of and lived for ever since Papa's death? Was she going to be so *foolish* just because she had fallen in love?

"I have taken you by surprise," Viscount Wroxley said. "I have rushed you. I ask your pardon, madam. I had thought my intentions to be clear to you. I thought you ready and willing to receive my addresses. Can you say yes to what I ask? Or can you at least give me hope?"

If she said no, he would go away. She would never see him again. Was that what she wanted? Would she preserve her freedom at such a cost? But if she said yes, she might regret her answer tomorrow or even later today.

"I need time, my lord," she said. "You *have* taken me by surprise, I must confess, and I am bewildered. I will not say yes, but I cannot say no."

He half smiled at her. "I have never known another lady as honest as you," he said. "How long do you need? I am impatient for your answer, but I dare not press for it for fear a pressed answer might well be no. Will tomorrow be too soon?"

She would see him for the rest of the day. She would see him this evening and tomorrow morning. She would never be able to think straight. If she saw him, she would be overwhelmed by her feelings for him, as she was in danger of being now—the beguiling smile lingered in his eyes. She looked away from him. She had to think. She refused to be a weak-minded woman who allowed passion and romance to rule her judgment.

"A week, my lord," she said. "A week away from you."

He was silent for a while. "We will return to the house," he said then. "Within the hour I shall be on my way. I have acquaintances in Bath whom I shall visit. I shall reckon the week from the moment I leave here, madam, not a moment later."

"Thank you." She looked up at him again. The smile was still in his eyes. She found it unreadable. Was it amusement she saw there? Confidence in what her answer would be at the end of the week? Self-mockery? Self-defense? She realized how very little she knew of him—almost nothing at all, in fact, except that he had been Papa's friend. And now he wanted to be her husband. But now was not the time to start questioning him. Her mind was in too much turmoil.

He fetched her hat while she stood up and brushed out her skirts. And after she had put it on and tied the bow at the back of her neck, he took her hand, raised it to his lips, and then grasped it firmly so that he could help her climb the path again—not that she needed assistance, of course.

She had not, she thought with a start of guilt, spared a single thought to Patience since reaching the pool.

They walked in silence. The climb was a breathless business. But the silence, she felt, was deliberate on both their parts. There was nothing more to say until next week. But there was the awareness that there would be that week—a whole week without a sight of each other. She was alarmed—and partly thrilled—at the realization of how much the thought of his absence mattered to her. Three days ago she had not even met him. Now, after he had left, there was going to be a restlessness, an emptiness in her life that might well prevent her from thinking clearly at all.

Perhaps when she could no longer see him or hear him or feel the touch of his hand, she would find it easier to make a rational decision. But how did one decide sensibly between passion and good sense, if indeed the two were opposed?

"You let this be a lesson to you, Nige," William Stubbs said, one massive hand on each of his massive thighs as the carriage swayed down the sloping driveway toward the valley and the village and the main road beyond.

Nigel raised haughty eyebrows, though he fully expected a scold for being weak-willed enough to allow himself to be driven away from Kedleston for a whole week by one small woman. But Will could scold his fill. He might be perfectly well able to flatten his master with one jab of just one of those fearsome fists, but he had always found that same master impossible to shift even one fraction of one inch from a decision once he had made it.

"You write 'er a letter if you cawn't say it face-to-face,"
William said. "Better yet, send one of them lawyer coves
to tell 'er for you. You don't owe 'er a single blessed thing
now, lad. You arsked 'er and she said to 'old on for a week
while she played 'ard to get, and so she 'as lost 'er chance.
Don't you be soft in the 'ead, Nige. Don't you arsk again."

Was that what she was doing—playing hard to get? She
had taken him by surprise, he had to admit. He had thought
his mission about to be accomplished with remarkable ease.
She had wanted to be alone with him, even after his confession with regard to her cousin's sprained ankle—and he
really had felt guilty about that. She had wanted to be
kissed, and she had responded to the kiss with heat, even
though he had embraced her with nothing except his mouth
and his tongue and his body against hers. He had not used
his hands. She was not ready for that.

He had fully expected her to accept his marriage offer.
Even after she had blurted out the suspicions with which
her uncle and aunts had poisoned her mind, he had expected
that his answer would have soothed her doubts.

The carriage swung out through the gates of the park and
onto the road that wound through the village, and he stead-
ied himself with a hand on the leather strap. A mocking
smile played over his lips.

Why had he not forced the issue? He could have done
so. He could have done it with words. He could have done
it with another embrace. She had been clearly wavering.
She had even admitted as much. He could have tipped the
scales with very little effort. Why had he not done so? It
was not as if she really had any choice. She did not. He
might even, as a last resort, have told her so. She would
have to know the truth sooner or later after all.

Was it cowardice that had kept him silent on the main
issue?

Or was it concern for her feelings? Her feelings had always concerned him. Hence the plan and the yearlong delay. But his feelings had concerned him in an academic
more than a personal way. He had been concerned with
justice. He had been wronged. He had achieved his re-

venge. He did not wish to leave an innocent party wronged
in place of him. He knew too well what that felt like.

His concern for her had perhaps become a little more
personal in the past few days. She was so damnably *innocent*. And so very—amiable. It was a weak word. There
was nothing even remotely mean in her character, nothing
that would help him believe that perhaps she deserved a
little suffering.

She did not.

And hence, perhaps, this drive away from Kedleston—
for a whole week.

He closed his eyes tightly when he realized suddenly that
his right foot, resting on the floor of the carriage by the
heel, was turning in large, slow circles anticlockwise. He
could feel the restriction, could feel the pain. He could feel
the frustration and the panic and the hopeless despair. He
could feel the hatred cold in his nostrils. And the two sustaining obsessions—England and revenge.

He stilled his foot and rested it flat on the floor. His hand
reached out to open the window to let in some air. He could
feel the perspiration clammy on his face and beneath his
cravat. He muttered an obscenity.

"Gawd awlmighty!" William said. "You don't even
need to be asleep to 'ave the nightmares, do you, lad? Wot
the 'ell are you doin' to yourself?"

"I was the foolish young sprig," Nigel said, leaning his
head back against the cushions and closing his eyes. "Nineteen years old and out to conquer the world. I would have
been content to have an amicable acquaintance with Worthing, Will. I would have been delighted to strike up a friendship with him. I looked for no more. But from the start he
saw me as his deadliest enemy and took great pains to make
himself mine. I walked into his trap with my eyes wide
open and a smile on my fool lips."

"You 'ad your revenge," William said with a grunt.
"And sweet it was, Nige. 'Twould be sweeter yet if you
'adn't started to feel sorry for the filly."

Yes, she had taken away much of the sweetness from a
victory for which he had waited and plotted for almost eight

years. And yet there was a certain rightness in her existence and in his dilemma and the solution he had devised. More of a rightness than Will realized. There was more justice in what he had planned than Will knew.

"You don't want to go 'itching yourself up with 'er," William said. "You don't want to go planting nothing under them petticoats to take root and bear fruit, lad. There is tainted blood there, nonetheless for the fact that she is a pretty little piece and would prob'ly make for good lusty riding. You do your planting in some good honest 'ore, Nige, someone wot knows 'ow to get rid of it quick and neat."

Nigel's hands clenched into fists on the seat beside him, though he did not open his eyes. "Shut your mouth now, Will," he said quietly, "if you value our friendship. It will end completely and irretrievably if you ever again in my hearing speak with disrespect about the Countess of Worthing. I swear it."

Tainted blood. His blood would be mingled with hers in their child. And something would be cleansed. Something would be put right even if the original wrong—the one Will Stubbs knew nothing about—never could be. When his child was born—hers and his—he would finally be at peace with himself. Justice would finally have been served.

A week. He had to wait a whole week.

And then what?

"Gawd in 'is 'eaven," William said, "you been and gawn an' done it, 'aven't you, Nige? The filly may not be 'ead over buttocks for you yet, but the Viscount bloody Wroxley as sure as 'ell is ears over arse for 'er. Well, never say old Stubbs didn't warn you, 'cause 'e did."

"Thank you, William," Nigel said, sounding infinitely bored. "I never will. But as usual you entirely mistake the matter. You have been without a woman yourself for too long. Perhaps you can rectify the situation when we reach London."

"London?" William said, his voice hopeful. "I thought we was going to Bath."

"London," Nigel said. "For one week. Then we will be back here to stay."

"Bloody 'ell," William said. "I will just 'ave time to remember 'ow to do it again and then we comes back 'ere."

"There are women here, too," Nigel said. "Of course, you might have to marry one here, Will. There is altogether more morality in the countryside."

William snorted.

TEN

Mr. and Mrs. Havelock returned home to Willow Hall two days later, satisfied that their niece had avoided a great danger and convinced that she might yet see the good sense of marrying Robin. Neither would be dreadfully upset if the marriage did not take place—Mr. Havelock secretly thought that perhaps Cassandra should marry someone closer to her in rank than his stepson while Mrs. Havelock thought it might be wiser for her son to marry someone slightly below him in rank. Both were content in the conviction that all would be settled by the following spring, when they would remove to London for the Season and Cassandra would finally marry. Kedleston would have a master again.

Robin stayed on after his mother and stepfather had left. He felt the need to offer his male support to his female relatives—though they were only *step*-relatives, Cassandra reminded him, laughing—both at Kedleston and at the dower house. Cassandra would need his knowledge and advice as she struggled to understand and take a hand in the running of her own estate—a foolish whim he expected her to outgrow very soon. Aunt Beatrice and Aunt Matilda would need the reassurance that he was there to offer both to their newly headstrong niece.

And Patience—well, Patience, who lived up to her name

in the days following her accident, was to be visited and
talked to as often as he could spare the time. She had never
once blamed him for causing her to sprain her ankle—quite
the opposite. But he blamed *himself* and wished desperately, as he told her more than once, that he could take her
pain on himself. The physician had directed that she not set
her foot to the ground for at least a week. It was Robin
who carried her from her bed to a chaise longue in the
sitting room late every morning and back to her bed again
every evening.

"I do believe," Cassandra said to him one evening as
they walked back to Kedleston together, "you are growing
fond of her, Rob."

He looked at her in incomprehension. "Patience?" he
said. "I already am fond of her, cous. I always have been."

Cassandra laughed. Steady, dependable, unimaginative
Robin would not recognize love if it curled itself into a fist
and crashed into his nose, she thought. But she had high
hopes. There was a gentleness in his treatment of Patience
that did not often show itself in his day-to-day behavior.
Robin needed a woman with whom he could feel protective, and the woman was certainly not she, though he had
broached the topic of marriage again on the day of his
parents' departure. Patience would be perfect for him—and
of course she adored him.

Cassandra kept herself very busy from early morning until late at night. She took charge of the running of the house,
as she had done for the past several years. She visited
neighbors and friends and was visited in return. That, too,
was part of her normal routine. She called upon poorer
tenants and laborers. She had often called upon the women
and taken them gifts of food. She had sometimes read to
the elderly and played with the children. Now she talked
to the men, too, listening, learning, planning. And she spent
hours of every day with her steward, with the estate books,
on the farms, beginning the slow and often painful process
of learning a way of life that would have been taught her
from infancy if only she had been a son.

She was determined to learn. She was determined to be

respected as an equal by the landowners whose land marched with Kedleston's. She was determined to be independent and free.

Freedom! She thought about it often during that week even as her mind tried to concentrate on the matter at hand. How fortune had smiled on her, giving her choices that most other women never knew. She would be foolish to give up her freedom so soon, before she had had time to savor it and to nurture it. And to a stranger. Now that he was no longer in her daily sight she understood just how much Viscount Wroxley was a stranger. She knew almost nothing about him.

She had behaved as foolishly as women were expected to behave, she thought. She had met a handsome stranger, who was also elegant and charming and experienced in gallantry, and she had tumbled into love without a single rational thought. The only sensible thing she had done was to delay giving an answer to his marriage offer, to send him away so that she would have a chance to gather her wits about her. She wished now that she knew where he had gone in Bath so that she could write him and ask him not to return. It would be embarrassing to come face-to-face with him again.

She had told no one about the marriage offer. Everyone assumed that they must have been mistaken about his intentions or that she had been so discouraging that he had decided to search out greener pastures, as Aunt Bea had phrased it. They had all congratulated her on not falling prey to a man who clearly had nothing to offer her but charm and polished manners and probably expensive habits, too.

She had come close to telling Patience. Her cousin had been upset when he took his abrupt leave, and clearly felt that somehow she was to blame. Cassandra had told her that he had confessed the full truth of his little conspiracy with Patience and that he had kissed her, Cassandra. When Patience had clasped her hands to her bosom and declared that surely then Lord Wroxley would return, Cassandra had not contradicted her.

"He has gone to speak with his father and with his family, you may be sure, Cass," Patience had said. "Oh la, he is asking for their blessing and then will come to ask for Uncle Cyrus's. Though he does not have to do that, does he? He has to ask only you. Oh Cass!"

But Cassandra had answered quite firmly. "I am not going to marry him," she had said, "or anyone."

Patience had smiled softly and leaned back against the cushions of the chaise longue. Her expression said that she did not believe for a moment that all was lost.

Cassandra was going to say no. A very firm no before she could be tempted again. She would be sorry if his feelings were hurt, but he would recover quickly. They had known each other for such a short while and really there was nothing in her to attach a man's deeper feelings. She had little beauty and she certainly had none of the sophistication to which he must be so accustomed in London. He would forget her within another week. Indeed, perhaps he would not even return. Perhaps once he arrived in Bath and met his acquaintants and his own sort of people again, he would realize what a narrow escape he had had.

Good sense prevailed during that week. And if her nights were disturbed by dreams and her days by occasional daydreams, she convinced herself that they were natural—she was a flesh-and-blood woman, after all. There were her needs as a person and her needs as a woman. She had decided to put the former needs first, to put the others firmly aside at least for a few years. They could not be entirely denied, of course. She was human. But she was a human who could put reason before passion. She was proud of herself.

She walked over to the dower house with Robin on the afternoon before the week was at an end. But she could not stay long. There was some reading she had promised herself she would do today since tomorrow was likely to be an emotionally turbulent day—how she wished it would come and go so that she could begin to forget about it, about *him*. Robin, on the other hand, decided to stay with Patience since Aunt Matilda had gone into the village. Cassandra began the walk home alone.

It was a lovely day again. She soaked up the warmth, occasionally tipping back her head so that the sunshine could get past the brim of her hat to warm her face. In truth, she thought, it was difficult to concentrate on anything today. The more she tried not to think about tomorrow, the less she could think of anything else.

She was walking along the lime grove, admiring the straight tall trees to either side, the wide grass avenue between, when her attention was distracted and she stopped walking altogether, her heart thumping erratically, her thoughts becoming immediately scrambled. He was almost at the far end of the grove, standing quite still as if he had seen her before she saw him. He was dressed fashionably and attractively in varying shades of light gray. His hair was powdered. He carried no hat or cane—he must have left both at the house. He looked rather like a prince from a fairy tale, Cassandra thought foolishly.

He also looked achingly familiar, as if he were someone she had known—and loved—all her life. She realized in a rush of purely irrational emotion that her week had been horribly empty without him, that her *life* would be unbearably empty. . . .

She walked slowly toward him, trying desperately to remind herself of all the sensible thoughts she had had during the week. But all she was really aware of as she drew closer was that his eyes were very intent on her and that they smiled. It was a foolish thought. She was not close enough to read the expression in his eyes.

He did not move until she came to a stop again twenty feet from him. He did not open his arms to her even then, just his hands. He spread them at his sides, palm out, in a gesture of surrender and welcome.

She ran the rest of the way, her arms lifting of their own volition, it seemed, to twine about his neck. His arms came about her waist like tight steel bands and their mouths met in an open, hot, yearning kiss. All she could feel—she could not think—was a sense of homecoming, such a welling of happiness that there was as much pain as there was joy.

And then they were gazing into each other's eyes—but he was not returning her smile.

"Give me my answer," he whispered to her. "I cannot live with the suspense. I could not stay away for the full week, by my life. Say yes or say no. Say *something*."

"Yes." There was no hesitation in her voice, no doubt in her heart—her mind had not even been consulted. "Yes, yes, yes."

And then they were both laughing and he had her off her feet and was swinging her about in a complete circle. The world had never seemed so bright a place or happiness so filled with joy.

She was two persons. Some dispassionate part of herself was fully aware of the fact. There was the heedless, passionate woman who had recognized her man, the one and only love of her whole life—the woman who would give up everything else that had meaning in her life for the sake of love. And there was the thinking woman of sense who stood back and knew that the sacrifice was going to be too great, especially when it was being made for a *stranger*. The passionate part of herself knew him from of old, from long before infancy or even birth, as the lover of her heart. The rational part of herself spurned such sentimental drivel and could see a man she really did not know at all.

But the passionate part of herself had taken control.

"I have not stopped thinking of you for a single moment," he said. "I have been unable to sleep and when I have slept from sheer exhaustion I have dreamed that your answer would be no. That it *must* be no. What do I have to offer someone of your beauty and sunny nature but my heart?"

" 'Tis all I want," she told him.

"Then 'tis yours," he said. "For a lifetime and beyond."

"And mine," she said, "is yours." She laughed again. "What is your name, my lord? I do not even know it."

"Nigel," he said.

"Nigel." She said it aloud and savored it in her mind.

Nigel. It was the name by which only those very close to him knew him—his parents, his family, his closest friends. It was the name by which she would know him in the intimacy of marriage. He was no longer Viscount Wroxley to her. He was Nigel.

"Yes, Cassandra," he said.

He pronounced her name as everyone else did. It sounded different spoken by him. It sounded like a caress.

"We will marry tomorrow morning," he said. "I have a special license with me. I did not stay in Bath, you see. I could not. I rode to London. If I kept moving, I told myself, I could keep my promise to stay away for a week. If I purchased a license, I could convince myself that your answer would be yes."

"Tomorrow?" She finally loosened her hold of his neck and leaned back away from him. "Tomorrow? Oh no, 'tis too soon."

The reality of what had happened during the past couple of minutes was beginning to intrude upon the euphoria of seeing him again—of touching him again. Tomorrow they would *marry*? But she needed time to think.

"Too soon?" he said. "I'faith, Cassandra, one hour from now would not be too soon. We must be apart for a whole night before tomorrow comes."

She moved her lips but she could not formulate words to express her tumbling thoughts. What was she *doing*?

"I have frightened you again." He loosened his hold on her until his hands rested lightly on either side of her waist. "What must you think of me and my impetuosity? Your uncle and aunt are not still at Kedleston, are they? You will wish to summon them. You will wish for a few days to organize a wedding breakfast and invite your neighbors. You will wish to plan your bridal clothes at some leisure. Perhaps you will wish to decorate the house and the church with flowers."

"And your family?" she asked him. "You will wish to send for them. From where? I do not even know where your home and estate are."

"I have only a sister," he said quietly. "She is far away.

Too far. 'Twould take too long to send for her. You will meet her later.''

He had no family but a sister? And he did not want even her at his wedding? Or any of his friends?

''Come,'' he said, releasing her and offering his arm. ''Let us walk to the house and tell our news to Lady Beatrice. If you write to your uncle, we can have the letter sent on its way today. Perhaps he will come tomorrow or the next day.''

But she felt that events had moved beyond her control. She felt a certain panic. ''Please,'' she said, ''let us wait. Just until tomorrow. There are guests expected for dinner tonight and for cards and music in the drawing room afterward. Let us keep the secret to ourselves until tomorrow.''

''And why, my little coward,'' he asked, his eyes laughing at her, ''have I returned so soon after leaving? How are we to explain it? What will your aunt think? And your neighbors?''

''And Robin,'' she said. ''He is still here. They may think what they will, my lord. I am mistress of Kedleston. I am answerable to no one.''

''*My lord?*'' He raised his eyebrows.

''Nigel.'' She smiled at him. And felt a welling of love for him. And an uneasiness. Her two selves were firmly at war.

'' 'Twill be our secret until tomorrow, then, Cassandra,'' he said. ''Your neighbors will think I am a sorry fellow, unable to bring you to the point. But your neighbors may go to the devil with my blessing. I will have our secret to hug to myself.''

She laughed and felt suddenly totally happy again. She rested her hand on his cuff and he bent his head and kissed her lips before they moved in the direction of Kedleston.

By tomorrow she would have sorted out her whirling thoughts. By tomorrow she would be ready to send for Uncle Cyrus and ready to deal with her aunts and with Robin. Tomorrow she would be ready to plan her wedding. There could be no alternative, she knew. She loved him. She would never be able to live happily without him. Her choice was between freedom and loneliness on the one hand and happiness and the confines of marriage on the other.

Really there was no choice at all.

"I am so glad you came a day early," she said, turning her head and smiling up at him with the whole of the sunshine in her eyes. "The wait until tomorrow would have been interminable."

"Too long an eternity," he agreed as they emerged from the lime grove onto the lawn, and the blazing glory of the tiered flower garden came into sight.

He would not sleep, Nigel thought later that night, even if he lay down. He stood at the open window of his bedchamber, his hands resting on the sill, looking out on a quiet moonlit scene.

He was back where he belonged—the feeling of homecoming he had experienced earlier when his carriage began the climb from the village had been almost overwhelming. He would not go away again—not for a long time. He would have no reason to go away and no need to do so. Everything he could ever want in what remained of his life was here.

Peace was in sight for him at long last.

All had been accomplished as he had planned it except that it had taken a few days longer than it need have taken. And except that even yet she was a little skittish. It was understandable, he supposed. He should have realized that a woman, even a woman in love, would need longer than half an afternoon and an evening to plan her own wedding. And of course she would want her family and friends about her and they must be summoned from ten miles and more away. Although he had been patience itself for a full year, he had noticed a strong tendency in himself to rush things now that he was so close.

Her aunt had looked horrified. Barr-Hampton had looked murderous. They did not know yet, of course, why he had returned. But they must very strongly suspect. Why else would he have come back so soon? Had there not been guests at the house all evening, he did not doubt that Barr-Hampton at least would have cornered him and demanded, as his stepfather had done a week ago, what his intentions were. The in-

terrogation would come in the morning. And before the day
was out, Havelock would have been sent for and would have
arrived, breathing the proverbial fire and brimstone. Indeed,
news of his return had perhaps already been sent to Willow
Hall.

He should be able to sleep tonight, Nigel thought, knowing that all was finally accomplished—all that he had
dreamed about for many years. She was in love with him.
She would marry him without fuss. When she knew the
truth, she would perhaps accept it. And if she did not, then
she must learn to live with it. He would never be unkind to
her.

Even Will Stubbs seemed reconciled to the inevitable.
He had done nothing on hearing the news except toss the
glance of his one eye ceilingward and mutter dark predic-
tions of doom beneath his breath.

When they married, Nigel could finally set right an ancient wrong. In his child—and hers—all would finally be
set to rights. It was perhaps a sentimental dream he had,
since he himself would not be the one to benefit, but dreams
were important.

Sometimes dreams were everything. For many years
dreams had been everything to him, reality having been
intolerable—an understatement if ever he had heard one.

Oh yes, the Countess of Worthing must marry him. And
he was very close—another few days, a week at the outside.

And then something beyond his window caught his attention. He leaned forward and peered intently out across
the lawn to the trees beyond. Yes, he had not mistaken.
There was something moving down there—*someone*. A
woman with light-colored clothing and dark hair loose
down her back. She must have come around from the back
of the house and was making her way toward the trees. She
was not moving either quickly or furtively.

Like himself, she was finding it difficult to sleep. Wiser
than he, she had chosen to step out of doors for air and
exercise. He could not see her clearly, but he had no doubt
who she was. She was certainly no servant. Perhaps she
wished for solitude, he thought. Perhaps she needed time

alone to think about the day's happenings. And perhaps she
would think too much.

It was a warm night. He did not pause to pull on either
his waistcoat or his coat. He ran down the stairs, let himself
out through the French windows of the ballroom, hurried
down the steps of the flower garden, and crossed the lawn
in time to see where she had gone among the trees. She
had not gone far. She stood against a tree trunk, looking
up at the moon and the stars.

She did not look startled when he circled about the tree,
careful to make his approach audible, and came to stand in
front of her. She looked at him with a soft half smile, almost as if she had expected him. She was wearing a silk
robe without stays or hoops. With her hair down she looked
seductively beautiful.

He could begin speaking, he thought, quietly tell her the
truth after all. Perhaps she would listen quietly with that
smile still on her face. Perhaps he had made mountains out
of molehills. Perhaps she would not be particularly upset.

Or he could refrain from speaking. He could put to rest
the doubts that were surely the cause of her wakefulness at
an hour that must already be well past midnight. He could
make sure of her—very sure.

" 'Tis dark," she said softly.

"But the moon gives light enough," he said.

"I meant your hair." She reached up with both hands
and pulled loose the ribbon that held his hair back at the
nape of his neck. His hair fell in waves over his shoulders
and about his face, and she threaded her fingers into it and
drew his face down toward hers.

There was no further decision to make. Seduction was unnecessary. He kissed her softly until he knew for sure what
she offered, what perhaps in her indecision she needed, and
then he untied the silk sash at her waist, slid the robe off her
shoulders with the straps of her shift, and took her naked
breasts in his hands. She whimpered against his mouth as he
set his thumbs featherlight against her nipples. He hardened
into instant arousal as she arched into him, hot with untutored desire.

He would not take her fiercely, though her passion seemed to demand it. He would not have her remember her first carnal experience as something violent, even though he could also make it satisfying for her. And he would not use her as she thought she wished to be used, merely because doing so would give him intense pleasure. She was to be his wife. Tonight would set the tone of their future relationship.

He gentled her with his hands and his mouth and with soothing words, and then he wooed her until she was languid with desire, ready to cope with the shock of the first penetration.

"Lie down," he murmured to her. He had backed her against the tree trunk several minutes before, his body holding her there. He had eased his legs between hers so that she straddled him and could feel his arousal, understand its significance many minutes before it might seem too stark a threat to her. "Let me make love to you properly."

He would force nothing. He eased his weight away from her. She could withdraw from what was to come if she wished. She looked down at the soft moss at their feet and lay down on her back. He knelt beside her, lifted her shift, opened the buttons of his breeches to free himself, and positioned himself between her thighs and against her opening before lowering himself on top of her, keeping his weight on his elbows.

He watched her face—her eyes were closed and she was biting her lower lip—as he thrust slowly and firmly up into her, past the barrier that had her flinching in pain, until he was embedded in her to his full length. He waited for the tension of pain and shock to go from her body and from her face. He breathed slowly through his mouth, imposing control on himself. She was moist and hot and tight.

He began to work her with firm, deep strokes. Her initial wild passion had gone. She was relaxed and lay still, her hands spread on the grass at her sides. But there was no revulsion in her. She was experiencing the new sensations, he thought, with quiet enjoyment. It was what he wanted for her tonight.

He worked with steady, controlled rhythm until he knew

that he could hold back the moment of release no longer. He held still and deep in her, sighing with the gushing of his seed.

But he would not allow himself to be mindless with his own carnal satisfaction—not even for a moment. He withdrew from her, moved to her side, drew her against him with both arms about her, and kissed her softly on the lips.

"My love," he whispered. "Thank you."

"Nigel," she said softly.

"Did I hurt you?" he asked her.

"Yes." She sighed. "I think I like it."

Her candor always took him by surprise. "I will persuade you to *know* you like it before many more nights have passed," he told her. "You understand that there can be no going back now, do you not?"

"I think I am glad of that, too," she said. "I always feel so uncertain except when you are with me."

"I will be with you, my love," he said, "for the rest of our lives."

She sighed again. "I think I like that most of all," she said.

So trusting, so innocent, he thought, holding her as she slid into sleep. With so strong an assumption that sex equated love.

It had been good sex. He had taken care to make it as good for her as a first experience—on the hard ground— could be. And it had been unexpectedly good for him. For the past two years he had chosen his mistresses with care from among those with reputations for skill and experience.

Innocence and ignorance and awkwardness had felt unexpectedly erotic.

But it had, when all was said and done, been only sex.

Except that he felt a certain protective tenderness for her. Her innocence would be fully gone soon. But he would hold her close, protect her from the abyss that had swallowed him at the age of barely twenty.

ELEVEN

THE WEDDING OF THE
Countess of Worthing to Viscount Wroxley was set to take
place five days after his return to Kedleston. All of her
family and neighbors and friends were invited and almost
all returned instant acceptances. Such grand occasions did
not offer themselves often in this particular corner of Somersetshire. None of his relatives and friends were invited, not
even the acquaintances in Bath with whom he had planned
to stay the week before. There would be plenty of time to
invite them, Cassandra assured him, almost desperate that
he should have someone of his own with whom to share
such an important day in his life. But he replied that *she*
would be there, and she was all that mattered to him.

They met with opposition from all the expected quarters
with all the expected arguments, of course. She was behav-
ing with remarkable foolishness, they all told her—except
for Lady Matilda, who thought the whole thing hopelessly
romantic. She should at the very least, they all pleaded, wait
until her uncle or Robin or her man of business, if she
insisted upon acting independently of her male relatives,
had discovered more about Viscount Wroxley and his position in society and his property and fortune. She should
have a detailed marriage settlement drawn up.

She refused all their advice. A marriage settlement was

unnecessary. She was independently wealthy. She would not depend upon her husband for any of the material things in life. As for investigating his identity, she would learn more about him after their wedding. She frequently asked him about himself, about his family, his home, his upbringing, his travels. He never refused to answer. He was never even curt or obviously secretive in his replies. She was only partly aware of the adroit way he had of turning the questions, giving interesting and witty replies without ever giving the information she had asked for.

It did not matter. She felt that she knew him at a far deeper level than knowledge of the details of his past would give her. He was an interesting, an amusing, a witty companion. He must have felt the hostility of her family—they did little enough to conceal it—but he treated them all with unfailing good manners.

More important than anything else, she had committed herself to him. She had committed herself with a verbal promise in the lime grove on the afternoon of his return. And she had committed herself with her body later that same night. There were no more intimate moments between them during the five days preceding their marriage, and sometimes the events of that night seemed unreal to her— not only what had happened, but the fact that she had not protested or even thought of doing so. It had seemed so right, so—so inevitable.

But it had been the ultimate commitment. She had known that at the time and had not wavered from it afterward. It gave serenity to the frantically busy days of the wedding preparations. She had given her body. She might even now be with child. There was no question now of avoiding the marriage even had she wanted to. She was thankful that that night had put all doubts, all inner debates to rest.

She had not particularly enjoyed it physically. There had been shock, pain, discomfort, embarrassment. But emotionally she had found it far more powerful than she could possibly have imagined. She had not realized that what happened between a man and a woman involved such a prolonged and vigorously active intimacy. She had not realized that he would come so very deep inside or that he would then proceed with such masculine strength and vigor to take away any remaining vestiges of privacy or possibilities of secrets.

She had become a part of him that night. She had her body back to herself, albeit a tenderly sore body that would never be quite the same again. But having possessed her body, he would forever possess her. And having known his body, having received it into her own, she would forever be bonded to him.

She did not need marriage settlements. She did not need to probe into every aspect of his life as it had been lived before she met him. Her knowledge of him went too deep for such trivialities. Her *love* was too deep.

And so the marriage preparations went forward and she prepared herself despite the very obvious worries and misgivings of everyone who had helped her live her life until her one-and-twentieth birthday just two weeks before.

In his new capacity as husband of the Countess of Worthing, Nigel was to move after the nuptials from the guest chamber originally assigned to him to the earl's rooms, adjoining the countess's. He dressed far earlier for the wedding than was necessary and left for the church long before he need have done so. It seemed important to everyone that he not see his bride until she came to him at the altar of the church. And so he obliged them by taking himself out of the way.

William Stubbs, who would not go too early to the church himself and thereby raise eyebrows belowstairs— he had raised enough as it was by his appearance and his manner of speaking—decided to move some of his master's belongings to his new quarters. He was in the earl's dressing room, arranging his friend's shaving gear on the washstand, when the door adjoining the countess's dressing room opened and the lady herself came through it.

She was not yet dressed for her wedding. She wore a white silk dressing robe with bare feet. Her hair, still unpowdered, lay loose down her back. She was carrying a long-stemmed red flower and lifted it to her nose as she crossed the dressing room and set a hand on the knob of the door leading into the earl's bedchamber. Only at that moment did she become aware that she was not alone. Her head turned sharply, her face became an instant mask of terror, and she squeaked in alarm.

"Who are you?" she asked.

William was quite accustomed to evoking terror in women—and in quite a few men, too, for that matter. Even the toughened, streetwise whores with whom he occasionally consorted to quieten his appetites usually came with him more out of a fear of refusing than an eagerness to earn their fee, until by his actions he made clear to them that it had never been his way to treat women roughly or to demand of them anything more than a swift and lusty, very basic performance of their skills. There were even a few whores of his acquaintance who were quite happy when he went back to them for a second or third time.

William Stubbs smiled—it was more of a leer than a smile, Nigel had once told him with a laugh and a hearty slap on his back—and bobbed his head in a strange approximation of a bow. "I am 'is lordship's man, my lady," he said. "William Stubbs."

"Lord Wroxley's valet?" She looked at him in total amazement—he was accustomed to *that* look, too, from those who had just made a similar discovery about his position.

"I am, my lady." He bobbed his head again. This little filly, he thought, he could pick up with one hand if he so chose and not know that he had more than a feather in it.

And then she smiled and he saw her dimple. "Mr. Stubbs," she said, "you startled me. I did not know anyone was in here. I am pleased to make your acquaintance. Welcome to Kedleston. I hope you will be happy here."

"Thank you, my lady." If he stood with his face full to the sun, William thought, he could not feel so bathed in light as he did with the little filly's smile directed at him. She was smiling at *him*—old Stubbs—and welcoming him to this palace.

She looked down at the flower in her hand. " 'Tis customary," she said, "for a gentleman to give his lady a rose. But I have decided to put one in my lord's chamber for him to find later today. Will he be pleased, do you think, Mr. Stubbs? Or will he think me remarkably foolish?"

William Stubbs gaped mutely. He had the distinct impression that the few brains he possessed had been scrambled, just like eggs. There was color in her cheeks and a soft look of love in her eyes—for that Nigel she was going to marry within a couple of hours. And she had asked his opinion—*his*.

"I'll shove it in a jug of water for you if you cares to leave it in my keeping, my lady," he said. "And if 'e don't like it, I'll tell 'im 'e must be dicked in the nob."

"Dicked . . . ?" she said. "Are you from London, Mr. Stubbs?"

William bobbed his head.

"You use London talk," she said. But just as William felt chastised she smiled once more. " 'Tis most colorful and charming. *Will* you fetch water? That would be very kind of you. I shall place the rose where I want it and you can put it in water when you return so that it will remain fresh."

She proceeded on her way into the bedchamber.

The whole interview had lasted for maybe one minute. But William Stubbs, standing rooted to the spot for several moments after she had disappeared, a shaving mug clutched in one huge fist, knew beyond a doubt that his life would never ever be the same again.

He had been for the first time close to a tiny little lady with a dimple and a sunny smile, a little lady who had called him *Mister* Stubbs in her soft, refined voice, and had bidden him welcome and said that his way of talking was charming, a lady who had called him kind for offering to fetch a jug of water for the red flower—that rose or whatever it was.

It would be inaccurate to say that William Stubbs had fallen instantly and irrevocably in love. There was no element of romance in his feelings for his friend's soon-to-be

wife. It would be more accurate, perhaps, to say that he
had fallen quite irreversibly into a deep and reverential devotion.

If that Nigel ever made the little lady shed one tear—
even *one*, he thought as he hurried from the room on his
mission, then old Stubbs was going to be sorely displeased
with him. Sorely displeased!

Cassandra wore white for her wedding—a white open
gown, its robings heavily embroidered with silver thread, a
white petticoat draped over wide hoops, and a white stomacher glittering with silver embroidery. Her hair was
powdered white beneath her lace-trimmed cap. Its silver-
threaded lappets reached to her waist.

By coincidence her bridegroom wore dove gray and silver and white. It was, she thought as she approached him
down the long aisle of the village church, her hand on her
uncle's arm, like an omen of compatibility and harmony.
He looked like the prince in a fairy tale, and she felt like
the princess.

He was not smiling. Indeed he looked pale, even severe.
He looked very intently back at her. She had not been smiling either, she realized as she reached his side, though she
had had eyes for no one else since entering the church. She
smiled now—and realized the full reality of the moment.

She was about to marry the man she loved more than
life, the man who had transformed life for her in a two-
week period and would fill the rest of her life with warmth
and meaning and love. If she had felt any lingering doubts
in the five days since his return—though really there had
been none—they all fled before the enormous significance
of this moment.

"Dearly beloved," the Reverend Hythe began.

It was the first moment of her happily-ever-after. She
very consciously voiced the thought in her mind.

Nigel was thinking about his home and his family. He
had cut himself off from them two years ago—after discovering that *they* had cut themselves off from *him*. He had

cut them from his memory and from his heart. He had not even bothered to fight them.

They were dead to him.

He had a new home and a new family. He had schemed and planned and worked for them, and by God, they were his. They were all he would need for the rest of his life.

And *she* was his. Very nearly his. He watched her from the moment she entered the church. As a bride, she surpassed even herself in beauty. She was pale and nervous— and yet when she finally smiled, he could see all the happiness, all the love, all the trust that were tucked away just behind her eyes.

The fierceness of his own sense of exultation and triumph took him by surprise. She was *his*. All that he had achieved would have been worth little—nothing at all, in fact—if she had escaped this moment.

She was his. Or very nearly his. His mind touched once more upon his own family and upon the late Earl of Worthing, her father.

None of them mattered now. He was safely entering a new world, embarking on a new life.

"Dearly beloved," the vicar said.

They looked, Lady Matilda said, her hands clasped to her bosom, tears in her eyes, like a prince and princess stepped out of the pages of a fairy tale. She said it when they stood on the steps of the village church after the service, the church bells pealing out the glad news of their marriage. Mrs. Havelock, softened and smiling now that the deed was done, told them they were the most handsome couple she had seen in many a long year. Even Lady Beatrice had suspiciously bright eyes as she hugged her niece and submitted to the kiss on the cheek her new nephew offered. Patience, leaning on Robin's arm, though she had declared just the day before that her ankle was as good as new again, was all smiles and tears. Robin was grave and. courteous—as was Mr. Havelock.

William Stubbs, lingering in the background with the other upper servants who had been granted permission to attend the service, nodded gravely to his friend when Nigel looked his way and held his gaze, though he did not try to approach the newly married couple.

They did not linger on the steps. Nigel hurried Cassandra through the churchyard, along the pathway cleared for them by the guests who would follow them to Kedleston for the wedding breakfast. The roadway beyond the churchyard gates was crowded with villagers, all cheering and applauding their countess on her wedding day and throwing rose petals.

It was the happiest day of her life.

They rode in an open carriage back to the house, the sunshine warm and bright. Cassandra turned her head to smile at the man beside her as the vehicle lurched into motion and he took her hand in both his own. He was smiling back at her. He lowered his head toward hers and kissed her softly. There was renewed cheering from behind them.

"My wife," he whispered to her.

"My husband."

They both laughed. And then sobered. And gazed at each other. The carriage turned into the park and began its ascent through the woods.

"You are happy?" he asked.

"Yes." She nodded. "And you?"

"Yes."

They laughed again.

"Such profound conversation," she said.

"Sometimes," he said, "there are no words. Sometimes the English language—or any language, for that matter— is quite inadequate. Sometimes there is only the heart."

Yes, it was true. That was what it was. There was no way of expressing the happiness of one's wedding day. They were married. They would live happily ever after. It was such an absurd phrase, such a cliché, such an impossibility. She was not so unrealistic, so blinded by romance, that she really believed that every day of the rest of their lives would be filled with unalloyed happiness. But for today it was the only phrase that would fit. Or rather, he was right, there were no words. She spoke anyway.

"I will remember this day, this moment, this *feeling*," she said, "for the rest of my life. The memory will sustain me. I will never allow myself to forget the rightness, the— the . . . Ah, you are right. There are not the words."

" 'Tis why," he said, "the wedding day is busy with the entertainment of the wedding guests and the wedding night is busy with a more private activity, which requires no words at all."

She blushed.

"Tonight, by my life," he said, "you will *know* that activity to be enjoyable, Cassandra. I pledge you my word."

It had been such an earth-shattering experience. The thought that it would happen again tonight in her own bed was somewhat overwhelming. Somehow it would seem more alarming and more embarrassing there, especially when she would know exactly what was to come. And infinitely more exciting, too. She was throbbing in that most private place where he had invaded her body. She sank her teeth into her lower lip.

"The servants will be waiting to greet you," he said. "Doubtless they will all be formally lined up. Someone will be on watch at the doors. Kiss me now before we can be seen and before any other carriage comes up behind us. A private kiss, my wife."

It certainly was a private kiss. He opened her mouth wide with his own and pressed his tongue inside. He breathed warmly into her mouth so that she felt a near merging of bodies. She murmured appreciatively and cupped her hand about the side of his face.

And then he was looking down into her face, his eyelids heavy. " 'Tis not something to be feared, you see," he said, "though in the space of five days your apprehensions might have grown again. There was pain on that night—you were virgin. Tonight there will be none. Only a fulfillment of the promise of that kiss."

He had read her like a book. She smiled at him. "I do not fear, Nigel," she said. "I am your wife. You are my husband. We belong together. We are part of each other, with nothing secret or hidden between us. I have given you my heart and my hand and my body as you have given me yours. Nothing will ever come between us to spoil what began two weeks ago and has come to fruition today. I am not afraid. I am happy. Utterly happy.''

He did not answer her. He continued to gaze into her eyes, a smile in his own. And yet for a moment it seemed that there was something else there, too—a certain wariness or look of calculation. The expression was gone even before she could begin to grasp what she thought she had seen, and he raised her hand to his lips.

''I'faith, madam,'' he said, ''I will devote my life to preserving your happiness.''

If he had not come, she thought, if he had not made the effort to travel all the way to Kedleston to greet her on her birthday just because he had been Papa's friend, how very different life would be today. It would be just an ordinary day. She would not know of his existence or of the existence of such a deep and glorious love. He could not have known what his courtesy visit had in store for him. Perhaps his decision to come had been a spur-of-the-moment thing, made because there had been no more pressing engagement to keep him in town. What sudden and fragile decisions and events could determine the whole course of the rest of one's life.

'' 'Tis as I thought,'' he said, nodding ahead of the carriage. They had come out onto the open lawn and into full view of the house. All the servants, indoor and out, were lined up on the terrace.

They laughed gaily together. They would not have another moment of privacy for several hours. But it was their wedding day and they would enjoy the company of relatives and friends and the good wishes of servants—and look forward to the privacy the night would bring.

It was their wedding day.

William Stubbs was sitting in the taproom of the village inn, tipping back a celebratory mug of ale with one of Kedleston's senior gardeners, and privately contemplating his future.

Nigel would probably be able to manage his own life quite nicely from this day on. He had got everything he wanted—and everything he deserved, in William's opinion. If he did not fall in love with his little bride and if he did not hang on to her love, then he was an idiot and could be helped no more.

It would be difficult to leave, of course. He had felt an obligation to Nigel ever since he had almost killed him that time. But his sense of obligation had long ago given place to genuine friendship and something stronger than mere friendship. Nigel felt more like a brother than any of his own numerous brothers and half brothers and stepbrothers had ever done.

But what was there in the countryside for a man who had grown up in London's crowded and fearsome rookeries? He eyed the skinny little barmaid, who was sporting a fat lip and one multicolored eye today, and looked away again to tip up his mug and drain off his ale before raising his arm to summon more.

All the maids at Kedleston were off-limits. He was a toff, a gentleman's man, and was not expected to consort with milkmaids and their like. Not if he paid them, at least. It seemed it was quite respectable simply to take what he wanted. But fair was fair, William always thought. What he took he liked to pay for. Even wenches had a living to earn.

The innkeeper—Mrs. Dorkins, a widow—delivered the fresh ale in person and congratulated William on his master's marriage. She also bent unnecessarily low as she set down the ale, giving William a privileged view of a very ample bosom indeed beneath the low neck of her gown.

The gardener dug him in the ribs and gave him an exaggerated wink.

Mrs. Dorkins had discovered Will Stubbs's strength just two days before when he had offered to carry two barrels of ale from a wagon outside her door into the cellar and had declined any assistance. She had made the simultaneous discovery that he was valet to the aristocratic gentleman who was about to marry Lady Worthing.

William drank in a mouthful of the fresh ale. Mrs. Dorkins would undoubtedly provide a fine and frisky armful. But she was hardly the type of woman who could be invited into the nearest shady doorway to hoist her skirts and allow him his pleasure in exchange for a coin of appropriate value.

The thought of the alternative set William to gulping down another mouthful. Neither his mother nor any of her numerous assorted "husbands," his own father included, had ever been married. He felt no particular inclination to break family tradition.

The goddamned countryside went quite against nature, he thought illogically. Human nature at any rate.

By late afternoon the wedding breakfast was over, most of the guests had left, and the house was almost quiet again. There was time for a man to slip away with his bride for an hour or so alone together. Nigel took his wife into the rose garden and seated her on the bench beneath the willow tree where they had sat before. He took her hand in his and raised it to his lips. He was feeling well satisfied with the day. He was feeling almost mellow.

Almost.

We are part of each other, with nothing secret or hidden between us. . . . Nothing will ever come between us to spoil what began two weeks ago and has come to fruition today.

Her words had been repeating themselves in his mind all afternoon. Her dreadful innocence was becoming a burden to him. It weighed on his conscience.

. . . nothing secret or hidden . . .

"Alone again at last," he said, breathing in deeply the scent of the roses. "And you still put the roses to shame, by my life, madam."

She smiled at him. *I am happy. Utterly happy.* He had felt those words, too, as something of a burden ever since she had uttered them. He could see the truth of them in her eyes.

"And you are still a shameless flatterer, my lord," she said. "I love it."

There was a sparkle of enjoyment in her eyes. Total trust. Total love. He kissed her hand.

"I believe Papa would have been happy today," she said.

He held her hand to his lips, lacing his fingers with hers as he did so. He did not particularly wish to think about Worthing today of all days—except with a certain triumph, perhaps. He just wished that Worthing could have *known*.

"His friend and his daughter," she said. "I wonder if he ever dreamed of this day, ever hoped for it, ever planned for it. He talked about me to you. Do you think he played matchmaker? Had he lived, would he have brought you here and promoted a match between us?" She did not wait for him to answer. She assumed his answers, his total compliance with her happy mental vision. "How delighted he would be if he could know that it happened anyway."

"You rarely saw your father in the last years," he said. "Did he mean so much to you even so?"

"He was my father," she said simply. "As a child, I worshiped him. But I did not realize quite how much he still meant to me until you spoke of him, Nigel. I did not realize how unhappy he was, how much he wished to protect me from his own low spirits. Do you understand how much you restored him to me by coming here as you did? For that alone I must love you."

He wanted to turn the subject then.

"My memories of Papa have now become very precious to me," she said, "instead of being a source of puzzlement and even bitterness. And they are all the more precious for the fact that *you* gave them back to me. My dearest Nigel, how happy I am that you knew him and will be able to talk to me about him from time to time as I will to you. We both loved him."

He bent his head and kissed her lips.

"I have been thinking," she said. "Until my birthday, you know, and even for a day or two afterward, I was determined that I would never marry. I had been given the gift of freedom, which so few women ever enjoy, and I was going to treasure the gift. I was going to run my own life and run this estate and prove to all the scoffers that I was the equal of any man. My life—my happy, free, independent life—was all planned out. But you came to Kedleston.'' She laughed at him, her dimple deepening, her eyes shining with love.

He kissed her palm, her wrist.

''You are a rogue, Nigel,'' she said. ''You spoiled everything.'' Her eyes sparkled. ''But I have been thinking. You will wish to have a hand in the running of the estate—you are a man and would feel diminished if I did not allow it. The world will see you take charge of Kedleston, then, as a husband should. But I mean to continue to learn and to make some of the decisions. I mean to know constantly what is happening with the property that will be our son's one day.'' She blushed rosily. ''We will work together, Nigel, side by side. What do you think?''

What did he think? He thought she was going to be very deeply hurt, that was what. First Worthing, now Kedleston. She was not going to take easily what he had to say to her—but not today. Not yet.

''Estate management, decisions, work?'' he said, lifting one eyebrow and looking infinitely bored. ''Zounds, madam, what are they? 'Tis my wedding day and I have my head stuffed with more important matters, like wedding vows and church bells and the spellbinding beauty of my bride. I have brought my bride to the rose garden so that I might gaze my fill at her and kiss my fill. If there is a plan lurking somewhere in this brain, then 'tis how I will bed my bride tonight in such a way that she will *know* and not merely think that she likes it.''

She laughed at him—and blushed at the same time.

''I believe,'' he said, lowering his voice and looking very directly into her eyes, his own half-closed, ''I will love her very slowly at first—for we have all night, you know— with my hands, touching her in places she does not even know are made for pleasure. And with my mouth. Yes, definitely with my mouth—and with my tongue. My teeth, too. She will know that she likes it—she will tell me so—before I penetrate her body and convince her all over again from deep within of the truth of what she tells me.''

He watched the smile become arrested on her face and her lips part. He watched her swallow rather awkwardly and then bite on her lower lip.

''Oh Nigel,'' she said, ''what kind of a rogue were you? I say *were* because you will be no longer, sir. You are mine, and if you must talk that way, it will be to me if you please. You do it extraordinarily well and I do believe I like it. But 'tis very *naughty*, for all that.'' Her eyes were twinkling again.

''Naughty?'' he said. ''You think you have heard naughtiness, madam? Allow me to extend your education just a little.'' He set himself to entertaining her with a great deal more of such risqué talk while she alternately giggled and blushed—and sometimes told him how silly he was. She was enjoying herself enormously.

He had succeeded in diverting her mind from more serious talk, which he far preferred to postpone for another few days.

We are part of each other, with nothing hidden or secret between us. . . .

Nothing will ever come between us. . . .

I am happy. Utterly happy.

Do you understand how much you restored him to me by coming here as you did? For that alone I must love you.

My life—my happy, free, independent life—was all planned out. But you came to Kedleston.

Yes, she was going to be deeply hurt.

TWELVE

CASSANDRA WAS LOOKING out through the window of her bedchamber, smiling in self-mockery. She had been so very sure just two weeks ago that freedom and independence were what she wanted most in life. Love and marriage had not been in her plans. She had not even believed in romantic love.

And then Nigel, Viscount Wroxley, had come to Kedleston and stood her world on its head. She could see him now as she had seen him that first time, standing in the crimson salon, turning from the window to look at her—handsome, immaculately elegant, with an air of self-assurance bordering on arrogance, like a man from a different world from the one she had always known.

She had fallen in love with him at that very moment, she realized now. How very firm she had been in her principles, in her determination to be free of any man's domination! Not that Nigel would ever try to dominate her.

She was his wife. She set her forehead against the glass and let her mind dwell on that reality and on the memories of the day that had just ended—her wedding day. Two weeks ago she had thought her birthday the happiest day of her life—and so it had been. She had not dreamed then that there could be a day infinitely happier even than that and so soon after it.

And it was not at an end yet. The very best part was to come—soon. She swallowed once and then again. It was foolish to be nervous after what had happened on the night of his return. Though it was not nervousness she felt, she realized. It was excitement. It was desire. There was surely something quite improper in a well-bred bride feeling desire for her bridegroom. She should be feeling a quiet submissiveness. But the very thought brought a smile of genuine amusement back to her face.

She had never been one to dissemble. She would not do it tonight. She would not pretend to a demure modesty she did not feel. And he would not expect it of her. She would not hide just how eager she was to have him do some of the outrageous things he had promised earlier in the rose garden—she laughed softly even as she blushed at the memory. He had done his best to shock her, gazing at her with his lazy eyes, and he had succeeded admirably, the rogue. He had also made her ache with longing.

She did not have to wait long. He came through her dressing room, letting himself into her bedchamber after the merest tap on the door. He was wearing a long brocaded dressing gown. His hair, brushed free of powder, was tied back loosely at the neck. She could see, and she could remember from a few nights ago, that his hair was thick and wavy and almost waist length. Dressed formally, he always looked impeccably elegant and handsome. Dressed informally, he looked masculine and virile and knee-weakeningly attractive.

"I thought perhaps my valet had waxed sentimental," he said. "But he has assured me that the rose came from you."

She smiled at him. Had it been a silly gesture—a rose from a woman to a man?

" 'Twas the promise of even greater loveliness the width of two dressing rooms away?" he said. His blue eyes caressed her from beneath heavy eyelids.

" 'Twas a welcome," she said.

"A welcome," he repeated softly, drawing closer to her

across the room. "Thank you, my love. It warmed my heart."

She hunched her shoulders slightly. She was beginning to feel breathless. "Mr. Stubbs is a fearsome-looking man," she said. "Where did you find him?"

"At my elbow, so to speak, when I needed him," he said, "though i'faith I did not know it at the time. You need not fear him, Cassandra. He will never hurt you. Indeed, I do believe you enslaved him earlier today when you appeared in my dressing room with the rose. He directed me to be sure not to forget to thank you prettily for the flower. You must tell him tomorrow that I did as I was bidden."

Oh. Was he *joking*? Had Mr. Stubbs dared say any such thing? And had Nigel meekly allowed it? There was mockery in his eyes, but it faded as they roamed over her, heavy-lidded again.

She was wearing a white satin nightgown. Her hair was down and loose. She was barefoot. She could feel a tightening in her breasts merely at his look and wondered if her hardened nipples showed through the gown. But she could not expect that detail to escape his experienced eyes—and she knew beyond a doubt that he was very experienced indeed. She did not mind. That was the past. This was the present and the future. She was his present. She did not doubt his love for her.

"Today your beauty was spellbinding," he said. "To-night it defies words. In a few moments, after I have removed your gown, I do believe it will defy even thought. I will have to respond to it by sheer instinct, madam."

His eyes smiled at her as she tried not to show embarrassment at his words—or excitement either. He was so very clever. He could evoke both responses in her simultaneously and he did so quite deliberately. She knew it and he knew that she knew. She walked toward him. He might be very much more experienced than she, but she was not going to allow him to orchestrate every move. She smiled at him as she opened the buttons of her nightgown, hesitated for the merest moment, and then shrugged it off her shoulders and let it fall to the floor.

He looked amused and very appreciative. He pursed his lips and his eyes moved over her as slowly and thoroughly as they had done just a minute before.

" 'Tis your turn," she said. She rather thought he must look very beautiful without his clothes. She wanted to see him—and touch him.

But he merely raised his eyebrows. "Not so, madam," he said. "You will discover that there is something exquisitely erotic about an embrace in which one of the partners is clothed and the other is not."

"And I am elected to be the unclothed one tonight?" she said.

" 'Twas a part you chose for yourself, madam," he reminded her. "I have not yet touched you, as you must agree. You threw off your own clothes in your eagerness."

Perhaps, she thought, she had better not even try to match moves with him. Not until she had learned considerably more. She bit her lip.

"Lie down on the bed," he told her, touching her cheek with the backs of his knuckles, his expression softening to tenderness. "Let me love you, Cassandra. Let me show you how much you will like it."

He extinguished the candles before joining her on the bed. He had removed his dressing gown but still wore his nightshirt. He slid his arms about her, drew her against him, and kissed her. He was, she decided, all hard muscle. He was warm and smelled musky. She knew she would like it. He did not have to prove anything at all. She could remember quite clearly and could scarcely wait for it to happen again even if there had to be pain again and discomfort. She could hardly wait.

"Easy," he was murmuring against her ear then. "Easy, love. It does not all have to be done in a minute. 'Tis better done over five minutes and better yet over ten. 'Tis blissful in fifteen minutes and world-shattering in half an hour. We will take an hour."

She shivered in anticipation.

He did take an hour or thereabouts—she did not time him. But she could not match his control. As he had promised, he touched her and caressed her with his hands and with his mouth long before he put himself inside her body. And as he had promised, he touched her in totally unexpected places and in ways that had her gasping and exclaiming and moaning and squirming with a pleasure that was almost agony—and shattering into mindless worlds beyond either pleasure or agony. She was helpless before his expertise. She knew no way of pacing or controlling her passions, no way of arousing in him any of the feelings he aroused in her. At first she tried apologizing for her uncontrolled responses, but he would not allow her to do so.

"I choose to give you pleasure," he told her. "Do you not know how it delights me to feel your losses of control, my little innocent?"

And so she came to understand that he gained sexual satisfaction for himself from what he did to her and from her own very obvious appreciation of what he did.

"Tell me now," he said at last against her mouth as she shuddered yet again into release from unbearable tension after he had stroked very lightly with his thumb a secret place that should have caused her great embarrassment but did not. "Tell me what I wish to hear."

" 'Tis good." She scarcely recognized her own voice. She seemed to be sobbing. " 'Tis good."

"And will be better," he promised against her ear. He moved over her, coming between her thighs, pushing them wide, and sliding his hands beneath her to tilt her and hold her firm while he thrust hard and deep into her. She was instantly on fire again, aching and yearning toward a final ending that she sensed had not yet been reached.

It was not after all as she remembered it. It was swift and fierce. His weight was heavy on her. They panted hotly and heavily from their exertions. She slid her hands up beneath his nightshirt and spread them over his back. She hid her face against his shoulder. She found herself moving with him in a wild riding rhythm—until he twisted his hands behind him, took hers firmly by the wrists, and pulled

them away from his back. He laced his fingers with hers
and spread her arms wide above her head. She lay still and
spread-eagled, her rhythm broken, feeling the power of his
climax coming, knowing that her own would come with it,
quieter and yet strangely more satisfying than the fierce
ones that had come before it.

He shouted out at the same moment as she felt the rush
of heat in her deep inner core and an exquisite shivering
toward total relaxation in herself. Thought had returned at
the final moment and with it the knowledge that this was
the happiest moment in the happiest day she would ever
know. For the merest minute—it was already in the past—
they had been perfectly one. Lover and beloved. Man and
wife. One flesh—she understood the term at last.

There would never, she thought—and somewhere in the
thought there was sadness, though she did not feel it now—
there would never again be a moment to match this one.
This was their wedding night.

He relaxed into instant sleep when he was finished while
she lay contentedly beneath his weight. She would have
lain awake herself to savor the moment, but she was totally,
deliciously sleepy. And sleep, she realized, was part of the
act that had preceded it. She sank toward oblivion.

But then she remembered something—something that
had not registered on her conscious mind at the time. It was
clear as day in her memory now. Her hands, spread wide
over his back, had discovered hard ridges there instead of
smoothness. All over. Not just in one place. As if he had
once sustained multiple wounds so severe that the marks
had not disappeared with the healing.

Long horizontal ridges.

As if he had been whipped. Savagely whipped.

He was kissing her softly, languidly. He had awoken
from a blessedly deep sleep only to grimace with shame
when he found that he was still lying full atop her, still
embedded in her. He was far too heavy and too large for
her. But in moving to her side, he had woken her—she had
grumbled sleepily and rolled onto her side against him. He

supported her head in the crook of one arm. His other hand was spread over her buttocks, holding her close.

He had married her, he thought, because there had been a few good reasons for doing so. Personal inclination had not been one of them. He had not even set eyes on her when he decided to marry her.

It was a pleasure, then, to discover that his marriage would bring him satisfaction. She was good to look at, she was an amusing companion, and she was a passionate lover, untutored though she was in the art of lovemaking. He enjoyed the prospect of being her tutor.

He was enjoying his wedding night. It was far from over. He was very glad now that he had had her the night of his return. She might have been too sore for a second mounting if tonight had been her first time. He could feel himself begin to harden. He concentrated his mind on the feeling. He would not arouse her this time, he decided. He would take her while she was warm and drowsy and relaxed. He would take her swiftly and then hold her again while she slipped back into sleep. She smelled deliciously of soap and sweat and woman.

"Nigel?" she whispered.

"Mm?" He opened his mouth over hers, tasting warmth and moisture.

"Nigel," she said when her mouth was free again, "what happened to your back?"

His mind exploded with an obscenity, which fortunately did not reach his lips. He had not been alert enough to realize where her hands had gone until it was too late. He had hoped she had not noticed.

"To my back?" he said foolishly.

"There are—ridges there," she said. "Scars. What happened?"

"Ah, those." He spoke carelessly. "I had a strict father, my love. And I went to a strict school. I was not always the most obedient of sons and pupils. Most boys have their stripes to boast of, you know. We will have to hope that our own sons will be less rebellious."

There was silence. But her body was no longer as relaxed as it had been.

"But fathers and schoolmasters do not leave stripes that last on into adulthood," she said at last. "Do they?"

"Little innocent," he said, kissing her, glad that she had no brothers. "Daughters are dealt with far more tenderly. But then they are more tender creatures. Sense and obedience and good manners and morality—and arithmetic—have to be beaten into sons." He kissed her again, murmuring endearments.

She drew her head back after he thought the crisis had passed. "Nigel," she said, "please light the candles."

"Why?" He had a premonition of why.

"I want to see your back," she said.

"No." He laughed softly. "Spare my modesty, madam. Besides, my back is not the finest part of my body. I was a *very* disobedient boy."

But he had lost her. She was out of the bed and stooping in the darkness for her nightgown. He watched her pull it over her head and push her arms into the sleeves.

"Please light the candles," she said. There was no humor in her voice, only the quiet command of someone who was accustomed to being obeyed.

He lit the candles. And since her next command was inevitable, he did not wait for it. He pulled his nightshirt off over his head and dropped it to the bed. He stood with his back to her and waited through the long silence that ensued.

He knew what his back looked like. He had seen it often enough in the looking glass, though he hated doing so. For a long time he had looked in the hope that the marks would have faded. But they never had and never would. They were lividly white and crisscrossed his back in innumerable ridged stripes. Whip marks sometimes left no permanent scars—the ones dealt out piecemeal over the top of one's shirt. Those dealt more formally while one was stripped and tied by wrists and ankles to a tripod never disappeared.

"What happened?" she said at last, her voice calm and seemingly quite dispassionate.

"I have told you," he said, sounding bored. And then the blood pounded at his temples. *Do not look down*, he cried silently, suddenly remembering. He willed her not to look down his right leg to the ankle.

"No," she said. "You have not. These are the marks of whips, Nigel, such as soldiers and sailors sometimes bear. Were you a soldier? But you would have been an officer. Officers are not whipped."

There was no point in lying further, though he was tempted. He would not tell the truth, but it would be pointless to lie.

"I was never a soldier," he said, "or a sailor either. It happened, Cassandra. It no longer matters how or why. 'Tis in the past. I have forgotten about it."

"It matters," she said. "And you could not forget when you bear such marks."

"But they are all behind," he said, turning to her and smiling. "In more than one sense. This is my present. You are my present."

She gazed at him for a long time before tipping her head to one side. "I do not know anything about you, do I?" she said softly. "I *know* you, but I do not know *about* you. And you will not tell me this one thing. I can see that you will not. You will keep it a secret. There is something horribly dreadful in your past, and I will never know about it."

"You overdramatize, by my life," he said. " 'Tis over and done with, my love. This is my wedding night and I would not have it spoiled. What did I say earlier about one lover being clothed while the other was not? You have neatly turned the table on me, i'faith."

But she would not be coaxed into smiling. Quite the opposite happened while he watched. Tears welled in her eyes and her lower lip trembled.

"I do not want anything secret between us," she said. "And I do not want you hurt."

He reached for her and drew her against him. He tipped back his head and closed his eyes, sighing inwardly.

"It was a long time ago," he said.

Her hands were on his back, stroking gently as if she feared to open the old wounds. "Nevertheless," she said. "I do not want you hurt even in the past. I do not want anyone hating you enough to do this to you."

She was not crying. But he felt her need to lean against him, to hide her face against his chest, to suffer through the knowledge that his past held a savage secret. He held her close, rocking her until finally she tipped her head back, looked at him, and smiled.

" 'Tis our wedding night," she whispered.

"Yes."

"It has not been spoiled," she said. "It has not, has it?"

"No, my love." He held her eyes.

"I will not let it be spoiled," she said. "It has been the most wonderful day and night of my life. And the night is not over."

"No." He smoothed the backs of his fingers lightly along her jawline, from her chin to her ear.

"Make love to me again," she said, "if you can bear such ignorance as mine. I did not know what to do except simply to enjoy. You are so very skilled. I have much to learn. I would have you teach me, Nigel, to give pleasure as well as to receive it."

"And yet, by my life," he said, "I thought I was the one simply enjoying. There is nothing else to do but that."

"I do not believe you for a moment," she said. "But for tonight I will accept it. Make love to me."

She needed comforting. She needed to be held. She needed closeness. He knew that she could sense a certain loss, a certain awareness that she had married a stranger, though she had just assured him—and herself—that she knew him even if she did not know a great deal about him. He removed her nightgown and blew out the candles while she lay down. But when he joined her on the bed again, he gave her what she needed. He put himself deep inside her without foreplay and rode her very slowly, taking her gradually, over many long minutes, through warm appreciation to moaning tenderness to a quiet cresting of pleasure.

She slept almost immediately after but not before whis-

pering first in his ear. "One secret," she said. "I will allow
you the one. But no more. Ever. Not after this."

His poor naïve little innocent. She thought that because
they had shared bodies, giving up all their physical secrets
to each other's touch, they would forever be open to each
other—one body, one mind, one heart.

She believed in romantic love. She loved him and
thought he loved her. She was not privy to all the secrets
even of his body. She had not noticed his ankle. Not yet.
And there was so much else.

He stared into the darkness. The exertions of his marriage
bed had tired him but not brought sleep. But then he had
a long acquaintance with insomnia. Insomnia was at least
better than the nightmares.

"I seen 'er awready," William Stubbs said, setting down
the open razor and waiting for his master to seat himself
to be shaved. "She poked 'er 'ead around the door 'alf an
hour ago to see if you was 'ere."

"I went out for a ride at dawn," Nigel said. "I could
not sleep."

"The wicked usually cawn't," his valet commented.
"She sez, 'Good morning, Mr. Stubbs,' she sez, as pretty
as you please, Nige, and then sez that she thought 'is lordship might be in 'is rooms 'cause 'e was gawn from 'er
bed wen she woke up. And she blushes up all rosy like,
realizin' what she just said. You must of done it gentle and
proper, then, 'cause she weren't weeping."

"Zounds," Nigel said haughtily, "I have no intention of
discussing with you if or how I did it, Will. A man is
entitled to some privacy, even from his valet. You are not
by chance casting yourself in the part of her ladyship's
champion, are you?"

"Wen are you planning to tell 'er?" William asked.

Nigel sighed through the soap that covered the lower half
of his face. "She has seen my back already," he said. "Actually she felt it first but then she took a good look."

"And?"

"And nothing," Nigel said. "I am telling her nothing

about that, Will. How would she feel knowing just what she has married? She does not need to know. Besides, if I told her that, I would soon be telling her who made it all possible—and *I will not have her know that.*"

"Gawd!" William said. "You got it bad, Nige. Serves you right. But for once old Stubbs agrees with you. The little lady don't need to know that. And you be gentle wen you tells 'er the other, Nige. You should of told 'er before she 'itched 'erself to you, but since you didn't, you do it gentle. Pretty little fillies like that oughtn't ever to cry or find out wot a ugly world this can be. They should be pertected, lad, an' I 'xpect you to pertect 'er. Keep yer gab still now or I'll slice you a good one without ever meaning to."

Nigel kept his gab still. How did one reply to the voice of conscience, anyway?

How did one destroy another person's world gently?

He wished suddenly that she need never know. She was sweetness itself. He had never wanted to hurt her, but he had not expected to dread doing so.

He remembered how it felt to be betrayed. He wished he did not.

THIRTEEN

M<small>R. AND</small> M<small>RS.</small> H<small>AVELOCK</small>
returned to Willow Park the day after their niece's wedding,
Mr. Havelock with mingled relief over the fact that his
responsibilities toward her were now quite indisputably at
an end and unease over his fear that she had made an over-
hasty and unwise marriage. Mrs. Havelock was only too
happy to return home yet again to her younger son and her
daughters.

Robin escorted Lady Beatrice to the dower house, where
she was to spend a few days with her sister and niece.
Robin was to stay there for a day or two also before returning to his own home. The aunts might have need of
him, he offered vaguely by way of an explanation for staying. And Patience, whose ankle must still be weak, might
have need of his arm for a turn about the garden. It was
his fault, after all, that she had sprained it.

Cassandra and Nigel saw them all on their way from the
terrace.

"And so we are all alone," she said, turning to her new
husband with a smile as Robin's carriage disappeared down
the driveway. "And no one will come calling for a few
days, you know. They will all tactfully leave us to ourselves. We will have to entertain each other. Will we be
able to do it, do you suppose?" She laughed.

"I'faith, madam," he said, bowing to her and extending his arm for hers, "I do believe if I set my mind to the task, I might think of one or two ways of entertaining you."

She linked her arm informally through his and they strolled by unspoken assent away from the entrance toward the side lawn. She felt rather as if she were living in a happily-ever-after. This morning she was more in love than ever, if that were possible. But this morning the euphoric feeling of romance was enhanced by the deep satisfaction of physical knowledge. The gentleman beside her, elegant and immaculately clad as ever—his hair was even powdered—was also last night's lover. She had liked it well enough that first night, beneath the tree which she could see now across the lawn, but until last night she had not known—oh, she had not *known*.

Happily-ever-afters, of course, could not last. She was well aware of that. But she wanted to cling to hers for as long as possible. And even afterward she would fight to maintain the happiness, the love, the—the everything. Not that there would have to be any great struggle. They shared the sort of love that would last until eternity.

She could not forget his back. The feel of it had been alarming enough. The sight of it . . . She hated even to remember. It had been a savage whipping indeed. If it had all been done on one occasion, it was truly amazing that he had survived. Indeed, she did not think he would have survived. But if it had been done over more than one occasion, then . . . Then dear God, what had been *happening*? And he would not tell her.

The fact that there was a secret between them, however far in the past, set a small blot on her happiness. She tried to forget. She thought about their wedding at just this time yesterday, about the wedding breakfast and their guests, about last night's lovemaking, about the happily ever after that they would fight to maintain.

"You are very quiet, my love," Nigel said. "Might I pride myself on having exhausted you with last night's, ah, exertions?"

She laughed at him.

"Derision, madam?" he said, and his quizzing glass was in his hand and at his eye. "By my life, I must try harder tonight. And perhaps you will permit me to practice once or twice this afternoon. You surely know what is said about practice."

She laughed at him again, though she felt a sharp stabbing of desire at the very thought that tonight—and perhaps even this afternoon—would be a repetition of last night. He was doing what she was trying to do, she realized. He was holding on tightly to their happily-ever-after. He would tease her and flirt with her as they walked. When they reached the lime grove, to which their steps appeared to be leading them, he would probably kiss her.

The day should be allowed to develop so. Just today. And perhaps tomorrow. There would be time enough for reality after tomorrow. But she remembered last night's frightening realization that she had married a stranger. A stranger she knew, but one about whom she knew almost nothing at all.

"Nigel," she asked, and wondered even as she spoke if she would be content with the one question and the one answer, "where is your home?"

There was a momentary tension in his arm, but he relaxed again so quickly that she might have imagined it. He did not answer immediately, though.

"In Lincolnshire," he said. "It *was* my home. I have not been there in ten years."

"You have no property there, then?" she asked him.

He hesitated—a strange fact when the question was such a very simple one. "No," he said at last.

"And no family except one sister?" she asked. "Is she older than you or younger? Is she married? Does she have children? What is her name?"

"Barbara," he said, answering her last question first. "She is seventeen and unmarried."

"If she is your only close relative," she said, "it must have been hard to leave her behind when you came here. And it must have been hard on her to see you leave. She will never forgive you for marrying without giving her time to come to the wedding. Invite her to come here, Nigel. Write the letter today. I have a *sister*—I have just realized. She may live here as long as she wishes. Oh, do send for her. Let us return to the house without any further delay.'' She pulled on his arm to stop him.

''I saw her two years ago, Cassandra,'' he said, stopping but making no move to turn back. ''Once. I called upon her at the school she attended. Before that it had been almost eight years. I have not seen her since.''

Her eyes widened. He had a sister—a young girl of seventeen—and he never saw her? She frowned. He was looking back into her face, a strange half smile curling one side of his mouth.

''I also have a brother,'' he said.

She stared at him mutely. He was a man with a title but no property, he had a brother, whose existence he had not acknowledged to her until this moment, a young sister whom he had seen once in ten years. He had been savagely whipped more than once. Who was this man she had married?

''Bruce,'' he said. ''He has the property—Dunbar Abbey in Lincolnshire. Barbara lives there with him.''

''He is older than you, then?'' she said.

''No.'' Again that rather twisted smile. ''Younger. I have the title, you see, and he has the property and the guardianship of our sister. 'Twere well, madam, to ask no more questions. Suffice it to say that we are not a close family.''

But she could not leave it alone. How could he expect her to? They were walking again, side by side, not touching. They were walking along the lime grove.

''How can your brother have the property if you are the elder?'' she asked.

''Dunbar is not entailed,'' he said.

''As Kedleston is not,'' she replied. ''But in effect such properties are always left to the heir.''

''Not always, madam,'' he said quietly. ''Though 'tis true that my father died before . . . He left Dunbar to me, but there were—complications later. But by my life, you look far too serious for a bride of scarcely one day.'' He had stepped in front of her and set his hands on either side of her waist. "You have discovered that you have a new brother and sister from whom your husband is unfortunately estranged. Am I not enough for you, my love? Have I been such a failure in four-and-twenty hours?" His eyes smiled into hers.

She shook her head, overwhelmed suddenly by her love for him. He had been dealt with unfairly and cruelly in his life, of that she felt no doubt, and his family had turned against him. She would make it all up to him. She would wrap him about with her love for the rest of their lives. He would never know unhappiness again.

She returned his kiss with desperate tenderness.

But what had *happened*? What could possibly have been drastic enough to have caused the overturning of his father's will and of tradition? He had lost Dunbar Abbey, which had been his.

She would not think of it. Not for the rest of today. Or tomorrow. She would think of their wedding, of their wedding night, of their love for each other. She coiled her arms about his neck and sighed with contentment as he prolonged the kiss.

He had wanted to keep the tone of today light, flirtatious, companionable. For his own sake he had felt the need of such a day—alone together, reveling in their new intimacy. And for her sake he had wanted a brief interlude of unclouded happiness. Her happiness had become a new responsibility to him, a new burden.

He kissed her, warmly, deeply, though without sexual passion. And she kissed him back openly and eagerly. Perhaps this day could be saved after all, he thought. But really for what? Tomorrow or the next day would inevitably come.

"Nigel." She moved her head back from his though she kept her arms about his neck, a feat she accomplished by standing on her toes. Her face was glowing with eagerness. "You do have a home again. You do have property. You have Kedleston."

He stiffened. Had Will Stubbs—?

"We will live here together," she said. "We will be happy here and bring up our children here. The time will come, you know, when our son—*your* son—will inherit Kedleston and be Earl of Worthing. In the meantime we will live here as if it belonged to both of us. I will not even think of it as exclusively my own from this moment on. I have worked very hard in the past few weeks learning about the running of the estate. You must help me. Perhaps you do not know much more than I since you were very young—nineteen?—when you left Dunbar Abbey. But you surely know as much as I and probably more. We will work together. There is a great deal to do both in the house and on the farms. It will be ours, Nigel, yours and mine. You have a home again."

He kissed her. It was tempting. Very tempting, if only for today.

He released his hold on her and her arms dropped from about his neck as he stepped away. He went to stand beside one of the lime trees and propped one shoulder against its trunk. He looked across the tops of trees to the valley and the hills opposite. And even now he wondered if he would turn the moment.

"Did I upset you?" Her voice came from just behind him. "Did I seem patronizing? Does it hurt very much that you own nothing while all this is legally mine? I am sorry. I would not have the disparity in our situations come between us, Nigel. Are you also—" She was silent for a few moments. "Are you also impoverished? You do not dress as if you were, and you *said* you had a fortune, but—my love, we must not allow such matters to come between us. But you are proud, of course. All men are proud. What can I say to—"

He rounded on her, his eyes blazing, and she fell silent. "You can say *nothing,* madam," he said sharply. "You can stop presuming to know my thoughts and my feelings."

His loss of temper took him by surprise. He had come prepared for this moment. He had waited for it for longer than a year. Even now he felt intense satisfaction at being able to say it at last. He just wished it could be to anyone but *her*.

She stared back at him wide-eyed and pale-faced.

"Zounds," he said. "You make this difficult."

"You *are* hurt," she said. "Nigel, *please*."

"A few moments ago," he said, holding up one staying hand, "you mentioned the fact that Kedleston is unentailed. I knew it before you said it. The late Earl of Worthing doubtless willed the property to you. But by the time the will was read, the property was no longer his to leave. He had lost it in a card game. To me."

—you be gentle wen you tells 'er—

And now he had told her—abruptly, badly, and coldly. He knew that he had retreated behind the old mask of icy arrogance. She was standing quite still and staring at him as if she was frozen in time and would soon jolt back into motion and take up her life from where she had left it just before he spoke.

"What?" The single word was whispered

"Kedleston is mine, Cassandra," he said. "It has been mine for longer than a year. I won it from the Earl of Worthing in a card game. I have the deeds to prove it."

"The deeds are lost." She was still whispering. "Papa's lawyer could not find them. But he said it did not matter."

"They were not lost," he said. "They were given to me, and all was made legal by my lawyer and his—obviously not his usual lawyer. Kedleston is mine, though as my wife you are still its mistress."

The words he had come to say were spoken so quickly, so easily. They had not been difficult to say at all. He stood indolently propped against one of the lime trees, a half smile on his lips, one hand on the handle of his quizzing glass, only half-aware that he leaned for support more than effect. His legs were weak under him.

With a smile on his lips he watched her world collapse about her. He inwardly cursed her very expressive face. He almost hated her.

A few times he saw her lips move as if she would speak to him, but no sound came. Even her lips were parchment white. She did not remove her eyes from his own—until suddenly she whipped about to face away from him. He considered reaching for her, turning her to his will. Could it be done? Could it be that easy? Was she that shallow?

Somehow—though matters would be infinitely easier for him—he did not want her to be that shallow.

He liked her, he realized. He admired her. He was even fond of her.

But before he could make up his mind what to say or do, she picked up her skirts and hurried away from him in the direction of the house. After the first few steps she broke into a run.

He stood watching her go. Should he go after her, try to explain—but what was there to explain?—try at least to force her to talk to him? Or should he let her go, give her a chance to digest what he had said before confronting her again?

He stayed propped against the tree.

Yes, she had always been the problem. He had very carefully planned that card game—he had spent eight years planning it—and it had turned out according to his plans. He had won Kedleston from Worthing. He had *won*. He could still revel in the feeling of triumph he had felt then. His revenge had been complete.

Except that there had been a daughter, an only daughter, living at Kedleston, and soon after the card game she had inherited, or apparently inherited. Worthing had died a scant two weeks after losing his home and two weeks before the end of the grace period Nigel had given him to break the news to his family and move out his personal belongings from Kedleston.

There had been only one way for Nigel to salve his conscience while keeping his winnings—and he had been through far too much to consider giving those up. He must marry the daughter, allow her to keep her home as his wife. Will Stubbs had disagreed with him—he owed nothing to the late earl's family, Will had always argued, and there was really no way of putting things to rights for the girl. Certainly if he must offer her marriage, Will had advised,

she should know the truth first so that she could marry—
or not marry—with her eyes wide open, so to speak. But
she had had no choice—to present her the appearance of
one would have been more cruel than to offer none at all.
If she had not married him, she would have been destitute,
totally dependent upon her uncle.

And so he had salved his conscience.

Nigel laughed softly, without humor.

Of course, he had soon realized that there was another
very good reason for marrying her—perhaps an even more
powerful reason than pity.

He wondered if she loved him enough, if enough could
be salvaged from their marriage to make life together at
least bearable. It was the question he had faced from the
start, of course. Was Kedleston large enough for the two
of them if they hated each other?

He did not hate her.

But there was little he could do to help her. He had given
her the bare facts, all that she needed to know. He was not
prepared to tell her any more. Nothing else was her concern.

Besides, she had loved her father very dearly. It had become unexpectedly important to him that she retain some
of her illusions. She might hate him now, of course—she
probably did, but that was her problem. He would always
treat her kindly.

He would not tell her more. She might think of him what
she would.

And yet he pushed himself away from the tree a few
minutes later, knowing that he must try speaking to her
again, try comforting her if he could. Nigel slowly followed
his wife back to Kedleston. Back to the house that had been
his for longer than a year.

She had to stop running when she was halfway up the
lawn. She had a stitch in her side. But she hurried onward,
breathless and still half running. She tried to hold her
thoughts blank. If she did not think, it had not happened.
If she did not think, it was not true, it would go away.

It was not hers, she thought, glancing up at the house as she sped along the terrace toward the front entrance. It had never been hers.

Yes, concentrate on that thought if you must think at all, she told herself. Kedleston was not hers. It had not been Papa's when he died and therefore it had never been hers. The house and the estate were unentailed. Her father had been free to sell them at any time if he had so wished. Or to lose them in—no, she would think no farther.

She brushed past the footman in the hall without offering him her usual smile and verbal greeting. He was not her servant. None of the servants were hers. She sped up the stairs and along the hallway to the blessed sanctuary of her own room—*it was not her room.* She almost collided with William Stubbs, who was coming out of his master's dressing room, a razor in his right hand. Cassandra jumped back, and all the confused emotions of the past fifteen minutes or so converted to instant and blinding terror.

"Go away!" she half screamed. "Oh, who *are* you?"

William Stubbs smiling and holding a razor would have struck terror even into Goliath, champion of the Philistines. The smile did not last.

"No, no, little lady," he said gently. "Will Stubbs won't do you no 'arm. Not never."

"Who *are* you?" she demanded again. "You are not a valet. I *knew* you were not a valet. What are you going to do with *that*?" She waved one shaking finger at the razor. She did not recognize her own voice. It panted and wobbled and squeaked.

William looked down at the razor in his hand as if remembering for the first time that it was there. "It needs sharpening to a fine slicing edge," he said. "I always does it myself. I knows all about knives and razors. I *am* 'is man, my lady, and I am your servant, too. Nobody'll never do you no 'arm while Will is nearby. Not even 'im. Not that 'e'll ever try."

"Who *is* he?" she asked in a fierce whisper.

The incredibly ugly giant looked at her steadily from his one eye. "Did Nige make you cry?" he asked. "I told 'im not to make you cry. I'll 'ave a word with 'im, m'lady. You go into your room now an' shut the door. Old Stubbs will get your maid to fetch you a nice cup of tea.''

Nige? *Nigel?* He called his master *Nige?* He had told Nigel not to make her cry? He would have a word with him?

William Stubbs playing gentle, solicitous mother was no less terrifying than William Stubbs smiling and wielding an open razor. Especially when he called Nigel *Nige.* Cassandra edged past him and dashed for her bedchamber, only to find that her husband's valet had sidestepped in order to open the door for her. He also closed it behind her—far more gently than her maid ever did.

She paced. She must think. No, she must *not* think. Not yet. She could not block from her conscious mind the constant refrain that repeated itself over and over like background music at a card party. Kedleston did not belong to her. It never had. But somewhere beyond that was an even worse thought—one she could not cope with. Not yet.

But she had no choice.

She turned when her maid tapped on her door. She would welcome a cup of tea. But it was not her maid. She turned quickly away again and walked to the window. She did not want to look at him. Suddenly his immaculate elegance— he did not look one mite disheveled even now—seemed somehow like a shield, hiding the real man.

She did not know the real man.

But he was her husband, whoever he was.

''Cassandra—'' he said softly.

''You are a gamester,'' she said. Ah, there it was, that thought. It could not be avoided after all. ''You are an adventurer and a gambler. You play for high stakes and fleece men of their livelihood and their dreams. And women, too—you have taken my life and my dreams from me. You are a liar and a cheat. And you are my husband.''

''Yes,'' he said after a heavy silence.

The loss of Kedleston was enormous. She knew that she had not even begun to digest the enormity of the loss. But there was another loss far greater. Perhaps more than one. She had lost her father, too—again.

"Everything you told me about Papa was a lie," she said. "You were never his friend. He never spoke of me."

"No," he said.

"He was a gamester, too, then," she said. "But he was not as skilled as you. Or perhaps he played honestly and you cheated. He was willing to wager Kedleston and my future for the pleasure of a game."

He did not answer her, though she waited for him to begin to defend himself. She wanted him to try defending himself so that she would have something to lash out at.

"I wonder why you waited a whole year," she said, "and why you came here to woo me and marry me. No, I do not wonder at all. I know. I was an extra ornament to your triumph, was I not? The jewel in the crown. I have the title and I am known in the neighborhood. You would have been seen as a cruel man indeed if you had evicted me from the place that has always been my home—and that has always been the home of the Earls of Worthing. But now you are married to the Countess of Worthing. She will be your hostess here. And of course you will be the father of the future earl—'tis too bad you could not wrest the title from me, too, my lord. But doubtless you are a realist. And you may well have your wish. Perhaps you got me with child last night or even a week ago. If 'tis so, then your triumph is complete."

"Cassandra," he said, "I do not like to see you so distraught. Come, look at me, my love."

She smiled out at the lawn and the trees, and then turned to smile at him.

"You may relax now, my lord, and enjoy your triumph," she said. "The time for pretense is over. Kedleston is yours, I am your wife, you may have me with child, and even if you do not, you may force yourself on me anytime you wish. Doubtless I will conceive sooner or later. Most wives do. You no longer have to woo me. You did it well and I, naive innocent that I was, did not even put up a token fight—unless sending you away for a week was a token fight. How you must have laughed at the joke of being sent away from your own home! I am your wife now, my lord. Men do not need to woo their wives. They own them. I am your property.''

"And you hate me," he said.

"Are you surprised?" She raised haughty eyebrows. "And does it matter to you? I think not, my lord. I think you are probably ice through to your very heart. I suppose you do have a heart if only to pump the cold blood through your veins.''

"What happened was between your father and me, Cassandra," he said. " 'Twas regrettable, by my life, that you had to be caught in the middle. I am sorry about it. I could think of no other way of protecting you from the consequences of—of that card game.''

"Marrying me was protecting me?" She smiled. "Forgive me for not being grateful, my lord. Am I to be permitted any privacy? This house is yours. This *room* is yours. And of course I am yours. You must tell me, if you please—am I to be allowed any privacy at all? I do not know the answer without asking. I do not know *you*.''

"This is your home," he said quietly. "You are my wife, Cassandra, not my slave or even my servant. And this chamber in particular is *your* room. I will come here in future by invitation only. Do you wish me to leave?''

"Yes," she said. "Yes, please.''

He did not leave immediately. He fingered the handle of his quizzing glass though he did not lift it to his eye. He was, she thought dispassionately, coldly handsome. So very cold. He seemed almost always to dress in shades of gray and white. Even his hair was almost always powdered white. How foolish of her not to have seen the essential coldness from the start.

And how foolish even to think of her behavior as foolish. What a totally inadequate word.

"We will speak further," he said, "after you have had time to digest what must be shocking news to you. Nothing need change for you. Nothing at all. You were happy before I came. You were happy afterward. You were happy yesterday and this morning. Nothing is different from what it has been for longer than a year. You may continue happy here as you always have been.''

She smiled at him. ''But there is one small impediment to my happiness, my lord,'' she said. ''I wed you yesterday.''

She stood looking into his eyes, scorning to be the first to look away. Finally he made her a deep and elegant bow before turning and leaving the room without another word.

—one small impediment—

I wed you yesterday.

For a long time she dared not move. She had the strange notion that only by standing very still where she was could she prevent herself from disintegrating into a thousand pieces.

In this very room, in that very bed—she could not turn her head to look at it—they had lain together just last night. They would never lie there together again if his word was to be trusted. He would never be invited into this room again.

As much as she had loved him just one hour ago—just an eternity ago—so much and more she hated him now. And with just as consuming a passion.

Another tap at the door heralded the arrival of her maid with the promised cup of tea. That ugly, terrifying man of his, who looked frighteningly at home with an open razor in his hand, had kept his word, then.

FOURTEEN

Nigel would have sworn that he had not had a wink of sleep all night if he had not woken up just before dawn in a cold sweat, jerking upright from his prone position on his bed, gasping for air.

Certainly he had not expected to sleep. The day had been a disaster—especially in contrast to the day before and last night and even this morning. He had convinced himself that he had done rather well, that when she finally knew, she would recover quickly after a few tears, a few words of reproach, an hour or two of shocked adjustment to the new order of things. She was deeply in love with him, after all. He had felt no doubt of that.

It was that very fact, of course, that had caused such a total disaster. Had her feelings not run so deep, perhaps she could have better coped with what he had told her. Love and hate were not at opposite ends of the spectrum. They were in very precarious balance with each other, sometimes indistinguishable from each other, easily exchanged for each other.

Her love for him had been total just yesterday, just last night—just this morning. Now her hatred for him was just as passionate, just as total.

She had not come out of her room for all of the rest of the day. When he had summoned her maid to make sure that at least she was receiving her meals, the girl had informed him that indeed her ladyship was—on orders from Mr. Stubbs. Nigel had raised his eyebrows but made no comment.

Will Stubbs had scolded in person, of course, and had offered to pop his master a good one if he tried forcing himself on his wife before she was good and ready to receive him again.

"If she ever is ready, Nige," he had concluded, "which I seriously doubts she ever will be on account of you give 'er a good tender ride under 'er petticoats last night and broke 'er 'eart this morning. Little ladies don't take kind to being made fools of, and nor should they, lad. 'Tis our dooty to pertect them from all wot is ugly."

He did not appear to deem it necessary to explain whence his sudden knowledge of the gentle female mind had come, and Nigel did not ask him.

Nigel had sent a note to her room during the evening, but he had received the expected response—delivered by word of mouth.

"Her ladyship says no, my lord," her maid had told him with a curtsy and a look of pure fright.

He had not expected her to agree to receive him. Or particularly wanted her to. The very last thing he felt like doing was making love to her. But they should talk again. He had hoped that at least they might exchange a few words before going to their separate beds.

Her answer had been no.

He would respect his promise to her, he realized, even if she never again came out of her rooms. They were her private domain. He would never enter them again without an invitation. Even without Will's prediction he was well aware of the fact that it might never come.

But she was married to him. She was safe from destitution. Her home was still hers even though she had lost ownership of it today—or a perceived ownership anyway. His carefully laid plans had come to a successful conclusion. He had no reason to feel out of sorts. And he had no reason to worry about Cassandra. He had done all he could for her. If she would never see him or speak to him again, it was regrettable. But he would still be in possession of all he had ever wanted—including her.

The sensible thoughts were not enough to allow him to get to sleep with any ease. He went to bed late, he tossed and turned, he went outside for a walk, he lay down again and tossed and turned. He was clearly in for a totally sleepless night he decided. And then he woke up in a cold sweat, gasping for air.

It had been the old nightmare—one of them. The old, lifelong nightmare of frustration, trying to run from danger to safety, finding himself unable to move at anything faster than a snail's pace, almost as if the air through which he moved had become thick and nearly impenetrable. And the old panicked feeling that whatever it was that threatened him was moving up behind him without any of the impediments that held him back.

Another nightmare had become all mixed up with that one over the past nine years. The need, the compulsion to defend himself from slander when no one would listen to him but would only stare back at him with amused disbelief or open contempt. And the panicked awareness that danger was creeping up on him from an unknown quarter—far greater danger than just loss of reputation.

The nightmare had been vividly visual—as always. That room—full of his smiling enemies. That mousetrap—that mantrap! Its walls and its ceiling had closed in upon him, and with them the people, until there was no possibility of escape and no air to breathe.

No air to breathe . . .

He panted for breath and clutched the sheet on either side of his perspiring body. For several moments he did not trust the vast airiness of the bedchamber in which he found his waking self.

God in heaven! If only he could be free of the nightmares. As if more than seven years of sheer hell had not been enough punishment for whatever it was he had done wrong. Youth was what he had done wrong. He had been a wild, eager, gullible, dangerously innocent youth—nineteen years old and confident that he could shape the world to fit his dreams.

He had been delighted to discover that the Earl of Worthing was in London when he arrived there himself to conquer it. He had thought—with an almost incredibly gauche naïveté—that Worthing would be equally delighted to find that he was there—after he had explained who he was.

Worthing had set out to destroy him and had succeeded with frightening ease. Or almost succeeded. It was Nigel now who slept in the earl's bed at Kedleston and who owned the property—and the earl's daughter.

Yes, he owned her, too.

In a sense his revenge had been complete when he married her less than two days ago. He might relax now in the knowledge that his goals had been attained—all except one, and that was impossible to attain. It was a dream more than a goal. There was no proof. . . .

He found himself thinking about Cassandra, alone in the next bedchamber. Awake, too? he wondered. Last night— such a short time ago, though it seemed now to be an eternity—had been her wedding night. And his, too.

He wished she had not had to be hurt.

But there had been no avoiding it. And he was not going to brood on her sufferings. He might have made it a great deal worse for her. He might have ordered her off his property immediately after Worthing's death.

He certainly did not need to have Cassandra on his conscience.

What had she called him? *You are an adventurer and a gambler. . . . You are a liar and a cheat.*

. . . you have taken my life and my dreams from me.

He threw aside the bedcovers and got out of bed. It was very obvious that he was not going to sleep again tonight. He was going to go for a brisk ride. And then he was going to start his new life. There was much to be done.

Kedleston was his. A lifetime's dream had come true.

Cassandra would come around. Just this time yesterday she had been lying naked in his arms. . . .

• • •

Cassandra awoke sometime after dawn and knew from the feeling of deep depression that pressed down upon her like a physical weight that there was something she really did not wish to face. She had been very deeply asleep— almost as if some benevolent power had granted her the gift of total oblivion from something quite unbearable.

She remembered, of course, within a few seconds and then she was sorry for the fact that she had slept and lowered her defenses. The pain that rushed at her felt so like despair that she knew fear in addition to the depths of misery.

She had thought herself so sensible, so mature, so wise.

She had been free and happy and secure.

She had married a man she did not know at all after a mere two weeks' acquaintance—not even two. She had married him because he was handsome and elegant and charming and very, very experienced at seduction.

Against the advice of her older and wiser relatives—*who loved her*—she had rushed headlong into disaster. She had married a gamester, a cheat, a liar, a man who had destroyed her father for the mere love of a game. She had lain with him—for a few moments she felt dizzy with nausea at the very thought. She might very well be with child by him.

She was safe from him only in this room and presumably in her dressing room and private sitting room, too. She was safe here *if he was an honorable man*. She laughed bitterly. He had left her alone last night, of course, even though he had requested permission to visit her in her room.

If she spent the rest of her life in these rooms, perhaps she could avoid ever seeing him again.

But the thought when verbalized in her mind struck her with its absurdity. She could not spend forty or fifty years in these three rooms. And she *would* not even if she could. Oh, she would not cower from him. He would think she was afraid of him. She could show her contempt of him— her utter contempt—only if she could look him in the eye.

She wanted above all else this morning to show him her contempt.

She rang for her maid, but she was unwilling to wait. She hesitated at the door that adjoined his dressing room but decided that she would not knock and wait for an answer. She knocked and opened the door.

He was not there. But his valet was, brushing out a riding coat. She felt an instant fear bordering on terror—the man was so huge and so evil looking and so incredibly ugly—but she was in no mood to cringe from anyone. He smiled. She wondered if he knew that he looked far more terrifying when he did so and concluded that he probably did.

"Good morning, m'lady," he said.

"Good morning, Mr. Stubbs." She did not smile back at him. "Where is Viscount Wroxley?"

" 'E is out with 'is steward," the valet said. "That is to say, with *the* steward. You must not mind, little lady. Nige will do good things for your 'ome 'cause 'tis 'is 'ome too and 'e 'as been eager for an 'ole year to get at it. You sit back and let 'im pertect you."

His impertinence rendered her almost speechless. But of course he was not a real valet. She had realized that last night.

"You are his bodyguard, are you not?" she said. It was not really a question. "I do not imagine that many men get past you—or women either. But if he needs you with him constantly, he must have done more vicious deeds than just the one involving my father. I hope he pays you well."

"Nige will never 'arm you, little lady," he said. " 'E should of told you the truth before 'e married you. I told 'im that he should of, but Nige can be one stubborn son of an 'ore—oh, Gawd a-lordy, now wot 'ave I said? 'E married up with you 'cause 'e didn't want to see you 'urt. 'E wouldn't never 'urt you, and if 'e did, 'e'd 'ave old Stubbs to answer to and 'e knows wot that feels like. We're not never going to 'arm you, m'lady."

"Thank you, Mr. Stubbs," she said coldly. "When I want information or an opinion from you in future, I will ask for it." She was proud of the steadiness of her voice. Despite his words, she was terrified of him. He had *beaten* Nigel? And she was very aware that that open razor he had been clutching yesterday was lying on the washstand almost within his reach. But she would not show her terror. Only her contempt for Viscount Wroxley and all who were connected to him.

William Stubbs tipped his head to one side and regarded her steadily from his one working eye. "I understands, little lady," he said. "I understands better than you knows."

"You will inform his lordship," she said, "that I wish to speak with him in the library two hours from now. Do you understand?"

"I understands, your ladyship," he said. If he had been anyone else she would have sworn that there was tenderness in his voice.

She lifted her chin and the hem of her dressing gown and swept out of her husband's room and back to her own, where her maid was pouring hot water into the bowl on the washstand.

She wished her mind had not betrayed her and thought of him as her *husband*. She shuddered.

Nigel had spent a few hours with Coburg, riding out to parts of the home farm, discussing in very general terms estate business, familiarizing himself with what was now his. He did not inform the steward that it was his—that could come later. He let Coburg assume that he was acting on his wife's behalf. It was what the man and everyone on the estate and off it would expect anyway.

He would not humiliate her by announcing the truth so soon. Perhaps eventually he would inform only those who needed to know, Kedleston's steward among them, and allow word to spread of its own volition.

He could not help remembering how she had talked to him with great enthusiasm about how she would run the estate herself, though she had been generous enough to want to include him so that his feelings would not be hurt.

He sighed as he arrived home and stepped inside the house. He wondered if she would come out of her rooms or agree to receive him there today. He must try. Life would be so much more comfortable for both of them when she accepted reality. He would write her another note.

But there was no need to do so. Will Stubbs answered

his summons to his dressing room and as usual did not wait to be spoken to.

"The little filly wants to see you in the library prompt like, Nige," he said. "Two hours ago she said two hours."

"You spoke with her?" Nigel asked. But he stopped himself from asking his friend how she had looked.

"She 'as a stubborn little chin," William told him. "She lifts it as cool as you please, even though she was shaking in 'er slippers and 'er voice was all breath. 'You will tell 'im I wants to speak to 'im, Mr. Stubbs,' she sez. 'And wen I wants your opinion I will arsk for it. Do you understand?' And all the time I seen by 'er eyes, Nige, that she knowed I could pick 'er up with one fist and crush all 'er bones. She's goin' to chew you up and spit you out, lad. You 'ad better get down there and face the music." He chuckled, a fearsome sound to anyone who had not heard his laugh before.

Nigel went back downstairs without stopping to change. He went to face the music. She was there in the library before him, her back to the door, her fingertips resting on the desktop. She stood facing the chair on the other side as if she realized this morning that she had no right to go around there to take the master's chair. She stood like a supplicant. She did not turn her head.

"Cassandra," he said after the footman had closed the door behind him. He did not insult her by injecting any heartiness into his voice. "Good morning."

She swung around then and looked him full in the eye—and he knew instantly what Will had meant by a stubborn little chin. He also knew that he was to deal with no tearful supplicant, with no weak woman whom he could comfort and pet. She looked at him with such dislike and such contempt in her face that he stopped himself only just in time from taking a step back and colliding with the door.

"I have failed to see anything good about it yet," she said, "but thank you for the sentiment."

"Come." He walked toward her, one hand outstretched. "Let us sit by the fireplace and talk. We need to talk." She had, he realized, taken the time to dress very smartly indeed this morning. Her hair was even powdered beneath her fetching round-eared cap.

"I shall sit here, I thank you," she said, indicating a straight-backed chair on her side of the desk and suiting action to words. "Please take your rightful place, my lord." She gestured toward the comfortable armed chair on the other side of the desk.

Well, he had not expected this interview to be easy. She was determined to give visual emphasis to the fact that he was now master and she in a subordinate position. He humored her.

"You said it was something between my father and you," she said. "Was it something personal? Or was it just a card game in which he played too deep? Did you have an acquaintance with him before that game? Was there some animosity between the two of you? Did you set out to strip him of all he held dear and all with which he supported himself and me?"

He sat and looked at her across the desk, considering his answer. There was the temptation to tell her everything. But he had never intended to do so and he still thought on the whole that he had been right. She would not understand all those events anyway—he still did not himself. He might have understood Worthing cutting his acquaintance, but he did not understand the hatred, the vicious compulsion to destroy. It was unlikely she would see those things in her father, anyway. She would not believe the truth even if she heard it. No one else ever had—except Will Stubbs. Not even his own family.

"I had an acquaintance with your father," he said. "We had played for high stakes before." That at least was the truth. "We were foxed, Cassandra. Men do reckless things when they are in their cups. They even wager their estates. Your father did and lost it. I was the fortunate winner."

"If you were drunk," she said, "then perhaps you could be forgiven for accepting such a wager. But you were sober the next day. Why did you not simply give it back?"

"Egad, madam," he said, "you do not know the ways of men. I would no more have dreamed of returning my winnings than your father would have dreamed of taking them back. He would have been shamed by the offer—dishonored.''

"But not by his recklessness?" she said. "Did you hate him, my lord?"

It had not escaped his notice that she no longer called him by his given name. It was a trivial point. He raised his eyebrows. "I do not hate *you*," he said. "By my life, I missed you last night. Have I been punished sufficiently?"

He knew the pointlessness of his words even as he spoke them. Light flirtatiousness had worked like a charm on her when she had thought him her father's friend and hers, too. Now it made her lip curl with scorn and her chin move just a little higher.

"You might ask that of someone else after an eternity or two in hell, my lord," she said. "How dangerous is your man? I will not call him your valet. He is your bodyguard, is he not? Has he killed?"

Very, very dangerous indeed as an enemy. Nigel half smiled. "Oh yes," he said, "I would imagine so. But you are perfectly safe with him. He is unfailingly gentle with women. He will be more than gentle with you. You are my wife."

"I wish for a lock on my dressing-room door," she said.

The half smile remained on his face. "To keep Will Stubbs out?" he asked her. "Or me?"

"Both of you," she said.

"Then you shall have it today, madam," he said, "though I shall never try the door to see if 'tis locked against me. I have given my word that I will not enter your rooms again uninvited."

"Then you have seen them for the last time," she said.

"So be it." He inclined his head to her. His wife was a woman to be admired, he thought. She was suffering dreadfully. That was perfectly obvious. During the past day she had suffered the loss of her home and of her love. She had found herself locked in a marriage with a man she deeply despised. She had lost her newfound faith in her father—though not nearly as much as she would have done had he told her the full truth, by God—if she had believed him. But she looked at him with steady eyes and cool contempt.

He had married a woman of character. She was not the helpless little ball of sunshine he had first taken her to be.

"I wish to know how much freedom I am to have," she said, "and what my role is to be exactly. Am I free to come and go as I please, or must I ask your permission whenever I wish to leave the house? Am I to run the house as I have done for the past several years? If I am not already with child, will you exercise your marital rights in order to get your son on me? If so, when and where and how often? I need to know. I would have all settled now, today, so that my life will not hold daily unpleasant surprises. When we are in company I shall not shame you—and I would ask you not to shame me—by showing my true feelings for you. When we are not in company, I would ask to be left alone as often as possible, as I have no ability to pretend to a regard or to a respect that I cannot feel. Please give me your instructions."

He sat back in his chair, his elbows on the arms, his fingers steepled against his mouth. He liked her more than ever, he realized.

"You are my wife, Cassandra," he said, "and by my life you will not goad me into treating you like a servant. This is your home and you will continue to live and behave here as you always have done. When we are in company and when we are alone together I shall treat you with the regard I feel for you. Now—the estate is prospering once more. In addition, I have a sizable fortune—won at the tables, of course. We will have more such interviews in the coming days to discuss together how best our money is to be spent on all that needs doing. We will try to divide our resources between the needs of our tenants and farms and the needs of our home. We will decide together, madam."

"Kedleston is yours," she said disdainfully. "I am merely your wife, your possession. I am merely a woman, incapable of deciding matters of such significance."

"I am sorry in my heart that you are bitter," he said quietly. "But petulance does not become you, my dear. I said that we will decide together. I will make it a command. You will doubtless remember that just two days ago you promised to obey me. We will decide together all matters of importance that concern our estate and our home.''

She said nothing, but she did not lower her eyes from his. And then she did say something.

''What happened to your back?'' she asked him. ''Who whipped you? Did it have anything to do with my father?''

He took his time replying. '' 'Twere better if we laid that topic to rest for once and all,'' he said. ''You would not wish to know the answers, Cassandra. And they do not concern you.''

''I know one answer at least,'' she said. ''You would have been swift to deny it if 'twere not so. My father had something to do with it. He discovered something about you and brought you to justice. I am glad he had the courage to do it, though he suffered for it. You took a dreadful revenge. You tricked him into that game, did you not? And you cheated him out of what was his. I am married to an evil man, am I not? And that is *not* a question I expect answered.''

He rounded the end of the desk, and reached out a hand for hers.

''Come,'' he said. ''I will escort you to your room or to wherever you wish to go. I will not subject you to my company any longer for today.''

''Thank you,'' she said coolly, ''but I can rise without assistance, my lord.''

He watched her do so and leave the room unhurriedly, her head high, her back straight.

He watched her appreciatively. And he liked her immensely. He had thought her as fragile as a sunbeam. There was nothing fragile about sunbeams. One could grasp them with one's hand and see only shadow on the ground. But one removed one's hand—and the beam of light streamed unbroken to the ground.

Cassandra was not fragile. She would survive. But she might forever hate him.

There was a strangely exhilarating challenge in the thought.

FIFTEEN

CASSANDRA HALF RAN DOWN
the hill to the dower house. She had left Kedleston immediately after the interview in the library. There had been
luncheon to wait for, but she had chosen not to wait. She
had asked him if she was free to come and go as she
pleased, and he had said that her life must continue as it
had always been. It was a relief to know that she did not
have to ask his permission for every move she made—if
there was any relief to be found in this whole situation.

It was a chilly, blustery day, with low, dull clouds—a
perfect day for her mood. But she was not cold. She had
hurried all the way from the house, just as if she had expected that he would come after her to tell her that after all
she was not free to leave the house or to visit her relatives.
And now she was running. She forced herself to slow
down. It would not do to arrive breathless and disheveled.
Or pale and frowning. She practiced a smile. She felt more
as if she were grimacing.

She hoped Robin had not yet returned home. He had
intended to stay at the dower house only a day or two, but
she did not believe he would have left without calling at
Kedleston to take his leave of her. Except, of course, that
everyone was avoiding Kedleston for a few days, tactfully

leaving the bride and groom alone to their newly married bliss.

They were all in the dining room at luncheon—Aunt Matilda, Aunt Bea, Patience, and Robin. They all got to their feet at the sight of her.

"Oh la," Cassandra said, removing her hat and handing it to the servant, who had shown her in, "do not let me interrupt you. I shall have a cup of tea if I may. I am parched. No, I will not eat. I just ate with Nigel and left him to his work. He is determined to play the master of the house, odious man, and run the estate for me. Uncle Cyrus will be prodigiously pleased. And I am, too, though I must *pretend* to be chagrined. Rob, *do* sit down."

She was talking too loudly and too fast. She sparkled on the edge of hysteria. None of them seemed to notice anything amiss.

"I knew there was more to that young man than met the eye," Lady Matilda said. "Gentlemen who are all amiability and charm on the outside generally possess good sense and steady principles on the inside."

"Have a seat, niece," Lady Beatrice said. "Can you not see that Robin will not sit down until you do? I hope Wroxley had the good sense to send a maid with you."

Cassandra laughed. "I escaped when he was not looking," she said. "You know how I hate having maids and grooms trailing along behind me when I am walking or riding, Aunt Bea. I daresay Nigel will be annoyed with me when he finds out. But I shall tease him out of the mopes."

" 'Tis more like he will stand his ground better than Worthing ever did while he was alive," Lady Beatrice said. "That is a young man who knows what he wants, Cassandra, and has got it, too. He is not like to tolerate a disobedient wife."

"Aunt Bea." Cassandra laughed again and leaned across the table, her eyes sparkling. "Nigel *loves* me. A man in love will tolerate a great deal."

"You look so very—happy, Cass," Patience said, and blushed. There was envy in her eyes. And then, as if the subject had been changed: "Robin is to leave for home tomorrow morning."

Cassandra turned her smile on him. "And I suppose 'twas your intention to slip away without a word to me," she said. "For shame. But I have come in time to say good-bye. You have finished eating?" She got to her feet. "Come and stroll in the garden with me, then. I need your advice on how to manage a husband who is determined to manage me." She laughed lightly.

"If that is what Wroxley is doing, cous," Robin said gravely, "then he has my respect. And my advice to you is to accept reality and relax and be a lady, as you were meant to be."

" 'Tis a conspiracy involving all males," she said with a mock sigh. "But come stroll with me, Rob, and convince me that 'tis right for me to be enjoying myself here while my poor Nigel is incarcerated at Kedleston trying to make sense of the books. They are written in Arabic, I am convinced."

She did not know why she had not simply spilled out the whole truth as soon as the dining-room doors closed behind her. They would know soon enough anyway. They would learn that Kedleston belonged not to her, but to Viscount Wroxley, and it would not take long for them to discover the rest. Including her permanent estrangement from the man she had insisted upon marrying just two days ago.

Perhaps pride kept her quiet.

But not to Robin. Her total aloneness had threatened to suffocate her this morning and she had felt the all-too-human urge to confide in someone. She had rejected her maid, both her aunts, and even Patience as confidantes. They could not help her. They were all female and shared her essential helplessness. Uncle Cyrus was ten miles away and it would be unfair to ask him to return so soon when she had taken so much of his time during the past year. He had his own home and his young family to attend to. Besides, she dreaded the thought of facing Uncle Cyrus once he knew the truth.

Robin had been the obvious choice—steady, solid, dependable Robin, who had always been more like a brother than a cousin. She wished now—oh, *how* she wished—that she had given more serious consideration to his marriage proposal. No, she did not, of course. A marriage with Robin would never have worked. She would have made him dreadfully unhappy.

But she had come rushing to Robin as to the only anchor in a stormy sea.

She slipped her arm through his as they stepped outside and climbed the sloping lawn to the orchard.

"You should not have walked over today," he said. " 'Tis downright cold, Cass. You will catch a chill. I cannot think what Wroxley is about, not keeping a better eye on you."

"Rob," she said, "please do not scold."

"I suppose," he continued, "you did not even leave word where you went. He will be looking for you. He will be annoyed with you, and rightfully so. You are a married lady now, Cass, and must learn to rein in this alarmingly independent streak. I would not put it past Wroxley to make his point with a heavy hand. You are so blinded by his charms that you have not learned yet—"

"Robin." She had turned her head to set her forehead against his shoulder—she had not put her hat back on to come outside. "Stop scolding. Please stop scolding."

"Well really," he began. Then his shoulder stiffened. "Zounds, Cass, you are *crying*. What the devil—? What has the blackguard done? Has he beaten you? Already?"

"Robin." She looked up into his face. She was not actually crying. Her misery was too deep for tears. "Robin, he *owns* Kedleston. He won it from Papa in a card game a few weeks before Papa died. 'Tis all legal. He has the deeds. And of course Kedleston is not entailed. I had forgot it because it has always gone to the heir. But 'tis not entailed. And Papa wagered it and lost. Viscount Wroxley *owns* it."

Robin stared back at her rather as she must have stared

at the viscount himself when he told her yesterday, she thought.

"He is a gamer," she said, "and a liar and a cheat and I think something worse, too. There was something between him and Papa—something for which he was taking revenge. I think Papa apprehended him in some sort of wrongdoing. Rob—there are whip marks on his back. Hundreds of them. Welts. They are livid white. He said he had them from his father and from school, but that cannot be true, can it? Oh Robin, whom have I married?"

She had not meant to sound so abject. She had meant to give cold facts—she had needed to give them because she had something to ask of him.

Robin had dropped his arms to his sides. His hands were in fists. "Why did he marry you?" His voice came out as a whisper.

"I am the Countess of Worthing," she said, "and Papa's daughter. Think of the perfection of the revenge, Rob. Think of the triumph."

"Has he beaten you?" He was still whispering.

"No," she said. "No, of course not. Rob, will you help me? I know I have no right to ask, especially after what you so kindly offered me just a few weeks ago. But I have no one else to turn to. I cannot go to Uncle Cyrus. Will you help me?"

He looked haggard. She was touched. Did she really mean so much to him? He might have washed his hands of all concern for her after her rejection of his suit.

"I am not sure I can, Cass," he said. "He is your husband. You married him. He—he owns you."

"I have to know," she said. "He will not tell me. He says 'tis in the past and best left there. But I have to know. Who is he? What was between him and Papa? What *happened*? And did he win Kedleston fairly? Or did he cheat? If he cheated—"

"And if it can be proved he cheated," he said harshly. "I would not hold on to any hope in that direction if I were you, Cass."

"Rob," she said, taking his arm in both her hands, "help

me. Find out for me. Oh, but how can I ask it of you? 'Twould mean traveling to London and asking a lot of questions. You have been from home for long enough and I know that you abhor the city. You are right. I married him and I must take the consequences of my choice. He will not be cruel, I think. He has granted me the privacy of my own rooms and freedom of movement. He has—oh Rob! He has a *bodyguard* with him, a man who calls himself his valet. He is a fearsome giant. I do not believe there can be a more terrifying man in all England. When I asked Ni—when I asked Viscount Wroxley if Mr. Stubbs had ever killed, he *laughed* and said he did not doubt it, or words to that effect.''

Robin was patting her hands reassuringly. ''I am going to London, Cass,'' he said. ''Tomorrow. I shall not even go home first. Zounds, but I will find out the truth. If he cheated and it can be proved, if there was something in his past to which Uncle took exception, perhaps—egad, cous, I know pitifully little about the law but surely there would be a way of freeing you from the marriage. Have you—'' He stopped abruptly and flushed.

''Yes,'' she said, understanding the unspoken question. ''Yes, I have. He did not tell me until yesterday, you see.''

''I am not sure 'twould make matters any easier anyway,'' he said. ''And I am not sure that discovering your husband is a scoundrel is grounds for divorce or annulment or anything else. It might be better not to hope too strongly, Cass. But I will discover the truth for you. I swear it.''

''Oh, Rob.'' She rested her forehead against his shoulder again and he wrapped one comforting arm about her. ''Will you? How very dear you are. I wish I had never loved you as a brother. Perhaps then—but no, you are better off without me.'' She lifted her head and smiled into his face. ''I wish you *were* my brother. You would be the dearest brother a woman ever had.'' She stood on her toes and kissed him on the cheek.

He looked beyond her and smiled. ''Patience,'' he called, and he stretched out his free arm toward her. ''Are you going to cry all over me, too, just because I am going away? Zounds, I should come here and leave more often.'' He chuckled.

But Patience was looking rather white-faced and did not come close enough to take Robin's arm. ''I do beg your pardon,'' she said. ''I did not mean to interrupt.''

Cassandra realized in a flash what Patience must be thinking. And how selfish of her to take Robin's time when it was his last day at the dower house. Patience's heart must be breaking in two.

Cassandra laughed gaily. ''Rob has done nothing but scold ever since we came out here,'' she said. ''He *approves* of the fact that Nigel insists upon doing all those things for me that gentlemen believe women incapable of doing for themselves. It seems, Patience, that I shall have to settle into being the average helpless lady and allow my husband to order my life and my estate for me. How tiresome! I was just forgiving Rob and bidding him farewell. And now I am pining for Nigel. I have been away from him for all of an hour—longer. I wonder if he misses me as much as I miss him. I must go home and see.''

''I shall escort you, Cass,'' Robin said.

''And I accept, sir,'' she said, ''not for my own sake but for Patience's. I do not need to be escorted home, you see, but Patience will after she has walked to Kedleston with me.''

Patience bit her lip and blushed and looked wistful. There, Cassandra thought, she had atoned. They would have all of half an hour alone together, the two of them. And if Patience had any sense in her head, she would make sure that somehow it was considerably longer than just half an hour. Though it would not be, of course. Patience did not have enough courage, and Robin had altogether too strong a sense of propriety.

How she longed for the mutual happiness of these two people, perhaps the two most dear people in the world to her. But the thought did not bear dwelling upon.

''Give me five minutes,'' she called gaily, setting off back down the lawn, ''to take my leave of the aunts and to tell them where Patience will be.''

• • •

It seemed somehow strange to Cassandra during the following three weeks that life could go on and even seem almost normal on the surface. Perhaps, she thought, having a houseful of servants and a countryside full of neighbors helped—not to mention a resident aunt and another, as well as a cousin, at the dower house nearby.

There were, after all, appearances to be kept up.

The Countess of Worthing was seen by her neighbors—when they saw her again, that is, after the week of seclusion following her wedding—as a radiant bride, touchingly in love with her handsome husband. She had always been sunny-natured and charming, but now she never stopped smiling. Her eyes never stopped sparkling.

Viscount Wroxley was seen as a man devoted to his lovely bride. Although he was well bred and even amiable in company and soon very well liked indeed by almost all his neighbors, it was obvious to all—and all were charmed by the fact—that he had eyes for no one but his wife. He watched her with a tenderness that had many people yearning for such a love relationship in their own experience. No one thought any the worse of him when rumor began to spread that he was making himself master of Kedleston. Indeed, they thought the better of him. He was clearly not a man to be overset by the superiority of his wife's fortune.

He was a real man, the ladies said approvingly—and had the looks and physique to match, the bolder among them added when there were no male ears to listen in. He had asserted himself so that matters between him and the countess were as they should be, the gentlemen said with equal approval.

Even Lady Beatrice had been largely won over—perhaps because Nigel was wise enough not to try to charm her. He talked to her with intelligent good sense, with the result that within a few days of her return to Kedleston she had reversed her early impression that he was a mindless fop. She approved of his meetings with Coburg and of the hours he spent traveling about the estate, learning as much as he could about it before trying in any way to manage it for himself.

Lady Matilda, of course, had liked him almost from the start. His warm charm continued to endear him to her as well as his offer to be at her beck and call at any time of the day or night now that her brother was ten miles away and her nephew twelve.

Patience simply adored him.

"Are you quite sure there is no permanent weakness in your ankle?" he asked her while escorting her as far as the lime grove on her way home one day—her maid walked a few paces behind. "By my life, I would never forgive myself if there were."

" 'Tis as good as new, my lord," she assured him, smiling up at him. "And 'twas my silly fault that it happened, not yours. But 'twas in a good cause. You went down to the pool with Cassandra and now you are married to her."

"And I have you to thank," he said, raising her hand from his cuff and touching the back of it to his lips. " 'Tis by far the most romantic setting I have ever seen, madam. 'Twas admirably suited for the marriage proposal that I made there."

"Did you?" She looked at him with wide, smiling eyes. "But you went away the same day. I was *so* disappointed."

"I was sent away," he said, "while my dearest love decided if she could live without me or not. 'Twas my good fortune that she decided she could not."

Patience was charmed by his confidences. "I am so *glad,*" she said. "La, I am so glad. But how could she even think there was a choice to be made?"

"How indeed?" he agreed, winking at her. " 'Twas the most anxiety-filled week of my life. And how is it with you, madam? Is a certain gentleman going to be content to live twelve miles away from the dower house?"

Patience blushed and bit her lip.

"Some gentlemen, i'faith," he said, "are blind in both eyes and deaf in both ears and have a mere pump for a heart. Some gentlemen need a swift boot in the seat of their—of their sensibilities."

Patience laughed at his deliberate attempt to amuse her. "To Robin I am merely a very young cousin, my lord," she said.

"Someone," he said, fingering the handle of his quizzing glass, "should inform Mr. Barr-Hampton that time does inevitably pass and that very young cousins equally inevitably grow up and transform themselves into handsome young ladies who are in fact not one's cousins at all."

They parted on the best of terms, well pleased with each other, like coconspirators.

Patience expressed her happiness to Cassandra while they were in the rose garden one morning, cutting a dozen blooms to be carried home to Lady Matilda. "La, Cass," she said, "how like a fairy tale 'tis, Lord Wroxley being so very handsome and so very amiable and so very devoted to you. Yet just a month ago you had not met him. How delighted Uncle would be if he could only know."

Cassandra merely smiled with the vibrant smile she had perfected since that morning, two days after her wedding, when she had rushed over to the dower house. She could not confide the truth to Patience. She was beginning to regret that she had told even Robin and begged his help. Her marriage was hers alone—and *Nigel's*—and something she must endure alone for the rest of her life. Besides, she was reluctant for others to know what a foolish disaster she had made of her first—and last—important decision as an independent woman.

She changed the subject. "Robin was very attentive to you while your ankle was sprained," she said. "And he was reluctant to return home, I do declare. He has never stayed at the dower house before."

"I could not ask for more kind concern even from a brother," Patience said.

Cassandra grimaced. "Someone is going to have to teach Robin how to open up his eyes," she said, unconsciously echoing her husband.

"His eyes already are open," Patience said sadly. "But 'tis not me that he sees, Cass. I fear you have broke his heart."

"Oh, no." Cassandra sat down on a bench, eight long-stemmed roses spread along her arm. "You are thinking of that scene in the orchard, Patience? 'Twas not what it seemed, I do assure you, not for me and not for Rob. You must not think it."

"And yet," Patience said, "he did not hug *me* when he took his leave. And he was frowning and preoccupied—even Mama noticed it."

"Because he was leaving you and did not wish to show unmanly emotion," Cassandra said.

"Cass." Patience looked at her with quiet dignity. "Do not persuade me that there is hope when there is none. I am not a child to be consoled by promises. I am a woman even if I am only eighteen. Robin cannot be made to love me. He cannot be tricked or bullied into it. I will not pine away into a decline. I daresay I will marry someone else eventually and find contentment in my own home with my husband and family."

Cassandra tipped her head to one side. If only she had such a hope.

"But I will always love Rob," Patience said, lowering her nose to sniff at the single rose that she carried. "I always will, though I will never say so to a living soul after this moment. There. 'Tis over and I am still alive and the world is still a beautiful place. And roses still smell sweet." She smiled so brightly that Cassandra was reminded of the image that had faced her in her own glass for the past couple of weeks.

But Patience was right. Life went on and the world was still lovely. Roses still smelled sweet.

She watched her husband with unwilling fascination whenever she was in company with him—and it was difficult to avoid being frequently in his presence once Aunt Bea had returned to Kedleston and visitors and invitations began to arrive again. She saw his elegant good looks and his polished charm differently now. She saw them as a shield behind which the real man—the stranger—hid from view. But nevertheless she was drawn to him totally against her will.

He treated her with unfailing courtesy even when the necessity of acting the besotted husband in company was not there to motivate him. Twice he asked if he might visit her in her bedchamber. Both times she refused. He accepted her decision without comment and without apparent annoyance. He carried through his decision to include her in all plans for change to the farms and house. And it was no token agreement for his own plans that he looked for. He asked her opinion and waited until she gave it. If he disagreed with her, he said so and insisted that they discuss the matter. Sometimes she won the argument, sometimes he did.

The drawing room and the dining room were to be the first rooms in the house to be refurbished—she had suggested the library and the crimson salon. The new colors and fabrics were her choice, though he had had differing opinions on the matter. On the farms a large drainage project was to proceed, though on a slightly smaller scale than he had wanted. The rest of the money was to be spent on reroofing some laborers' cottages, a project more dear to her heart.

As business partners—he insisted on describing them as such—they worked well together. She grew, despite herself, to respect his energy and his willingness to work long hours when necessary. He came to respect her taste and her compassion for the human element of their property.

Perhaps, she thought as the weeks progressed—though she tried to avoid the weakness of thinking so—she had judged him wrongly. She knew so little of the harsh world of men. She supposed that fortunes were won and lost daily at the card tables of the gentlemen's clubs and at the gaming hells in London. Perhaps not all men who won such fortunes were villains.

He watched his wife during those weeks and found himself intrigued by her beauty and her grace and dignity. He had expected when he saw her running in the direction of the dower house that morning that she would enlist the support of her whole family against him, that she would hide behind their righteous wrath. He had expected that she would turn all her neighbors and friends against him. He had expected to lose his newfound admiration for her.

But she had apparently said nothing.

There was a total estrangement between them as far as personal relations were concerned. But nothing of her unhappiness was allowed to show in public. Even her aunt, he would wager, was convinced that she was deeply in love with him and deep in the throes of the blissful early weeks of a love match.

He had hopes that in time she would accept reality and realize that life could be a long process. He had hopes that they could settle into a more comfortable amity and he could enjoy fully and in peace the property and the life for which he had paid very dearly indeed.

He wanted a child of her—a son, preferably, though a daughter would be hardly less welcome. Even a daughter could inherit her title, if not his own.

If they could but have a child together, all his plans would have come to fruition. No, more than a plan—a dream.

He would not force her—not ever. But he had hopes that in time she would issue that invitation for which he waited and he would get her with child.

He hoped that sometimes dreams, as well as more carefully laid plans, came to fulfillment.

SIXTEEN

I<small>T WAS A HOT AND SUNNY</small>
July day. It was impossible, Cassandra thought, to dwell
upon all the negatives of her life. Life at Kedleston was
much as it had always been—as tranquil, as comfortable,
as filled with a pleasing combination of duties and social
pleasures.

Sometimes, treacherously, she felt that life was better
than it had been before. There was all the challenge of
adjusting her life to a stranger's—a handsome, charming,
compellingly attractive stranger, who happened also to be
her husband. He had asked her again last evening as they
rode home in the carriage from a card party at Mr. Wintersmere's. . . .

She had said no again.

She had been horrified by the power of the temptation
to say yes.

Her wedding night had come to seem more like a dream
than a nightmare.

If only she did not have to see him so often, she thought.
But today she had not seen him since breakfast. He was
away with Mr. Coburg, making arrangements about that
drainage scheme. Perhaps he would be back soon. Perhaps
he would come looking for her in the rose garden or in the
park or in one of the dayrooms in the house and sit down

to converse with her as he often did or suggest a stroll outside.

She would feel her defenses crumble just a little more, as they did with each passing day. She was no longer sure what she wished to hear from Robin when he wrote or came in person. She was not sure she wished to hear anything at all. Perhaps he had failed to discover anything. Card games like the one in which her husband and her father had been involved were perhaps common occurrences.

She felt as if she were living in suspended time. Sometimes she wished it could remain suspended.

But she was quite determined to remain strong. He had heartlessly fleeced her father of all he had owned. Papa had died of a heart seizure a mere two weeks later. She did not doubt that it had been brought on by the loss of Kedleston. That made Viscount Wroxley . . . Especially if he had cheated . . . It made him a murderer.

She was weakening toward the man who had first cheated and then murdered her father. And then lied to her and married her.

Oh, she was determined to remain strong.

And so she did not linger in the rose garden or in the house or in any part of the park where she would be visible at a glance. Aunt Bea had gone over to the dower house in order to pay some afternoon calls with Aunt Matilda and Patience—Cassandra had declined the suggestion that she go with them. She went alone to the pool.

It had always been her favorite retreat, a place in which to be alone to hug to herself some secret joy or to nurse a secret hurt. The perfect beauty, perfect seclusion of the clearing was admirably suited for both purposes.

She remembered telling him that.

She stood on the spot where she had stood with him only a month before, looking into the pool, which was a very deep green today, looking up the long waterfall, which sparkled in the light from the sun, listening to the soothing, rushing sound of the dropping water, and remembered.

Remembered his kiss, the feel of him, the smell of him. She remembered wanting him here with her so that in a sense he would always be a part of her favorite place in all the world.

She had been right. She ached with memory.

She sat on the log and set her hand where his foot had rested.

She had asked for time. She had been overwhelmed by the romance of it all, by her love for him, by her desire to make it all permanent. But she had asked for time. She had thought herself so wise, so cautious, so sensible.

She had not seen past the mask at all.

She had not even seen that he wore a mask.

She could so easily love him again, she thought, closing her eyes. Perhaps she could be forgiven her naïveté in falling in love the first time. He was, after all, a very experienced seducer. She had no doubt about that. And everyone else in the neighborhood had been deceived by him and still was—except for her family at the start, of course. She could never forgive herself if she fell in love with him again, knowing what she now knew.

But what *did* she know?

She knew nothing. And he would tell her nothing. Why? Why did he not invent lies to impress her, even if he was not prepared to tell her the truth? Why would he tell her nothing?

Why must she believe the worst?

But what else was there to believe?

It was very hot. At first she was tempted to strip off her clothes down to her shift and swim in the pool. But she remembered a blistering scold she had had from Robin one day when he had come down and found her swimming alone. He had made her promise on her honor that she would never do anything so foolhardy again. But there was another way to get cool. She had almost forgotten. It was something she had not done in years. She looked at the waterfall and at the steep, rocky drop over which the water fell. The rocks were dry to either side of the water and really quite climbable, though they looked dangerous from down here. No one had ever forbidden them to climb— perhaps because no one knew that they ever had. But they had climbed up a few times as children just for the sheer pleasure of it or in order to edge their way behind the water in that one spot about a third of the way up, where they would be shaded from the sun and cooled further by mist from the waterfall.

She kicked off her shoes and pulled off her hat to drop on top of them. Ten minutes later she was up in the old perch, feeling warm and breathless after the climb but exhilarated by the view down to the clearing and by the cool droplets of water that were already soothing her face and her arms.

She must be strong, she thought. She must at least wait until Robin wrote to her to tell her what he had found out. Perhaps there had been nothing so very heinous after all, except for a reckless card game. She would hope. She found herself hoping fervently. Or perhaps he had found out something so dreadful that it would be grounds for a separation or perhaps even grounds for suing to have her property restored to her.

Perhaps she could be a free woman again. Perhaps she could have a second chance. She would not squander another.

She really did not know what she most hoped for.

She had been sitting on the broad ledge, half behind the waterfall, for almost an hour when he appeared in the clearing below. He was wearing the riding clothes in which he had gone off with Mr. Coburg that morning. His hair, tied back with a black ribbon but not bagged, was unpowdered. He looked as handsome and virile as he always looked. Cassandra sat very still and watched him.

He stood on the spot where they had kissed and where she had stood just an hour before, and looked all about him. Then he spotted her hat and her shoes beside the log. He walked toward them and looked around again. He even looked up, but she knew she must be virtually invisible from down there.

"Cassandra?" he said.

She did not answer him. She hugged her knees.

"Cassandra?" His voice was louder. *"Cassandra?"*

There was fear in his voice. She saw him looking at the still waters of the pool and knew what thoughts must be going through his mind. She should call down to him. But she did not want to come face-to-face with him here. Not here of all places. She bit her lip.

"Cassandra?" His voice echoed about the clearing while he tore at his coat and his waistcoat and boots. She drew breath to call down to him, but he had plunged into the pool before she could make up her mind to reveal her hiding place.

He dived under three separate times, each time staying down so long that her heart raced with fear. The third time he came up she could hear him gasping and sobbing for breath. She bit hard on her forefinger, appalled by the power of his panic and by her own cruelty in causing it.

It was marvelous punishment, part of her thought. Part of her gloated.

"I am here," she said. She scarcely raised her voice, but he heard her. He looked wildly about him, treading water, shaking droplets from his eyes. "I am up here."

She slid outward along the ledge and turned face in to the cliff in order to make her way carefully downward. Going down always seemed more perilous than going up. She did not look down at all. She thought she must be almost at the bottom when hands grabbed her, lifted her away from the rock face, and set her on her feet on firm ground. The same hands turned her, grasped her painfully by the shoulders, and shook her until her head flopped beyond her control and she clutched at him in panic. His shirt was cold and wet.

"Damn you," she heard at last, when her ears began to register the words he was saying. "God damn you to hell. You enjoyed that. You enjoyed letting me imagine that I had driven you to taking your own life. God damn you, Cassandra." His voice was harsh and fierce, unrecognizable.

And then her face collided nose on with his chest and was held there with a hard hand pressed against the back of her head. She listened to his harsh gasps even as she felt the utter rigidity of all his muscles.

"God damn you," he said again.

She was no longer gloating. She stood very still, waiting for violence. The shaking he had given her had been a frightening warning of her utter helplessness in his hands.

But after a whole minute or more of silence, during which she could feel his only just-leashed passions, he released his hold of her abruptly and turned from her without a word or a look. She watched as he strode back to the edge of the pool and dived in again.

She was, she realized, almost paralyzed with terror. And with horror at his violent reaction to the thought that she might have committed suicide as a way of being free of him. And with something else that she could not and would not even try to analyze.

But clearly terror was not the predominant emotion. If it had been, she would have made her escape while she had the chance. She could have grabbed her shoes and been a good way up the slope back to the house before he could climb out of the pool and pull on his coat and boots over his wet clothes. She might have made it back to the house and the sanctuary of her own rooms before he caught up to her.

She did not even try. After standing very still where she was for several minutes, she reached for the laces that held the bodice of her gown closed and pulled them loose. Her dress and her petticoats were too heavy to swim in. She stripped down to her shift.

Nigel dived under the surface of the pool again and swam a few breaststrokes, trying to concentrate on the coolness of the water on his whole body, trying to relax, trying to force the wheels of his mind to slow down. Even when he lifted his head above the surface, he did not look toward the bank. He hoped she had made her escape.

He had been about to—he really was not sure whether he had been about to punch her senseless or rape her. He had been about to do something violent. He, who had always avoided violence even when it was virtually impossible to do so, who had always thought his icy self-control to be his greatest strength. He had wanted to *hurt* her.

He swam with powerful strokes toward the base of the waterfall. He wanted to feel the water pounding down on his head. Perhaps he could knock himself senseless if he tried hard enough.

This was her place of retreat. She had told him that. He had known that he should not come after her here. He had promised her freedom of movement, after all, and a measure of privacy. But he had been tempted when Will Stubbs had told him she had come in this direction. For several weeks he had tried to be patient. He had hoped that patience would eventually wear down her resistance and they could proceed to live in something approximating contentment.

But he had been tempted. The clearing at the bottom of the hill with its pool and waterfall really was one of earth's beauty spots. It was not only beautiful—it was perhaps one of the most romantic places on earth, too. He had kissed her there and proposed marriage to her there. Perhaps she had gone there today—*if* she had gone there—to remember. Perhaps if he went after her, he would find her in a softened mood. Perhaps they could talk, settle something, come to some arrangement more satisfactory than the present one.

Cassandra had a romantic soul. She had shown it without any attempt at concealment before their marriage. He could take advantage of that fact, perhaps, if he could meet her at the pool. He could play upon her memories.

And so he had come. And had found the clearing deserted—except for her hat and her shoes.

He swam out from beneath the waterfall, gasping for air and shaking his head like a dog to clear his eyes. He had thought she was dead. He had thought her drowned, probably in a deliberate suicide. He shuddered, finally feeling the chill of the water. He would have gone mad. It was as simple as that. He would have lost his sanity.

He would have been the destroyer, not only of innocence and happiness, but even of life.

Of Cassandra's life.

And then he saw her, poised on the bank in her thin shift, diving headfirst into the water.

She had not run away, then. Quite the opposite. She had dived into the pool with him. He might have guessed it. Cassandra was nothing if not a courageous woman. And it had taken courage to stay, he knew. He had both seen and felt her terror—and it had been fully justified. He still did not quite know where he had found the sense to turn away from her and get himself underwater before he could explode into mindless violence. The memory of his anger disturbed him.

She could swim well, he saw at a glance. She swam across the pool ahead of him in a graceful crawl. He was aware again suddenly of his surroundings—of the deep water itself, the fern-draped banks, the green, mossy clearing enclosed by trees and hills on three sides, by the steep cliff and waterfall on the fourth. He was aware of blue sky above and sunshine, of the contrast between the warm summery air and the cool water. Invisible birds were singing merrily. He could hear them above the constant rushing sound of falling water.

Ah yes, it was the loveliest place on earth. Something inside him relaxed. He dived under the water and swam the breaststroke again, his eyes open. He broke the surface just ahead of her. She looked startled and stopped swimming. He grinned at her and she laughed.

It was one of those precious moments in life that came from nowhere and with no warning and no fanfare.

There had been so little lightheartedness in his life for years and years past, he realized.

He set his hands on her waist and drew her against him. They both trod water while he kissed her. Her body felt sensuously warm against his, her mouth hot. She kissed him back, her hands on his shoulders.

He released her and without a word or any eye contact they swam together, side by side, slowly, almost lazily.

This was not really a place, he found himself thinking. And it was not really time. They had entered a different dimension—heaven perhaps, where they did not have to think or justify themselves or settle any problems. It was a nonplace and nontime, where they could simply be.

They climbed onto the bank together after what might have been ten minutes or perhaps an eternity and stood side by side, dripping wet, until they turned to look at each other. But time and place were there, he realized, waiting to rush back to claim them. What seemed the inevitable next step was not inevitable at all. He had promised her. . . .

But what he had felt for the last ten minutes—or eternity—was too powerful to have been felt alone. He could see in her eyes a sharing of his own feelings and an equal reluctance to let reality in.

"Yes," she said quickly, reaching out one hand to set her fingertips against his chest. And lest he did not understand the meaning of the one word, she said it again. "Yes."

She might regret it. She probably would. And perhaps she would blame him. But he was in no mood to think sensibly or even to think at all. And clearly neither was she.

He spread his coat and his waistcoat on the ground and stripped off his wet clothes. She had crossed her arms and was peeling her shift off over her head. He was struck by her beauty, by its perfection in these most perfect of surroundings. She seemed a part of nature, like a water nymph. Her hair, wet and sleek, lay loose down her back.

They came together wordlessly above his spread clothes. They kissed hotly and deeply, widemouthed while their hands feverishly explored and aroused. Their tongues clashed, circled, embraced. He was ravenous for her, on fire for her. And he exulted in her own answering hunger and heat.

The ground would be hard and he was in no mood for gentleness. Neither was she. When he had her mounted, he knew, he would pound his passion into her. The ground would be too hard.

"Come," he said, lowering himself onto his dry garments, lying on his back, bringing her over him. "Come astride me. 'Twill be good. I swear 'twill be good." He drew her thighs in to hug his sides and set a hand behind her neck to pull down her head to his again. He kissed her long and deep before raising her and taking her breasts into his mouth, one at a time, sucking, rubbing her hardened nipples with his tongue, pulsing his teeth about them, while she gasped and moaned with desire.

And then he raised her again and looked up into her face. She looked back at him, her drying hair like a curtain on either side of his face. There was heavy-lidded passion in her look as there was in his, he knew. There was also awareness—of who he was, of what they were doing together and about to do, of the fact that she had consented.

Mindless passion had somehow been suspended for a brief moment. They gazed knowingly into each other's eyes as he grasped her hips and slowly impaled her, bringing her down onto him. She frowned very briefly but did not look away from him. And then he felt her inner muscles clench tightly about him. Her eyes closed and the passion was back—in both of them.

"Ride me," he told her urgently. "Ride me hard."

She rode him with uninhibited passion, her hands on his shoulders bracing her above him. But he could not lie passive beneath her, as he had intended to do at least for a while. He pumped upward into her, matching the rhythm she had set, gasping with pain and need and pleasure.

He was not sure who cried out first. Perhaps it was simultaneous. She was shuddering about him while all his own tension was gushing out into her with his seed. He wrapped both arms about her and drew her down to lie full on top of him. He eased her legs down one at a time, straightening them to rest on either side of his own. She pillowed her head on his shoulder and lay relaxed and warm against him.

He gazed up at the blue sky and knew that heaven—at least in this life—was neither a time nor a place to be grasped and made into a possession. It came in fleeting moments and then went away again to leave one nostalgic and yearning and on the verge of tears.

Very much on the verge of tears.

And very frightened.

For several mindless minutes the long-dead boy who had been himself had come back to vibrant life and occupied his body and his mind and his emotions. A boy capable of love and tenderness and commitment.

An innocent boy who must be hidden away once more if he was not to be hurt again beyond bearing.

For several minutes he had loved her—and allowed her to love him.

He closed his eyes and brought himself back to earth. He was glad she was sleeping—after good sex. That was what it had been.

That was all it had been.

Neither of them had spoken a word since he had told her a long time ago—she remembered the words now with some embarrassment—to ride him hard. They had made love in a frenzy of desire and lust and then they had slept with the exhaustion of satiety. She had woken to find in some surprise that they were still joined. He was lifting her off him—he was sleek and still long though no longer hard —and turning her to lie beside him.

She lay there for a time, her eyes closed, while one of his hands gently smoothed the hair back from her face. She did not open her eyes. She did not want to look into his. She did not know what she would see there—triumph, amusement, tenderness?—and did not really want to find out. If she looked into his eyes, she would feel obliged to say something or at the very least to think something. She did not want to think. She did not want to face the fact that she had allowed lust more power than conscience. And she certainly had felt lust—the raw desire to be naked with him, to be touched sexually by him all over—and to touch, to feel that long, hard part of him deeply embedded in her, thrusting her to the point of madness.

She did not want to think. She did not want to imagine that it might be tenderness she would see if she looked into his eyes. She did not want his tenderness.

His hand stopped touching her eventually and his body

heat was gone. She opened her eyes tentatively to find that he had got to his feet and was standing on the bank of the pool, his back to her.

He was magnificently built, she thought grudgingly, her eyes roving over him. He was perfectly proportioned and well muscled. The livid whip marks crisscrossed his back from the shoulders to the buttocks. She felt slightly dizzy for a moment as she imagined the whistling of the whip, the bloody cut, his groan. She looked down hastily. She did not want to imagine. She had always been squeamish about violence. And though she no longer loved him as she had on their wedding night—this afternoon had not been love, but only lust—she still did not want him hurt or permanently scarred.

She found her eyes focusing on his right ankle. There was a deep red-and-purple scar there, too, a couple of inches thick, in an almost perfect circle about the ankle. She frowned. What—?

She opened her mouth and drew breath. But she did not ask the question. He would probably not give her an answer if she did. And she was not sure she wanted to know the answer anyway. She felt dizzy again. She was quite sure she did not want to know the answer. She looked at the heavy scar again and up his leg to his back.

She felt suddenly very frightened indeed.

She got to her feet and dressed quickly with fumbling fingers, leaving off her wet shift. Her hands trembled. He must have heard her get up. He must know what she was doing, but he did not turn. She hesitated for a moment when she had slipped on her shoes and gathered up her shift and her hat. She bit her lip. He was still standing, naked and proud and magnificent at the edge of the pool, looking away from her toward the waterfall.

She turned and half ran toward the steep path back up to the house. She climbed quickly, almost in a panic, hardly pausing to catch her breath. She looked back when she was at the top, but he was nowhere to be seen.

Who was he? she wondered as she hurried up the lawn. Who was this stranger she had married?

SEVENTEEN

"You FOUND 'ER, THEN," William Stubbs said. He clucked his tongue over his master's wet breeches, which had just landed on the dressing-room floor at his feet. He frowned darkly at the moss-stained coat and waistcoat that had been tossed carelessly over the back of a chair. "Any valet wot looks after you for any length of time, Nige, deserves a chestful of medals—or else 'e needs to 'ave 'is noggin read. 'Ow am I supposed to keep you looking like a regular gent?"

"I went swimming," Nigel told him.

"You went a-riding, too, lad," William said, tackling the coat with a brush. "And I don't mean on your 'orse with that there Coburg fellow. I just 'opes as 'ow you arsked nicely, Nige, and waited for the little filly's say-so before tumbling 'er. And there's no cause to poker up for old Stubbs. It 'as been as plain as the nose on your face that you 'aven't been getting any since your wedding night, and don't think that me and 'er maid 'aven't noticed, 'cause we 'ave. I cawn't say as I blames the little lady. You didn't force 'er, did you, Nige? If you did, I'll pop you a good one in the nose."

"You are her ladyship's self-appointed watchdog," Nigel said, his voice bored as he shrugged into a clean shirt without waiting for William's assistance. "I would not put it past you to know the answer firsthand, Will. But if you do, by my life, I will be the one popping you a good one, to use the vernacular.''

"Wotever the verny-wotever might be," William said. "Is all well, then, Nige? Is the little lady 'appy again? I 'opes she don't let you forget that you owes 'er a big favor every day for the rest of your life. But I 'opes she lets 'erself be 'appy with you, much as you don't deserve it. You are a fine figure of a man, I'll grant you that, and always was—once we got some fat back on your bones. But we was all pretty scrawny by the time we got back, wasn't we? Remember old Leddbetter? Skin and bones was all 'e was.''

"And just too stubborn to die," Nigel said. "I have strong hopes, Will, though if you expect me to discuss the state of my marriage with you, then you are to be sorely disappointed, my friend. But what of you? I remember your swearing that if you could only get your feet back on London pavements, you would never venture off them again— and that was two years and more ago. Now that you have seen me safely to my happily-ever-after, would you prefer to go back there?''

"Trying to get rid of me, are you?" his friend asked.

"Not so," Nigel assured him. "But you are restless, Will. It has not escaped my attention that you have disappeared to the village almost every night for the last few weeks. You were not even back here to attend me one night, if you will remember.''

"I remember, lad," Will Stubbs said. "I was 'elping Mrs. Dorkins move some more barrels.''

"Mrs. Dorkins?" Nigel frowned and then laughed. "Are you *courting*, Will?''

"She is the innkeeper," William explained. "A widder. And a sharper-tongued, shorter-tempered, bigger-bosomed, rounder-bottomed 'andful of woman it 'as not been my pleasure to clap eyes on this side of my deflowering wen I was thirteen, lad. Quite an 'ore *she* was.''

"And you were helping the widow move some barrels.''

Nigel laughed again. "You *are* courting, egad. Fancy yourself as a country innkeeper, do you?"

"She took me for a vagabond or a footpad," William said, chuckling. "She let fly with such abuse as would put the lowest moll to shame, Nige. Wen she found out I worked 'ere, she 'it me over the 'ead with a tankard she 'ad in 'er 'and and told me she would 'ave me arrested and 'anged up for a thieving lying tramp. But I soon showed 'er that I could talk 'er language just as good as 'er—and better. Then she found out as I was your man."

"Dear me," Nigel said. "A tender courtship indeed. *Do* you intend to be an innkeeper? Am I to lose the best valet I have ever had and the most impertinent one *any* man has ever had?"

"There is a feast to satisfy the 'ungriest of men under them petticoats," William said, holding the coat at arm's length and frowning while he examined it for stains that might have resisted his brush strokes. "Not wot I 'ave made up my mind to get under them yet, Nige. Wen she seen 'ow strong I was, she looked me over like I was a slab of meat or one of them new machines wot can do the work of ten men. And then she started acting real nice with 'Mr. Stubbs this' and 'Mr. Stubbs that.' She thinks Will Stubbs would dance to 'er tune if she was to make 'im the second Mr. Dorkins—or maybe there 'as been more than one, lad. She could wear out any normal man, wot with 'er tongue and wot she 'as under them skirts."

"We must be thankful that you are abnormal, then, Will," Nigel said. "Does she know your credentials?"

"My cree—?"

"Your past history," Nigel explained.

"None of 'er business, lad," William said. "Not till I decides to make 'er the first Mrs. Stubbs. And I 'aven't decided no such thing."

Nigel chuckled. "We are in a fair way, you and I, to settling into domestic bliss, Will," he said. "We are on the verge of living happily ever after. Who could have predicted it when we first met?"

"I once thought I could live 'appily ever after if I could

just see you filthy and 'ungry and sniveling for mercy and for your mother in that gentleman's voice of yours,'' William said cheerfully, tackling the waistcoat. "I thought it would be the 'eight of 'appiness if I could see your spirit and your body both broke and if I could 'ave an 'and in the breaking. I didn't think 'twould take long, neither.''

"And I once thought it would be happiness,'' Nigel said, "to see from your face and all the others—but especially yours, Will—that you knew it could not be done. I fully expected to die. I would have died happy knowing that *you* knew I had not been broken.''

"Old Stubbs is a stubborn cove,'' William said, looking up from his task to view his master with a fond eye. "It took me a long time to admit it, lad. The more you 'ung tough, the more determined I was to see it 'appen and to make it 'appen. You 'ad us all down on you, Nige, every last one of us. You 'ad no friends, only vicious enemies—of which number I was the viciousest. I don't know 'ow you done it.''

"I'faith, Will,'' Nigel said, "you did not break either, you know, even though you had me as a constant annoyance at your side. And I *did* have a friend eventually, a powerful friend. The best friend a man ever had—and formerly the worst enemy.''

William wagged a finger at him. "Now don't you go talking about 'appily-ever-afters, Nige,'' he said. "That little filly was badly 'urt, and I won't 'ave you imagining that giving 'er a good lusty ride between 'er legs will fool 'er into forgetting wot you done to 'er before. There is more to winning 'er little ladyship than giving 'er an 'ard working over even though I don't doubt your skills, Nige, and I knows very well that you got superior tools.''

"Thank you, egad,'' Nigel said dryly. "I had not realized that I might need more than tools and skills, Will. You have become an expert, of course, on a woman's sensibilities.''

"That there dull squire is back,'' William said.

Nigel raised his eyebrows. "Havelock?'' he said.

"The young 'un,'' William said. "The one wot 'as two

names 'cause 'e is so dull no one would remember 'im by just the one.''

"Barr-Hampton?" Nigel said. "He is *here*?"

"At that there other 'ouse," William said.

Nigel smiled. "Is he, by Jove?" he said. "I can think of one young lady who will be mightily pleased, Will. And *she* does not consider him dull, by my life."

" 'E 'as sent a note to your little filly," William said. " 'E arsked 'er to marry 'im once upon a time, you know, and 'e 'ad 'er family's blessing. You watch out for 'im, Nige."

"They are a close family," Nigel said. "Of course he has sent my wife a note. And of course he asked her to marry him—and *was refused*, Will. She married me instead, remember?"

"That was wen she thought you was one of them gods wot stands on a block of stone, Nige," William said. "The dull squire prob'ly looks an 'ole lot better to 'er than wot 'e did before you told 'er 'ow you tricked 'er. You watch 'im, lad. She's gawn awready."

Nigel raised his eyebrows once more.

"She come back all rosy-cheeked from 'er tumbling with you," William said. "Five minutes later, after 'er maid 'ad taken 'er the note, she was tripping off to that there other 'ouse as fast as 'er legs would carry 'er."

"Of course she did," Nigel said, getting to his feet after combing and bagging his own hair—he would not have it powdered until the evening, when he was to attend an assembly in the village with Cassandra. "Barr-Hampton is like a real cousin to her ladyship, Will. Like a brother, perhaps. Of course she has gone to see him."

But so soon after the strenuous climb up from the pool? he thought as he left his dressing room. So soon after her swim—and after their very energetic lovemaking? And with an assembly to prepare for in the evening? Would Barr-Hampton not be attending that with Lady Matilda and Patience? Could Cassandra not wait until then to see him?

Perhaps it was his betrothal to Patience that had been announced in the note. That news would doubtless have sent Cassandra running. But just the announcement of his return to the dower house? Would that have sent her back out in a hurry for the rather lengthy walk there?

After recovering from his strange mood following their coupling, he had felt cautiously hopeful about the future. She had very clearly consented—he had not even asked the question she had answered. And she had been quite as ravenous as he for what had ensued—and quite as satisfied at the end of it all.

She had recognized her need for him. And the pleasure she had taken from their lovemaking had ensured that it would be a recurring need. It was a start on the road to peace and contentment—and the begetting of a child.

He had certainly not needed Will's warning. He did not believe in happily-ever-afters. But he had hoped for a resumption of his marriage.

Now he felt uneasy.

Had she rushed to the dower house to confide all in Barr-Hampton? Had the past three weeks made her realize her own loneliness despite the nearness of her aunts and her cousin? Had the events of the afternoon disgusted, even frightened her? Had the note from Barr-Hampton found her at her most vulnerable?

Strangely, it appeared that she had told no one in her family the truth. The truth would come out, of course. He had confided it finally only yesterday to Kedleston's steward. But Cassandra had not wanted anyone to know. The desire for sympathy from her family had been offset, perhaps, by a reluctance to incur their pity—or their censure for so hastily accepting his suit.

If she had not, of course, she would have become dependent upon Havelock.

Now perhaps she was spilling out all her troubles, all her misery, to Barr-Hampton. Perhaps the lovemaking at the pool should not have been seen as a sign of hope. Perhaps it had been the final disaster.

Nigel decided not to follow his first instinct, which was to go after his wife to the dower house. He stayed at home instead.

• • •

Robin Barr-Hampton did not realize how very good it felt to be back on Kedleston land until he alighted from his carriage outside the dower house early on a brilliantly sunny July afternoon. All the way from London he had dreaded the coming encounter. He had wished he could go to his own home, bury himself in work there, and forget all the turbulent events of the last couple of months.

Unfortunately he had been unable to do any such thing. From a very young age his stepfather's family had been his own. He loved them as if they were his own. He felt a sense of responsibility toward them stronger than mere duty.

But throughout the journey he had dreaded arriving.

Until he stepped down from his carriage.

Someone was in the middle of the flower garden to one side of the house—someone who would have made a pretty picture under any circumstances. But to a man who had just spent three unwilling weeks in a city he hated, she was a sight for sore eyes indeed—all rustic wholesomeness and beauty. Patience with a basket of cut flowers over one arm and cutters in her free hand. Patience without hoops or frills, with an old, unadorned straw hat tipped forward over a plain cap. Patience with her lithe, coltish grace, so different from the voluptuous, bejeweled, painted beauties of London society.

Robin, disoriented by weariness from his journey and the busy weeks that had preceded it, felt that he had come home.

Patience had spotted him. At first she merely stood and stared. Then she took a few hasty steps toward him before stopping again. Finally she dropped both the cutters and the basket, caught up her skirts, and came hurtling toward him, like the hoyden he had sometimes been unkind enough to call her in former years. Except that she did not look at all like a hoyden. She looked like a delicious and delightful little piece of home.

Her face, he saw when she came closer, was lit up by surprise and wonder and welcome.

She hesitated when she was a few feet from him and would have stopped if by some strange power beyond his own volition Robin's arms had not opened to her. She rushed into them, and he lifted her off her feet and hugged her so close that he had the fanciful thought that perhaps he could fold her right into himself and keep this bright little piece of home next to his heart for the rest of his life.

He set her back on her feet and kissed her heartily on the cheek before releasing her—and remembering that his upbringing had taught him that a gentleman never greeted ladies, even his cousins—especially perhaps his not quite cousins—with anything more physical than a touch of the hand.

Patience was rosy pink all the way from the frill of her cap to the part of her bosom that was visible above her stomacher.

"Rob," she said, "what are you *doing* here?" There was a strange light in her eyes, a strange breathlessness in her voice.

"Zounds," he said, pressing a finger down between his cravat and his neck, "but 'tis good to see you again, Patience. Where is Aunt Matilda?"

Her flush deepened and she bit her lip. "Why do you need to speak with Mama?" she asked him. He had the curious impression that the light in her eyes might leap out at him and set him on fire. "And what has brought you back so soon?"

He laughed, feeling uncomfortably embarrassed. "What?" he said. "You are not glad to see me, cous?"

"I am," she told him, smiling. "Of course I am. I am always glad to see you, Rob. Why have you come?"

"I have to see Cass," he said. "Is she here by any chance?"

She did not immediately answer him. He watched, fascinated and somehow disturbed, as her eyes changed. The light died in them very gradually until she was again his sweet young cousin, Patience. For a while, he realized in retrospect, she had looked far more woman than girl. She had looked—almost beautiful.

"No," she said. "Neither is Mama. She has gone visiting with Aunt Bea. I begged to be excused. Come inside, Rob. You must be ready for some refreshments. 'Tis a hot day. Why do you need to see Cass?"

"I must send word to her that I have come," he said. "Take me to some paper and pens, cous?"

"You must remember that Lord Wroxley is there with her now, Rob," she said quietly.

Zounds! As if he could forget. He felt again all the anger, all the fear, all the panic he had lived with throughout the journey. Wroxley was with Cass at Kedleston. He was her husband.

He had to talk to her.

"Who is your fleetest-footed servant?" he asked. "Summon him for me, Patience, while I write. I must see her just as soon as possible. Without Wroxley. I would rather he did not even know I am here."

Patience, he noticed, was pale-faced and tight-lipped as she led him to the small escritoire in the morning room and indicated the writing things laid out neatly there.

"I wish now that you had not come back," she said. "I thought you had come for a different reason. How foolish of me."

She left the room before he could reply, presumably to summon a servant to deliver his note.

He was going to have to explain his return somehow to Patience and the aunts, he thought as he sat down at the desk. Patience was obviously unaware of the reason—Cass must have said nothing to them. He did not know if secrecy was still desirable or even possible. He would have to discuss the matter with her.

If only she was at home—alone.

If only she came quickly.

He dipped the quill pen in the inkwell.

"Well?" Cassandra gazed anxiously, impatiently, into Robin's face. Conveniently they were out of doors, where they could be assured of privacy. He had been strolling outside with Patience when she had come over the hill.

Patience had not waited for her arrival, but had gone running back to the house.

She willed Robin to have no news or good news. What disastrous timing for him to arrive today of all days, she had thought all the way from the house. She did not want him to come today. She did not want him bringing bad news.

She could see from the drawn look on his face and from the way his eyes did not quite meet hers that it was bad news.

"Well?"

" 'Tis not good, Cass," he said unhappily. "Where should I begin?"

"With the worst," she said quickly. "What is the worst you have discovered?"

He blanched and closed his eyes.

"He is a convicted felon," he said, his voice toneless, as if he were reciting something he had rehearsed, something he could not bear to think about, only recite by rote. "He was in transportation for seven years—in the American colonies. He has been back for two years."

She felt strangely unmoved, unsurprised. She had known it. Surely she had. There had been the whip marks as evidence. And the mark of the iron ring about his ankle, to which a chain would have been attached, which she had discovered just today. Her husband had been convicted of some crime nine years ago and taken in a chain gang to the hulks and transported to the American colonies for seven years of hard labor and harsh discipline as punishment. He had survived and come back.

For revenge.

"What was the crime?" she asked.

"Theft," he replied. "Theft by cheating at a card game. Theft of the property of other gentlemen who had attended the game but not participated in it. The property was all discovered in his rooms before he could rid himself of it, as well as the marked cards he had used. He was fortunate indeed not to hang. Though perhaps for you 'twas not so fortunate."

Cassandra closed her eyes.

"Whom did he cheat?" She was whispering. "At cards, I mean. Whom did he cheat?"

She knew the answer. Robin's long silence merely confirmed her in it. His words when they came were quite unnecessary. They hit like a lightning bolt. "Worthing," he said. "Your father, Cass."

She heard herself moan and had a sudden vivid memory of Nigel's face bobbing up before her in the pool earlier as she swam, startling her, making her laugh. Making her happy. Making her want him with a longing that was not to be denied. A mere couple of hours ago.

"And last year?" she asked. "When he played a hand with Papa again?"

"I have been able to find no evidence that he cheated, much as I have tried," Robin said, "though I daresay he did. None of the men who were at that first game, except Worthing himself, of course, was at this one. And if anyone saw Wroxley cheat, he is not saying so. There were half a dozen ruffians with Wroxley on that occasion—not gentlemen, you will understand. I have the feeling that everyone has closely buttoned lips on account of those ruffians, Cass."

"I daresay Mr. Stubbs was one of them," she said quietly.

"I beg your pardon?"

"Nothing," she said. "I have been cheated out of my land, then. And out of my freedom." She could remember the feel of him, hard and long and sleek, as she rode in obedience to his command—and her own lust—just a short while ago. She still held a physical awareness of him and his seed inside her.

"If we could only find proof of his having cheated, Cass," he said, "surely this time they would hang him."

She shuddered.

"I will go back," he said, "and tackle the witnesses one by one until I find one with the courage to defy those ruffians and speak the truth before a magistrate. I will see you free again, Cass. I will see Kedleston yours again. But in the meanwhile I fear for you."

She swallowed.

"I want you to come with me," he said, "to Willow Park. Now, today. I want you safe with Stepfather."

"I am his wife, Rob," she said. "I am his property. He could come and take me back and no one could stop him."

"I would kill him first," he said with quiet conviction.

"No." She shook her head. "You have done what I asked, Rob, and I thank you from my heart. I know 'twas not easy for you. But I do not want you to do more. 'Tis not your concern or Uncle Cyrus's or anyone's but mine. He is my husband. I will deal with the matter myself."

"How?" he asked. "You are just a woman, Cass. You need a man."

"I have one." She laughed without humor. "Go to Patience, Rob. Tell her that you had a message from someone that had to be delivered to me personally—wedding greetings, perhaps. Make something up. Be cheerful. Be glad to be back here for a day or two. Come to the assembly at the village this evening. Dance with Patience. Make her happy. Do not say a word of any of this to anyone. He is my husband. I would not have anyone know that I am married to a thief and a cheat, a convicted felon who has spent seven years of his life in transportation." She felt dizzy for a moment but fought to stay steady on her feet so that he would not see and pity her.

"I fear for you," he said again.

"Do not," she said. "I am in no danger from him, Rob. I am his prize, his ultimate triumph, his crown. No, not quite the ultimate triumph, I suppose. That will come when I bear him a son, the future Earl of Worthing. I have to be alive and healthy to do that. You do not need to fear for my safety."

He looked at her with an unhappy frown.

"Go," she told him. "Find Patience. Make my excuses. Tell her I cannot bear to be away from my beloved Nigel for one moment longer than necessary. She will believe you. She adores him—almost as much as she adores you. Go.''

Robin went after gazing at her, troubled, for a long while.

Cassandra felt curiously calm, curiously detached. She had dreaded Robin's return. But he had merely told her what she felt she must have known all along—except for the transportation. She had not suspected that, not until an hour or so ago at the pool perhaps, when she had seen his ankle.

How he must have been laughing at her there, she thought, while he had slaked his appetites on her and she had panted with unbridled passion for what he did to her.

How she hated him.

Hatred was like nausea at the back of her nostrils and throat.

Her hatred was too strong for fear. She was not afraid of him.

She turned and made her way slowly but firmly up the hill toward the lime grove.

EIGHTEEN

H<small>IS</small> WIFE HAD NEVER
looked more beautiful, Nigel thought appreciatively as they
set out for the evening's ball at the assembly rooms above
the village inn. Although it was a country affair and not a
grand ball, as her birthday celebration had been, she was
dressed magnificently in pale blue and white. Her hoops
were wide, her hair was carefully curled and powdered
white. She wore a black patch again, in the same spot next
to her mouth as she had worn it before.

She sparkled with eager vitality.

He sat opposite her in the carriage so as not to crush her
skirts—or his own silver-brocaded evening coat. They had
dined earlier with Lady Beatrice. There had been no chance
of private conversation since they were at the pool together.
Looking at her in the dusk light, dimmed further by the
interior of the carriage, his eyes stripped her of the formal
garments and clothed her again in sun-bright nakedness.
And he took her look of bright sociability and mentally
replaced it with one of dreamy-eyed passion.

Yet memories of the afternoon made him uneasy.

She looked back and locked eyes with him.

"You rested in your room after returning home this afternoon?" he asked her. "You were not to be found anywhere else in the house."

"Yes," she said. "I fell asleep."

Ah. A lie. It was unlike Cassandra to tell anything less than the bald truth.

" 'Twas a tiring afternoon," he said. "Climbing the falls, swimming, and—climbing the hill back home."

"Yes," she said.

"And a vigorous lovemaking in the midst of it all," he said.

"Yes." Her eyes had slid from his. But suddenly she pushed the bright mask back into place—it *was* a mask, he realized—and plied her fan before her smiling face. "La, 'tis scarce cooler than it was this afternoon," she said. "The assembly rooms will be stuffy. But no matter. I long to dance again. I have not danced since my birthday."

He wondered why Barr-Hampton had returned. Because of Patience? Nigel doubted it. The man did not have a romantic bone in his body.

"We will dance then, madam," he said. "The first set and at least one other."

Why had she gone running to the dower house the instant she had received word of Barr-Hampton's return? Why had she not told him of her visit? Why had she accepted so eagerly the lie he had offered her instead of admitting that she had gone to her aunt's?

"We are married, my lord." She smiled brightly at him. " 'Tis not customary for married couples to dance together."

"Because they may dance together altogether more privately and intimately every night of their lives?" he asked.

The motion of her fan was suspended and her eyes gazed back into his, wide with shock.

"Though you and I do not," he said softly. "Unless this afternoon was your invitation to me to return to your bed and resume the dance."

"No," she said hastily but quite firmly. "This afternoon was a mistake."

"A sweet error, madam," he said. "We will dance together—at least twice—at the assembly, then."

"Yes, my lord," she said with what he recognized as deliberate docility. She smiled dazzlingly.

He had changed her, he thought as the carriage rolled to a halt and he waited for the door to be opened and the steps set down. Just a little over a month ago there had been no artifice at all in Cassandra. She had been startlingly candid and quite disarmingly happy.

She looked happier than ever tonight. She smiled warmly about her, her hand in his, as he helped her down outside the inn. There were a group of children and a few adults standing at a respectful distance, admiring the show. Cassandra looked like a newly married young lady on her way to a ball, glowing with love and exuberance.

Perhaps, Nigel thought, he would be the only one present tonight to realize that she wore a mask, that the innocent gaiety with which she had enchanted her family and neighbors and suitors on the night of her birthday had been shattered on that very night and during the few days following it. Shattered forever. By him.

He wondered if he would ever see her truly happy again.

And he wondered why he was suddenly feeling guilty about the changes in her. He had shown her more kindness than cruelty in his dealings with her. And growing up was a necessity of life. Loss of innocence was an inevitable part of growing up.

He reached into a pocket and withdrew a handful of coins. He tossed them toward the children and watched as they scrambled to retrieve the treasures. His wife laughed gaily.

The coachmen and accompanying servants of the neighboring gentry enjoyed an entertainment almost as much as the gentry themselves. There was always plenty of food and liquor and congenial company with which to while away the potentially tedious hours. The village assemblies were perhaps their favorite entertainments, since they enabled the attendant servants to await the return journey in the inn taproom itself—while their masters danced and feasted in the far more handsome assembly rooms above their heads.

William Stubbs had not come with the carriage from Kedleston, but he nevertheless put in one of his frequent appearances before the evening was far advanced. He enjoyed company and he enjoyed his pint of ale. And for the first time in his life a respectable woman had set her sights on him—a buxom, not unhandsome woman who promised more in the way of carnal delight than any of the London whores with whom he had been accustomed to consort when the need was on him. And who offered him besides a more-than-respectable livelihood—not that she had made the offer in words yet. But Will Stubbs recognized a cap when it was set in his direction.

He was just not at all sure of the price that must be paid for such a tempting feast.

He also recognized Robin Barr-Hampton's coachman, the hue of whose nose suggested that the glass of ale he clutched in one fist was not his first or even his second of the evening. William plumped himself down beside the man and slapped him on the shoulder. He felt at liberty to behave with such jovial familiarity since valets were above coachmen on the social scale. It still tickled William's fancy that he was a gentleman's valet.

"Another pint for my friend 'ere, missus," he roared to Mrs. Dorkins above the noise of conversation and laughter about them. "And one for me." The scrawny, pockmarked little maid, who always looked at him in blank terror, delivered the drinks a minute later and slopped some on the table in her haste to be gone. She ducked away before anyone had a chance to cuff her. " 'Ere, lad, 'tis good to see your ugly face back 'ere again. Where you been, then?"

It was as easy as that. No subtlety was needed at all. William listened with interest as the inebriated coachman proceeded to describe the journey to London and some of the people and places his master had visited while there.

William bought him another glass of ale.

The fat had certainly splashed into the fire, he thought. That Nigel was in for it now, all right. The greatest pity, though, was that the little lady would suffer for her knowledge. William had already watched the innocence and the happiness die from her eyes. Pretty little ladies like Nigel's filly should be protected from the knowledge even of the existence of such things as treachery and hulks and transportation. They certainly ought not suddenly to find themselves married to a convict, innocent or otherwise.

William watched idly as the barmaid delivered brimming tankards to the next table. She did not duck away fast enough this time. One drunken coachman wrapped an arm about her waist and thrust his free hand down the bosom of her dress. The man next to him slipped one arm up under her skirts, exposing one thin leg. There was a roar of raucous hilarity from the other men gathered about. William pursed his lips and watched the maid's impassive face and blank eyes. Had he not been thinking soft thoughts about Nigel's wife, perhaps he would have minded his own business as he usually did these days. Doubtless the little maid had been pawed and laid a few score times. It was one of the hazards of being a female servant.

"I don't think the wench is enjoying the joke," he commented in the voice with which he had commanded an army of ruffians for years before he had been transported, and an army of convicts while he was in transportation. It was not a particularly loud voice. But it always brought attention snapping his way.

"Are you, wench?" he asked her. Her eyes registered terror when they alit on him.

"If you want to paddle or poke her," the man with a hand in her bosom was unwise enough to say—the other man had surreptitiously removed his hand from beneath her skirt, "you can wait your turn, you ugly bastard."

William rose unhurriedly to his feet. "I got only one eye, lad," he said—the "lad" was at least ten years his senior, "but I got two ears and they works pretty sharp like. You better tell me quick that they didn't 'ear wot I thought they 'eard just now, and you better get your 'and out from where it don't belong if you don't want your nose to have a bend in the middle and blood gushing out the end to spoil that fancy shirt of yours."

The coachman was not so inebriated that he failed to

realize his grave error as soon as William got to his feet and launched into prolonged speech.

"Lord," he said, feigning bored annoyance as he returned his hand to the table, "some people cannot be jested with. I beg your pardon, my friend, if you are one of them." He shrugged his shoulders and looked haughty—and uneasy.

The crisis would have passed off without significant incident. William was poised to resume his seat. But Mrs. Dorkins decided to jump into the fracas by rushing up to the little barmaid and delivering a resounding cuff to the side of her face while shrieking out the pronouncement that she was a lazy slut among other even less complimentary things. The maid toppled sideways, hit the unslapped side of her head against the table edge, and collapsed, senseless, on the floor. A few of the inn's clients banged their hands appreciatively on their tables.

"Jolly well done, Mrs. Dorkins," someone roared.

"That's the way to keep 'em under control, Mrs. Dee," someone else bellowed. "That'll learn 'er."

But Mrs. Dorkins was not amused. She turned toward William. "Here, Mr. Stubbs," she said, "haul the slut up to her room for me and lock her in, if you will be so good. I'll give her a good strapping tomorrow when I have the time and she has decided to wake up. Then I'll send her packing. I will employ only respectable help in this inn."

William got to his feet again, obedient to his lady love's call, and lifted the girl gently into his arms. She moaned but did not open her eyes. He followed Mrs. Dorkins's directions up to a tiny attic room through whose damaged ceiling he could see the sky. There was a bare and filthy mattress on the floor and one thin rag of a blanket. There was nothing else. William set the girl down on the mattress, removed her large cotton cap, and examined the lump on the side of her head with gentle fingers. She moaned and opened her eyes.

She gazed at him blankly for a few moments before the terror returned to her eyes and she began to wail.

"No, no, lass," he said, "I won't 'urt you. Nobody's not going to 'urt you."

But she put her arms up protectively before her face and rolled away from him, curling her legs up against her as she did so. She was whimpering.

William Stubbs had grown up in the tough rookeries of London. He knew all there was to know about violence and abuse. He had been a violent man himself through much of his life, though he had never hurt a woman. He got to his feet and left the room without locking the door behind him. He went back downstairs and out the back door in search of the carriage from Kedleston. He returned to the attic five minutes after leaving it, a heavy lap robe over one arm, two cushions in the other hand. He would explain to Nigel later.

The girl started wailing again at sight of him.

"No, no," he said soothingly, setting the two cushions where her head should be and spreading the lap robe over her. "Will Stubbs won't never 'arm you, and that there Mrs. Dorkins won't neither—not ever again. Wot's your name, then?"

"Sal," she said. "Please, sir. Please, sir, if you want it, I'll give it and you don't have to pay me. But don't tell her. And don't beat me. I'll do it like you want it. Just tell me what."

"'Ave you done it before, then?" William asked. He did not doubt that she had done it many times and with many partners—and never willingly.

"Yes, sir," she said. "I'll do what you tell me—whatever you want. Don't beat me."

"You put your 'ead on the pillows, Sal," he said, "and you 'ave a good sleep. I'm not going to beat you or do it to you. Nobody's going to beat you or shout at you. None of those men down there's going to try doing it to you ever again unless you wants it and tells 'im so. Will Stubbs is going to pertect you."

She moved her head onto the cushions and stared up at him, the terror muted to simple fright. "You don't want to do it to me?" she asked in some amazement.

He looked at the thin body, the pale, pockmarked face, the lank dirty hair, the frightened eyes, and knew that he had enjoyed whores with far less physical appeal.

"I wants you to stop being frightened, Sal," he said. "I wants you to go to sleep. A lass like you will find a fine strapping lad one day and be 'appy with 'im. Big old ugly Will Stubbs won't never 'arm you."

She surprised him then before she closed her eyes. She smiled at him.

Once upon a time, he thought—but then the same held true of countless women among whom he had grown up— she must have been a pretty little girl. With pretty brown eyes. A long time ago.

So much for the countryside being kinder and healthier and more respectable and innocent than the town, he thought.

And so much for his incipient dream of becoming a village innkeeper.

In three weeks of marriage the bloom had not worn off the happiness of the Countess of Worthing, her friends and neighbors concluded as she danced her way through the evening. Quite the contrary, in fact. She sparkled and talked and laughed a great deal. Her eyes strayed to her husband frequently through the evening, even when she was not dancing with him—and she danced with him three separate times.

And in three weeks of marriage Viscount Wroxley's fascination with his bride had not dimmed. His eyes, lazily heavy-lidded, watched her all evening, though he conversed with his new neighbors and even danced with a few of their wives and daughters.

Cassandra was well aware of the impression they made, an impression that for her part was quite deliberate. She did not want her friends to know that Kedleston had belonged to Viscount Wroxley long before he married her. She did not want the humiliation of her situation to become general knowledge. And she certainly did not want them to know . . .

It was a strange, unreal evening, the familiarity of her surroundings and companions and the bright gaiety of her demeanor quite at variance with the horror that hammered at her mind and her heart.

He had cheated Papa and robbed both Papa and his friends. He had been caught and tried and convicted. He had been chained to other convicts and sent in one of those dreadful, inhuman hulks—she had once heard that only the strongest of men survived them to begin the sentence assigned them—sent to a penal colony in America. There he had been kept in chains and set to hard labor and savagely whipped over and over again—did that mean he had continued rebellious, depraved, recalcitrant? He had survived and returned to England to complete what he had begun before he went. He had taken everything from Papa, but this time he had surrounded himself with ruffians in order to intimidate both Papa and any other potential witnesses to the truth of what had happened.

And then he had masqueraded as a respectable gentleman and come to Kedleston to woo and marry her. Like the green girl she was, she had fallen into the trap with a smile on her lips and a sparkle in her eyes. She had given him her heart and her body, too, even before the wedding. In retrospect it seemed somewhat surprising that he had not laughed at her after that night beneath the tree and ordered her off his land while buttoning his breeches.

But he had not done that. He had married her instead and so sentenced her to a lifetime of imprisonment. His own had lasted for only seven years.

She did not dance with Robin, though he asked her. But she did converse with him and Patience and Aunt Matilda for several minutes after the opening set of dances and made a great show of surprise—Nigel was at her elbow at the time—at seeing Robin so soon returned.

"And to the dower house rather than Kedleston, Rob?" she said archly, looking significantly at Patience.

But Patience was looking back at her with puzzled and hurt eyes and Cassandra felt instantly contrite. Sooner or later, she thought, she must take Patience into her confidence. They always had been close friends. Besides, the truth—all of it—was going to become common knowledge at some time or other, she supposed. Even in remote Somersetshire one could not expect such spectacular truths to remain hidden forever.

"Of course to the dower house, Cassandra," Lady Matilda said with equal archness. She smiled almost coquettishly at Nigel. "Poor Robin would feel decidedly *de trop* at Kedleston. He would feel obliged to spend all his time with Bea."

"I trust," Nigel said, addressing Robin, "that you found all in order on your own estate? You must have been happy to be home again for a short while."

"Yes, indeed," Robin said stiffly. "I would have been happy to stay there, but with my stepfather at Willow Park, I felt concern for Aunt Matilda and Patience and rode over to see that all was well with them."

"A paragon of a nephew and cousin, i'faith," Nigel said, and made Patience an elegant bow while he favored her with his most charming smile. "May I beg the favor of the next set, madam?"

" 'Tis mine," Robin said quickly.

"But 'tis not, Rob," Patience told him. "I danced the first with you."

Robin, unlike herself, Cassandra thought, found it difficult to dissemble. He looked like thunder while his young cousin was led away by a man who had spent seven years in transportation for theft.

"Zounds," he muttered, "he had better stay away from Patience if he knows what is good for him."

Cassandra plied her fan, smiled dazzlingly, and engaged her aunt in conversation.

It was an interminable evening, with the constant necessity of juggling her inward horror with outward artifice. And with constant memories intruding of the afternoon at the pool and of the fact that even now, even despite the horror, she could not keep her eyes—and something more than just her eyes—from appreciating his beauty and his almost overpowering sexual appeal. She had to keep reminding herself that beneath the fashionable and immaculate evening clothes were the whip-scarred back, the iron-scarred ankle, and the cheating, lying, scheming heart.

She wished as she was handed into the carriage at the end of the evening that Aunt Bea had not been kept at home by a slight cold. She settled back against the cushions and closed her eyes. She would indulge in one more pretense this evening. She would pretend to be sleepy.

"And so, my dear," her husband's pleasant voice said from the seat opposite after the door had been closed and the carriage had lurched into motion, "we have to decide how to proceed now that you know everything."

Her eyes snapped open and she was surprised that she could see him quite clearly despite the darkness. Beyond the windows a bright moon and stars made the night almost as light as day.

"Your champion has been busy on your behalf," he said. "You must be proud of him."

She was sorry then that she had not confronted him as soon as she returned home that afternoon. She did not know why she had not done so or why she had lied about sleeping in her room after returning from the pool. She did not know why she had allowed Robin to lie at the assembly. She did not like being put on the defensive. *She* had done nothing wrong, except behave like a fool.

"I have always been proud of Robin," she said. "Now more than ever. He was eager to go home again. He hates London. But he was willing to postpone going home and to spend as long as necessary in London merely to oblige me."

"Perhaps," he said, "you are sorry you did not marry him, Cassandra."

"He deserves better," she said.

She could see that he was smiling at her. "And he would not be able to satisfy you," he said.

She set her lips in a tight line as she remembered just

how obvious she had made her satisfaction while she had knelt astride him by the pool that afternoon.

"I suppose," she said, "it was my father who brought the charges against you nine years ago." He must have been only nineteen or twenty, she thought suddenly.

"Of course." He was still smiling.

"It was not wise," she said, "to cheat at cards and to steal money and jewels all on the same evening and in the same place."

"Not wise at all," he agreed.

"Or to leave the evidence in your rooms to be found by your accusers," she said.

"That was the most foolish part of all," he said. "But I was a very young and very foolish man, my love."

"And so you were convicted," she said, "and went away vowing revenge against my father."

"Ah yes," he said. " 'Twas the thought that sustained me, madam—to destroy him as he had tried to destroy me."

"And to have me to crown your triumph," she said, trying to keep the bitterness out of her voice.

"A bright crown indeed," he said. " 'Tis intensely satisfying, madam, to know that all of those who turned on me nine years ago and very firmly cut my acquaintance two years ago must now acknowledge the fact that I am owner of Kedleston and husband of the Countess of Worthing. I would say I have effectively thumbed my nose at them. Would you not agree?"

She looked at him with compressed lips. She hoped he could see her as clearly as she could him. His face was alternately in light and darkness as the carriage moved among the trees of the driveway. She wanted him to see her scorn.

"You were a viscount," she said. "I would have thought it possible for you to avoid common justice."

"They managed to conceal my true identity," he said, "until I was safely away from English soil. No one listens to a common felon when he claims to be a titled member of the nobility. Not even when his speech reveals him to be a gentleman—or a man with aspirations to gentility.''

"Is that what happened to you?'' she asked. But she did not want to know, she thought even as she spoke the words. She did not want to give him the satisfaction of knowing her curious at all. Besides, she knew all she needed to know.

He merely smiled.

"How did you persuade him to play cards with you again?'' she asked. "He must have recognized you.''

"In seven years,'' he said, "I acquired certain persuasive powers.''

She shivered. Her father had been coerced into playing with him and had then been cheated out of Kedleston.

"And so you achieved what you had failed to do years before,'' she said. "You cheated your way to property and fortune.''

"And to an aristocratic wife, my love,'' he said. "You must not forget that. Except that I have never cheated in my life—or stolen anything either.''

"I believe,'' she said, looking into his eyes with what she hoped again was visible scorn—the carriage was past the trees and moonlight streamed through the windows, " 'tis common for felons to protest their innocence of the crimes for which they have been convicted.''

"Ah yes, by my life,'' he said, " 'tis true, madam. There was scarce a man of my acquaintance during my seven years in the colonies who was not as innocent as a newborn lamb.'' He laughed softly. "Yet we were all in chains and all paying dearly for the crimes we did not commit.''

She turned her head to look from the window, feeling a wave of nausea. If she stretched her eyes wide, she thought foolishly, would she finally wake up from this bizarre nightmare? Would she find herself napping on her birthday, before any of the celebrations had begun? Before any guests had arrived?

"We will go to the library on our return to the house," he said. "We have some matters to settle."

"I am tired," she said. "I am going to bed."

"Ah, but you are my wife," he said in his pleasant, soft voice, "and you promised me obedience, madam."

She drew a slow breath and turned to look at him.

"We will go to the library," he said. He was still smiling.

NINETEEN

WILLIAM STUBBS HAD SUM-
moned Nigel outside the door of the assembly rooms during
the ball to confirm what both of them had begun to suspect—that Barr-Hampton had been to London on a mission
and that he had spoken with at least some of the right people. Or the wrong people, depending upon how one viewed
the matter.

It was the truth Nigel least wanted Cassandra to know.
Though he supposed it had been inevitable she find out
sooner or later. Better sooner, perhaps.

He had not pressed the full story on her and she had not
picked up on his single protestation of innocence. She
would not believe it anyway. No one ever had—not even
his own family. And she was her father's daughter.

It did not matter. He had learned to live with injustice.
He had hardened his heart to scorn and distrust and hatred.
Sometimes he thought his heart must be made of ice—
except that ice could melt. Stone, then.

She would not believe him. He would not even try to
convince her. But there were certain things that needed to
be said—tonight. He did not choose to wait until morning,
to give them both a whole night in which to brood upon
the situation.

"Have a seat," he said to his wife when the library door

had closed behind them—he had given instructions that the servants need stay up no longer.

"I prefer to stand," she said, walking toward the window. Her chin was up, her face pale and set.

He admired her courage. It must have been terrifying for her, to say the least, to discover this afternoon just whom she had married. Yet she showed no visible fear, and was even prepared to defy him. But he had brought her here to settle a few things between them.

"Have a seat, madam," he said more quietly.

She paused, clearly considering further defiance, and then crossed to the chair before the fireplace that he had indicated and seated herself straight-backed on it. She raised her eyes to look directly into his.

"There are certain realities of our lives, Cassandra," he said, "and neither of us can dive back into the past even by as much as a day to change any of them. I had a quarrel with your father, which he appeared to win quite spectacularly, though I had the last word. Kedleston is mine. You are my wife. And you, my lady, are married to the man who had that last word. You are married to a man once convicted of a felony and punished for it in such a way that he will carry the marks to his grave. Those are the realities."

"Yes," she said. "And so is the fact that you have a wife who will hate and despise you for the rest of your life, my lord."

"Our marriage must continue, Cassandra, regardless of your sentiments toward me," he said. "We have proved during the past weeks that we work well together as business partners and that we can be civil and even more than just civil when we are together in other people's company. We have proved—on our wedding night and again this afternoon—that we work well together in more intimate ways, too."

"That was lust," she said, her cheeks flushing.

"Lust is a part of marriage," he said. "A healthy part. Lust bonds two people with pleasure. Lust begets children."

She had no answer for him except to thrust out her chin and refuse to drop her eyes from his.

"We will share a bed from this night on," he said.

Her lip curled with scorn. "Why would I even have expected you to be honorable in this?" she said. "You promised that you would not come to me except by invitation. Foolishly I gave that invitation this afternoon. I am not giving it now. But that does not matter, does it? The master has spoken and issued his command."

He remembered the smiling, vibrantly happy young woman who had come to him in the crimson salon that first day and invited him to her ball and to stay at what she believed to be her home. This was the change he had wrought in her, he thought, looking at her bitter, contemptuous face. And did he really intend to force her?

"I promised you the privacy of your rooms, madam," he said. "That promise will stand. I did not promise you the privacy of your body. That is mine—as my body is yours. We will exercise our right to each other in my bed."

"My only hope is to keep to my rooms for the rest of my life, then," she said. "Will you allow me to retire to my dressing room to get ready for you, my lord? Will you trust me to come out again?" She half smiled, though there was no amusement in her eyes.

"Yes," he said, and she raised her eyebrows. "Because you fear me, Cassandra. You fear what I would do when you eventually came out."

"Why would I fear you?" She laughed disdainfully.

"Because of the scars on my body," he said, "and the constant reminder they will be to you of what was happening in my life when they were acquired. Because you will always wonder how I survived such inhuman conditions and such prolonged violence. Because you will suspect that I did it by being tough and inhuman and violent myself. Because you will believe that such experiences killed all finer feelings in me and fitted me well for disciplining a defiant wife."

For a moment the fear that he knew must have been concealed behind her social image all evening was visible in her eyes. But only for a moment. He would never have suspected on that first day, he thought, that behind the smiles and the gaiety and the beauty of the woman he had come to meet and to woo were firmness of character and an implacable courage.

"How *did* you survive?" Her voice had become a whisper.

"By being too stubborn to die," he said. "By having a goal to be accomplished after my return—one whose achievement I constantly reminded myself, even when it was most difficult to believe, was more desirable than dying."

She looked steadily into his eyes, her own unreadable. But the fear was gone, or at least it had been brought very firmly under control.

He walked closer to her chair and held out a hand for hers. "Come," he said.

She looked at his hand but did not immediately place her own in it. "I will not come," she said, "because you command it, my lord. I would not enjoy being beaten or otherwise—disciplined. But I believe I would risk your violence rather than go always in fear of what you might do to me. I choose not to be controlled by fear."

Ah. She had called his bluff. He would have no choice now but to take hold of her and carry her, against her will, to his own rooms. He did not believe he would be able to rape her when he got her there, though.

"I will come," she said, "because there is sense in some of what you say. There are realities. And the future will perhaps be a long one. I am appalled when I think of whom exactly I have married. But I married you freely despite my family's warnings against being seduced by charm when I knew almost nothing about you. I have nowhere else to go and I doubt you would allow me to go there even if there were. I will be your wife, then, my lord, in every way, and the mother of your children. But not because you command it or because I fear you. Because I *choose* to do it." She had looked back into his eyes as she spoke and held them now as she placed her hand in his and rose to her feet.

He had never admired her more. He had wrought all sorts of negative things in her life, but he had also brought out in her a strength of character that he doubted anyone had suspected her capable of. He had destroyed her innocence, but he had not destroyed *her*.

He bowed over her hand and touched his lips to the back of it. He chose not to notice, when he raised his head, that her eyes were bright with unshed tears. He did not want to know what painful reality had caused them.

It seemed to Cassandra that she had slept for only a few minutes before she woke up again. But the first signs of dawn—a slight lightening at the window, a loud chorus of birdsong—told her that she must have slept for a couple of hours.

His bed was more comfortable than hers and smelled of him—a mixture of his cologne, his shaving soap, *him*. The bed was warm from their shared body heat.

She thought of how treacherously her body had responded to his lovemaking. She had expected a fierce, masterly possession. She had expected passion, lust. She had steeled herself to be cool, dutiful, dispassionate, a wife making the best of a bad situation.

He had caressed her with warm, gentle hands. He had relaxed her rather than aroused her. Then he had moved over her and come inside her long before she had expected it, and had proceeded to work in her slowly, unhurriedly, keeping the rhythm unbroken for so long that she had marveled at his control. He had worked in her until she was slick and silky with wetness and there was sound to the rhythm as well as feeling.

She had not shared his control. She had been unable to keep herself steeled against gentleness and exquisite sweetness. She had lost herself in pleasure. She had not even realized that she was moaning with each exhaled breath until he had shushed her with whispers and silenced her with openmouthed, almost languid kisses.

He had won again, she had thought afterward, with what might have been bitterness if she had had the energy to feel

bitter. He had proved to her that it was not always lust.
There had been no great excitement, no shattering climax.
It had been the most wonderful bedding yet.

She had slept—though she had intended asking coolly if
she might return to her own room, the performance of her
chief marital duty completed for the night.

But now she had woken and almost instantly she understood why. He was thrashing and muttering and moaning
on the bed beside her, deep in the throes of some nightmare.
She touched his arm to find it on fire and wet with perspiration and rigid with tension.

And then she cried out in alarm as he surged over to pin
her beneath his rigidly hard body, and his hands circled her
neck like an iron band. She lay beneath him, unable to
breathe and mindless with terror while he went very still
and gradually—very gradually—began to relax as he
panted for breath. He rolled suddenly off her and off the
bed and went to stand at the window, his hands braced
against the frame on either side of his head. She was very
aware of his scarred back, his marked ankle.

"Out!" he said to her so harshly that she scarcely recognized his voice. "Get out of here."

She sat up on the bed, feeling her heart like a trapped
bird fluttering wildly against her rib cage and in her throat
and her ears and her temples.

"Out!" he said again, even more harshly.

" 'Twas a dream," she said. "You were having a nightmare."

"I might have killed you," he said. "Never *ever* touch
me when you see me like that, Cassandra. It happens often.
Never touch me. Leave me while 'tis safe to do so. Leave
me now."

She looked longingly at the door to his dressing room—
and her own. If she left now, instinct told her, he would
reverse last night's decision. He would allow this aspect of
their marriage to lapse again. She would have a large measure of freedom again. And if he had nightmares, then there
was some justice in the world.

"No," she said. "I will not go."

He rounded on her then, his face a mask of distorting passions. "Madam," he said, "my commands are not negotiable. Especially the ones that are given for your own safety. Leave me."

"No," she said, and swallowed to try to stop her voice from shaking. "What is it you remember? Will it help to speak of it?"

He laughed harshly. "Do you think I would sully your ears with even the mildest of the memories?" he asked her, though it was clearly not a question he expected answered. "You are a woman, a *lady*. You are my wife."

"They are merely memories," she said. "They are in the past, and the past, as you said downstairs in the library, cannot be changed. It need not be allowed any power over the present, though. The present is now and there is the future like an empty land or an unwritten book ahead of you. Come back to bed."

She wondered why she was trying to comfort him. She should revel in the fact that he still suffered and perhaps always would. He deserved to suffer. And indeed he might yet get to relive the past in all its nightmarish reality if she allowed Robin to go back to London to try to find the proof he had been unable to find this first time. He might even hang, viscount or no viscount.

"If you will not leave me, then I must leave you," he said. "I shall go riding. 'Tis dawn already."

"Come back to bed." She held out her arms to him.

She could see his indecision, his longing to accept even a small measure of comfort.

"Please," she whispered. She was capitulating to the enemy. She knew that. But she knew, too, that she must live with him for the rest of a lifetime. And unwillingly she remembered with what deep love she had married him.

He closed his eyes and she could see him shudder. "You are a fool, madam," he said. "Promise me you will never again touch me while I am asleep and dreaming."

"I promise," she said.

He came to her then, his body cold and noticeably trembling, and she took him into her arms and wriggled upward on the bed until she had his head pillowed on her bosom. She rested her cheek against the top of his head and massaged his scalp through his thick, long hair with her fingertips.

"This is the present," she told him softly. "The past is over. For both of us. 'Tis over. There are just the present and the future." She forced herself to say the one remaining word, her eyes closed, her arms holding his warming, relaxing body close to her own. "Nigel."

"What am I going to do with you, Cassandra?" he asked.

Neither of them answered the question. He slept. She stared at the ever-lightening window, wondering how she could possibly love the man who had so deceived her, the man who had wreaked such a wicked revenge on her father that he had probably killed him in the process.

Except that I have never cheated in my life—or stolen anything either.

It would be better not to believe him, not to begin to hope. It would be far better just to accept reality and learn to live with it.

But she knew that she wished to know more. That she *must* know more.

Nigel had gone out and was likely to be gone for several hours. He had given Lady Beatrice his escort to the village, riding beside her carriage, and was then to continue on his way to a distant tenant's cottage to discuss some matter concerning the drainage project. Cassandra was always content to let him handle that business alone.

She waited almost half an hour to be sure that he would not return for some forgotten item before summoning his valet to the morning room.

William Stubbs looked disconcertingly large and rough and ugly standing just inside the doors. He also looked thoroughly out of place and uncomfortable.

"Good morning, Mr. Stubbs," Cassandra said.

He ducked his head. "Morning, m'lady," he said, and frowned. "Did that Nige go out and ferget to tell you—"

"His lordship told me where he was going, I thank you," she said. She had risen from the escritoire and the letter she had been writing and had come to stand facing him, some little distance away. She was no longer afraid of him, despite his fierce looks. She had *chosen* not to be afraid of him. "Were you a prisoner with my husband?"

He was instantly wary. "Wot does 'e say?" he asked.

"I have not discussed the matter with Lord Wroxley," she said. "I am asking you. Were you in transportation together, Mr. Stubbs?"

"We was," he admitted. "We was chained next to each other. We was close companions, so to speak, for seven years."

"And always close friends?" she asked.

His lips twitched for a moment with what she imagined might be amusement. "Not always, m'lady," he said. "We was mortal enemies for a year and more."

"Why?" she asked him.

"Look at me, little lady," he said, spreading his huge hands to his sides. "And look at 'im. It was a joke they played on the two of us, putting us together like that. 'E thought I was—now wot was that fancy word 'e always used? Unc—"

"Uncouth?" Cassandra suggested.

"The very same." William indulged in one of his fearsome grins. "An' I thought 'e was a pretty boy wot would break if I snapped my fingers at 'im. I thought the fun would be over too fast like to be real fun at all."

"But it was not?" she asked.

"We *all* thought 'e was a pretty boy," William said. "Even them guards. Especially them. We all tried to break 'im, but none of us ever could. We was finally let free of our chain, 'im and me, so that I could give 'im wot for and 'e could blubber for mercy. But 'e wouldn't even fight me. 'E just laughed at me. I means just that, m'lady. 'E laughed while I thrashed 'im within a inch of 'is life—'e says now 'e thought it was more like 'alf an inch. And then when 'e finally woke up and I tried to give 'im a drop of water, 'e knocked the cup out of my 'and and spit in my face. I put 'im right back to sleep with one pop, but I knowed then that 'e were a man to respect, a man to follow. We all knowed it except them guards. They kept on trying.''

"Do you have the scars of whips on your back as he does, Mr. Stubbs?" she asked.

"Some," he said. "But not like 'im, m'lady. They wasn't content with just cutting 'im with the whips while 'e worked like they done with the rest of us. They knowed 'e was a gentleman and a cut above them. They kept saying 'e done things 'e 'adn't done and then they could tie 'im to them tripods and make us all watch while they flayed the flesh off 'im. I begs your pardon, m'lady. I oughtn't to of told you that. 'E would flay me with 'is tongue if 'e knowed I was saying this. They never could make 'im scream or beg 'em to stop. 'E always laughed wen they was finished and cut 'im free before chaining 'im to me again—if 'e was still awake to laugh, that was.''

"Mr. Stubbs." She was almost whispering. "Was he guilty?"

" 'Course 'e—" William Stubbs stopped abruptly. "Wot 'as 'e said, m'lady? You got to arsk 'im. It was between 'im and your pa. 'Tis not for me to say wot I don't know about 'cause I didn't know 'im till we was chained together.''

"Thank you," she said. "Thank you for being willing to talk to me, Mr. Stubbs.''

He nodded kindly, like a parent to a child. "You loves 'im," he said. "Will Stubbs understands, little lady. You don't 'ave to worry about loving 'im. 'E won't 'urt you nor never let you down. Old Stubbs will always pertect you, but 'e don't need to do it wen there is Nige to do it so much better.''

But she had stiffened. "Thank you, Mr. Stubbs," she said. "That will be all.''

He did not turn immediately to leave as she expected him to do. He regarded her speculatively out of his one working eye, his head cocked to one side. "I would arsk something of you, m'lady, if I might," he said.

"What is it?" she asked him.

"There is a young woman," he said, "wot is being treated bad in 'er place of employment. She is 'alf-starved and froze and beaten by 'er mistress even though she does 'er dooties to the best of 'er abilities. And she is treated bad by the men wot she 'as to serve in ways I cannot describe to no lady."

Cassandra's eyes had widened. "Close to here?" she asked. "There is a woman so treated close to Kedleston?"

"She is a barmaid at the inn in the village," William said. "I 'ave talked to Mrs. Dorkins wot runs the establishment, my lady, and I knows that I 'ave her afeared to lay a strap to the wench like she intended to do today. But tomorrow she will likely forget. And them there men, once they gets into their cups, will think they can paw and poke—they will think they can misuse the maid if Will isn't there to stop them. I was wondering, my lady—"

But Cassandra's eyes were flashing. "I can assure you that Mrs. Dorkins will not be in business at the inn for much longer, Mr. Stubbs," she said, "if it is true that she mistreats her employees and allows her customers to—to *use* her barmaids unlawfully. Are you speaking of Sally? I arranged that employment for her to get her away from her father. Her father—" She could feel herself flushing hotly.

"I understands," William Stubbs said gently, and Cassandra had no doubt at all that he did. "I was wondering if you could see your way to employing one more maid than is needed 'ere, m'lady. The 'ousekeeper told me this morning wen I arsked that there was no opening."

"I shall have a word with her," Cassandra promised him. "Sally will be here before the day is out."

William set his head to one side again. "You are a kind little lady," he said. "I told Nige you was gentle and innocent and 'e 'ad better treat you right and pertect you from the wicked world. But you already knows something about wickedness and tries to pertect them wot is weaker than yourself. That Nige is a lucky man."

Cassandra was too startled to reply to his impertinence. But there was something else that must be said before she attempted yet again to dismiss her husband's valet.

"Mr. Stubbs," she asked, "what is your interest in Sally?"

For a moment she was afraid of him again. For a moment he was dangerously angry, though the closing of his huge fists at his sides was the only outer sign. " 'Tis a fair question," he admitted after that moment had passed. "I 'ad a sister wot was dead of overuse and disease at fourteen, m'lady. I couldn't 'elp 'er. I was only eight. I *can* 'elp Sal. I promised 'er that I would pertect 'er and I will."

Cassandra smiled at him. It was hard to believe that she was having this conversation with her husband's strange valet—another convicted felon. It was even harder to realize that she had come to trust him.

"Then finally Sally will be safe," she said. "Thank you, Mr. Stubbs. That will be all."

He left then after bobbing her another of his awkward bows.

The world was indeed full of wickedness, she thought with a sigh. She had congratulated herself less than a year ago on having rescued Sally from an unthinkably dreadful fate. She had always thought Mrs. Dorkins to be a strict but fair employer. But if Mr. Stubbs was right—and she did not doubt that he was—the woman was not only cruel but failed to discourage her customers from making free with Sally's unwilling favors. Cassandra shuddered.

And even those on the side of the law—those who administered the law—were not always to be trusted. Nigel had acquired those ghastly whip welts entirely because his gentleman's ways had offended his guards.

William Stubbs, just before he stopped himself, had been about to say that her husband had been innocent of the charges against him.

Not that he could know the truth of it any more than she did, of course. He had not known Nigel at the time. He had admitted that himself.

Except that I have never cheated in my life—or stolen anything either.

She could not forget those words, though he had not gone on to try to convince her of their truth.

If he *was* innocent—

If he was innocent, then what exactly had happened? What had happened before his arrest and transportation? What had happened after his return?

Oh yes, she thought, she had to know more. But there was no point in asking him. She would have to discover the truth in other ways.

But in the meantime there was Sally to be rescued from yet another situation of abuse. She turned to the bell rope to summon her housekeeper.

TWENTY

CONTENTMENT, WHEN IT came, Nigel found over the next few weeks, was just a little anticlimactic. He had not expected happiness or anything as trite as a happily-ever-after. All he had dreamed of were peace and security and contentment. He had all three.

Something was missing.

Nothing was lacking. All the improvements to the farms that he and Cassandra had agreed upon had been set in motion. The renovations inside the house were to begin before winter set in. Their neighbors were welcoming and amiable and eager to both issue and accept social invitations. Lady Beatrice always had interesting conversation. Lady Matilda was warmly affectionate. Patience was sweet and quiet—and unhappy. Robin Barr-Hampton had returned home.

Will Stubbs had no immediate plans to desert and return to town, though it seemed that his courtship of the Widow Dorkins had turned sour. Indeed, the woman was trying to sell the inn so that she might move to a nearby village to keep house for a prosperous brother who had begged her to come. That at least was the story she told to cover her dignity—Cassandra and Will told a different story. And it seemed that Kedleston had acquired a new scullery maid.

Nigel watched in some amusement the steady transfor-

mation of his friend from coarse, dangerous ruffian and
bully to the decent man who must always have lodged deep
inside him. But the circumstances of his life before his
transportation had made it impossible for the real man to
develop. Only the tough and the ruthless survived in London's rookeries. Now Will was friend to an aristocrat, devoted servant to a countess, champion of an abused,
downtrodden little serving girl, and prospective innkeeper.
He was considering trying to take over the inn himself.

And Cassandra?

She seemed as full of energy and almost as happy as she
had appeared on her birthday, when he had first met her.
She ran the household with the ease of long experience and
carried out her duties in the neighborhood in the same way.
She treated their servants with courtesy and compassion,
their neighbors with amiability and charm, her aunts and
her cousin with warm affection. When he consulted her on
estate business, she discussed the matter at hand with sense
and understanding—she had continued her self-imposed
education, he came to realize. She was determined to know
all about the running of the estate that no longer belonged
to her.

She had not invited him back to her rooms. But she came
to his bed each night without having to be commanded to
do so and was an apparently willing participant in what he
did with her there. Certainly he found that when he woke
during the nights she was almost invariably curled up
against him, though the nights were warm and shared body
heat was not necessary to comfort. And she never protested
even by as much as a quiet passivity when he needed and
took her a second and even a third time in one night. He
needed her more than once when the nightmares threatened.
He had somehow trained himself to wake up before he
became too deeply immersed in their darkness.

She was life and warmth and comfort to him. He did not
believe he could face a night without her any longer.

She asked no more questions about the past. Sometimes
he thought that it might have been better after all to tell
her everything. Had she asked again, perhaps he would

have. Or perhaps not. She would probably not have believed him. She had loved her father. Telling her and having her call him a liar would put a further strain upon their marriage.

It was best left alone. Best forgotten about. It was obviously what she considered best, too.

All his plans had come to a successful conclusion. There were peace and security and contentment to be enjoyed for the rest of his life.

It all seemed somehow anticlimactic.

Something was missing.

Cassandra was restless—and oppressed by her own selfishness. She had sent Robin back to London. Oh, she was not being quite fair to herself, she knew. He had wanted to go back. Perhaps even if she had said no he would have gone anyway. But she had said yes. She had been desperate for more information.

After a few weeks she was desperate no longer. She still wanted to know. She still *needed* to know. But she should have contented herself, she thought, with the conviction that sooner or later Nigel would tell her everything himself. It seemed somehow disloyal to go behind his back as she was doing.

It *was* disloyal.

She loved him. If she really thought about her feelings, she could perhaps despise herself for loving a man who had wreaked so much havoc in her life and her father's, a man who had spent seven years in a penal colony plotting revenge, a man who had tricked and deceived her and still held his secrets to himself.

But love, she knew, was not a rational thing.

If none of the truth had come out, if he had withheld it all from her, even the essential fact about the ownership of Kedleston, she would still be as blissfully in love with him as she had been on her wedding day. And her liking and respect for him would have deepened tenfold. He showed every sign of taking his responsibilities at Kedleston seriously. He carried out the social obligations that a man unaccustomed to country living might well find tedious. He was already well liked. Even Aunt Bea had passed judgment on him by describing him to Cassandra as a sensible young man with a head on his shoulders even if he did pay a little too much attention to his appearance.

If she could ignore the past and forget about all the mysteries surrounding him, she could perhaps be happy, Cassandra thought. He was an interesting companion and a wonderful lover. And if his dress and his behavior were more immaculate and more formal than was customary in the country, they were also powerfully enticing. Just seeing him could make her heart beat faster. Just hearing his voice could make her breathless.

Sometimes she despised herself. Was she so weak that a skilled villain could make a willing slave of her? Or was she merely a realist who understood that life was a long process and that people did grow and sometimes even changed? He was her husband after all and would be the father of her children. She rather suspected that he would be that latter before their marriage was ten months old.

She was restless and watched the driveway for Robin's returning carriage, though she did not know if he would come directly to Kedleston or go to the dower house.

He went to the dower house and walked over to Kedleston with Patience one afternoon while Cassandra and her aunt were entertaining some visiting ladies. Nigel was in the drawing room with them, too, charming everyone—something he always accomplished with great ease. He raised his eyebrows when Robin entered the drawing room behind Patience, and pursed his lips and looked amused. But Cassandra scarcely noticed his reaction—or Patience's almost fearful happiness.

"Rob." She crossed the room to him and took his arm while Nigel was kissing Patience's hand and seating her beside Lady Beatrice. "How lovely to see you again so soon. La, 'tis quite like having you as a close neighbor. Have you seen your mama and Uncle Cyrus lately? How do they do?"

"I have not seen them, Cass," he said gravely. "I came

over to the dower house to see how Aunt Matilda and Patience did.'' He turned away from her to bow his greetings to the other ladies and accepted a cup of tea while he politely discussed the weather and the health of some mutual acquaintances.

"One wonders, by my life," Nigel said, his hand on the handle of his quizzing glass while he looked lazily at Patience, "at the devotion to duty a mere cousin is capable of displaying. Pardon me—I meant a *step*cousin, of course."

But Patience only blushed and looked down into her cup.

Fifteen minutes passed before the departure of some of the guests gave Cassandra the excuse to draw Robin aside to stroll in the tiered flower garden with her. The remaining two guests had come to see Aunt Bea more than her anyway and were quite contented to have Nigel entertain them.

"Well?" she said, and had an alarming feeling of déjà vu. She had greeted him in the same way the last time he had returned, on that afternoon when she had rushed over to the dower house. Pray God he did not bring news as bad this time.

"I am sorry, Cass," he said. "I have no good news for you."

Her heart sank and she closed her eyes briefly. What would she do now? Confront Nigel with the fact that he had cheated Papa out of his land? Find out if she could institute legal proceedings to recover her property? Would that involve criminal proceedings? Would he be tried again? Convicted again? Was cheating enough to constitute theft? Was it a capital offense? Would they hang a viscount?

The thoughts and the questions all flashed through her mind within a few seconds.

She did not want to know.

"Has he treated you very badly?" Robin was asking. "Has he ever beaten you, Cass? But there is no way of helping you now. Egad, I wish there were something I could do for you."

Her mind registered what he was saying. "You cannot

help me?'' she said. ''What do you mean, Rob? Is there
nothing with which we can make an appeal to a magistrate?''

''I am afraid not.'' He shook his head sadly and apolo-
getically.

Hope returned with a painful lurching of the heart.

''Exactly what have you discovered?'' she asked.

''Nothing,'' he said, ''except more of what I discovered
before. No one will admit to having seen Wroxley cheat at
that card game. And one of them—a baronet, Cass, a respected man—was so annoyed that I would return to ask
the same questions again that he insisted on writing you a
letter.'' He patted the pocket of his coat. ''And that lawyer,
Croft, merely confirmed what I knew must be true. The
transfer was indeed made and quite legally. Kedleston belongs to Wroxley. Uncle signed everything.''

''Nigel did not cheat, then?'' Cassandra had released her
hold on his arm and stood very still on the path between
two tiers of flowers. '' 'Twas a fair game? 'Twas merely
that Papa wagered recklessly and lost?'' She bit her upper
lip hard. She could no longer see Robin, though he stood
not six feet in front of her.

''I am sorry, Cass,'' he said quietly. ''I wish you would
not cry. You cannot imagine how rotten I feel. I feel as if
I had let you down. There is still the question, of course,
of why Uncle agreed to play against Wroxley. They were
the only two players in a roomful of men in a private res-
idence.''

But she was not prepared to worry about that question.
Not yet. It had been a fair game. There had been no cheating involved. Papa had lost and Nigel had won. Nigel had
somehow persuaded Papa to play against him, of course,
and his motive had been pure revenge. But he had done it
fairly. Papa might as easily have won—she wondered
briefly *what* he would have won.

''I am sorry, Cass.'' Robin sounded genuinely miserable.
''I would challenge the scoundrel to meet me if I thought
I had any right to do so. But I do not. Not unless he has

been beating you. And even then—egad, cous, he has the right to do even that if he wishes.''

She fumbled through the slit opening in her petticoats for the handkerchief she kept in the pocket taped about her waist. She smiled at him as she dried her tears.

''He has never beaten me, Rob,'' she said, ''and never will. He has been good to me. And I cry because I am glad. I so feared you would bring news that would force me to take action against him. You cannot know how much I have hoped for just the news you have brought.''

''Egad,'' he said, ''you *love* him, Cass? Even knowing who and what he is?''

''He is my husband,'' she said.

Robin drew a deep breath, held it, and let it out rather noisily. ''He cheated and robbed nine years ago, Cass,'' he said. ''He spent seven years among villains. Such an experience usually brutalizes men rather than reforms them. And somehow he persuaded Uncle to play that game. I still think he must have cheated. 'Tis all that makes sense.''

''I do not care what happened nine years ago,'' she said. ''And I care about those seven years only because he still suffers all their horrors in his nightmares. I do not know how he persuaded Papa to play him again, but I will believe that 'twas a fair game. And he has not been brutalized, Rob. Neither has Mr. Stubbs.''

''Stubbs?'' he said.

''Never mind.'' She blew her nose and put her handkerchief away. She had remembered something. ''You have a letter for me?''

He drew it out of his pocket and set it in her hand. ''Aunt Matilda has already engaged me to escort her and Patience to various entertainments for the next three days,'' he said. ''After that I will go home, Cass. I hope you are right about Wroxley. I hope he is a reformed man. There is not a great deal I can do for you if he is not, I am afraid. But if you ever need me—''

She smiled and touched his arm as she stood on her toes and kissed him on the cheek. ''I will not,'' she said. ''I will no longer be a burden on you, Rob, just a loving cousin. You must stop taking the burdens of your extended family on your shoulders and attend to your own personal happiness. I shall look forward to seeing you marry soon and settling to domestic bliss.''

''Egad, Cass,'' he said, ''I am not even considering marriage yet.''

''There is no one special to tempt you to change your mind?'' she asked.

He laughed. ''Who?'' he said. ''I have not even been home or in one place for any length of time for longer than I care to remember. 'Twill be a few more years yet before I think of looking about me for a suitable helpmate.''

Ah, poor Patience, Cassandra thought. But she would undoubtedly do more harm than good by mentioning her name and trying to play matchmaker. She said nothing.

''I will leave you to read your letter,'' he said. '' 'Tis time I escorted Patience back home. She is to go to town for a Season next spring. She will take well there—she is growing prettier. Have you noticed? I just hope she can find someone to appreciate her good nature and her tender heart. She *cried* when I left two weeks ago and she cried again when I arrived back earlier today. Can you believe such tender sensibilities?''

''She is fond of you, Rob,'' Cassandra told him.

He nodded. ''Something else,'' he said, frowning. ''I almost forgot. That fellow Croft said he needed to see you in person. He asked me how long 'twas since Uncle's death and said he was alarmed to realize that more than a year had passed. He asked if you were in town and when I said no he said that he must come down here, then. He would not tell me what his business was. But it appears that you are to expect him, Cass. He seemed quite adamant about the land transfer being legal, though. I would not be too hopeful about that if I were you.'' He looked at her with level eyes. ''But you would not hope that any longer, would you?''

''No,'' she said.

He nodded and turned back to the house, leaving her alone with her letter and her questions.

Why did her father's lawyer—not even the lawyer he had used to conduct most of his business—need to speak to her so badly that he would come all the way from London to Somersetshire? Would not a letter do? He might have sent one with Robin.

But she had a letter to read—from a baronet, a respected man, who had been present during that card game. She was a little afraid to open it. What if he was willing to admit things in a letter to her that he had denied to Robin? What if—

She broke the seal and unfolded the sheet of parchment.

Sir Isaac Snow wished to inform Viscountess Wroxley, the Countess of Worthing, that he was present at the card game in which the late Earl of Worthing wagered and lost his estate to Viscount Wroxley. He had been invited to attend by the earl himself as one of six men to stand his friends and vouch for the fairness of the game. Viscount Wroxley had had the same number of men with him, though Sir Isaac found himself unable to assure her ladyship that any of them had been gentlemen.

He was able to assure her ladyship, though, that there was no foul play during the course of the game. Sir Isaac had some little experience with cards and knew all the tricks by which an unfair advantage might be gained. He had provided the cards himself and had been the last to inspect them before the game began. He was confident in asserting that there had been no cheating. The wagers had been made in advance—Worthing's Kedleston against Wroxley's promise to leave Britain within two days of the game and to stay away for the rest of his life with no further communication with anyone living in the Isles.

Viscount Wroxley had fairly won the game. The wager was fairly and legally paid two days later when Sir Isaac had gone with the late Earl of Worthing to witness the transaction.

He hoped that this letter would finally satisfy her ladyship about the circumstances that had brought her late father and her husband into unhappy rivalry. He hoped with all due respect not to be called upon again to receive the very persistent Mr. Barr-Hampton on her behalf. He remained her obedient servant.

Cassandra folded the paper and held it against her mouth while she closed her eyes very tightly.

There had been no cheating. It was very clear that her father had chosen Sir Isaac as one of his six witnesses because the man was an expert at cheating. If there had been the slightest suggestion of anything suspicious, he would have spotted it. There had been nothing.

Nigel had not cheated.

There was the whole question, of course, as Robin had reminded her, of what had happened nine years ago. There had been evidence enough on that occasion—marked cards and stolen property all discovered in Nigel's rooms. He had been convicted of the crimes and punished for them. But that was a long time ago. Last year he had not cheated or stolen.

Except that I have never cheated in my life—or stolen anything either.

Did he realize that she *knew* about that stolen property being discovered in his rooms? Evidence like that did not lie. But he obviously did.

And then she felt rather than heard movement behind her and turned her head sharply.

He was standing at the end of the path on the same tier as the one she stood on. He was all gray-and-white elegance, she thought, all mask and mystery. He was looking at her from beneath half-lowered eyelids. She had come to recognize the look as one that combined an apparent laziness with an actual closeness of scrutiny. It was an enigma, a paradox, like everything else about him.

Sometimes she felt that she knew him very well indeed. She knew him with the intimacy of a marriage partner.

Sometimes she knew that she did not know him at all. Sometimes he was an almost frightening stranger.

She slid the letter through the slit in her petticoat, where it joined her rather damp handkerchief in her pocket.

• • •

Obviously she had *not* put the past behind her and accepted the reality of the present. He had assumed at first that it was Patience who had brought Barr-Hampton back this time, but it had not taken him long to realize that he was wrong.

Barr-Hampton had escorted Patience home. Lady Beatrice was seeing the remaining guests on their way. Nigel went to find Cassandra. She was standing alone in the middle of the flower garden outside the ballroom. As soon as she saw him, her head turned back sharply over her shoulder, and she slipped something beneath her petticoats. He strolled toward her.

" 'Twould seem," he said, "that the courtship between Patience and Barr-Hampton progresses satisfactorily. Do you believe 'tis why he returned?"

"Yes." She was looking in the direction of his chin. "Yes, I suppose so."

He set one hand beneath her chin and lifted it until her eyes met his. "Why did he return?" he asked gently.

"He feels a responsibility for Aunt Matilda and Patience," she said.

"Cassandra." He set the pad of his thumb against her lips. "Why did he return?"

"You did not cheat." She was whispering. She closed her eyes. "I have a letter from one of the witnesses. You did not cheat." She opened her eyes again. "How did you persuade him to play against you and make such a wager?"

He drew breath and let it out slowly before replying. "By making the alternative seem very unattractive indeed to him," he said.

"Unattractive." She looked blankly at him. "You threatened him?"

With doing to Worthing exactly what Worthing had once done to him. And with allowing Worthing to be uncomfortably aware of the band of ruffians with which Nigel had surrounded himself, courtesy of Will Stubbs. Would he have carried through on the threats if Worthing had chosen to call his bluff? Nigel wondered. He was not at all sure. But he thought he would have. The memories of his own

ordeal had still been very fresh in his mind. He had still
been habitually limping from the shackles and the chain
that were no longer attached to his leg.

"He agreed to my challenge," he said.

"If you had lost," she asked him, "would you have gone
away never to return?"

"Yes," he said. "But I had no intention of losing, Cassandra. I had always had unusual skill with cards. I waited
almost a whole year after my return from the colonies before making the challenge in order that I might sharpen my
skills again. I won a fortune during that year."

"Did you also," she asked him, "challenge the other
men from whom you stole nine years ago?"

"Only Worthing," he told her. "Only your father."

"Why?" She looked very steadily into his eyes, his hand
no longer beneath her chin.

She could no longer be protected, he thought. There was
no further point in hiding the truth. "I have never cheated
or stolen in my life," he said. "Someone planted marked
cards in my rooms and costly jewels that various gentlemen
had worn the evening I played your father and won a large
sum. If I had been guilty, I would hardly have been fool
enough to leave the evidence in the first place that would
be searched. But no one at my trial could see the logic of
that argument. I was framed, Cassandra."

Her face, which had been calm, almost cold, was showing signs of distress. He clasped his hands at his back and
looked at her through half-closed eyelids.

"Why did you think Papa was the guilty one?" she
asked him.

"He was the one who accused me," he said, "or so I
assume. Certainly he was the one who did not know me or
answer my pleas for help after I had been arrested and
dragged away. He had been my friend—or so I thought.
He had led me into a trap."

"But why?" There was torment in her eyes now. "You
were just a *boy*, Nigel, young enough to be his son. Why
would he do something so heinous to you? Tell me."

That was the part he had never fully understood. He had

never been able to think of a motive strong enough for such a ghastly betrayal.

"Because I had won over two thousand pounds from him, I suppose," he said.

"He sold you unjustly into seven years of—of hell for two thousand pounds?" she said. "No. Papa would not do that. Papa was—he was my *father*. I *loved* him."

"You have a choice to make, madam," he said, feeling a chill creep about his heart. "You can believe in your father or you can believe in me. You have insisted on making this moment of choice inevitable. You might have left the past where it belonged and made something workable of the present. I have not played the tyrant with you, and by marrying you I ensured that you keep the home and the way of life to which you are accustomed. 'Tis your fault if you have walked into the nightmare."

"Yes," she said, lifting her chin. "And you make it easy to choose, my lord. I loved my father. I do not love you. Perhaps I should trust my heart. I believe I will do so. I do not *believe* that Papa could have dealt with you so."

"So be it, madam." He made her a formal bow and turned to stride back along the terrace—alone.

He had trained himself to be alone—always alone—to keep the ice about his heart, numbing him to pain. After the nightmare of his trial and conviction—worse than nightmare because he had known that there was no possibility of waking up—and the terrifying realization that he had no friends or allies or even protectors in the new life to which he had been sentenced, not even his jailers and guards, he had set about ensuring his survival and sanity in the only way he could think of. Physically he had not been strong enough—or free enough—to fight either his fellow convicts or the guards. And so he had set about achieving a mental and emotional superiority, laughing—literally laughing—at the worst they could throw at him. He had made things worse for himself by such an attitude, of course, but the extra kicks and whippings had been almost worth enduring. Because slowly it had worked. He had gained the supremacy.

But in so doing he had isolated himself and learned to live entirely alone even while chained permanently to other human beings and watched constantly by still others. Even Will's unexpected but much-valued friendship had not made much difference to his essential isolation.

Only Cassandra had worked her way through the ice and through his aloneness to curl warmly about his heart. He had not defended himself against her because he had not realized until this very moment what was happening—what had happened. He had grown long accustomed to steeling himself against violence and hatred. He had never had need to build defenses against tenderness and sympathy.

Until she had shown him both.

And like the fool he was he had fallen into yet another trap.

She believed in her father, not in him. She loved her father, not him. She had chosen her dead father over her live husband.

He felt rather as if he were shattering into a few million pieces. He must find some place where he could somehow piece himself back together again.

He kept on walking when he came to the front doors. He hurried past the house and across the rose garden. He half ran down the back of the hill, jumping recklessly from stone to stone. He threw off his clothes even as he crossed the clearing, letting them drop where they landed.

He dived naked into the pool.

TWENTY-ONE

It was a strange irony, Cassandra thought, that her discovery of what she had wanted desperately to believe—Nigel's innocence of cheating in that final game—had also wrecked her very fragile marriage.

She had rejoiced when he had come to her in the flower garden and they had begun to talk—finally to talk—about what had happened between him and her father. She had quite earnestly wanted to get to the bottom of it all, to understand exactly what had happened and why. Especially why.

She had believed Nigel. But she had believed equally in her father. He could *not* have done what he had seemed to do, or if he had, he must have felt that he had good reason. He could not have played such a ghastly trick on a new friend, a man young enough to be his son, merely because of two thousand pounds. He had drained a great deal of money from the estate during the previous few years, but he had not drained it dry. The loss of two thousand pounds would not have made him that desperate—or that evil.

She had wanted Nigel to help her solve the problem or at least to admit that there *was* a problem. But he had turned on her with all the cold arrogance she had known him capable of, though she had never witnessed it with quite such force before—and had offered her a choice. She had been distraught enough to allow herself to be goaded. She need not have allowed it. She could have looked back at him scornfully and told him not to be so foolish. It was not a simple matter of choosing between him and her father.

Deeply hurt and bewildered, she had spoken to hurt. And she had succeeded—she had hurt herself more deeply yet. She had ruined any chance that their marriage might settle down into something workable.

She had not touched anything human in him, of course. He had gone striding off without a word and had stayed away until after she and Aunt Bea had finished their dinner. He had not returned until it was almost dark, and then he had closeted himself in the library instead of coming to the drawing room. She had waited later to be summoned to his bed—she had never waited before, but she was too proud to go uninvited.

The invitation—the command—had not come.

And the following day, though everything was normal on the surface and to any outside observer, he was like marble. Or granite. Whichever was the hardest and coldest. Strangely, to Cassandra he seemed more handsome, more elegant, more charming than ever. But something—some essential part of him, the part that was *himself*—seemed to have gone, whether vanished into space or hidden deep within she did not know.

He had shut her out of his life. It had been that simple for him. But then he, of course, had not been foolish as she had been. He had not mistaken amity and sexual pleasure for that deeper emotion called love. She would have been better served to have held to the conviction she had had even up to her birthday that there was no such thing as romantic love.

Except that her feelings about him, with the exception of the few days surrounding her wedding, could hardly be described as romantic. They could not be so lightly dismissed.

She had lost him.

And she had lost her father.

She wished she had never allowed curiosity to prompt her into setting a whole string of events into motion. She would have been far better off accepting the present for what it had been and leaving the past where it belonged.

Except that she could not quite believe that either.

Mr. Herbert Croft, the lawyer, arrived at Kedleston the next day. He arrived late in the morning, when Cassandra and Nigel were in the study with their steward, discussing the renovations to some of the laborers' cottages that were about to begin. Mr. Croft was shown into the room after the butler had come ahead of him to announce his arrival.

"Croft?" Nigel said after the lawyer had made his bow. "This is a, ah, pleasant surprise." He was looking arrogantly indolent, Cassandra noticed, and was therefore at his most alert.

"Mr. Croft," she said, "I am pleased to make your acquaintance. You were my father's lawyer on occasion, I understand?"

"I had that honor, my lady," he said. "I did ask to speak alone with you on a matter of some importance."

Nigel could not be expected to resist that pointed setdown, of course. He already had his quizzing glass to his eye.

"In a moment I will escort her ladyship to the crimson salon and summon her maid," he said. "There you may speak with her in private to your heart's content, Croft. You will give us the pleasure of your company at meals for the rest of the day and stay at Kedleston at least for tonight, I take it?"

"Yes, please do, Mr. Croft," Cassandra said, smiling at him.

"And I shall avail myself of your professional advice later today, if I may—in private," Nigel said, before bowing to her and extending an arm for her hand.

She wondered, as she had several times during the past two days, what business her father's former lawyer could have with her that would bring him all the way from London. Had there been something wrong with the transfer of

Kedleston from her father to Nigel? Some loophole? Yet he had assured Robin that all had been legal. What else could there be?

"Well, sir?" she asked him when she was finally alone and seated with him—apart from her maid, who sat quietly in the darkest corner of the room. "What may I do for you?"

He cleared his throat. " 'Tis a strange commission, my lady," he said, "and one I am late executing. I very humbly beg your pardon on that score. My head clerk, who was with me and with my esteemed father before me for longer than forty years, died suddenly just six months ago, and his successor has not yet learned to be so reliable in prodding my memory on matters that are not constantly before my attention."

Cassandra raised her eyebrows in polite inquiry.

"I ought to have called upon you exactly one year after the sad passing of his lordship, the Earl of Worthing, your dear father," Mr. Croft continued. "The delay of two months is unpardonable. I beg your forgiveness, my lady," he added illogically.

"Of course," she said. "My father left something with you, Mr. Croft? Something that he could not leave with his usual lawyer?"

"Not his lordship, my lady," he said. He reached into a deep pocket of his rather ill-fitting frock coat and drew out a flat package. "And not with me. This was left with my grandfather by yours. No, that is not right, either. 'Twas left by his late lordship's grandfather. He would have been your great-grandfather, my lady, the Earl of Worthing."

Cassandra frowned and then laughed. "Am I to understand, sir," she said, "that my great-grandfather left a package with your grandfather with instructions that it was to be put into my hands one year to the day after the death of my father? 'Tis something of a bizarre story."

" 'Twas not nearly so simple as that, my lady," Mr. Croft said, taking a large handkerchief from the same pocket that had held the package and discreetly dabbing at his forehead with it. "And though I would agree with you that 'tis a somewhat unusual story, 'tis not my place to judge, but merely to carry out instructions.''

Cassandra waited for him to explain.

''The Earl of Worthing, your great-grandfather,'' he said after putting the handkerchief away again, ''delivered three identical packages to my grandfather, my lady. The first was to be put into the hands of his son, your grandfather, one year after his death. We were to instruct his lordship that he might act upon or not act upon the information he would find within, according to his conscience. But he was to know that destroying the package would not solve the problem since two more identical packages were in existence, to be delivered with similar instructions to his son one year after his death and to *his* son after that. That is you, as it happens, my lady—not a son, but a daughter who has nonetheless succeeded to the title.''

What strange game had her great-grandfather been playing? Cassandra wondered, eyeing the package, which was still in the lawyer's hand.

''The package was to be presented to the current earl for three generations,'' he said. ''You are the last who will receive it, my lady. I am to tell you that you may act or not act upon its contents, according to your conscience. And yours will be the final decision. If you destroy the package, the information it contains will be gone forever.''

Cassandra felt strangely frightened.

''Do *you* know the contents, Mr. Croft?'' she asked.

''No, my lady,'' he said. ''But I am to make myself available to follow any instructions you may have for me. Your father before you and his father before him had none. But I shall stay in the area for a week. I have taken a room at the village inn for that long, though I shall be honored to avail myself of his lordship's kind invitation for tonight.''

He got to his feet and handed her the package.

It burned in her hand—a strange, fanciful impression given undoubtedly, she told herself, by the fact that it had been in his pocket and his hand and was warm from his touch.

Curiosity burned in her, too. But curiosity had been her enemy during the past two months. And her life certainly needed no further complication. But what could be so frightening about a package that had been prepared by an ancestor she had not even known? For a moment she could not remember even which one he had been. But yes, she could. He had been one of the twins—the set that had preceded her father and Uncle Cyrus.

She was the last of three generations of earls to receive the package. If she decided to destroy it, it would be gone forever. She might act upon it or not act, *according to her conscience*. It sounded like something more serious than a foolish game.

But foolishly her first instinct was to rush from the room, find one in which a fire was burning—there would be a *huge* fire in the kitchen—and toss the package into the heart of it. She did not want to know. Whatever it was, she did not want to know.

But she did, of course. Curiosity had always been one of the strongest of temptations to her.

"Thank you, Mr. Croft," she said, getting to her feet, her hands closing about the package. "My maid will see that you are conducted to a guest chamber and informed about mealtimes."

She took her package to the rose garden. There was a chill breeze blowing even though the sky was partly blue. But the high hedges offered some shelter, and she sat with her back to the wind.

She shivered anyway.

"You have completed your business with her ladyship to your mutual satisfaction, Croft?" Nigel asked, nodding dismissal to his wife's maid and taking his guest in the direction of the library.

"Yes, indeed, my lord, I thank you," the lawyer said. But being a lawyer, of course, he offered no unnecessary information.

Barr-Hampton would, of course, have called upon Croft just to assure himself—and Cassandra—that all had indeed been done up right and tight. Nigel wondered if the man's coming to Kedleston had been her suggestion or Barr-Hampton's. What remained to be said that the lawyer had agreed to come?

Croft's arrival had taken Nigel by surprise. But he had been jolted even more by the fact that he had been thinking about the man for the past day and a half and had almost made up his mind to make a journey to London to consult with him. Yet here he was at Kedleston.

"I understand," he said after a footman had closed the library doors behind them, "that her ladyship's relative Mr. Robin Barr-Hampton has paid at least one call upon you within the past month or so?"

The lawyer visibly stiffened. "With all due respect, my lord," he said, " 'tis against my policy to discuss any of my clients with a third party."

Ah. A man of honesty and integrity. Nigel had always suspected so. He raised his eyebrows and fingered the handle of his quizzing glass.

"I'faith," he said, "you are right, sir. Will you discuss Kedleston with me, then? 'Tis a property that is unentailed, though it was the principal seat of the Earls of Worthing for several centuries. But it is now mine. There is no disputing that fact?"

"None whatsoever, my lord," the lawyer assured him, accepting the glass of port his host handed him and taking the offered seat. "Your lawyer and I drew up the papers and they were duly signed. I pride myself on not making errors in such matters. The property is yours."

"But it *is* unentailed," Nigel said softly.

"Assuredly, my lord," Mr. Croft agreed.

"Then," Nigel said, "we have business to discuss, sir."

The handwriting was old and difficult to read. But not impossible.

"I have something on my conscience," a former Earl of Worthing—her great-grandfather—had written, "something that I have persuaded myself is not a matter for conscience at all. I have reasoned with myself that I was right

to agree to what was done, that I owed it to my father, to
my family, to my dependents. But conscience is not so
easily appeased. I have decided, then, to involve you, my
descendants for three generations, in my decision. Was I
right? Am I right? What happened is not irreversible. For
three generations—longer, perhaps—the evidence will be
fresh enough to be used to effect change. Any of the three
of you may decide that I was wrong—and act or not act
upon what your conscience tells you. If all three of you
decide as I have decided, then there will be an end of the
matter. An ancient wrong, which I have decided was no
wrong at all, will be allowed to pass into history. You, the
third of my descendants, my great-grandson, may destroy
this letter and the contents of the small accompanying package, and all will be gone. Only you will have the original
in that package. My son and my grandson will have mere
copies. So perhaps the gravest responsibility rests upon
your shoulders, my great-grandson. I can only hope that
they are broad.''

Cassandra, intrigued, had almost forgotten that she was
reading something that concerned her personally. But now
a gust of wind chilled her and she shivered again. She
should have brought a shawl outside with her.

She could still destroy the letter without reading further.
A foolish thought, of course. She read on.

''I was born a twin, only half an hour separating my birth
from that of my brother—my elder brother, or so everyone
believed. He was brought up as the heir. There was a closeness between us, as there almost always is between identical twins, but we were very different from each other.
Graham was rebellious, wild, irresponsible. He went off on
his Grand Tour at the age of twenty and stories soon
reached our father of his wild excesses and debaucheries.
Finally word came that he had married imprudently and
was bringing his bride home.

''That was when I was injured in a riding accident and
the attending physician made the remarkable discovery that
I had a large diamond-shaped mole on my right hip—as
had the elder of the twins he had delivered more than

twenty-one years before. He swore to this in writing, as did the retired housekeeper of Kedleston, who was present at my birth and my brother's. The midwife, who had also attended, was found and confirmed what the other two had sworn to. An attorney took her statement, since she was illiterate, and she signed it with her mark.

"I was the elder son and heir. Within the year I was the sixth Earl of Worthing. My brother returned and raged to no avail. He disappeared with his bride and I have never heard of or from him since.

"This is the hard part to write, my descendants. And perhaps I should not do so but keep to myself what only I know now among the living. But I will keep to my decision to let this be a family decision—a family across the generations. It was all a lie, you see. My father had favored my steadiness of character over my brother's wildness for years before Graham's marriage drove him into instituting a plan that had long tempted him. I was persuaded into agreeing and the three witnesses were easily bribed.

"I married well and believe myself to have been a good husband, a good father, and a good landlord and master. I have been upright and sober in character, a devout servant of God, and a responsible leader of men.

"Did I do right? My reason tells me that I did, although I lost a dear brother, a part of myself, perhaps. My conscience tells me that I did right—or maybe I tell my conscience that I did. Only one person who knew the truth could not be persuaded or bribed to deny it. Our old nurse, who lived fifteen miles from Kedleston when my father died, came soon afterward, bringing with her a blue silk ribbon with 'Graham' written on it. She had tied it herself about the wrist of the first twin to be born, and my mother had written my brother's name on the ribbon a few hours later. I took the ribbon, affecting deep concern, promising to investigate further and put right the wrong. The ribbon is in the package that accompanies this letter. The first two packages, remember, contain copies of the ribbon and not the original.

"Am I really the Earl of Worthing? Are you? You must

each decide for yourself. This letter and the ribbon will surely be powerful evidence against your claim if you choose to make them public. The choice is yours. I leave it with you and your conscience.''

There was an official seal beside the signature.

Cassandra let the letter fall to her lap and left the little package unwrapped. She looked about her at the roses and the clipped hedges and the trees beyond. A message from the grave, she thought. The strangest of messages.

At first she did not realize the full implications of what she had read. In reality she was not the Countess of Worthing. That much was clear. The title belonged to some distant cousin—if there was such a person—she knew nothing about. It had been stolen from the rightful heir years and years ago.

It was strange—she even smiled. Just two months ago she had thought herself to be the Countess of Worthing, owner of Kedleston. She had thought herself to be a favored being indeed. But first Kedleston had been taken away from her, and now her title. In reality she was a nobody and always had been.

Except, of course, that only she knew this truth. She was the only living person. And she was the last of those to receive this confession. If she destroyed it, no one else would ever know. She would remain Countess of Worthing. Her son would be the earl after her time. She unconsciously spread one hand over her abdomen.

At least Kedleston was safe, she thought. It was no longer hers to lose. It had already been lost by her father. Except—

Except that *it had not been her father's to lose.*

If the title belonged to someone else, then so did Kedleston. Neither the title nor Kedleston was hers—or Nigel's either.

Unless . . . Unless by his will her great-great-grandfather had specifically stated that the estate was to go to her great-grandfather. It was unentailed. But that fact had been ignored down the centuries—until her father had discovered it and wagered Kedleston in a card game. In all probability that will had merely stated that Kedleston was to be the new earl's.

If she made public the contents of this letter, Cassandra thought, instead of destroying it, then she would lose her title and Nigel would lose Kedleston. He had already lost his own property. They would have nothing.

Aunt Bea would lose her home. Aunt Matilda and Patience would lose theirs.

She felt panic well up behind her nostrils like nausea.

But how foolish she was being. This letter had been written years ago about events that had happened even longer ago—eighty years ago. If she were to show it to any lawyer, she would be laughed at. No one would take it seriously. Even if the original fraud was accepted as the truth, everyone would agree that too much time had passed to make any change possible.

It was a hair-raising story that she might tell her grandchildren and laugh over.

A man had disinherited his own son through lies and bribes, and the son who had benefited had connived at the fraud. She was a direct descendant of that man and his son. She, too, had benefited from their dishonesty. And could continue to benefit if she so chose.

She would be foolish to do otherwise. It was far too late to put right such an ancient wrong. It had not been *her* wrong. It was none of her business.

What *had* that will said about Kedleston?

Her thoughts whirled into incoherence. She needed to talk to someone. But there was no one to talk to. This was *her* concern, hers alone.

Well, she thought with bitter humor, she had wanted independence. She had wanted to make her own decisions. She had wanted to take on responsibilities that only men usually bore. Now she had more than her share.

"Bad news, madam?" Nigel's voice behind her was pleasant and cool—and so unexpected that she crumpled the old letter and swung around, her eyes wide with dismay.

"No," she said. "What are you doing here?"

He raised his eyebrows. "I'faith, madam," he said, "I

am walking here. In my own rose garden. Are you well?''

She was very far from well. It was not his rose garden. Or hers. They had nothing. They had nowhere. She lurched to her feet and ran, stopping only when she came to the archway farthest from the house—and bent over to vomit ignominiously and quite wretchedly against the hedge. Nigel and her letter and her package had been left behind.

A cool hand came against her brow as she heaved.

"Zounds, Cassandra," he said, "it *was* bad news. May I help, my dear? Will you share it with me?"

"No!" she said sharply, and fumbled for her handkerchief, but his own much larger one appeared in her hand before she could locate hers. "There is no bad news. Why would there be?" She held the handkerchief against her mouth and closed her eyes for a moment.

"Are you with child?" he asked quietly.

"Yes." She could hear the petulance in her voice. "Of course I am. 'Tis what happens in marriage, I understand."

Until two days ago she had pictured herself telling him when they were warm and quiet together in his bed or down at the pool perhaps. What a horrid moment for them to share such precious knowledge.

Their child would have no inheritance. Nothing at all.

She had opened her eyes, but her vision darkened about the outer edges.

She must have lost several minutes after that happened, she thought, her mind in a strange confusion. She was being carried up the stairs inside the house, in Nigel's very strong arms. She turned her face into his shoulder.

"My letter," she wailed. No one must see it. He must not read it.

" 'Tis safe in my pocket," he said, "as well as the package that was with it."

"Give them to me," she said.

He had paused outside the door to her room. But he did not open it, perhaps remembering his promise. He walked on to his own room, carried her inside, and set her down gently on the bed.

"Give me the letter," she demanded, sitting up in a panic.

He handed it to her with the package. His eyes, she noticed, behind the heavy lids, were as cold as ice. "No, madam," he said, "I have not read it or any part of it. I will not pry into your secrets as you have pried into mine. I shall send your maid up to tend to you."

"Nigel—" she said when he was half out the door.

He looked back at her with raised eyebrows, but she could not think of a single thing to say.

"I am pleased with you, madam," he said. "You will, of course, be very careful of your health in the coming months. Kedleston needs an heir. So does the earldom." He continued on his way out of the room.

She lay back against the pillows and closed her eyes. She had imagined joy—shared joy because of what they had done together in the intimacy of married love.

He had married her and bred her and she was now in the process of performing her main function as his wife.

There was nothing else.

There was *nothing* else. Not unless—

Oh yes, she thought, she was going to destroy that letter. It was only foolishness. Utter foolishness. She was going to destroy the letter and be happy for the rest of her life.

She laughed. And then cried. She was doing both when her maid arrived, wide-eyed and timid at having to come into the master's bedchamber.

TWENTY-TWO

ROBIN QUARRELED WITH Patience before leaving the dower house and Kedleston for home. They had never come remotely near to quarreling before. She had always been all quiet, docile sweetness. And he had always treated her with amiable indulgence.

They were walking back to the dower house together on the morning of his planned departure, after he had paid a farewell call at Kedleston. Patience had gone with him and had been very serious and silent, as she had been ever since his return from London.

"Zounds," he said, finally breaking the silence, "you are quite right to be out of spirits, cous. She has made a disastrous marriage and is desperately unhappy and there is little I can do to help her."

That was when the quarrel started. Patience did not make the expected sympathetic reply.

"I am glad you are going away," she said, her voice trembling. "You must stay away this time, Rob. You must not come back. 'Twould be dishonorable to come back."

"*What?*" He looked down at the top of her straw hat, his brows snapping together in a frown.

"Cass is married," she said. "And I think it a wonderful marriage. Lord Wroxley is charming and exceedingly fond of Cass, and she adores him. Anyone can see that. Except you, of course.''

''Why me, *of course*?'' he asked irritably.

''Because you wanted to marry her yourself,'' she said, ''and she refused you. She married Lord Wroxley instead. You should have gone home after the wedding as Uncle Cyrus and your mama did. You should not have stayed here and kept coming back even after you did leave. 'Tis not right.''

''Zounds!'' he exclaimed. ''You think I am sulking. You think I am moping because she refused me.''

''I did not expect it of you,'' she said. ''I thought you had more pride and more of a sense of honor.''

Robin stopped walking and lifted his three-cornered hat to scratch his head before replacing the hat. Cassandra had not given him leave to tell anyone the truth about Wroxley.

''I offered because she needed protection,'' he said, ''and because Stepfather and Mama and the aunts were worried about her. I am not sulking, Patience. Cass means nothing to me. She means no more to me than you do. She is just my cousin.''

''Except that she is not,'' Patience said, sounding uncharacteristically cross. ''And I am not. We are not your cousins, Rob. We are nothing to you and you are nothing to us. Less than nothing.''

He raised his eyebrows. She had lifted her head to glare at him, the color high in her cheeks, her eyes bright with unshed tears.

''Leave her alone,'' she said, before he could think of a reply to such a magnificent setdown. ''Leave her alone to be happy with Lord Wroxley. Go away and never come back.''

Robin's feelings were deeply hurt. He had one half brother and two half sisters, years younger than himself. He had his stepfather's two nieces as cousins. He had never had anyone quite his own, it seemed. But he had always thought of Cassandra and Patience as very nearly his own. They had felt almost like his sisters. Yet now he was being told that he was less than nothing to them.

"You do not know the half of it, Patience," he said. "Have you wondered why Cass has been so pale lately?"

"I *know* the reason," she said. "Cass told me herself. She is increasing. Of course she is pale. And happy. So is Lord Wroxley. Did you not notice how he jumped up to pour a second cup of tea for Aunt Bea himself a little while ago so that Cass would not have to get to her feet? 'Tis you who do not know the half of it, Rob—because you choose not to see what is before your eyes."

He spared a thought of sympathy for Cassandra. But his own feelings were wounded, and he was angry. He had done so much for his female cousins, and see how he had been rewarded. Cass had turned down his perfectly decent, self-sacrificing offer for a common felon, and Patience had dismissed him from her life and told him he meant less than nothing to her.

"You will be pleased to know that I will be on the road within half an hour," he said, with all the dignity he could muster. "I will not be back. I wish you happiness, Patience. Doubtless you will find a suitable husband when you go to London next spring. 'Tis to be hoped he is someone who will mean *something* to you. 'Tis a good thing that I mean nothing since 'tis unlikely our paths will cross again."

"I am very happy to hear it," Patience said, sounding anything but.

On which mutually satisfying note they proceeded down the hill to the dower house in stony silence and parted before they reached the door. Robin went inside to collect his valet and his baggage, to have his carriage brought around, and to take his leave of Lady Matilda. Patience went to examine a distant flower bed for new blooms and stayed there, intent on the plants while all the bustle of departure proceeded outside the house.

She did not look up even when the carriage rolled on its way. Not that Robin knew it. He did not look out the window.

He was furious and he was upset. He looked about him for something to smash. There was nothing.

He was not a man given to extremes of temper. He did

not know quite what to do with this one. He did nothing except remove his hat and knock it several times against his knee as if there were a whole sackful of dust to dislodge from it.

He was going home. At last. He had longed for it for what seemed like forever. He was not a man made for the city or for excitement. All he wanted of life was his own home and hearth, his own farms and horses and livestock, his own family.

His own nonexistent family.

A wife who belonged only to him. Children who belonged only to him. Cozy winter evenings about the fire in his small drawing room, a book in his hand, reading to his wife, who would be bent over her embroidery, while his children would be in bed or gathered about the table if they were a little older.

Robin sighed.

Patience.

The wife opposite him had raised her head and smiled at him with Patience's gently beguiling smile.

Patience was his sister. No, his cousin. No, neither. She was nothing at all to him. He was nothing at all to her.

Except that during his last brief visit to the dower house and during this one they had been virtually inseparable. And both times, on his arrival, he had seen her with a deep welling of gladness, with a feeling of totally happy homecoming. That first time she had come rushing toward him and he had opened his arms to her and she had come all the way into them.

It had been a bewildering moment. Disturbing. He had pushed it from his memory in some embarrassment. It had been one of the most wonderful moments of his life. No, it had not. It had been *the* most wonderful moment.

He had had Patience where she belonged, folded right against his heart.

She had come running to him. She had had that look of radiance that had made her almost unrecognizable. And then, when he had mentioned having to see Cass in a hurry, she had lost the look and said something about thinking he had come back for another reason. She had been angry this morning. Upset. She had told him to go away and never come back—because she thought he was in love with Cass. She had told him he was less than nothing to her—with tears in her eyes as she said it. She had not come to say good-bye to him even though she had been in sight, bent over a clump of flowers. She must have heard all the commotion of his departure. She had shown no sign.

Was he blind?

Was he an idiot?

He was blind and an idiot.

He leaned forward and rapped sharply on the front panel for his coachman to stop.

She was still at the same flower bed when he returned. She seemed not to have moved. It was the same flower bed she had been at the other time, when she had dropped her basket and cutters in order to run to him. She did not come running this time. She did not even look up, though she must have heard the carriage. It would be difficult to hide the sound of a large traveling carriage and four horses on a country road even if he wished to do so.

She showed no sign of being anything but stone-deaf and blind as a bat.

He strode toward her. He came to a halt at the edge of the flower bed. She was arranging the petals of one of the flowers, just as if nature had not already done a good enough job of it. He stood and watched her for fully half a minute. He had never been good with words.

"I am glad I am not really your cousin," he said at last. "Or your brother."

Apparently he had said nothing to give her a burning desire to reply. He tried again.

"I have never loved Cass," he said, "except as a sort of sister or cousin. I offered because I wanted to help her. I am glad she said no. I hope she can find happiness with Wroxley. I really do."

Patience was plucking off a few outer petals and watching them flutter to the ground.

"You are a baron's daughter," he said, "with a respectable dowry. Aunt Matilda must have high hopes for you. Indeed, I know she does.''

She patted the flower as if in apology for the mutilation she had begun to wreak on it.

''I have only a moderate fortune and a moderate estate,'' he said. ''I am a dull fellow.''

''No, you are not,'' she whispered to the flower.

''You do not want me, Patience,'' he told her.

She looked up at him then. Her eyes were reddened by tears. Her cheeks and lips were swollen and blotched red and white. She must have been weeping bitterly since even before he left. He had never noticed before, he thought, how incredibly beautiful she was.

''How do you know, Rob?'' she said. ''Have you ever asked me?''

''Do you?'' he asked her. ''Do you want me?'' He felt unbelievably uncomfortable. How did other fellows go about this sort of thing? How had he gone about it with Cass? But he remembered suddenly and rejected *that* as a suitable method.

''Am I being offered you?'' Patience asked him.

He nodded.

''Why?'' she asked. ''Because you knew I was crying over you and you felt sorry for me?''

Her eyes, he noticed, were fathoms deep—with doubt, longing, suffering, hope. It would be very easy to fall into them.

''Because I cannot go home without you,'' he said. ''Because there can be no home for me without you. Because you *are* my home. Zounds, Patience, I never was any good with words. Because I love you. There. Is that better? But they are foolish words. They mean nothing. They do not even begin to express—''

Fortunately he did not have to torture himself any longer with the inadequacy of words. A little missile had launched itself at him, knocking off both his hat and her own in the process. She locked her arms tightly about his waist and burrowed her head into the hollow between his neck and his shoulder and nestled there as if she had always belonged there but had only just found her way home—to stay.

"But you would be far better off going to London next spring and meeting other fellows," he said, folding her very firmly in his arms and making it perfectly obvious to her that he meant not a single word of the nonsense his mouth was speaking. "You have never met other fellows, Patience. When you do, you will realize what a dreadfully dull dog I am."

She lifted her face to him then, and it was all sunshine and laughter and tears and radiance.

"If you say so, Rob," she said. "But you are all mine and I am going to hold tightly to you for the rest of our lives. Be warned. I think I would like you to kiss me now, please. On the lips. I have dreamed for so long about you kissing me on the lips that I can scarce believe the reality is this close."

Robin kissed her on the lips. And lifted his head after a few moments, wondering if he should have spoken to her mother and even his stepfather before taking such a liberty with her person.

But Patience smiled at him and kissed *him* on the lips.

He would think about Aunt Matilda and his stepfather later, he decided before thought abandoned him. Preferably much later.

For two days following the arrival of Mr. Croft, Cassandra felt dreadfully ill. She could scarcely eat, and when she did she could not keep the food down. She could scarcely sleep, and when she did she was disturbed by strange, muddled dreams. Everyone soon knew about her pregnancy, of course. How could they not when she displayed such symptoms?

But she was not just ill. She was irritable and short-tempered. In a single day she complained to the chambermaid who brought hot water to her dressing room because the water was not hot enough and to her personal maid because her hair was not styled quite to her liking. And she frowned at a footman who was slower than he might have been in opening the dining-room doors for her and then snapped at another footman who was unfortunate enough to splash one tiny drop of wine onto the cloth beside her wine glass.

She *always* treated servants with smiling courtesy.

It did not help to know that everyone was making excuses for her because of her condition. Servants who were mistreated had no business making excuses for their employers.

She did not know what to do. She conducted so many inner debates with herself that she soon had a permanent headache. And every time she came up with a different conclusion and always for a new reason.

She would make the contents of her letter public simply because it was the right thing to do.

She would say nothing because too much time had passed.

She would invite Uncle Cyrus to Kedleston and confide in him. She would let him make the decision.

She would make discreet inquiries about the descendants of her great-grandfather's twin—and base her decision on the results of that inquiry.

She would destroy the letter and the package without further ado. She would not even *think* about it anymore.

She would find out if her great-grandfather had been specifically named as heir to Kedleston. If he had, then she would allow the title to go to its rightful holder. If he had not, then she would destroy the letter.

She would—she would lose her mind!

She had realized one thing—with perfect clarity. She now knew why her father had changed so completely. Her mother had died not long after her grandfather. She had always assumed that grief and his new responsibilities had brought about the changes in her father. Perhaps they had been partly responsible, but not mainly. It had been the letter and the decision that had had to be made.

Her father had decided to ignore the truth. So had her grandfather, another bad-tempered man who had not always been that way, if her grandmother was to be believed.

They had both made their decision, and both had suffered

for it. Both had been guilt-ridden. Her father had spent very little time with her after that and had not invited her to join him in London, as he should have done in order to find her a suitable husband. He had been unable to face her, knowing that the decision would be hers to make all over again after his death.

Both her grandfather and her father had known themselves to be impostors, but both had been unable to give up a way of life that had always been theirs. They had been unable to face the alternative to keeping silent.

She longed to confide in Nigel. But Nigel was cold and courteous and haughty and solicitous about her health. Nigel was so self-contained that he might as well have been a marble statue. If she told him, he would force her to destroy her package. And she would know for sure that he was still an opportunist, a dishonorable man.

As she was a dishonorable woman.

He was having the nightmares again. It was her immediate thought when she heard his door click shut very late in the night, while she lay sleepless on her own bed, and footsteps passed her door and receded in the direction of the staircase. He went outside. She watched from her window as he walked across the wide lawn in the direction of the driveway. A whole hour passed before he returned— she had stood there the whole time. She could tell from the droop of his shoulders that he was tired, but that being up and walking was preferable to the nightmares that came with sleep.

She rested her forehead against the glass of the window and closed her eyes. She was tired, too. Exhausted. Bone weary. She wondered if life would ever seem a bright and wonderful thing again.

She needed—someone. She needed—him. And he needed her. After that first night she had spent in his bed, he had stopped having such violent nightmares. He would be back in his room by now. Perhaps he was standing at his window as she was standing at hers.

How foolish it was to be apart. She could not really remember why they were apart. There were many reasons

why they should be, she knew. And only one overwhelming
reason why they should not be. Or perhaps more than one.
They were married. They were to have a child. They were
both tired and lonely.

He was not at the window, she found when she opened
the door from his dressing room and stepped into his darkened bedchamber. He was lying on the bed, one leg bent
at the knee while his foot rested flat against the mattress,
one arm across his eyes. He turned his head to look at her,
but said nothing.

And she said nothing. She climbed into the bed beside
him—he moved over to make room but left his arm
stretched out beneath her pillow. She burrowed against him,
her palms spread flat against his chest, while his arms
folded warmly about her.

They said nothing. They did not make love. She was not
sure which of them fell asleep first.

By the time morning came her decision was made. She
felt rested and calm and knew there would be no changing
her mind this time. She would dress and have breakfast—
she was ravenously hungry—and summon Mr. Croft to the
crimson salon. Conveniently he was still staying at Kedleston, as the inn had temporarily closed down. She knew
exactly what she would say to him, what she would have
him do.

She was alone in the bed. She must have been sleeping
deeply not to have heard Nigel get up. But she knew he
had slept as deeply and as well as she had. She had not
woken, but a part of her had known that she slept only
because he slept with her, his arms about her.

Life would be bright and worth living again, she thought.
Nigel was tough and resilient. He had proved that quite
conclusively over the past nine years. And she would wager
that she was, too. She would prove that she was a worthy
match for him. She loved him and they were to share a
child. Sometime, sooner or later, but *some* time, he was
going to love her, too. She was going to make him love
her.

She no longer cared a fig about the past. She really did

not. There was a future to fight for now and she was going
to fight. She felt strangely exhilarated by the challenge. The
sky was a clear blue, she saw. It was still summer. It was
going to be a beautiful day.

Nigel was inside the village inn with William Stubbs and
Coburg, though the steward had just been excused to return
to his other duties and left without further delay.

"You think you can make a success of life as a village
innkeeper, then, Will, do you?" Nigel asked, looking about
him.

"I don't see wot it will be so difficult," William said,
"despite wot old sobersides there says about books and
accounts and things like that wot 'as nothing wotsoever to
do with serving people their ale and dishing up their beef
and tucking them up in their beds at night. 'Course I can
manage, Nige." He rubbed his big hands together and also
looked about him. "And as for the money wot you lent
me, it will all be repaid, every last farthing of it."

"Consider it a gift," Nigel said.

"Oi, oi," William said, deeply offended. "I never took
nothing from you wot I didn't earn, lad, and don't think I
plans to start now. Every last farthing, Nige."

"You will not miss London?" Nigel asked. "And the
old life? You can be happy here, Will?"

"I did without London for seven years," William said
with a great bellow of a laugh. "I s'ppose I can manage
without it for the rest of my life. I fancies this life, I do.
I'll stay out of trouble 'ere. And I'll see that you keeps out
of trouble, too. You got to, Nige, with a little nipper coming
along."

"I am leaving," Nigel said quietly.

"Eh?" His friend's brows snapped together.

"You heard me," Nigel said again. " 'Twas a mistake,
Will. All of it. I should have contented myself with giving
him a good thrashing. Or with letting him simply die of
fear in the knowledge that I was back and knew where I
could find him anytime I wanted him. I should have taken

more account of the fact that there was someone else involved in the revenge I had decided upon.''

"You're queer in the attic, Nige," William said. "It's too late to 'ave second thoughts now. You've 'itched yourself to the little filly and you've give 'er a good one and got 'er belly swelling up. If you abandons 'er now, my lad, you goes with a broken nose and smashed teeth and raw meat for a face—courtesy of your old chain mate, Will Stubbs."

"As you wish," Nigel said coldly. "I am going to earn my way, Will, so that I can support my child."

"Support—?" William looked at him incredulously. "All the money from your lands will support the nipper, Nige, and the filly and the army of servants wot works for you."

Nigel looked back at him, grim-faced. "I never did have a right to this land, Will," he said. "Not anything that would be recognized as a legal right, anyway. Winning it in a card game that was forced upon Worthing has proved remarkably unsatisfactory. It was won at Lady Worthing's expense more than at his—and she was innocent of all wrongdoing."

"Eh," William said, suddenly suspicious. "Wot are you up to, Nige? Wot are you planning to do? Wot you been and done?"

Nigel's smile was rather arctic. "By my life, Will," he said, "I mean no offense, but you may mind your own business and leave me to mind mine."

"You aren't going to 'urt that little lady," William said sternly. "You wronged 'er once and now you are going to wrong 'er again. She don't need you in no London playing cards to support 'er baby. She needs you in 'er bed putting more babies in 'er belly. Now don't you be one stubborn son of an 'ore as you always used to be, Nige. You listen."

"William." Nigel looked at him with arrogant disdain from beneath half-lowered eyelids. "You may go to hell, my friend."

He left the inn taproom and closed the door behind him.

TWENTY-THREE

SALLY, THE NEWEST AND lowliest of the kitchen maids at Kedleston, was a marked woman, it seemed. She was known as a woman of easy virtue who should never have been allowed the respectability of employment even at the inn. But for some unfathomable reason she had become a favored charity case of her ladyship's and had finally achieved dizzying heights of success in the form of employment at Kedleston itself.

She was given the most menial and the least pleasant of tasks to perform and annoyed several of the more senior servants by performing them all conscientiously and uncomplainingly. No one would have dared cuff her since violence to fellow servants meant instant dismissal at Kedleston, but it would have been pleasant to some to have an excuse for giving her the sharp edge of a tongue once or twice a day.

Some of the lesser menservants planned to get her into a quiet corner for a few minutes one of these days. She came easy, it had been said at the inn, with no squawking and no hysterical tears and no noisy demands for more money than was offered her.

William Stubbs kept an eye on her. She would never be pretty and she would never have a buxom body or ample curves to compensate for her lack of looks, but it pleased him to see her clean and neat and decently dressed. She kept her distance from him, always lowering her eyes whenever he looked at her to find her gazing back, and bobbing curtsies to him just as if he were the King of England. Of course, he reminded himself with some amusement, he *was* his lordship's valet and therefore a superior being indeed to a mere kitchen maid.

He spent the rest of the day in the village after Nigel had left, making his preparations for opening the inn again as his own, excited by thoughts of the new life he had not even been able to dream of less than three years ago, and worrying about Nigel. He had certainly never intended to care for the frightened, bewildered gentleman who had been chained next to him when they had been taken to the hulks. He had hated him on sight with a ferocious passion and had amused himself—and all their fellow prisoners—with ever-new, ever-more-painful ways of annoying and hurting his foe until finally he had almost killed him. But he had learned something, almost without realizing it. He had learned the power of quiet dignity and inner strength and moral courage and nonviolence. He had grown to admire and even to love his former adversary—and to worry about him.

He worried because Nigel had built a very hard shell about the core of his real self, but it had begun to crack, and William was afraid that if it broke—not by violence but by something far more dangerous—the man himself might break, too. William feared that even inner strength had its limits.

But there was no helping Nigel unless he chose to be helped. He really was, William thought with frustrated exasperation, the most stubborn son of a whore he had ever encountered. Pounding him to a pulp certainly would not help. Nigel would just laugh and disappear even farther inside himself.

But there was someone who could and would be helped. Sal was approaching the stables as William walked home in the early evening, obviously sent there on some errand from the kitchen. She was carrying a pail of something, which was clearly too heavy for her slight frame. William speeded his pace in order to take it from her, but one of the undergrooms, a stooped and skinny and spotted youth, stepped out of the shadows into her path, wrestled the pail from her grasp, set it down, backed her into the shadows from which he had come, and pressed his body and his mouth to hers. All in the twinkling of an eye. Sal whimpered and flailed her arms before they were imprisoned against her sides.

William lengthened his stride and grasped the groom with one huge hand on the seat of his breeches and the other on the neck of his shirt. He lifted him bodily away from Sal and set him down an arm's length away.

"Wot you got to learn, lad," he said pleasantly enough, "is that wen a wench says no, she don't mean yes or even p'raps. She means no."

The boy was terrified but no sniveling coward. "I was just kissing her, Mr. Stubbs," he protested, rubbing his rump.

"And in a minute you would 'ave just been feeling 'er," William said, "and a minute after that just poking 'er and a minute after that just finished with 'er and buttoning your breeches. You go about your business now, lad, without another lying word and Will Stubbs will not give you the thrashing you arsked for. And don't you never come near this little wench again."

"Yes, Mr. Stubbs. I mean no, Mr. Stubbs." The boy was shaking with relief, but he was not going to slink away without some show of bravado. "I beg your pardon, I am sure, Mr. Stubbs. I didn't know she was your bit of petticoat." He left at a run.

So did Sal. She went blindly racing away in the opposite direction from the safety of the house. She was already disappearing among the trees when William, after hesitating for a few moments, went after her. She was not difficult to follow even though William had no experience at stalking anyone in the countryside. Twigs cracked under her panicked feet until finally there was silence except for the sobbing gasps of someone who was winded and very frightened.

William stopped some distance from where she hid, her body flattened against the trunk of a tree, her eyes wild with panic.

"No, no, Sal," he said quietly. "I am not going to come any closer, lass. I am not going to touch you or 'arm you. I just come so you wouldn't be frightened of the woods and the shadows and every sound you 'eard. Will is 'ere and will keep 'is eyes on you. You are safe."

"Mr. Stubbs," she said several moments later, "I have tried so hard to do my duty and be a good girl. But I am bad through and through. I think I should do away with myself. Everybody would be happier if I did. I would be happier."

William's brows snapped together. "Now wot kind of talk is that?" he said in the voice that had often made the toughest of London's ruffians quake. "Don't you never talk that way again. You *are* a good girl, Sal. Just because you been cuffed and poked by riffraff wot never learned 'ow to behave proper with women don't mean you are bad. And some people would not be 'appy if you was to kill yourself. 'Er ladyship would not be 'appy. Will Stubbs would not be 'appy. And you would not be 'appy, lass. Wot kind of daft idea is that? 'Ow can you be 'appy when you are dead and stiff and six feet under?"

"Mr. Stubbs," she said, turning her eyes on him, "*would* you be unhappy?"

"Course I would," he said. "If you kills yourself, Sal, old Stubbs will be very cross with you."

"But why would you care?" she asked. "You are such a grand, important man."

"Not me, lass," William said, laughing softly. "You don't want to go thinking grand thoughts about me. You are shaking. Are you afraid to step away from the tree? It 'appens sometimes after something bad 'appens. For a few minutes you thinks everything is over and back to rights, and then you seems to lose control of your own self."

She was crying with soft, desolate sobs.

"I am coming over there," William said, "unless you says no, Sal. Just to 'old you till the feeling passes. Not to 'urt you. I won't never 'urt you."

"Please," she said through her sobs, "come quick."

He held her thin, shapeless little body against him while she wept and trembled, and then rocked her quietly when she was finished.

"I tried so hard to be good," she said eventually, her voice muffled against his coat.

"You *are* good, lass," he told her.

"Mr. Stubbs." She raised a wan, tearstained, pock-marked face to his and gazed at him with her big, wounded brown eyes. "Mr. Stubbs, do you want to do it to me?"

William was indignant, perhaps because the answer was yes. "I come 'ere to comfort you, Sal," he said, "not to 'urt you."

"You said once," she said, "that I didn't have to let any man do it to me again unless I wanted it and told him so. I want you to do it to me."

William looked at her sorrowfully. "That is not something to give just because you thinks you owes somebody something, Sal," he said. "You don't owe me nothing."

"Mr. Stubbs." Tears had welled into her eyes again. "I want to feel clean again. Make me feel clean. Do it to me and make me clean."

His sorrow deepened. "I am a bad man, Sal," he said. "I grew up from a nipper on 'urting people and bullying them and taking wot was not mine to take. I got caught and chained up and sent in one of them great 'ulks across the sea, where they kept me chained and at 'ard labor for seven years. I been in transportation, girl. I am no man for you."

"You are the most wonderful man in the world," she said. "I worship you, Mr. Stubbs."

"And I am ugly as sin," he said.

"And I am pretty as a princess," she said with the only venture into humor he had heard from her. "Please do it to me—if you want me. Make me feel clean again."

"Ah, lass." William moaned and lowered his head to set

his mouth against her throat. "I do not even know how to be gentle."

"Yes, you do." Her fingers stroked lightly over his head. "You are the gentlest man I have ever known, Mr. Stubbs. You have always been gentle with me. I do not care what you were. I know what you are."

William was in many ways a very innocent man. He knew nothing of foreplay. His big hands trembled as they gentled her, made her feel feminine and desirable. He clenched his teeth in the effort not merely to follow instinct. He wanted to make her feel clean. He wanted to redeem all men in her eyes.

He almost forgot when it came to the point to lay her down on the moss at their feet. And when he had her down there, he was painfully aware of his weight, which would crush her if he put the whole of it onto her body, and of his broad bulk, which would put a severe strain on her thin legs when he forced them wide. He managed to keep much of his weight off her, and she spread her legs wide without any forcing on his part, and lifted them to twine about his massive ones. And then he was aware of his great size.

"I will 'urt you, Sal," he said with something very like a sob. "I am too big for you, girl." She was such a fragile little thing and had been so dreadfully used by her father and numberless others.

"No, you are not," she said, very cool and practical now that she was about to be cleansed. "Put it in, Mr. Stubbs. I want to feel it."

He groaned as he put it in, and Sal gasped. He rested inside her and cursed himself for allowing lustful desire to give in to her very generous invitation. He did not realize that he was sobbing. He was far too big for her, even though she had stretched around him, causing him almost unbearable desire.

He would do it to her very slowly and gently, he decided. Perhaps he would hurt her less that way. For her sake he wished he could do it quickly and gently, but both simultaneously were not possible. And so with his teeth clamped hard together and every ounce of his will holding his body to obedience, he innocently ensured that Sal had several minutes of excruciatingly agonizing pleasure. She screamed at the exact moment his seed sprang.

William was still half sobbing after he had drawn himself out of her and lifted himself away from her to lie at her side, her thin body held against his bulky one.

"I am so sorry, Sal," he said. "I didn't want to 'urt you. I won't do it again. I won't never do it again, lass."

But she lifted her head and surprised him by kissing him square on the lips. "Thank you," she whispered. "I feel all clean again. And wonderful. You did it to me so nicely. You are the most beautiful man in the whole wide world, Mr. Stubbs."

Amusement pierced William's distress. "You be sure and forget now wot you said a while ago, Sal," he said. "No more talk about being a bad girl and wanting to kill yourself. You are a good girl and a beautiful girl and someday that 'andsome lad is going to come along wot will take you to live 'appily ever after somewhere."

"But I am not going to let any other man do it to me, Mr. Stubbs," she said. "Not ever. Only you. Whenever you need it, you can come to me for it. It will be just for you. They will be my happy times, when you come. But I will be happy even when you do not come because you have been good to me and made me feel like I really am beautiful and worth something again. They will be my *happiest* times, when you come to me." The pretty little girl she must have been once upon a time smiled out of her eyes again. They were eyes that shone with happiness and trust and adoration.

"Lass," William said gently, a great ball of longing lodged somewhere in the region of his stomach, "I am just a great 'ulking lump of sin."

"No, you are not," she said, "for I just made you clean, too, Mr. Stubbs. Because I love you with all my heart. Forever I will love you. You can come to me anytime. I will always be waiting to give you ease."

"Sal, Sal." He hugged her close, remembered his great strength, and loosened his hold somewhat. "Do you know anything about books and accounts and figures and troublesome stuff like that? Can you read?''

"I can," she said proudly. "And I can do figures as quickly as you please. Mrs. Dorkins used to call me to help her when she couldn't get them to add up the same more than once in a row.''

"P'raps you will come to the inn with me, then," he said. "It is going to be mine, but that Coburg says I got to know about figures. You come and do them for me, Sal.''

"Oh." She smiled happily. "And I will serve tables and clean rooms and wash dishes and scrub floors, Mr. Stubbs. And I will be close by when you need me for yourself. Will you really let me come?''

"I got to talk to Nige," he said, frowning. "To 'is lordship, that is. I got to find out wot to do to get 'itched up. We got to go to church and do it proper, Sal. We are in the country and got to be respectable. We are going to own the inn and be people of property. If you means wot you says about loving me and wanting nobody but me to do it to you, then you got to be my lawfully wed woman. I am not going to 'ave you as my 'ore, lass, and nobody's not going to call you that no more. They are going to call you Mrs. Stubbs, as polite as you please. Or I will be arsking them the reason why not.''

Her arms were about his neck then, half strangling him, and she was kissing the underside of his chin with fierce passion. She was also crying silently.

"There, there, Sal," he said, patting her back, "it won't be so bad, lass. I won't never beat you just 'cause you're my lawfully wed woman and I will always try to be gentle on account of I am so big. And there will be maids to scrub the floors and wash the dishes for you. You will do them figures for me wen you are not giving our little nippers milk at the breast. It won't be so bad. You dry them tears now and give Will one of them smiles.''

She gave him one of dazzling brilliance even before she dried her tears. "Oh, Mr. Stubbs," she told him with fervent sincerity, "it will be *heaven*.''

"You better call me Will, Sal," he said.

"Oh yes, Mr. Stubbs," she said.

Nigel summoned Cassandra the next morning. She was to bring a hat, he instructed. They were to go walking.

She had not come back to his bed the night before. On the whole he was glad of it, though he had lain awake waiting for her and had even gone into his dressing room at one point and had his hand raised to knock on her door. If she had come to him last night, he would have made love to her. He did not need that complication in his life at the moment.

Her face was pale and set when she came to him in the hall. She had lost weight, he thought.

"Good morning, madam," he said, bowing to her. "You are well enough to walk?"

"I am quite well, thank you, my lord," she said.

"You have eaten this morning?" he asked her.

"Thank you, yes," she said.

"And have kept your food down?"

"Yes."

"We will walk, then," he said. "There is something I wish to say to you."

But he did not immediately say it. He took her hand on his sleeve and walked with her up the hill behind the house until they were among the trees. At the top, he knew, the trees thinned out so that there was a quite breathtaking view of the surrounding countryside and even of the waters of the Bristol Channel in the distance.

What a force of evil he had been in her life, he thought, looking at the slender hand resting on his cuff. She had been quite vividly happy on her birthday, the title and property hers—or so she thought—and her independence won with her majority. She had planned to remain unmarried and to prove to the world that she, a woman alone, could run both her life and her estate without a man's guidance.

He had taken the property from her, two weeks before she would have inherited it, and he had taken her freedom from her and even her person. Her person was suffering the invasion of his child. He had taken her exuberance from her and her dreams.

All because of a lifelong dream of his own to be able to call Kedleston home. And because the burning need to avenge himself on a man who had wronged him dreadfully had given him the chance of achieving that dream.

But Cassandra had been in the way. Innocent Cassandra.

"I find myself restless, madam," he said, opening the conversation at last. He had planned it during his sleepless night. She would never know his agony. No one would ever know. He had become an expert at hiding agony. "I find that life at Kedleston becomes tedious."

Beneath the forward-tilting brim of her hat he could see her lips compress. She said nothing.

"And that married life bores me," he said.

"I believe, my lord," she said, "that country living and marriage frequently bore gentlemen who are accustomed to wilder, faster living. I am not surprised."

"I shall be returning to London tomorrow," he said.

Her head dipped farther, so that he could not see even so much as her lips. "I would beg permission, my lord," she said, her voice so low that he could scarcely hear it, "to be allowed to remain at Kedleston."

"I'faith, madam," he said, injecting a world of boredom into his voice, "I never had the smallest intention of taking you with me."

Her hand jerked once against his sleeve and lay still again. "Thank you," she said. "When may I expect your return?"

"You may not," he said.

She looked up at him then, and her upper lip curled in scorn and distaste. "I almost believed in you," she said. "How I would despise myself now if I had done so."

He looked at her, his eyelids drooped over his eyes. "But you did not, madam," he said, "and so you may keep your good opinion of your judgment. You knew that your father was not to be doubted, and so your husband must be the villain."

"I did not say that," she said. " 'Tis just that you are

of weak character and have allowed adversity to further weaken it.''

''Ah,'' he said, ''I am honored to have my character so insightfully analyzed, madam. You will not be burdened by my company after today. After the child is born I shall have my man of business send monthly support for its keep.''

Her eyebrows shot up at that.

''A man of honor must insist upon supporting his own child,'' he said.

''A man of honor?'' Her voice was icy. ''Your estate will adequately support my child, my lord—unless you intend to drain it quite dry with your excesses.''

''I intend no such thing, by my life,'' he said. ''I have no estate, madam. The one that was my own was taken from me after my disgrace and I have chosen not to dispute the dubious legal maneuverings that accomplished the feat. The other estate I have disposed of.''

''*What?*'' She stopped walking abruptly and turned so pale that he lunged forward to catch her. She slapped his hands away and took a step back from him.

''I have disposed of Kedleston, madam,'' he said with a bow. ''I have signed it away. 'Tis no longer mine.''

She swayed on her feet, but she held up her hands sharply when he would have stepped forward again to support her.

''What are you saying?'' She looked barely conscious.

''Kedleston is yours, Lady Worthing,'' he said, raising one mocking eyebrow. ''With my compliments.''

''Why?'' she asked him on a mere breath of sound.

Because I have wronged you. Because I love you. Because I would die for you—and perhaps will find some way of doing so sometime soon.

''I'faith, madam,'' he said, '' 'twas amusing to own it for a while and to own, too, the daughter of the Earl of Worthing. But I have tired of both.''

''But you cannot so easily rid yourself of me,'' she said.

He smiled at her. ''And neither do I wish to,'' he said. ''Marriage bores me. I will never again wish to amuse myself with it, having tried it once. And I am happy to have been of service to you. You would not perhaps have married if I had not come here intent upon seducing you into wedded bliss. But now you have your title and your property and your independence—and your heir. It does not matter if 'tis a son or a daughter, does it? Only that it lives.''

She stared at him for a while, her face stony and quite unreadable. He wondered for perhaps the hundredth time why she had come to him the night before last and had lain with him, quiet and still, and had been asleep no more than five minutes after coming. The answer to the question might make all the difference in the world to everything.

She had probably been sleepwalking.

She had made a choice. She had chosen to believe in her father, because she had loved her father and *did not love him*. She had told him so in exactly those words. There had been no misinterpreting her meaning. And heaven knew she had little enough reason to love him.

No, he would not show weakness. Not now. Not showing weakness, not showing even a chink of vulnerability had become second nature to him.

''You may enjoy what is yours in peace, madam,'' he said. ''While I enjoy—living elsewhere.''

She startled him then. She started to laugh, at first softly, almost soundlessly, and then loudly and helplessly, even hysterically. He clasped his hands very tightly at his back and raised his eyebrows.

''What a joke,'' she said, finally bringing herself under control. ''What a marvelous, marvelous joke. So I am to lose my husband, too.''

She laughed again, but her face suddenly crumpled out of her control and she caught up her skirts and began to run back down the hill. He expected every moment that she would miss her footing, but she did not.

He stood where he was long after she had disappeared from sight. If she had not hated him sufficiently before, now she did. He had accomplished what he had set out to do this morning. It would be better if she hated him, if she had no niggling doubts in the future.

He turned at last and made his slow way to the top of the hill.

Cassandra continued on her way down, scarcely slackening her pace all the way to the house. She knew she was on the verge of hysteria, of total collapse. Her only hope was to keep all thought at bay until she was alone in her rooms.

But she did not get that far.

The butler bowed to her as soon as she entered the house and told her, a curious frown on his usually impassive face, that a visitor awaited her in the crimson salon. She was too distraught to ask who it was. Her first instinct was to tell Dexter to inform the visitor that she was not at home and not expected to return anytime soon. But even that instinct she rejected. Life could hardly get any worse than it was at this moment and the truth could not be held back from their neighbors for much longer.

She changed direction and made her way to the salon.

She stepped inside and turned her eyes in the direction of the man who was turning away from the window to look at her over his shoulder.

She stared at him in horror as her hands reached behind her to clutch the door handle, clawlike, behind her back.

Nigel was staring back at her.

She had left Nigel up on the hill a few minutes ago, dressed quite differently.

He was turning to look more fully at her.

Nigel.

But not Nigel.

TWENTY-FOUR

"THE COUNTESS OF WORTH-ing?" the man who was not Nigel asked.

"Who are you?" She was whispering and still clinging to the doorknob behind her back. But she knew who he was even before he spoke. Of course she knew. *She had written to him.*

"Bruce Wetherby, at your service, my lady," he said, making her a formal bow.

Nigel's brother. She had written to him at the same time as she had sent Robin back to London. She had almost forgotten. She had asked a series of questions, hoping for a reply and some information that would help her fit together the puzzle that was her husband.

Her husband no more, except in name. She pushed aside the thought.

His brother was so like him that it was somewhat disorienting just to look at him. And yet there were subtle differences. This man was immaculately and expensively dressed but with not quite the same exquisite elegance as his brother. His face was good-humored and lacked entirely the heavy-lidded cynicism of his brother's—and its powerful sensuality, too.

"I can see your shock," the Honorable Mr. Bruce Wetherby said. "He did not tell you that we are twins?"

He had once told her that there were no twins in his family. Yet he was himself a twin. She shook her head.

"From your letter," he said, "I understood that he has not told you a great deal about his family."

"Almost nothing," she said, "except your name and that of your sister." She closed her eyes briefly. He was considerably closer when she opened them. He was looking at her with concern.

"May I help you to a chair?" he asked. "You look as if you are about to faint."

"You look so like him," she said.

"Even our first tutor and most of the family servants did not know us apart," he said, taking her arm in a firm, comforting hold and leading her toward a chair. "We took full advantage of the fact." He seated her and took a chair close to hers. "Will sitting down help? Should I call a servant to send for your maid?"

She shook her head. "You came," she said. "I did not expect you to come in person."

"You are my sister," he said quietly. "And though you did not say so in your letter, I understood that all was not well with you and your marriage. My wife gained the same impression when she read the letter. How may I be of service to you?"

She looked at him and wondered how she could have mistaken him for Nigel even for a single moment. Had Nigel ever looked like this—with an open, untroubled countenance despite the very real concern in the eyes?

"Why did you not support him?" she asked. "Why did you cast him off and have him disinherited?"

His eyes fell before hers and turned to gaze into the empty hearth. He did not answer for a while. "May I assume," he asked at last, "that when you married Wroxley, you did not know the truth about him?"

"Yes," she said, "you may assume that."

"You did not know he had wrested your estate from the Earl of Worthing, your father?" he asked.

"No," she said.

"Or even about his—his criminal background?" he asked.

"I did not know," she told him.

"Then I am sorry in my heart that I was not in communication with him," he said. "I might have prevented it from happening. You must be desperately unhappy indeed. I beg you to allow me to be of service to you. You must return to Dunbar Abbey with me. My wife and my sister will be happy to receive you—and my children, too."

"Mr. Wetherby," she said, "Nigel is my husband. I am to have his child. Kedleston is my home."

He leaned back in his chair. "Of course," he said. "I do beg your pardon. I assumed you were in distress."

"You assumed," she said, "that he has mistreated me."

"If he has reformed his ways," he said, "sufficiently to treat his wife with some affection, then I can return home a great deal happier than when I came here." He looked sharply away again but not before Cassandra had caught the gleam of tears in his eyes.

With some affection. Nigel had returned Kedleston to her and her independence. Because he had wearied of them. Because he was bored with her. He was leaving her and never coming back.

She had lost everything. Everything but the breath in her body and the child growing there. Soon enough perhaps she would be glad to go to Dunbar Abbey in Lincolnshire to live with her brother-in-law and her sisters-in-law. And with her nieces or nephews. A dependent—though Nigel would support their child, she thought bitterly.

But this was not the time or place for such thoughts. She had come to the crimson salon instead of continuing on her way to her rooms.

"You have not answered my questions, Mr. Wetherby," she said.

"You have doubtless heard enough evil about my bro—about Wroxley to last you a lifetime, my lady," he said. "In your letter it seemed that you knew about the criminal charges and the—the punishment."

"Yes," she said. "I discovered the marks of the whips

on his back on our—on our wedding night.''

"The marks of—oh, dear God." She saw the brightness of his eyes again for a moment before he jerked to his feet and crossed the room to stand at the window again, his back to her. "He did everything to alienate us, to show his contempt for all that we stood for. He inherited the title and Dunbar when we were only seventeen. He was restless. He had always been dealt with a little more strictly than I was. If there were thrashings or lectures to be handed out, his were always a little more severe and a little more long-winded than mine were. Our father used to spend long hours with him that he did not spend with me. Nig—Nigel was fond of saying that I was far better suited than he to be the viscount and lord of the manor. 'Twas not true—or I thought it was not true. 'Twas just that all the pressure was on his young shoulders—and yet we were twins. We thought and talked and acted in tandem.''

There was a lengthy silence, which Cassandra would not break. Too late she was learning about Nigel things she had been hungry to know. She was still hungry, she realized, even though she had lost him. Even though he was not worth getting to know.

"Then he went away," Bruce said, "to London. I stayed at Dunbar to try to decide what I would do with my life. He went wild. We soon heard stories of the sorts of excesses very young men are prey to—gaming, carousing, womaniz— Ah, pardon me. I did not worry unduly. I thought I knew my brother. I did not expect anything blatantly dishonorable of him. Then, after a disturbingly long silence, we heard what had happened. Cheating at the tables—that was bad enough. 'Tis something from which a gentleman can never expect fully to recover his reputation. But theft . . .''

There was another silence. Cassandra watched him rest his hands on the windowsill and bow his head forward.

"He hid his identity," he said, "though how I do not know, when all the witnesses must have known who he was. He did not write to us. We might have done something for him if we had known in time, changed the sentence at

least. We might have arranged to have him sent into exile.
I would have gone with him. But he wanted nothing to do
with us. He was ashamed, perhaps. I have always liked to
think 'twas that. Though 'twas difficult to believe so after
what I discovered when I finally went to London—after he
had been taken away and we had learned the truth.

"He had sold some of the family jewels. Not all of
them—just the pieces that had the most sentimental value
to the family. He had laughed about my staid ways with
his friends and about the fact that he had wheedled me into
being his unpaid steward at Dunbar. 'Twas a minor detail,
but it hurt. We were *twins*. He was my beloved brother. He
arranged a match for Barbara—our sister—to be solem-
nized on her fifteenth birthday, to an old man, one of England's most profligate rakes. He was very wealthy, of
course. There were plans for selling Dunbar—I spoke with
the lawyer who was drawing up the papers. And there was
a young lady of good birth who had been ruined by my
brother—against her will. She was in Bournemouth, await-
ing the birth of her child. I was never allowed to see her,
though I tried."

Cassandra's hands were tightly clenched in her lap. She
could feel her fingernails digging into her palms and wondered idly if she was drawing blood.

"There you have it, my lady," Bruce said after another
heavy silence. "I was angry, suspicious, defensive, upset—
I thought I would go out of my mind with grief. He was—
my other half. But cool reason can finally prevail against
even the most intense emotion. And so I consulted a whole
arsenal of the best lawyers England has to offer and began
the proceedings that have led to this. Had I not taken Dunbar from Wroxley, perhaps he would not have coveted Kedleston. Or made dishonor doubly dishonorable by cheating
your father out of it and achieving a revenge to which justice and honesty did not entitle him."

"You love him," Cassandra said foolishly.

He laughed, though there was no humor in the sound.
"I *did* love him," he said. "But one cannot love such a
man. I beg your pardon. Perhaps you would disagree."

"He was innocent," she said.

He turned to look at her. "I would expect him to say so," he said gently. "And I would expect you to believe him. You are his wife. You are also my sister. Is there any way I can be of service to you? I am afraid I have done you a disservice by telling you what I have told you, but you did ask." He half smiled. "I shall not stay here. But tell me if there is anything I can do for you. And write to me anytime you find yourself in need of a brother—or sisters."

"You are very kind," she said. "Are there other twins in your family?"

"Not in recent memory," he said. "But in previous generations, yes. On my paternal grandmother's side. We appear once in a while. We are almost always male and almost always the eldest sons—a curious coincidence, perhaps. I suppose it could be annoying to the twins in my position—born a few minutes too late. It never annoyed me. I loved—Nigel and I could see the strain his position as the elder put on him. I tried to support him by being steady, by being always there for him. I should have gone to London with him."

"You are not your brother's keeper, Mr. Wetherby," she said. "You have your own—"

But she had no chance to finish the sentence. The door had opened and then closed quietly after Nigel had stepped inside.

He looked as elegant, as fashionable, as immaculate, Cassandra thought, as if he had just stepped out of his dressing room. With one eyebrow raised, his eyelids drooped over his eyes, and his quizzing glass to one eye, he also looked at his most arrogant and his most cynical—and his iciest.

"Zounds," he said, his voice heavy with boredom, " 'tis the very respectable Mr. Bruce Wetherby. My brother, by my life. And what do you do at Kedleston, sir, if I might be permitted to ask? I suppose my esteemed wife sent for you?"

"Her ladyship wrote to inform me of her marriage to

you," Bruce said. His face had turned quite white, Cassandra noticed. "I came to pay my respects to her. I was taking my leave when we were interrupted."

"Splendid," Nigel said. "Then I have been spared the discourtesy of having to ask you to leave my property, sir."

They were so very alike, Cassandra thought. And so very different. They had been virtually inseparable and almost indistinguishable once upon a time. Before the journey to London. Before the fateful meeting between Nigel and her father—both twins. Both the elder of the two.

A fateful meeting indeed. She felt dizzy and fought the feeling.

"Mr. Bruce Wetherby will be remaining on *my* property for at least a little longer, my lord," she said. "So will you. You will be remaining in this room, the two of you, while I leave it. 'Tis time you came face-to-face again—after almost ten years."

She swept from the room but turned to look back before closing the door. Bruce had turned back to the window. Nigel was looking after her, naked amazement on his face.

"If you need me afterward, my lord," she said, "I shall be down at the pool."

She closed the door.

The pool was the only place that would do now. Her rooms would no longer suffice. It would have to be the pool.

They were not just brothers. They were twins—identical twins. Losing his twin had not been like losing their mother or father, or even like losing their younger brother when he was five and they were seven. Those had been painful losses but had left him intact as a whole person. Losing Bruce, though Bruce had not died, had been like having a part of his body and soul amputated.

It was said that after an amputation one always felt the missing limb as if it were still there.

" 'Tis good to know," Nigel said, strolling toward the chair Cassandra had just vacated and seating himself on it, "that you reply to some letters at least, Bruce."

His brother stood staring out of the window. "For this I despise you most, Wroxley," he said. "For taking from that lady what was rightfully hers and trapping her into matrimony with a blackguard."

"She has not told you?" Nigel asked. "I have been victim of a painful bout of conscience, i'faith. I have returned her property and her independence. Had you arrived tomorrow, by my life, you would have found that I had quit the field."

Bruce turned his head. "You are leaving her?" he said, scorn heavy in his voice. "You have got her with child and you are abandoning her?"

"Ah, she has told you the happy tidings of my impending fatherhood, then," Nigel said. "You must hope 'tis not a boy, Bruce. And you must hurry and marry so that you may produce boys of your own. Dunbar Abbey *and* the title. You must have been disappointed to discover that the colonies and hard labor and the hulks had not killed me."

"You bastard!" his brother said very quietly before turning back to the window.

A hostile silence settled on the room.

"I have been married for five years," Bruce said at last. "We have three children, Charlotte and I—two sons and a daughter."

Nigel did not know why it hurt so much to know that his brother had carried on with his life—and that he himself had not even known it. Five years ago he had still been living in hell. He had not known that his family was still capable of hurting him.

"I had not realized how much you coveted everything you had lost by not being born half an hour earlier than you were," he said. "I was young enough and naïve enough to expect you to come running. I was foolish enough not to worry a great deal while I languished in prison. Bruce would come soon, I told myself and anyone who was willing to listen, and he would put all right. Bruce, the steady half of myself, the miracle worker. When I was in court I watched for your arrival with only slightly dwindling confidence. Even when I was being led away in chains I expected you to come riding neck or nothing after me. I expected a last-minute reprieve. Even when I was in the hulks, far below deck, I listened for you. Young men ought not to be allowed to be so foolishly innocent.''

"I am no miracle worker," his brother cried. "How could I come if I did not know? How could I save you if you did not call for help? Why did you not send someone? Write? Would they not let you write?''

"Damn you," Nigel said. "I wrote daily. At vast expense. They took the letters. They assured me they had been sent. They promised me. . . .''

Bruce turned his head again and they stared at each other.

"Who are 'they'?" Bruce asked.

"My friends," Nigel said.

"Friends," Bruce said softly. "Not a single letter reached me.''

He must still be suffering from incredible naïveté, Nigel thought. The possibility had never once entered his head until this moment. They had been his *friends*. But then Bruce had been his brother—his twin.

"You wrote?" Bruce's voice sounded somewhat strangled.

Nigel laughed. "But you were just a boy when all is said and done," he said. "You could have done nothing to help me.''

"Were you guilty, then?" Bruce asked. "Your wife says you were innocent.''

"Does she, by Jove?" A convenient lie as a sign of solidarity with her husband? "It does not matter now if I was guilty or innocent. The evidence was overwhelming. And the sentence has been served—and survived.''

"It matters." His brother's voice was fierce.

Nigel looked at him with raised eyebrows. "Well, then," he said, "if 'tis important to you, Bruce, I will say it. I was innocent of all but a young man's folly. I had friends as young and foolish as myself, and abandoned them for an older, faster crowd, who made me feel like one devil of a dashing fellow. I was far closer to hell than I realized. They made a hellish joke of me. I wonder if they have stopped laughing yet. Worthing has, of course.''

''You were innocent?'' Bruce was looking at him in some horror. ''How could you have been innocent?''

Nigel shrugged. ''By not being guilty, I suppose,'' he said. ''I was set up. Far more thoroughly than I realized until this moment. And very, very effectively.''

''But by whom?'' Bruce asked. ''By Worthing? But why?''

Nigel shook his head. ''I was young and green,'' he said. ''Perhaps they derived their jaded pleasure from destroying foolish little boys. Perhaps I was not their only victim. Who knows? All I know is that it *did* happen and that I lived to tell the tale—and to wreak my revenge. I was certainly not expected to survive, of course. The weak do not—and even a very large number of those who are not weak. I would have given a great deal to have seen Worthing's face when he knew I was back.''

''Why did you sell Mama's jewels?'' his brother asked.

''Mama's jewels?'' Nigel frowned.

''Why were you in the process of selling Dunbar?''

''Hm?'' Nigel looked blankly at his brother.

''Oh, dear God,'' Bruce said. '' 'Twas all part of it. You did not do either, did you? Or impregnate Miss Hickmore. She was probably not even increasing.''

''Who the devil is Miss Hickmore?'' Nigel asked.

''She probably did not even exist,'' his brother said. He closed his eyes briefly. ''Nige, show me the whip marks on your back.''

''She told you about those, too, did she?'' Nigel said. ''Forget about it and about them. I have.''

''Nige.'' His brother had taken a few steps closer. ''Show me. Damn you, show me.'' His eyes were bright with tears.

'' 'Twere best left,'' Nigel said. ''We were a pair of blind and innocent young lambs, Bruce. Perhaps we can shake hands.''

''Show me.'' His brother had taken up his stand directly in front of his chair.

Nigel recognized both the tone of voice and the look, even though the latter was marred by tears. He got slowly to his feet and removed his coat and his waistcoat and his cravat and shirt before turning around. There was a lengthy silence before he felt two hands rest very briefly flat against his back. And then his brother was sobbing awkwardly and noisily.

"And all the time this was happening," he said, his voice coming in gasping jerks, "I was taking everything from you and marrying Charlotte and getting our children and laughing and riding and dancing. And when you came back and went to see Barbara at school, I whisked her away from there and left a message for you should you go back."

"You did what I would doubtless have done if everything had been reversed," Nigel said, pulling his shirt back on over his head.

"No," Bruce said. "You would not, Nige. I always prided myself on using my head. You always acted from the heart. You would not have turned me off no matter what."

"But I did," Nigel said quietly. "I ordered you off Kedleston land in so many words just half an hour ago, Bruce."

"If your wife had not forced us to talk—" Bruce said.

"But she did." Nigel held out his right hand and looked steadily at his twin. "I did not die, but part of me has been dead for longer than nine years. Give me my life back again?"

Bruce ignored his hand. And then they were clasped wordlessly in each other's arms.

"'Twas Charlotte who persuaded me to come instead of just writing," Bruce said at last when they stepped apart. "To see your wife, of course, and offer her our support. But to see you, too. She told me I must see you and speak with you. Whatever you had done, she said, you were someone I could somehow not live without. I was not *going* to see you if I could help it, but she would have been very annoyed with me if I had not."

"I would like to meet her," Nigel said, "and your children. And I long to see Barbara again."

"You will see all of them," Bruce said. Suddenly he was looking his old happy, eager self again. "And soon. You must bring Lady Wroxley—Lady Worthing to Dunbar, Nige, if she is able to travel, of course. If not, I shall bring everyone here. We will—"

"You have forgot," Nigel said, "that I am leaving here tomorrow, Bruce. I am leaving Kedleston and my wife."

His brother stared at him. "But not now," he said. "Not any longer."

"I have discovered you again," Nigel said. "I have discovered that you did not betray me and you have discovered that I did not lose my honor. This does not change a thing between Cassandra and me."

"Egad, Nige," Bruce said, "she is your wife. She is with child. And she is beautiful and charming and—and Worthing's daughter. Is that it? Can you see only Worthing and your hatred of him when you look at the daughter?"

"I have tired of Kedleston and tired of her," Nigel said. "I am leaving."

His brother stood looking at him closely. "You still have that trick with your eyelids," he said. "I used to try to imitate it, but everyone used to tell me to stop squinting. Open your eyes and tell me you have tired of her."

"Zounds, Bruce," Nigel said frostily. "Do you call me liar again so soon, then?"

"Why are you leaving?" Bruce asked.

"I have told you—"

"No," his brother said firmly. "Why are you leaving?"

Nigel sighed. "I took everything from her," he said. "Everything, Bruce, including her very body. How ghastly it must feel to her to know that 'tis my babe she carries inside. She is Worthing's daughter and she loved him. She cannot bring herself to believe in his villainy. And so she must believe in mine. I cannot set her free and I cannot pluck the child from her womb. But I can do all in my power to restore to her what I took from her."

"And yet," Bruce said, "she told me you were innocent."

"She was being loyal in the face of outsiders," Nigel said.

"I am your brother," Bruce said. "She was talking to your twin. What if she does not want you to leave, Nige? What if she has greater strength of character than either you or I have? What if she loves you no matter what? What if she wants a father for the child? What if she simply wants you? Have you asked her? Have you given her a choice?"

"I gave her no choice about marrying me," Nigel said. "I made sure she fell in love with the man I pretended to be. She was just a young innocent. I have to make amends somehow."

"By punishing yourself—again," Bruce said. "Perhaps she would like to be given a choice this time, Nige."

Nigel closed his eyes. "What if she does not want me?" he asked. "What if she wants me to go away?"

"Then you will do the honorable thing," his brother told him, "and go away. 'Tis what you intend doing anyway."

Nigel looked bleakly at him. But if he went without asking her, at least he would not know for certain that she did not want him. At least he would be able to keep the shreds of his armor about himself. At least he would not have opened himself to pain that would finally, after all he had endured, be unendurable.

"Dear God," Bruce said, "you *love* her, Nige. Do not believe I cannot read your eyes just because I have not seen them for ten years. You love her. Go and *win* her."

"You will stay?" Nigel asked. "You will not simply disappear for another ten years?"

"I will stay," Bruce assured him. "I will get that butler of yours to show me to a guest room. Poor man—his eyes very nearly popped from their sockets when he saw me. Go. I am quite capable of seeing to my own comfort for an hour or two—or four or five. She said she would be at the pool, wherever that is. She would hardly have told you that, Nige, if she had wanted never to set eyes on you again. Is it a suitably secluded spot?" He smiled.

"The loveliest and most romantic place in the world, by my life," Nigel said. "Cassandra and I are both agreed on that."

His brother's smile had turned into a grin before Nigel hurried from the room.

TWENTY-FIVE

SHE WAS SITTING ON THE
log where she had sat when he proposed marriage to her,
gazing out across the pool in the direction of the waterfall,
her straw hat on the grass at her feet. It was an artist's
dream, the whole scene, with her at the center of it.

And he was not a part of it at all.

She seemed not even to have heard him coming. She had
not turned her head or shown any other sign of realizing
she was no longer alone.

It was her favorite place, the place where she liked to be
alone.

He had planned to give her back her aloneness, her independence, her happiness. If she could ever be happy
again.

The whole world seemed to have achieved happiness.
Barr-Hampton, it appeared, had finally opened up his eyes
and realized what a treasure was right in front of them.
Patience had won her man—he half smiled at the pun his
mind had unconsciously wrought. They were to be married
within the month.

And just one day after that Will Stubbs was to marry the
little kitchen maid he had rescued from the inn. She was a
thin and shapeless, lamentably plain, pale, pockmarked little thing, any bloom she might have had worn away by a

lifetime of physical and sexual abuse. But love, it seemed, did conquer all and was indeed blind—for both of them. And love there was in undeniable abundance. Will was puffed up almost to bursting with it, and when he had brought his beloved to the library that morning to present her to his friend, she had hung her head in terror until Will had said something to make her lift it and look into his eyes—and eyes had never been so filled with adoration and trust and sheer beauty as hers had been while she had gazed on Will. It had been an extraordinary moment.

An excruciatingly depressing moment personally, though Nigel was genuinely delighted for his friend.

Bruce had found happiness with his Charlotte.

Even he had found a measure of happiness today—a large measure. His brother, his twin, had been restored to him without even a remaining shadow lurking between them. It was a totally unlooked-for happiness, all the more precious perhaps for being so unexpected.

But it was a happiness that seemed of little account now as he stood at the edge of the clearing by the pool, his shoulder propped against a tree trunk. The clearing was bathed in sunlight. He stood in shadow. It seemed that the sunlight was not for him—or the beauty and peace of the scene.

Or the woman who was its centerpiece.

He did not know what to say to her. It had all been said on the hillside earlier, though of course he had not spoken from the heart there. Quite the opposite. He was not sure it would be to the advantage of either of them to reverse his position now.

There was nothing else to say.

And then she moved. She dipped her head downward to rest her forehead on her knees. It was a pose that told him as clearly as words that the scene was not idyllic after all. She was unhappy. But at almost the same moment something must have alerted her. She raised her head and turned it sharply in his direction.

He did not move.

She got to her feet and came slowly toward him. He

deliberately tried to memorize her form, her face, her way of moving. He tried to imagine her large with his child. He would never see her thus for himself. He half lowered his eyelids.

"Why did you lie?" she asked him. He raised his eyebrows. "About there being no twins in your family."

"My brother was dead to me at that time, madam," he said. "I had no wish to acknowledge the fact that I am myself a twin."

Her next question surprised him. He had expected her to ask about his meeting with Bruce.

"Why did you make my father's acquaintance?" she asked. "Was it accidental?"

Ah. Cassandra was certainly not lacking in intelligence.

"Not entirely," he said. "When I discovered he was in town, I went out of my way to secure an introduction to him and explain who I was."

"And who were you?" she asked.

"You have guessed, have you not?" he asked in return. "Merely on the knowledge that I have a twin? You and I are distantly related, madam. Very distantly. You must not disintegrate with fear that our child will be an idiot or be born with a harelip or donkey ears. To be exact, we share great-great-grandparents."

He watched her close her eyes and draw a slow breath.

" 'Twas one reason why I found your portrait gallery so fascinating," he said.

"You knew my father was a distant kinsman?" she said. "How? One would have to be a student of family trees to know it after so long. How did you know?"

He smiled at her. "You would not wish to know, my dear," he said. "You would find my motives even more sinister."

"I want to know." She spoke sharply, and her hands, he saw when she raised them, were clenched into fists. For a few moments she held them as if she was about to pound them against his chest. But she let them fall to her sides again. "I need to know, Nigel. Let me in. I need to know."

Let me in. It was the one thing he found most difficult to do. Almost impossible.

But she looked him full in the eyes and spoke again, very quietly, as if she realized she had suddenly found a key that the lock to his innermost self could not withstand.

"Let me in," she whispered.

"There was an old story," he said, "concerning my grandmother's family. She was an only child. 'Twas said that her father had been brought up as the heir of the Earl of Worthing, the elder of twins. But when he was already grown up, he was defrauded of his birthright when 'twas suddenly discovered, under very suspicious circumstances, that in fact his twin was the elder. The story has been passed down to the heirs of each generation—that in reality they should be heirs to the earldom. 'Tis a claim that cannot be proved now and obviously could not be proved then or it would have been—though I grew up dreaming about Kedleston being mine. I even went out of my way to read about it. I was excited to discover that the Earl of Worthing was in town when I arrived there at the age of nineteen."

"Did you tell him this story?" she asked.

"Oh yes, with great exuberance," he said. "Yes, I remember we made a famous joke of it, of my someday winning back my birthright and rendering him and his daughter destitute. 'Tis ironic, madam, is it not, in light of what happened later?"

"And you have no idea, do you," she said, "why he went to such pains to destroy you? Why he let go of all honor, all decency, all humanity in order to rid himself of you?"

He looked closely at her. Did she believe that her father had acted dishonorably, then? And that he had been purely a victim? "Perhaps," he said, and half smiled at her, "he believed my tale? I think not, Cassandra. Why would he do any such thing? No, we cannot explain what happened that way."

She slipped her hand then into the opening at the side of her petticoat and drew out a sheet of paper from her pocket. It was the letter Croft had brought her, the letter that had so upset her, if he was not mistaken. She held it out to him without looking at him.

"I would like you to read this," she said. "The package referred to in the letter is safe in my room."

He looked at her as he took the letter from her hand, but she would not raise her eyes. She was very pale. She turned and walked away, going on past the log almost to the foot of the waterfall. She sat down on the grassy bank, facing away from him, her arms clasped about her knees. She was not wearing hoops.

He unfolded the paper and began to read.

Somehow she had known the truth as soon as she saw Bruce and realized after the first disorienting moment that he was not Nigel. It had been somewhat foolish, perhaps. There must be thousands of twins in the world. But she had known. She had needed only to have a few questions answered to confirm what she already knew.

It had to be the truth. It was the only thing that would allow everything to fall finally into place.

She did not look away from the waterfall when Nigel came to sit on the grass beside her. He said nothing for a while.

"You must destroy this letter," he said quietly at last.

She laughed softly. "Now you have everything," she said. "'Tis just and right. You have suffered for it. You understand now why he did what he did, do you not? He must have been confident of the fact that only you knew the story. You had told him the part about its being handed down only to the heirs, I suppose?"

"Probably," he agreed. "You must not hate him, Cassandra. He had your security and your future to consider."

"Even knowing that I, too, would receive this letter?" she said. "He found himself unable to give up what he had been brought up to. He persuaded himself that what he did was right, that it was too late to put right an ancient wrong, that what had been done was not his concern anyway. When it came to the point, he was prepared to go to dreadful lengths to keep what was not really his."

"You do not know his thoughts," he said. "Perhaps you should not judge him. Perhaps you should simply keep on loving him."

She did not pause to wonder why he was suddenly defending her father to her. "I do know," she said. "I have faced the same temptations, you see. And I know how very strong they are."

"Kedleston is yours," he said. "The title is yours. I do not want either. You must destroy the letter and forget about it. I will be going away tomorrow. You may live in peace. If you do not want the child, I will take it. Then you can forget you ever met me."

It was the same message as he had spoken on the hillside earlier, taken one step further. He was prepared to take even her child from her. But it was spoken differently. He was not using his bored, arrogant voice. He was speaking softly and gently.

She set her forehead against her knees.

"I have sent Mr. Croft to find you," she said. "To find the descendant of that wronged man, that is, who should be the earl. I do not know what sort of legal proceedings will set things to rights. Even he seemed somewhat stunned by the whole prospect. But wheels have been set in motion. I am not going to stop them."

"Cassandra?" he said. "You did this even before you knew 'twas me? You were willing to risk losing—everything?"

"No, I was not willing at all," she cried, clasping her knees more tightly. "But 'twas the only thing I could do. Even in just two days the knowledge, the guilt, were tearing me apart. I could not live with them as my father lived with them and my grandfather before him. There was nothing else to do. There was only the right thing."

"Cassandra." His hand came to rest against the back of her head, and his fingers caressed her scalp through the lace of her cap. "How I honor you. Every day since our marriage I have come to see more and more that you are a woman of character. Had I suspected the depths of that character or the height of your courage, I would not have dared set foot on Kedleston land, even to kiss the hem of your gown.''

She swallowed, heard the gurgle in her throat, and swallowed again. His reverence was very sweet. But not nearly sweet enough.

"How can you bear even to touch me," she said, "when I am his daughter? Nigel, you were *innocent*. Totally innocent. The victim of another man's fright and power. He put you through *that*. I dare not even think of all you must have suffered—all the indignity and pain and exhaustion and despair.''

" 'Tis over," he said. "I survived it."

" 'Tis not over." She lifted her head and turned to look into his face. She noticed his eyelids immediately drooping over his eyes and with it the mask covering the rest of his features. " 'Tis still with you."

"The nightmares grow less frequent and less severe," he said. "In time they will fade altogether."

"I do not mean the nightmares," she said. "Nigel, will you now finally and fully—ah, fully, *please*—tell me the truth. Will you let me in? What are your feelings for Kedleston? For—" She drew a deep breath. She was taking a dreadful risk. She might well be destroying herself once and for all. "For me?"

The mask settled more firmly in place. "For Kedleston, madam?" he said. "Why, I love it, of course. In all my boyhood dreams I loved it. The reality surpasses the dream. And for you? Why, I love you, of course." He was using his indolent voice.

She was not as afraid as she might be. "You are speaking the truth," she said. "Are you not?"

His eyebrows shot up. "I bare my soul, madam, and you doubt me?" he said. "I speak the truth, i'faith."

"Then why are you afraid of it?" she asked.

There was a great blankness in his eyes suddenly behind the mask of his sleepy eyelids. "Afraid, madam?" he said. "I, afraid?"

She scrambled up onto her knees then, facing him, and she framed his face with her hands. "It must have been appallingly difficult to survive," she said. "Especially for someone like you."

"Someone like me?" He smiled at her. "You think me a weakling, madam?"

"Anything but," she assured him. "But you were just a boy. You had been brought up to be a gentleman. You survived. I know how you survived."

"Do you, by my life?" he said.

"You did it by becoming strong in the only way you knew how," she said. "You made yourself incredibly strong. So strong that finally you could put all your trust in yourself. There was no one else in whom to put it—except eventually, I believe, in Mr. Stubbs."

"And you, madam," he said, laughing and lifting a hand to cover the back of one of hers, "should take to reading palms. You would be very convincing."

"But in becoming strong you became weak," she told him.

He turned his head to kiss her palm and then smiled mockingly at her. "Zounds," he said, "a riddle."

"You are unable to trust anyone except yourself," she said. "You are unable to love freely or allow yourself to be loved. You *do* love. You love your brother—and your sister, I believe. You love me. You do. I know you do. You meant what you said even though you said it in that mocking tone of yours so that your feelings would be protected if your words were rejected. Nigel, I love you. *I love you.* You must let me in. Oh please, you must."

He tried smiling again but failed.

"Nigel." She was whispering to him. She leaned forward and set her lips to his. She kissed him softly, warmly. His lips did not move. "You have to let me in. You will not fall apart if you do. I am here. I am here, my dear love, and I love you. I am never going to stop loving you even if you go away tomorrow and never come back. I love you."

He tried to break away from her then. He jerked his head free of her hands and made to get up from the grass. But she slid her arms more securely about his neck and moved across the small space between them to sit on his lap. Some instinct told her that if she lost him now, he would be lost forever—not just to her, but to himself, to the life that remained to him.

Somehow they both lost balance, so that he lay flat on his back on the grass and she lay heavily on top of him. She was about to lift her head to smile at him and renew the campaign against him when she heard his first sob. It came from deep inside him and tore painfully at him, she knew. It was only the beginning. Soon he was convulsed by sobs, which he tried to control and failed. He was embarrassed—deeply mortified—by them, she knew. He would have got up and staggered out of sight and hearing if she would have allowed it.

But she would not. She lay on top of him, her arms about his neck, her head pillowed on his heart. She lay still for a long time. It was a long time before he was quiet again. Even then she did not raise her head or move. She would give him all the time he needed—but not the space he thought he wanted.

"Cassandra," he said at last, "I am so afraid."

"I know, my love," she said. "Welcome back to the world."

"I will not be able to make you happy," he said. "Everything I touch turns to darkness."

"No, it does not," she said, wriggling into a more comfortable position as his arms tightened about her. "Most of what happened to you for many years was beyond your control. But you have been a force of great good in what you could control. Mr. Stubbs is not going to return to a life of crime because you befriended him when you might have hated him with a terrible passion. He is going to be an innkeeper and he is going to marry poor Sally—did you know? He really loves her. Is it not amazing? I cried when my maid told me this morning—with joy. And though you made Patience sprain her ankle, you also made Rob realize that she is no longer just his little cousin but his love. You have begun improvements to Kedleston that have made a large number of people happy. You have won the affection of Aunt Matilda and even Aunt Bea. And Nigel—oh, Nigel, you came into my life and taught me how glorious love can be, a love shared between a man and a woman. Even if you leave tomorrow, you have given me more happiness than any mortal has a right to know in this life. And you have made me with child. I wish you could know the feeling. I do wish it. I have a child growing inside me—now. My love, you are such a very *good* person. A good person masquerading as a cynic. But you cannot fool me. Or escape me. You have touched me with sunshine.''

She lifted her head then and wriggled upward until her face was above his. His eyes were reddened. And wide open. And so naked with vulnerability that she almost became afraid herself—had she taken his defenses without being able to offer enough in return? But no, she had everything to offer that would be sufficient and more than sufficient. She smiled at him.

''My love,'' she whispered.

He gazed at her while his hands very gently, shaking ever so slightly, smoothed over the sides of her face, removing her cap as they did so.

''My love,'' he said back to her. ''My love.'' He drew her face down to his.

It was an achingly sweet lovemaking. And achingly erotic, both of them remaining fully clothed except in the area where they became one. He moved with slow, deep rhythm in her, leaning over her on the grass. They watched each other as they loved, making of the physical act an emotional bonding. She smiled dreamily at him. He gazed back unsmiling, his newly vulnerable eyes losing their fear, filling instead with an acceptance of the love she was giving him with her body, of the love and peace and security he could find here at Kedleston.

They sighed together when he reached his climax. She had not needed climax herself—what was happening had very little to do with sex and everything to do with marital love. She snuggled against him when he withdrew and lay at her side.

They were bathed in sunshine.

"My love," she said once more. And then with a low chuckle, "My Lord Worthing."

He kissed her. "There is no need," he said. "We will burn the letter and send new instructions to Croft."

"No, we will not," she told him.

"I suppose," he said, "you will never be a biddable, obedient wife, madam?"

"Never," she said. "I will still be the Countess of Worthing, after all."

"And owner of Kedleston," he said with a chuckle.

"Everything will be finally settled with our child," she said. "With him—or her—there will no longer even be question of what is whose."

"There is none now," he said. "What is mine is yours."

"And mine is yours," she said with a smile. "What are you going to do about Dunbar Abbey?"

He grimaced. "Fight my brother," he said, "and hope I have better success with him than I have had with you. He will move heaven and earth to try to return everything to me."

"He will not succeed," she said. "I will be fighting at your side."

"Zounds," he said. "Poor Bruce. I pity him from my heart. He has not the ghost of a chance."

She laughed.

"Ah," he said, gazing at her through half-closed eyes— though he was no longer using his eyelids as something to hide behind, " 'tis good to hear you laugh again. It seemed when I met you that you held all the sunshine inside you. How I wanted a part of it. And then I thought I had killed it."

She touched his cheek and shook her head slowly. "You are my sunshine," she said.

He smiled then. Not the old mocking smile, but one that held warmth and trust and happiness.

"I love you," he said.

"I know." She kissed him. "I know."

But for the moment the sunshine was almost too dazzling. She pressed her face to his waistcoat and breathed in deeply of the very essence of him. They had come so close to losing everything. So very close.

They had both given, expecting to lose.

And so they had both received. And gained everything. Each other. The whole world. Everything.

All the sunshine there ever was.

"I love you," he whispered again, against the top of her head.